D0240476

LANCASHIRE COUNTY LIBRARY

3011814015426 5

The Secrets Between Us

By Judith Lennox

The
Secrets
Between Us

JUDITH LENNOX

REVIEW

Copyright © 2020 Judith Lennox

The right of Judith Lennox to be identified as the Author of
the Work has been asserted by her in accordance with the
Copyright, Designs and Patents Act 1988.

First published in Great Britain in 2020 by Headline Review
An imprint of HEADLINE PUBLISHING GROUP

1

Apart from any use permitted under UK copyright law, this
publication may only be reproduced, stored, or transmitted, in
any form, or by any means, with prior permission in writing of
the publishers or, in the case of reprographic production, in
accordance with the terms of licences issued by the
Copyright Licensing Agency.

All characters in this publication are fictitious
and any resemblance to real persons, living or dead,
is purely coincidental.

Cataloguing in Publication Data is available from the British Library

ISBN 978 1 4722 6069 7

Typeset in Joanna MT Std by Palimpsest Book Production Ltd, Falkirk, Stirlingshire

Printed and bound in Great Britain by Clays Ltd, Elcograf S.p.A.

Headline's policy is to use papers that are natural, renewable
and recyclable products and made from wood grown in well-managed
forests and other controlled sources. The logging and manufacturing
processes are expected to conform to the environmental
regulations of the country of origin.

HEADLINE PUBLISHING GROUP
An Hachette UK Company
Carmelite House
50 Victoria Embankment
London EC4Y 0DZ

www.headline.co.uk
www.hachette.co.uk

To Macsen James Bethencourt-Smith

LANCASHIRE COUNTY LIBRARY	
3011814015426 5	
Askews & Holts	17-Jul-2020
AF AFR	£20.99
NGA	

Acknowledgements

Heartfelt thanks are due to:

Clare Foss at Headline, for being such a sensitive and inspiring editor.

Maggie Hanbury of the Hanbury Agency, for many years of stalwart support and encouragement.

Piper Verlag, my German-language publisher for the last twenty years. Bettina Feldweg has been my editor throughout that time – thank you for having faith in me.

Iain, with love and gratitude for all those magical visits to Scottish islands. I look forward to many more in the future.

PART ONE

A CHANGE IN THE WEATHER
1937–1939

Chapter One

December 1937

Rowan Scott's husband, Patrick, had not wanted to come to the Manninghams' cocktail party. Resentfully, she had put his refusal down to the quarrel they had had that morning over the breakfast boiled eggs and toast, he suggesting they travel on Christmas Eve to his father's house in Guildford, she preferring to put it off as long as possible and motor there on Christmas morning. In Patrick's absence, Rowan had come out with her usual set, the Charlburys, the Wiltons and the Vaughans – and Nicky Olivier, on good form tonight, making fun of their hosts as he sat in an armchair surrounded by half a dozen acolytes.

To one side of the large, crimson-papered drawing room, Davey Manningham's manservant was mixing fiercely alcoholic cocktails that were decorated with a scratchy sprig of holly to mark the season. A piano murmured arrangements of Christmas carols and the air was perfumed with the scents of cloves and oranges. Boughs of apple-wood smouldered in the fireplace. The women's frocks were a delicious froth of emerald, eau de nil, turquoise, orange and baby pink.

A voice said, 'Mrs Scott, how delightful!' and Rowan,

seated on one of the Manninghams' plump sofas, looked up and saw Simon Pemberton. Simon was a cousin of Artemis Wilton, who was Rowan's especial friend. She had come across him before at dances and concerts. She murmured a greeting.

'I've been out of circulation,' he told her as he leaned against the sofa arm. 'A relative of mine has been ill and required my company. I've been staying in the countryside for the past three weeks. Such a relief to return to civilisation.'

His shudder was theatrical; it pleased her that he should try to capture her attention. Caught in his gaze, she felt a thrill of excitement, an intimation of a possibility of solace and adventure. Simon Pemberton was tall and had close-cropped chestnut hair and navy-blue eyes. He had the profile of a handsome Roman senator: an aquiline nose, a slightly cruel curve to his lips.

She said, 'Do you dislike the countryside?'

A downward flexing of the corners of his mouth. 'I find little amusement in country sports, and really, what else is there to do? There are no reputable art galleries in Suffolk, where my uncle lives, and little opportunity to hear music of any but the most amateurish standard. As for the people one meets, what is it about fields and woodland that erases the capacity for conversation? Or perhaps those who have no conversation *choose* to bury themselves in the countryside.'

'I miss the countryside when I'm in town too long,' Rowan said. 'I feel stifled.'

'Yet you live in town.'

'We must, for Patrick's work.' Her husband was a barrister.

He sat down beside her. 'I've never been tempted by the institution of marriage. What does it offer but a narrowing of outlook and opportunity?'

4

Though her own marriage had proved to be a severe disappointment, and though she had for some time felt Patrick to be in every way indifferent to her, she still bridled at Simon's judgement.

'It offers security,' she said. Though, looking back, she wondered whether she, in marrying Patrick, had confused security with love.

'I've been fortunate enough never to lack financial security,' he said. 'It's different for women, you are dependent on men. As for love, is it to be found only in marriage? In all truth, is it ever, after the first blissful months, to be found in marriage?'

'How fashionably cynical of you.'

'Forgive me. Cynicism is a slippery and unattractive quality. You're right, optimism's harder work, particularly at the present time.'

He was referring to the news, Rowan assumed, to the horrors of civil war in Spain and the ominous grip of fascism in Germany and Italy.

'One is almost afraid to open a newspaper,' she agreed.

Swiftly, skilfully, he redirected their conversation. They spoke of contemporary art – he admired Ben Nicholson and Stanley Spencer but despised Henry Moore.

Art done with, they moved on to the theatre as the pianist thumped out 'The Holly and the Ivy'. Simon claimed to have seen every worthwhile play in London. 'Not that there are more than a handful,' he added. 'Theatre is a burned-out shadow of its Edwardian heyday. The West End is full of perfectly dreadful revues and vulgar musicals.'

'Don't you enjoy musicals?'

'Does anyone with a modicum of intelligence?'

'I adore them. And the cinema? Do you go to the cinema?'

'Never. I went once and I loathed it.'

She smiled. 'Perhaps you chose the wrong film.'

'I don't believe so. Warm, foetid air perfumed by penny cigarettes and cheap scent . . . the massed hordes, with their popcorn and ices. And then, the banality of the story unfolding on the screen. It was unendurable.'

'I like to go on my own, in the afternoons.' Simon was so confident in his opinions Rowan found it impossible not to challenge him. 'It feels so wonderfully decadent.'

'Do you admire decadence? I despise those who pursue decadence for the sake of it, who claim to revel in a seedy nightclub or screeching jazz band because they believe it will make them more interesting.'

'Dear me.' She gave him a mocking glance. 'Must I add jazz music and nightclubs to the list of things you don't care for?'

'How can such idiocies compare with an aria from The Magic Flute . . . or a painting by Velázquez? Or the scene in Giselle when the ballerina appears to float across the stage like the spirit she's pretending to be?'

Rowan had felt her own breath catch at such moments. She, too, admired intensity and passion and despised the vapid and half-hearted. That he had spoken with true feeling made her like him more.

'What you speak of is sublime,' she said. 'But it's rare and it's fleeting. And in the meantime, we have to keep our spirits up.'

'Yet you must surely agree that the cheap and shallow degrades us. It blunts our capacity to appreciate beauty, and what are we without that?' Amusement sparked his dark-blue eyes. 'I admit it, I can never resist beauty. Why do you think I'm here, talking to you, my dear Mrs Scott, though we appear to have little in common?'

6

A racing of the heart. 'You're very flattering,' she said.

He shook his head. 'I never flatter. When it comes to beauty, I always tell the truth. For instance, you shouldn't wear that colour. That shade of blue takes the fire from your hair. You should wear red. Auburn-haired women always shy away from red. They're afraid it will clash, but they're mistaken. You would look glorious in just the right shade of Venetian red. Like a flame, a tall, shimmering flame. Ah, I see you think me impudent.' His tone betrayed no hint of regret.

'Not at all,' she said, adding flippantly, 'practical advice about one's dress is always useful.'

They talked for a little longer and then he invited her to dinner. Leaving the Manninghams' house and her friends, Rowan knew she was taking a step down a treacherous road, but went anyway.

At Simpson's in the Strand, they were enclosed by dark panelled walls beneath an ornate plastered ceiling. As they dined on sirloin of beef, Rowan asked Simon about his plans for Christmas.

'I shall stay in my rooms,' he said. 'I never go away for Christmas. As for family Christmases, I find noisy infants and shrieking children unendurable. A few close friends will come to lunch, fellow dissidents from family life. I'll spend the evening in the company of Samuel Johnson's essays and a fine vintage port. I'm looking forward to it enormously. And you, Rowan?' They had slipped easily into using each other's Christian names.

'We always spend Christmas Day with Patrick's father and his sister, Elaine, in Guildford.' She was already dreading it: the infirm and querulous old man, the resentfulness and bitterness of Patrick's unmarried sister, who looked after him.

Heavy food and hot rooms and boredom. She went on, 'My younger sister, Thea, will be with us.' Thea, who was sixteen, always joined them for the festive season. Their father was a widower. He disliked Christmas and chose to spend it fishing or hill-walking with an old friend called Malcolm Reid, a recluse who lived in the remote Scottish Highlands and whom none of them had ever met. Rowan added, 'Then the three of us will go to Glasgow, for Hogmanay.'

'I've heard that in Scotland, the New Year is often celebrated more than Christmas.'

'Yes, that's so. Do you have family, Simon? Oh yes, the uncle in Suffolk.'

'Denzil prefers to spend Christmas Day on his own, too, at his home, Ashleigh Place. It is perhaps the finest small manor house in England.'

'Ah, beauty again.'

'I'm a slave to it.' His gaze latched on to hers. A clumsier man might have added some tiresome compliment. That he did not left her tense and on edge, wanting more.

She asked him whether Ashleigh Place had been in his family for a long time.

'Not at all. Denzil bought the house when he was twenty-five years old. It had been owned by a madman, an exhibitionist who liked to put on theatrical performances. Before that it belonged to an old Suffolk family, the Gardiners, who allowed it to fall into disrepair. Denzil restored Ashleigh Place. It was a huge undertaking, his life's work. You wouldn't think it now because his health is poor, but when he was younger he was capable of great energy and vigour.'

'You're fond of him, aren't you?'

He smiled. 'I am, yes. Apart from Denzil, there are not many of my family with whom I would choose to spend my time. I have a sister, Anne, who's married to a bore called Edwin. She has two children. Henry is a solid little chap. I shall send him a Fullers' walnut cake for his tuck box. My niece, Zorah, is featherbrained and insipid. What Christmas present should I buy her, do you think?'

'How old is she?'

'I forget. Five or six.'

Rowan considered. 'A box of paints, perhaps? I used to adore painting when I was a little girl.'

'Do you still paint?'

'Scarcely at all, now. Our house is very small and there's nowhere to put things down. Oh dear, I'm making excuses, aren't I?' She sighed. 'I can't think of anything to paint any more, and that's the truth of it. Do you think one runs out of ideas, when one gets old?'

'You're hardly old.'

'I'm twenty-three. Sometimes I *feel* old.' Twenty-three felt ancient to her. She had been almost nineteen when she had moved from Glasgow to London. It seemed an age ago. She remembered how excited she had felt, how full of enthusiasm she had been for the new possibilities ahead of her, and how she had adored exploring the city.

'I'm thirty-six,' Simon said. 'I feel no older than the day I left school.'

From the brief conversation Rowan had had with Artemis while collecting her coat, her friend had confirmed that Simon was unmarried and that he had no need to work. 'You're fortunate,' she said. 'You can just amuse yourself.'

'Do you disapprove of that or envy it?'

'Neither. At least, I don't think so.'

He laughed. 'What was that? A flash of Scottish Presbyterian censure?'

'Doesn't it feel rather . . . aimless, disorientating even, to have nothing to do but to please oneself?'

'No, it's quite delightful. Why don't you try it?' She began to speak, but he silenced her, placing his fingertips on her wrist. 'You're not going to be so dull as to remind me that you have a house to run and a husband to look after, are you, Rowan? How very disappointing that would be.'

Though he withdrew his hand, it seemed to have left an imprint on her, like an impression in clay. She should walk away now, she thought, tell him that she had an appoint-ment or that Patrick would be waiting for her – anything.

But she remained where she was. 'Everyone has duties,' she said. 'Even you must have some.'

'Everyone gives the *appearance* of having duties but most people are like me, they do only what pleases them. I speak of my own class, naturally. The lives of the lower orders are bound by necessity. One may play a long game, of course. I have my reasons for enduring the rigours of the Suffolk countryside.'

'Beauty.'

'Yes.' He studied her. 'And I presume that you, Rowan, you tolerate your domestic duties and social routine because . . . because they satisfy you.'

Marrying Patrick three years ago, she had assumed that because so much of what was involved in running a home was both piffling and tedious, it must also be easy. It was piffling and tedious, and yet it had turned out to be time-consuming and arduous as well. She had learned to organise the grocer and greengrocer, the butcher and fishmonger, the laundry delivery and daily woman. She had become a passable cook: their cook-general, Gwen, had taught her how to prepare several supper dishes which Rowan made for herself and Patrick on Gwen's evening off. She was considered by her friends to be an amusing and original hostess. Yet increasingly she found herself thinking – and now what? What outlet could she find for the energy that seethed and bubbled inside her, for the restlessness that made it impossible for her to sit quietly indoors in the evening, reading or sewing? More grocer's lists, more dinner parties, for another twenty or thirty years?

'Hardly,' she said, with a small laugh.

He lit two cigarettes and passed one to her. He said softly, 'Or you endure it for the sake of your husband, whom you adore.'

'*He* doesn't adore *me*,' she said, but immediately regretted the confidence. Knowing she was undesired, he might want her less.

But he raised his eyebrows. 'Then he's a fool.'

'No,' she said bitterly. 'Patrick is anything but a fool.'

'Then why?'

She gave a tight little shake of the head. She did not know why Patrick did not want her. Their conversations skirted round the subject. She was afraid to ask him in case she was to blame. She was cold. She was getting older. She lacked sex appeal. Beauty and desirability were not necessarily the same thing. More and more often, it crept into her mind that she was simply unloveable.

A kerfuffle in the corner of the restaurant, a patron who had had too much to drink knocking over wine glasses, provided a distraction that was a relief to her. Waiters rushed around with cloths and dustpans.

'You look sad,' Simon said gently. 'Tell me.'

The waiter came to clear away their plates. When he had

gone, she said, 'When I first met Patrick, I was living on my own in London. I was rather low . . . there was a love affair that hadn't worked out. With Patrick, I felt I had something solid to hold on to. I needed that. Have you ever felt cast adrift, with no idea which direction to take?'

'No, never.'

In those early days, she had been attracted to Patrick's goodness and calmness. She found it difficult to be calm and did not think of herself as especially good. But after three years of marriage, three years in which their physical intimacy, never frequent, had diminished to nothing, the silences Patrick took refuge in reduced her to anguish and fury.

Simon gave a gentle smile. 'But then, though I pretend to be an aesthete and a city dweller, scratch away and you'll find that a couple of generations back I come from a long line of stolid Hertfordshire yeomen. I should probably be tending my swine just now.'

She laughed. 'Simon, you would spoil your clothes.' His evening dress was immaculately tailored.

'So I would.' He patted her hand and it was all she could do not to grip his hard, to clutch it like a lifeline. She shivered as he ran his thumb across her palm. His voice low, he said, 'Rowan, my dear, I've admired your fire and splendour for some time now. I've only stood back for fear of being scorched.'

What response could a woman possibly make to such a declaration? She was relieved when the waiter came with the pudding menu, breaking the moment. Neither of them wanted pudding; she had lost her appetite and Simon told her that he never ate it. Over coffee and petits fours they spoke of this and that, but Rowan knew that a bridge had

12

been crossed, and that they were edging towards danger – no, there was no danger to him, a man and a bachelor, only to her.

Her anxiety fought against an intense longing. It seemed a long time since she had desired a man, since her senses and emotions had been stirred and caution had battled with urgency. A half-light was peeling away. She had mislaid the person she was capable of being and yet suddenly, here she was, back again, shaking off the ashes of her marriage, colour shining through the grey. That he wanted her, that he made no secret of wanting her, made her feel alive again.

They finished their coffee and left the restaurant. Out in the street, a pale, misty corona shimmered round the gas-lamps. She put up a hand to hail a taxi but it sped by. On such events your life turns, she later thought – had the taxi stopped, he would not have had the opportunity to kiss her. His kiss was passionate and shocking; helpless with pleasure and desire, she returned it.

In the early hours of the morning, travelling through the wintry London streets, she looked out of the window of the taxi and saw how the mist bled the advertising hoardings into a yellow blur. The faces of the people on the pavements became frozen, white and distorted, open-mouthed and sliced by shadows. A tramp, sleeping in a doorway, became a heap of rags and old blankets with nothing inside. The darkened shops and offices appeared hollowed out and empty.

Rowan ran the tip of her tongue over her upper lip, which felt bruised. Her euphoria had drained away, replaced not yet by remorse, but by melancholy. She dreaded returning home to Mallord Street. She had chosen the house on a whim, attracted by the raffish artiness of the Chelsea area,

13

but had come to dislike it for its claustrophobic flimsiness. Formerly an artist's studio, it was small and narrow. Downstairs, there was a kitchen and scullery, drawing room and dining room; upstairs, three bedrooms. The attic room was all sloping, inconvenient angles and used for the storage of the ornaments and furniture they had inherited on Patrick's grandmother's death. The guest bedroom, in which Thea always slept when she visited, was at the back of the house, overlooking the basement area. Rowan and Patrick's room was at the front. A bow window, installed by the builder who had carried out the conversion, leaked whenever it rained heavily.

When she crept into their bedroom, Patrick would pretend to be asleep. He wouldn't ask her where she had been and she wouldn't tell him. Neither of them would break the pact they had mutually and silently constructed, a pact which she increasingly felt imprisoned her. They tiptoed round confrontation, much as she herself would shortly tiptoe round the bedroom, quietly undressing and taking off her make-up, conspiring in the pretence that he was asleep.

Patrick could not easily be quarrelled with. If she shouted or wept he became more passive and distant from her. Their arguments were about minor matters – that she had forgotten a social occasion with his lawyer friends, that he had not yet found a tradesman to mend the dripping scullery tap. The gulf between them, those canyons of hurt and resentment, yawned too wide to be spoken of.

Patrick was slight, with fairish hair, small blue eyes and finely drawn features, handsome in a restrained English way. He was a good provider, a stalwart friend, an excellent host. To upbraid him for his absence of desire would, Rowan knew, hurt him terribly. Sometimes, before he turned away from her in bed, she glimpsed in his eyes both guilt and shame, naked and humiliated. Yet it was not only pity that prevented her from confronting him about the emptiness of their marriage. To talk about it must open barriers. All sorts of emotions and accusations might rush in.

This situation can't go on for ever. The words sprang into her head as the taxi drove through the streets of Chelsea. She and Patrick teetered on the edge of a chasm. Tonight she felt herself falling. Simon had reminded her of desire and its power, which overcame logic, sense and duty. Bitterly, she regretted the time she had wasted, the dry, desiccated years of her marriage.

The taxi reached Mallord Street. As she let herself into the house, she felt herself shrinking, as if to fit into the small rooms and the constraints of her marriage. In the hall mirror, she checked that her lipstick was not smudged. Patrick's papers were scattered across the dining table. The Christmas tree she had chosen was, she thought, too large for the drawing room. Rowan slipped off her shoes and went upstairs.

She slept for a few hours. Patrick woke her at seven o'clock in the morning to tell her that her sister was on the telephone.

So it was Thea who broke the news to her that their father was dangerously ill with pneumonia. Thea had come home to Glasgow from her boarding school in Yorkshire at the end of term, on 17th December. Their father had returned from a business trip in the south to the family home the following day. He had been unwell, feverish and coughing, yet had refused to allow Thea to send for the doctor, but his condition had taken a turn for the worse and Thea had

15

placed the call the next day. Dr Waring had diagnosed pneumonia. Their father was not responding to treatment. He had suffered from weak lungs since the Great War, the consequence of exposure to mustard gas.

Patrick called for a taxi to take Rowan to Euston Station to catch the Glasgow train. Folding blouses and skirts, putting jars of cream and lotion into a sponge bag, Rowan's hands fumbled as she was overwhelmed by fear. At the back of her mind hovered a suspicion that her father's illness was her fault, that it was some punitive consequence of her passionate encounter with Simon.

A horn sounded. She glanced out of the window; the taxi was at the door. Clasping her suitcase shut, she hurried downstairs.

Chapter Two

December 1937

It wasn't the first time that Hugh Craxton had been away from his family over Christmas. Some years ago, urgent business had taken him to Glasgow just before Christmas Eve (he worked so hard, poor Hugh) and had prevented him from getting home in time. And, on more than one occasion, when on a hiking holiday just before Christmas to see his reclusive friend, Malcolm Reid, in the Highlands, snowstorms and bad weather had closed in, blocking roads and railway lines, making it impossible for him to travel home. This year, it had been very cold in early December, with heavy snowfalls in the south of England, but during the week before Christmas the weather had become milder. His wife, Sophie, had listened intently to the forecasts but the announcer hadn't mention blizzards in Scotland, or anything like that.

Every other time he had been delayed, Hugh had phoned or sent a telegram to let her know that he was all right. He had always been good about that. Whenever he went away he telephoned home regularly. But not this time. That the phone did not ring cast a shadow over Christmas Day, making it a subdued and prickly affair. Though anxious herself, Sophie tried to reassure her sons about their father's absence. He would be home soon, something must have come up. Even so, Stuart, aged fifteen, was upset, while her elder son, Duncan, was resentful and angry.

During the past year, Duncan and his father had often clashed. He was eighteen, a difficult age, Sophie reasoned, no longer a boy nor yet quite a man. He was to go to university to study engineering the coming September. Hugh had insisted he stay at school in the meantime, a cause of friction between them. Wary of provoking another quarrel, Sophie had backed her husband up, though in retrospect she questioned whether she should have tried harder to persuade him to allow Duncan to do what he wanted, which was to leave school and find a job. Hugh might have found him a temporary position in the factory or the offices, to occupy him in the months before he started at university. The experience of earning money and taking part in the world of work might be just what Duncan needed. She had suggested this but Hugh had demurred.

It was the day after Boxing Day. Duncan and Stuart had gone out to see their friends, Michael and Thomas Foster. In their absence the house, which was in a cul-de-sac in South Kensington, seemed unnaturally quiet. The only sounds were the distant murmur of traffic, along with a faint soughing as air seeped through a leaky kitchen window. From a pot on the stove came a bubbling as bones from the roast chicken they had eaten on Christmas Day simmered for stock.

Sophie washed and dried the cake tin. Stuart, who was perpetually hungry, had polished off almost the entire Christmas cake last night, which meant that Hugh hadn't

18

had a single slice. *Your Christmas cake is the best in the world, my darling Sophie.* At the memory of his words, the sense of dread, of wrongness, that she was trying to suppress, flooded through her.

It came to her as she went through the house, mechanically tidying and putting things away, that the rooms felt *dead.* Sophie shivered and scolded herself for being morbid. The weather had delayed him. Or his work had.

But these comforting phrases no longer provided solace. *Face facts, Sophie.* Hugh had left London a week before Christmas. He'd been feeling under the weather throughout December and had developed a nasty cough, but there had been a problem at the factory in Glasgow that required his immediate attention so he had had to dash up north to sort things out. Kissing her before he left, he had promised to be home by Christmas Eve at the latest.

On the second night, they had had a brief phone call. Hugh had told her that he had reached Glasgow. His cough had worsened and he had thought he might be running a temperature. He had promised to go to bed and take care of himself. Since then, she had not heard from him and the ache of anxiety she carried inside her intensified hourly.

She smoothed out a sheet of wrapping paper lurking behind the sofa and put it away to use next year. Before Hugh had left, he had looked so pale and strained she had urged him to stay at home and cancel his meetings, but he had refused. Like so many men, he hated to admit weakness and was reluctant to consult a doctor. Had he gone down with bronchitis or influenza? Was he lying in a hotel bedroom, untended and alone? Or might he be in hospital, febrile and desperately ill, in danger of his life?

And yet none of these horrible imaginings made sense.

He could have phoned from his hotel. Even if he had been delirious and taken to hospital, someone would surely have phoned or sent a telegram. They might have posted one of those messages one heard on the wireless: *Would the family of Mr Hugh Craxton contact such and such a hospital, where Mr Craxton is dangerously ill.*

Instead, nothing.

Hugh had his demons. He was a drinker. The times of day for Hugh were marked out by snifters and noggins and jiggers and chasers and *one for the road, sweetie.* Drink was Hugh's bulwark against the world, the rituals of making drinks almost as important as the alcohol itself. Mixing an elegant cocktail took his mind off business difficulties; opening a bottle of champagne blurred a black mood. Had he had one drink too many before he had climbed back in the car? Had he gone on one of his occasional but spectacular benders and was he now lying in a stupor in some grim room in a roadhouse on the Great North Road?

She and Hugh were never very sociable over the festive season. Church on Christmas Day morning was about the limit of their mixing with other people. Hugh always preferred it to be just the four of them, regardless of the occasion. *Why would I choose to spend my time with other people when I have everyone I want here?* His words, spoken to her when Duncan and Stuart were little, had warmed her heart and made her love him all the more. Now it occurred to her that though the lack of social contact isolated her, it had this Christmas been a relief, because she had not been required to make awkward explanations for Hugh's absence.

In the drawing room, dry brown needles, shed from the Christmas tree, clogged the gaps between the floorboards.

The candles on the angel chimes had burned down to stumps. Glancing out of the window, Sophie saw that snow was falling, tiny flakes that dissolved as soon as they touched the pavement. The motor cars and vans had slowed and switched on their headlamps, around which a ghostly greenish aura glimmered. It had just turned three in the afternoon, but night came early during this, the dregs of the year. A crepuscular gloom was settling over London and soon the day would come to an end.

With shocking clamour the telephone rang; Sophie dashed to answer it. It must be him! Hope flared as she grasped the receiver.

'Hello?' she gasped.

'Sophie? It's Viola.' Viola Foster was a friend and neighbour of Sophie and the mother of her sons' friends, Michael and Thomas. 'I wondered whether you would mind if Duncan and Stuart stayed to tea?'

'Not at all,' Sophie managed as disappointment flooded through her. There was an exchange of pleasantries and she put down the phone. The silence returned, sour and unyielding.

She opened the door to Hugh's small study. She rarely went into this room, which was dusted and vacuumed once a week by Mrs Leonard, her daily woman, but otherwise used only by Hugh. 'My private kingdom' he called it, jokingly. As she opened the topmost desk drawer her heart began to pound.

Writing paper, envelopes, blotting paper, pens and pencils, and a small notebook which she leafed through carefully, but which only contained household accounts. A folder storing the boys' school reports safely and another for bills. The only surprise was the half-bottle of Scotch in the bottom

21

drawer, an inch of whisky inside it. There was no glass. A startling image popped into Sophie's mind of Hugh sitting at the desk, totting up their weekly outgoings, a Turkish cigarette from the box on the desktop between the fingers of his left hand, while he swigged whisky from a bottle.

The framed photograph on the desk was of the four of them, taken a couple of years before by a beach photographer on a day out in Ramsgate. In it, Duncan looked tall and handsome but ill at ease. Two years ago he had already considered himself too old for family seaside outings; she remembered that he had been that day in an uncooperative mood. In contrast, Stuart's face was lit up by a jaunty smile.

Her gaze moved to Hugh. He was standing a little apart from his family. Tall and well made, he was a handsome, striking man with an upright, military bearing. His long face, high forehead and hooded hazel eyes could make him seem distant, severe even, in repose, but his smile charmed and warmed.

Sophie delved into the pockets of the old tweed jacket on the back of the chair – 'my writing jacket' Hugh called it. Her search yielded only a handkerchief, comb and a ticket for the Glasgow subway. The destination on the ticket, Buchanan Street, meant nothing to her. She had never been to Glasgow. Hugh had never taken her or the boys to see Craxton & Sons, the stationery business he owned. 'Why on earth would you want to travel hundreds of miles to see noisy machines making writing paper and envelopes?' he'd said. 'You'd hate it, Sophie. I hate it. It's only saving grace is that it pays the bills.'

The resolve, the sense of rebellion that had been fomenting inside her during Hugh's absence, intensified. Sophie went into the bedroom. She opened his chest of drawers. He had kept the habit of neatness from his army days. Either she or Mrs Leonard, her daily help, would leave his laundered clothes on the bed and Hugh would put them away himself. If a button needed to be re-attached or a lining repaired he put the item of clothing in her sewing corner. Hugh liked everything just so; she had seen him fold every garment again if it was not done to his liking. She went through the vests and drawers and combinations knowing that she was invading his privacy. In the second drawer she found socks, scarves, gloves and gaiters. The drawer below that contained jerseys and a jacket she had knitted for him, which he claimed to love but rarely wore. It was too warm and heavy, she thought.

Inside the bottom drawer she found half a dozen parcels, wrapped in brown paper and tied with red satin ribbons. Sophie read the labels. *To my darling Sophie. To Duncan, with love from Dad . . . To Stuart, much love to my boy, Daddy.*

She sat back on her heels, clasping her Christmas present to her breast, while tears sprang to her eyes. Oh, Hugh, what's happened to you? Come home, I need you to come home! Please, please, come home!

Stumbling into the kitchen, Sophie put the kettle on the stove. As she spooned tea into the pot, her mind was in turmoil. Should she telephone the police? Should she tell them that her husband was missing, and that she was scared stiff that something awful had happened to him? At that moment she felt incapable of making a decision. She couldn't even decide whether to give Duncan and Stuart the Christmas presents from their father. Would Hugh want her to do that? She did not know.

But she could predict the questions the police would ask and the answers she would be obliged to give. Where did your husband stay when he was in Glasgow, Mrs Craxton? *I don't know. I never asked.* But you must have written to him, surely? *No, he always phoned me.* Do you know the address of his business there? *No, I don't know. I never needed to know.*

She poured boiling water into the pot and stirred it. After taking a few mouthfuls of tea she returned to the bedroom, where she knelt down by the bottom drawer once more. Among a jumble of miscellaneous objects she found the boxes containing Hugh's military medals, a torch, a couple of old pipes, a silver christening mug and some lengths of wire in a brown paper bag.

Beneath the paper bag was a small notebook, the sort one might keep in the inside pocket of a jacket as an aide-memoire. The blue leather covering had worn through at the corners. Sophie leafed through the pages. On them, Hugh had listed telephone numbers. Beside the numbers were initials. She frowned as she tried to puzzle them out. None of them meant anything to her until, turning a page, she saw a phone number. Beside it Hugh had written, *C & Sons*.

She hesitated, frowning. There was only one way to be sure.

She dialled the operator and asked to be put through to the Glasgow number. Minutes passed, the line crackled, then a girl's voice said:

'Craxton and Sons Quality Stationery and Office Sundries.'

Hope soared. 'I'd like to speak to Mr Hugh Craxton, please,' Sophie said.

'I'm sorry to have to inform you, but Mr Craxton has passed away.'

Had the receptionist misheard? Or had she herself misunderstood the girl's strong Scottish accent? '*Mr Hugh Craxton,*' repeated Sophie, loudly and irritably. 'I need to speak to Mr Hugh Craxton.'

'Mr Hugh Craxton's family has informed us that he died on Boxing Day of pneumonia,' said the girl, in a bored tone. 'We're passing on his calls to Mr Ross and Mr Paterson. May I put you through?'

'No. Thank you.' The words were a gasp.

'I beg your pardon, but are you a customer of Craxton's?'

I'm Hugh's wife. But she was seized by a horror that the girl might not have made a mistake, and that Hugh might indeed have died, and the phrase jammed in her throat.

The receptionist was speaking again. Her tone had softened. 'Mr Craxton's two daughters are making the funeral arrangements. Would you like me to give you the number of the Craxton residence?'

The impulse to shout down the line, 'Daughters? What daughters?' swelled and peaked and then collapsed like a badly set blancmange, and Sophie cut off the connection. Her legs buckled and she found herself sitting on the floor, nauseous and trembling. She pressed her knuckles hard against her teeth.

Mr Craxton's family has informed us that he died on Boxing Day of pneumonia. Mr Craxton's two daughters are making the funeral arrangements. Her head reeled. Nothing made sense.

It was a while before she was able to drag herself to her feet. In the drawing room, her hand shook as she poured brandy into a glass. Splashes of liquid blobbed the surface of the cabinet. Collapsing into an armchair, she drank the brandy in slow, steadying sips, her gaze fixed on the view through the window: the street lamps, the pale riming of snow on wall tops and post boxes. Everything seemed unnaturally vivid. Sounds jangled and vibrated, exacerbating her nerves.

Mr Craxton's two daughters are making the funeral arrangements. If Hugh was dead – surely it could not be true? – but if, God help them all, it proved to be so, Hugh had no daughters. Which meant – it *must* mean – that this was all a terrible mistake. The receptionist must have been referring to some other Craxton.

Yet the number she had phoned, the number in Hugh's notebook, had been for the stationery factory. And Craxton was not a common surname.

Mr Hugh Craxton's family has informed us that he died on Boxing Day of pneumonia. Sophie saw, through the blurry grey of the evening, two familiar figures approaching the house. Duncan and Stuart were coming home. She put the brandy bottle and glass back in the cabinet, then wiped up the spills. Leaving the room, she caught sight of her reflection in the mirror above the mantelpiece: she had a crazed expression, she thought. She ran a hand over her face as if to wipe it away, then went to meet her boys.

They came into the house jostling each other, arguing about something in a noisy, friendly way, pink-cheeked with cold and trailing mud and water on to the hall tiles.

'Has Dad come home?' Stuart asked.

Sophie shook her head. Duncan said, 'Shut up, you idiot.'

'I thought he might have.'

'He hasn't, you can see he hasn't, so shut up.'

Duncan went upstairs. Stuart dropped his shoes in the middle of the hall and headed for the kitchen. 'I'm starving,' he said.

'I thought you had tea at the Fosters.' She marvelled that she could speak so calmly as she trembled on the edge of catastrophe.

'It was just leftovers.' Stuart reached up to a high larder

shelf and took down a tin of Jacob's crackers. Duncan had reddish-brown hair and hazel eyes and took after Hugh in his colouring, but Stuart was her boy through and through, fair-haired and blue-eyed and sweet-natured. He was at that in-between stage that touched her heart, the boy metamorphosing into the man, tall and gangly and prone to outbreaks of scarlet spots, but still affectionate and eager to please.

He said, 'Is there any cheese?'

'Some mousetrap, that's all. The grocer's boy hasn't been.' Sophie had to think hard which day of the week it was. Monday, it was Monday. The grocer's boy usually called on a Monday. Nothing was right.

Stuart spilled half a dozen crackers on to a plate and unwrapped the cheese. He talked about the game of football he and Duncan and the Foster boys had played in the park, in the snow. 'If it keeps falling, we'll be able to make a snowman tomorrow.' Though he was more than a head taller than her, he was still excited about such things.

Sophie called up the stairs to ask Duncan whether he wanted a cup of tea and he shouted back a no thanks. She and Stuart sat at the dining table and Stuart got on with the Christmas jigsaw, an image of the Royal Scot flying over a bridge, and after a while Duncan came down and joined them. The wireless played a programme of symphonic music while Duncan did the sky and Sophie and Stuart started on the engine and carriages. Or, rather, Stuart did. Sophie felt so sick and shocked she couldn't even try.

Stuart said suddenly, 'Are you worried about Dad, Mum?'

Duncan said, 'Of course she's worried about Dad, you clot, he's been missing for over a week.'

'Missing', Sophie thought. Not 'away'.

'But he'll come back soon, won't he?' said Stuart.

Sophie squeezed her younger son's hand. 'Why don't we all have a cup of cocoa?'

'I'll make it,' Duncan said. He went to the kitchen.

She was relieved when, an hour later, Stuart, yawning, announced that he was going to bed and went upstairs. Sophie, too, stood up and said goodnight to Duncan, who liked to stay up late. She went upstairs and lay down on the bed fully clothed. Already, the bed was starting to seem as if it belonged only to her. The hollow in Hugh's pillow had been pummelled out by Mrs Leonard, and the room had been aired and no longer smelled of Hugh's cigarettes.

She had met Hugh during the war, in early 1918. She had been twenty-one years old and working in a hospital for convalescent officers, set up by a family friend in a house in Knightsbridge. Her duties were making beds, sweeping floors and scrubbing out bedpans, that sort of thing. Hugh was visiting a friend of his who had been wounded at Passchendaele. When visiting hour was over Sophie showed him out of the house and he asked her to dinner. She had said yes; there had never been any question that she would not say yes. During Hugh's fortnight's leave they went to the theatre and cinema and, hand in hand, walked by the Thames and window-shopped in Piccadilly. And they kissed, passionately, beneath gas-lamps and in frosty parks.

The day before Hugh was due to return to the Front, they embraced in the shadow of a bridge, where the misty grey river lapped at the muddy bank. He undid the top button of her blouse, then another. 'Hugh,' she said. 'You mustn't.' When he made to undo a third button, she said, 'Hugh, no,' and pulled away. 'Sorry, I'm sorry,' he murmured. He smiled at her and said ruefully, 'It's just that you're such a damned beautiful girl, Sophie, and I want you so much.'

It was not that she did not want him too, only that she was terrified, as every girl was, of the disgrace of finding herself pregnant and unmarried. It had been drilled into her since she was old enough to understand about such things that if that happened, her life would be over. Immorality led inexorably to ruin, degradation and exclusion from society.

And yet later, saying goodbye to Hugh outside the hospital, she clung to him, wishing she could turn back time. She was afraid she had offended him or that he thought her a tease. She might lose him, never having let him love her. What a prude she had been, what a fool.

Hugh returned to the carnage on the Western Front. He wrote to her twice a week; she lived for those letters and became sick with anxiety whenever they were delayed. In April he was entrained back to England after having been wounded at the Battle of Picardy. He was still woozy from the anaesthetic when he asked her to marry him. His right arm was heavily bandaged and in a sling when they were married by licence two weeks later. He never completely recovered from his injury; his writing remained that of a clumsy schoolboy.

Who on earth could they be, these *daughters* that the reception-ist had referred to? Might Hugh have been having an affair? Tears stung her eyes and spilled down her face. It occurred to her that if a man had wanted to keep a mistress, he might have constructed a life much like Hugh's. The fact that one of his businesses was in Glasgow meant that he had always travelled a great deal and was frequently away from home. Might he, a few years ago, have taken a mistress in Scotland and fathered on her a couple of illegitimate infants? But no, again that did not fit. *Mr Craxton's two daughters are arranging the funeral*. Any illegitimate daughter would have to be, surely, at least sixteen years old to be capable of arranging a funeral – and thus much the same age as Stuart. Sophie found it impossible to believe that Hugh could have kept a mistress for so long without her knowing about it. And surely any mistress, however low her morals and depraved her character, would have the decency to contact her, the bereaved wife, to let her know that her husband was dead. There was some mistake. She would sort it out tomorrow.

And yet doubt piled upon doubt. What did she know about Hugh? Not much. That he had had an unhappy childhood, brought up in a dim, damp, Devon parsonage which he had left at the age of eighteen and never returned to. His parents had died before Sophie had met him; he had no family. Her own mother had never liked him. 'Handsome is as handsome does,' Mrs Torrance had said, with a sniff, after meeting Hugh for the first time.

What else? He disliked crowds, so they did not go to the cinema or the theatre and took their holidays in quiet seaside or country towns. When they went out for a meal it was generally to a modest local establishment, though Hugh, who loved her cooking, preferred to dine at home. He was not a clubbable man and preferred the company of his family to evenings with male friends. He did not have any friends of his own so far as she knew, apart from Malcolm Reid. He found her friends and their neighbours dull, so she tended to visit them by herself. There were no supper invitations to each other's houses. Hugh had never introduced her to any of his colleagues. 'Tedious lot,' he had told her. 'I won't inflict them on you, my love. It may be selfish of me but I prefer to have you to myself.'

Hugh was clever and fun, inventive and generous. His presence could transform a run-of-the-mill day into an adventure. He was capable of stoicism and courage – those medals for his three and a half years' service during the Great War proved that. But he was also easily bored, and his restless streak meant that he went out for a walk on his own most evenings, even when it was dark and cold and rainy. He had no allegiance to any church or political party and had once told her that he had lost the capacity for any sort of faith during the war. He was affable, he was charming, but he could be quiet and inward-looking too. There were times when he shut himself off from her.

Hugh was a loving and passionate man but he had a wandering eye. Now and then she caught him looking at women in the street. This had always been a source of pain to her. Could he have done this terrible thing? Was he capable of fathering two daughters, half-siblings to Duncan and Stuart, and hiding them away for years? Surely not, she said to herself as she rose and took the pins out her hair. Surely such treachery was unimaginable.

She must have dozed off eventually because she woke at six the following morning in a tangle of sheet and blankets. The temperature had risen during the night and when she looked out of the window she saw that the snow had gone. The change in the weather contributed to the air of tension and division that hung over the household. The boys were surly and quarrelsome and Sophie had a headache.

But she had made her plan. Once Duncan and Stuart had gone out she called the operator and explained that she needed to find the telephone number of an undertaker in Glasgow. Her stomach gave a twist of anxiety as she sat in the hall, telephone receiver in hand. An old friend had died, she told the operator. She had had a note informing her of his death, but no further information, and she did not know who to contact about the funeral. Yes, it was very worrying. If the exchange would kindly put her through to some Glasgow undertakers, she might be able to discover which firm was dealing with the arrangements. No, she did not know in which area of the city to look first. Not the poorer parts, if that was any help.

It was funny, she thought later, how you could sit there, trying to find out whether your husband was alive or dead, and yet still feel a mild panic at the cost of the trunk calls. It was the eighth undertaker, a Mr Peasgood of Peasgood and Price, who confirmed the news Craxton's receptionist had broken to her the previous day. Sophie told her story again, giving her maiden name of Torrance to stave off any intrusive questions. The undertaker's soft voice informed her that yes, Peasgood and Price were assisting Mr Craxton's daughters in the arrangements for the funeral of Mr Hugh Craxton, who had passed away on Boxing Day, and yes, Mr Hugh Craxton had been the managing director of the stationery suppliers Craxton & Sons.

Disbelief and panic. Sophie had to take a deep breath to steady herself before asking Mr Peasgood a further question. Would he please confirm the deceased Mr Craxton's full name?

A ruffling of papers; then the honeyed tones resumed. 'Hugh James Dashwood Craxton, Mrs Torrance.'

She forced out a thank you and put down the telephone receiver. Though she might have expected to feel grief now that her worst fears had been confirmed and any room for doubt removed, instead, rage of a tempestuous ferocity ripped through her. She went into the drawing room and climbed on to a chair. Then, reaching up on tiptoe, she tore down the paper chains that hung from the ceiling and with a single sweep of the hand toppled the Christmas cards from the mantelpiece.

Gasping for breath, Sophie stood in the middle of the room, surrounded by a sea of coloured paper, robins and snowmen.

Chapter Three

January 1938

The astrakhan collar of Thea's black coat itched; she put up a hand to adjust it and her fingers, brushing against her father's maroon cashmere scarf, tucked round her neck, released a faint scent of Turkish tobacco and Blenheim Bouquet, fragrances she always associated with him. She gulped, and Rowan, who was sitting to one side of her, put a hand on her arm. Rowan had put down her black net veil so Thea could not properly see her comforting smile, but she knew it was there all the same. Her sister was wearing a beautifully tailored black coat, black hat, black stockings and shoes. The only flash of colour was the bright coil of hair at the nape of her neck.

Patrick was sitting on Thea's other side. As chief mourners, they were occupying the front pew. Thea would rather have sat at the back but that wasn't allowed. The church was desperately cold, and from the congregation seated behind them came a subdued murmuring. The sight of her father's coffin, in front of the altar, made such a flurry of awful thoughts run through Thea's head that she dug her teeth into her lower lip. She didn't want to cry here. There was, she recognised, an illogicality in that: surely, if one was ever going to cry at all, it should be at the funeral of one's last-surviving parent. But positioned so, in front of so many strangers, she felt on display, and she hated that. At school prize-giving, she always dreaded the moment of walking across the stage to receive her copy of *The Master of Ballantrae* or whatever. If she were ever to marry, she would prefer to go to Gretna Green so there would be no one to stare.

Thea tried to distract herself by thinking about the funerary practices of ancient lands – of Egypt, the mummi-fication of bodies, grave goods buried with the dead, magic spells cast by priests. Would it be sacrilegious to think of the vicar's prayers as spells? And the tomb chambers of Ur, with their sacrificial bodies, the expendable slaves and wives deemed necessary to accompany the important dead. The organ music droned on and her thoughts moved to Neolithic burials and the long barrows of Wiltshire and the cairns of Scotland, where the dead were laid to rest alongside those objects precious to them in life, the polished flint arrow-heads, ivory buckles and strands of beads. What grave goods would she place beside her father? His hiking boots, she thought, his binoculars, a packet of Turkish cigarettes and a bottle of whisky. But not the cashmere scarf; she could never have parted with his cashmere scarf.

The murmuring faded a little; the service was about to start. Thea, who had hardly slept the previous night – had slept little during the two and a half weeks of her father's illness, death and its aftermath – and was afraid of exploding very publicly into wails of grief, changed her mental subject and thought about psychopomps. She had been thirteen years old when she had first come across the word in a book of mythology. For a long time it had been her favourite word. It was the role of the psychopomp to guide the newly dead soul to the afterlife. A psychopomp could be a god or an angel or even an animal. Who would escort her father to Heaven? Her father hadn't believed in Heaven, so did that mean no helpful psychopomp would come for him? Tears blurred her vision again. What creature for her father, to take him through the lands of the Dead? A stag, she decided, recalling with a pang a glorious autumn day the two of them had once spent walking in the Highlands. They had stood on a hillside, watching two stags locked in combat, and the sound of antlers clashing had carried through the cold air. Her father had been enraptured. Stags were proud, handsome, strong and remote, like him.

A loud rumble of organ music broke through her thoughts and then a sonorous succession of chords gathered themselves into the introduction to 'Dear Lord and Father'. Thea wiped away her tears as she, along with the rest of the congregation, rose to her feet.

And it was over, the service and the burial, and she found that it was true, what some people had said to her beforehand, that she did feel a little relief. As they walked away from the graveside, the wind stung and their shoes crunched the snow.

Rowan put a hand on Thea's sleeve. 'Are you all right, darling?'

Thea nodded. 'Are you?'

'I'll be awfully relieved when today's over. But here goes. Could you bear to thank the secretaries and typists? I'll do the managers.'

The staff of Craxton & Sons had come out in force for the funeral of the firm's owner and were now scattered in respectful little clumps round the graveyard, talking quietly to each other. The factory and offices had closed that day as a mark of respect. Thea shook hands and thanked the female staff, in their funeral blacks. Though she murmured the polite questions Rowan had drilled into her that morning over breakfast she felt self-conscious and worried that she wasn't doing it very well.

She caught sight of a woman standing on her own near the porch, beside a headstone that blossomed with grey and orange lichen. She looked as if she felt much as Thea did and was finding the whole thing an ordeal. Thea walked over to her and offered her hand.

'Good morning. I'm Thea Craxton.'

Large sapphire-blue eyes studied Thea, then the woman shook her hand. 'Mrs Torrance.'

Question number one. 'Did you work closely with my father, Mrs Torrance?'

A shake of the head. 'I'm not an employee. I'm a . . . I'm a friend.'

Mrs Torrance was much the same height as Thea. Locks of her fair curly hair sprung out from beneath the brim of her hat. Thea, who had straight dark hair, always felt deeply envious of women with properly curly hair, which must save them all the tiresome messing around with pin curls and rags.

She moved on to question number two. 'Have you come far?'

'From London.'

'My sister lives in London, in Chelsea. Do you live there?'

'No, in South Kensington.'

Mrs Torrance suddenly looked terribly upset. Thea felt sorry for her. 'Funerals are so awful, aren't they?'

Mrs Torrance stared at her. Thea was afraid that she had said the wrong thing. She was trying to think how to retrieve the situation when Mrs Torrance spoke again.

'Did he . . . did he suffer?'

Thea murmured, 'Not too much, no.' It was a lie, but she couldn't bear thinking about the last week of her father's life, and anyway, that was what Rowan had told her to say. *I know it's not true, Thea, but some of them have worked for Dad for years and years, and there's no point making them feel even more miserable.* Mrs Torrance might not be an employee of Craxton's, but the same rule must surely apply.

Mrs Torrance's gaze swung across the churchyard to where Rowan was talking to Mr Paterson. 'Is that your sister over there? With the red hair?'

'Yes, that's Rowan. And that's her husband, Patrick, next to her, the fair-haired man.'

The haunted blue stare swung back to her. 'Your sister's married?'

'Yes.'

'How old is she?'

'Rowan's nearly twenty-four.'

'Twenty-four . . .' Mrs Torrance was staring at her, her expression – well, Thea could only interpret it as horror. 'And you?'

'I'm sixteen.'

A silence, then the older woman spoke again, suddenly, harshly. 'Where's your mother?'

'She's dead. She died when I was a little girl.'

'I'm sorry.' The eyes dropped at last; a shake of the blonde head. Mrs Torrance muttered, 'Forgive me.'

Thea was distracted by their neighbours, the Macdonalds, a couple in their sixties, attracting her attention to apologise that they would not be able to attend the funeral breakfast. When she turned back, she saw to her surprise that Mrs Torrance had gone. A movement caught her eye. A small, black-coated figure was heading fast along the road, away from the church.

She must have put her foot in it, Thea reflected glumly, though when she ran back the exchange in her head it seemed to her that her remarks had been gauche and clumsy rather than annoying or upsetting. She was unable to face any more talking to strangers – and besides, her eye was caught by a growth on a nearby gravestone, a nice little clump of golden crustose lichen: *caloplaca flavescens*, she thought, squinting at it.

Rowan extracted herself gracefully from her conversation with Mr Paterson, her father's manager at the stationery factory. Large black cars were drawing up by the roadside to take her and Thea and Patrick and the old and infirm to the hotel that was providing the funeral breakfast. It was only a quarter of a mile away so the rest of the mourners would walk.

Patrick was still engaged in conversation with Miss Naylor, her father's secretary. Rowan gave her husband his due, he was good at occasions like this. He did what had to be done and had been such a help with all the ghastly arrangements and sweetly comforting throughout. He was so perfect in some ways, she thought with a stab of misery, and she was such an awful person for cheating on him.

She yearned for this day to be over and to return to London. It was unspeakable of her to have found herself thinking about Simon Pemberton on the day of her father's funeral, yet she had and hated herself for it. She had not heard from Simon since they had parted at his flat on the night of the Manninghams' party. She was afraid that, failing to see her in the usual places, he might think she was avoiding him.

A voice saying her name broke through her thoughts. Rowan looked round and saw a distinguished-looking man in his fifties.

'Mr Ross,' she said. Mr Ross was Craxton & Sons' chief accountant. 'Thank you so much for coming.'

Mr Ross took off his hat and shook her hand. 'Forgive me for interrupting you, Mrs Scott, but might we have a private word when it's convenient?'

'Tomorrow?' Rowan suggested. 'Perhaps in the afternoon . . .'

'I'm afraid it's urgent. It's to do with the firm. I really do need to talk to you today.'

'Oh.' The day that stretched out before her was already unendurably long and full of dreadful obligations, but she smiled and said, 'This afternoon, then. Would five o'clock suit you?'

'Thank you, Mrs Scott.'

She looked round, trying to find Thea. What on earth did Mr Ross want to talk to her about, and why had he been so insistent? She knew nothing about the business. Dad had never talked about it much and, if she was honest, she had never been able to raise the slightest interest in envelopes and visiting cards. Rowan caught sight of Thea, crouching in the snow, peering at a gravestone, and went to join her.

Sophie was on the London train. When that girl had said to her, *Do you live in Chelsea, Mrs Torrance?* she had for a moment thought of replying, 'No, Hugh and I live in South

Kensington.' Perhaps she should have done, she thought savagely. Or perhaps, as they lowered Hugh's coffin into the grave, she should have burst through the circle of mourners and shouted, 'He was married to me!'

That she hadn't was due partly to an innate politeness and her dislike of the theatrical, and partly because she knew now that she and Hugh had never been married. Sophie broke off a chunk of the slice of Dundee cake she had bought from the café at Glasgow Central Station and popped it in her mouth. Having hardly eaten anything at all for days she was suddenly ravenously hungry.

She stared out of the carriage window at the rows of factories and tenement houses, with their icing of snow, and once more checked the arithmetic in her head. It was hard doing the sums when her brain reeled with shock, exhaustion and worry, but do them she must. The eulogy had been given by a Mr Paterson, who had begun by sum-marising the salient events of the deceased's life. Hugh had married his wife, Sigrid, in 1912, six years before she, Sophie, had met him. Six years! A daughter, Rowan, had been born in 1914 – the congregation's sympathetic gaze had turned to the front pew. Mr Paterson had then alluded to Hugh Craxton's heroic service to his country during the war before going on to mention the births of a second daughter, Thea, in 1921. Which meant that between the birth of his two sons, Duncan and Stuart, Hugh had fathered another child, that girl, Thea, who was now sixteen.

All that had put paid to any final, fragile hope Sophie might have had that Hugh had been widowed or divorced but had somehow omitted to tell her by the time she herself had married him in 1918. The bleak, cold mathematics of it all confirmed what she had known in her heart since she

41

had talked to Thea Craxton: that it was *her* marriage that was bigamous, *her* children who were illegitimate.

All this was too huge and too terrible for her to absorb. That Hugh had two grown daughters. That, when he had proposed to her, he had already been married to another woman. That her marriage had never been valid and that he had lied and lied and lied to her for two decades. She did not know how she had managed to get on the right train.

Mr Paterson had droned on, hammering nails into Sophie's heart. He had mentioned the death of Hugh's beloved wife, Sigrid, in a tragic accident, after which, according to Mr Paterson, a grief-stricken Hugh had carried out with stoicism and valour the task of bringing up his two young daughters on his own. Hugh Craxton had been a man of humour and good cheer, the eulogy had concluded. Here, Mr Paterson had slipped into cliché, describing Hugh as having bravely conquered life's vicissitudes. He had had a passion for the Scottish countryside . . . and for that other great product of the country, a fine malt whisky. Well, that at least was true, Sophie had thought angrily as a murmur of laughter rose from the congregation. Sophie herself had been afraid she might actually vomit. At least the roiling of her stomach had provided some fleeting distraction from the horror of discovering that the man she had thought she had known, the man she had believed to have been her husband, had in fact been a stranger to her.

Sophie finished the cake and leaned back against the headrest, closing her eyes. She had travelled from London to Glasgow yesterday, having told the boys a story about going to Cornwall to see an old friend who was unwell. She knew that Duncan hadn't believed her.

After her long journey, she had booked into a small guest

house a few roads away from the church where Hugh's funeral was to be held. She had not slept at all the previous night, kept awake by fear and dread and the icy chill of her bedroom, which had no fire. In the morning, she had walked to the church, a large, imposing red sandstone building, and waited in the bus shelter on the opposite side of the road as the mourners arrived. Some came by motor car, others by bus or on foot. Unable until the last moment to decide whether to attend the service, she had eventually been driven into the church by the cold (her feet were blocks of ice) and had taken a seat in a pew at the back. Somehow, she had stood for the hymns and knelt for the prayers.

And now she was tired beyond endurance, wrung out and aching and longing for home. She could find only one sour consolation, that the straws she had grasped at during the past two and a half weeks had finally been obliterated, incinerated to grey, ashy fragments. If the enormity of Hugh's betrayal was impossible to take in, at least she was now spared the task of inventing excuses for him.

When she thought about what he had done, whenever it drearily re-inserted itself into her head after some brief distraction, a fresh wave of pain and anguish washed over her. For the last twenty years Hugh had ruthlessly and methodically deceived her. He had deceived her sons, too, and that made her hate him most.

Presumably he had also lied to his daughters and their mother, though they were not her concern. She closed her eyes again and an image of Hugh's daughters sprang into her mind. The younger girl, Thea, had been small, slight and dark and brown-eyed; the elder, red-haired Rowan, was tall and elegant and strikingly beautiful. Both girls had been well dressed. Sophie, who cared about clothes, had recognised that the Craxton girls' garments were of superior quality and newer than her own. Perhaps Hugh's first family had been better off than his second.

She hated him for that too, not for her own sake (she had been brought up to be careful with money), but for her sons'. Well, I could break your comfortable world in two, Rowan Craxton, or whatever your name is now, Sophie thought meanly. I could wipe away that polite smile and serene expression with a few words. In the next moment, her anger was replaced by fear as she recalled something else Thea Craxton had said to her. Rowan and her husband, Patrick, lived in Chelsea, which was just around the corner from South Kensington. They were almost *neighbours*, her boys and Hugh's daughters. They might run into each other any day in the street. And that was too appalling to contemplate.

A blast of white smoke obliterated the landscape beyond the window, and then, as they rattled on, it thinned, revealing soaring hills and shadowed valleys, illuminated by snow as dusk fell. When she had asked Thea Craxton whether Hugh had suffered, Sophie could not have honestly said what she wanted the answer to be. He deserved to burn in hell for his lies and for a betrayal she could not imagine she would ever be able to recover from. And yet a sense of futility washed over her. Nothing could make any difference now. Nothing could ever make up for what he had done to her.

She must have groaned out loud, because the man sitting opposite her – fortyish, respectable-looking, grey wool overcoat – said, 'Forgive me for intruding, madam, but I was just going to the buffet car. May I get you something? A brandy, perhaps?'

Sophie murmured a polite refusal. The man in the grey

wool overcoat left the compartment. A woman wearing an ugly green hat, who was sitting beside Sophie, stared at her. Sophie stared back and the woman dropped her gaze. Did she look like the sort of woman who might accept a drink from a strange man on a train? If she did, it was hardly surprising. In the passing of a day, she had become that sort of woman. She was a mistress, a tart. There were worse words for what she was, for a woman who had lived with a man for more than nineteen years without being married to him.

How had Hugh kept up the pretence? How had the strain of living two lives not enervated and wearied him and reduced him to despair? Perhaps it had – or perhaps he had enjoyed it, she thought with a fresh rush of anger. Had he been ashamed of the secrets he had kept, or had he relished them? It wasn't hard to imagine Hugh enjoying the feeling of being in control and beating the system. He had always had a dislike of authority and a contempt for societal conventions. Perhaps living two lives had allowed him to feel that he was more interesting than most men. Hugh had always prided himself on his cleverness. Perhaps she had only ever been an antidote to the boredom and restlessness that had plagued him.

Her judgement of herself was quick and condemnatory. How could she have failed to notice that something was so badly wrong? Had he chosen her because she was stupid, besotted and blind? Because there had been clues, this she now saw as she recalled the sudden whims and changes of plan that Hugh had been prone to and that had sometimes unbalanced her. A restaurant they had visited on her birthday, where Hugh had reserved a table. When they had arrived there, he had glanced round the room and decided he didn't care for it and they had left without saying a word to the waiting staff. A summer holiday in Torquay; they had been walking along the esplanade when Hugh had without warning steered them in a different direction. Later that day he had insisted they book out of the hotel and return to London.

She remembered important occasions that Hugh had failed to turn up for, sports days and prize-givings and Founder's Days. He had been late for her mother's funeral. Hugh and her mother had never got on; at the time Sophie had thought it a deliberate slight. She and Hugh had lived as if on an island, cut off from the rest of the world. He had insisted they live like that, but she had enabled him.

A fresh onslaught of anger consumed her. Why was she thinking of Hugh – why was she thinking of wretched, damnable Hugh? She shouldn't waste another second on him. Only her sons mattered. She must find a way of protecting them, because they had no one but her now. Yet she dreaded telling Duncan and Stuart the truth about their father, a dread that magnified with every rotation of the train's wheels, bringing her closer to London. What Hugh had done was monstrous and would cause them unbearable hurt. Better to let them believe that Hugh had left her or that he had disappeared off the face of the earth. Better to let them believe anything at all apart from the truth.

But if she did not break it to them that their father had died, they might spend the rest of their lives looking for him. Stuart would, at least; Duncan's anger with Hugh was already palpable. Which was crueller, she wondered, to tell them that their father was dead, and that he had lied to them throughout his entire life, or to leave them with a hope that was entirely false? Wouldn't that make her as treacherous as Hugh?

It would be nine o'clock or so before she reached home.

It occurred to her that she could quite reasonably and truth-fully claim tiredness after her journey. She would go straight to bed and postpone any conversation.

No. As the train slowed to a halt at Carlisle station, she made up her mind that, whatever happened, she would always be honest with her boys. They had had enough lies. Telling them about Hugh was going to be awful anyway, no matter when she did it.

Whistles shrieked and doors slammed. No matter how much it hurt her, she would tell them the truth, as kindly and gently as was feasible. From now on her sons would have nothing but the truth.

Even the house seemed unfamiliar, thought Thea, as she went into the drawing room. Nothing was as it should be. A rather sickening scent of lilies perfumed the ground floor, and Jessie, the maid, was moving round the rooms with exaggeratedly light footsteps instead of her customary galumph as she laid the fires. Throughout the day, the sheer blinds had been pulled down over the three large windows and the willow-green curtains kept partly drawn. Jessie had seen fit to light only a handful of lamps, presumably judging the gloomy light appropriate to recent events, and now dark shadows daubed the grand piano, the cream-coloured bureau and pale-green upholstered armchairs, with their scrolled arms and curved backs, brought from Thea's mother's family home in Sweden on her marriage.

Mr Ross, her father's firm's chief accountant, had called in the late afternoon. They had received him here, in the drawing room, and a short conversation had followed. By the time it was over Thea had known that nothing would ever be the same again.

47

Mr Ross had told them that there wasn't enough money in Craxton & Sons' bank account to pay the staff wages. The stationery firm had been struggling for years, Mr Ross explained, after having been almost bankrupted earlier in the decade, during the years of the Depression. Since then, the business had sunk further into the red. Blow after blow had followed, with the force of a mallet striking a tent peg. Hugh Craxton had propped up the business by taking out a further mortgage on his house – this house. Mr Ross had advised Hugh against taking out the mortgage. He had pointed out that it would be unwise to use the family home as collateral to shore up an ailing business, but Hugh had insisted. Patrick had said, 'A further mortgage, Ross?' and Mr Ross had said yes, he had understood that the house was mortgaged already.

After Mr Ross left the house, Rowan had telephoned their family solicitor, Mr Macready, who with bleak courtesy had confirmed everything that the accountant had told them. And more: Mr Macready had informed them that there was nothing left in Mr Craxton's personal bank account. Both mortgages were in arrears. Hugh Craxton's daughters would have no alternative but to sell the family home. The money raised from the sale was unlikely to be sufficient in present financial conditions to pay off both mortgages.

Thea had known none of this. The business, the house, had been such constants in her life that even now, several hours later, a part of her questioned whether there had been some mistake. That they had lived precariously for years, that their seemingly solid life had been built on sand, was impossible to take in.

Rowan came into the room. She had changed out of her funeral clothes into a grey skirt and Fair Isle jersey. She flung herself on to a sofa beside Thea.

'Good lord, what a day,' said Thea.

'Yes.'

'So we're ruined.'

'That's rather melodramatic, but yes, looks like it.'

'Did Dad ever say anything?'

'Not a whisper.'

'Maybe he didn't want to worry us. Poor Dad.'

Thea remembered visiting the factory once, years and years ago, when she was a young girl: the smell of paper and oily machinery and the visiting cards that one of the men had made for her, with their goffered gilt edges. Her father hadn't even tried to economise. Though he must have known about their precarious financial situation, they had gone on living in the old lavish style.

She asked Rowan where Patrick was.

'He has some work to do. He must return to London tomorrow. A case has come up, some woman who hit her husband on the head with an iron and hid his body in the coal hole.' Rowan yawned. 'He had a quick look through Daddy's desk and he found a receipt for your next term's school fees. So that's been paid, thank goodness.'

With borrowed money, thought Thea. It was hard to imagine going back to her boarding school in North Yorkshire; she felt she had outgrown it, that too much had happened for her to be able to slip back with any ease into the routine of classroom and playing field.

Rowan was saying, 'When the spring term ends, you must come and live with us. You'll always have a home with us, you know that, don't you, for as long as you like.' When Thea tried to thank her, Rowan hushed her. 'There was never a question, Thea.'

Rowan's kindness made her want to cry again. But she

was tired of crying, so she said, 'Did you ever hear Dad speak of a woman called Mrs Torrance?'

'I don't think so. Why?'

'She came to the funeral. I spoke to her in the churchyard. She was small, about my height, with curly blonde hair and blue eyes. Very pretty.'

Rowan shook her head. 'I don't think I know her. Did she work for Daddy?'

'No. She told me she was a friend of his.' When Thea ran back their conversation in her head some of Mrs Torrance's questions seemed rather odd. Why on earth had she wanted to know how old she and Rowan were? Why had she asked her about their mother? If she had known Dad well enough to come all the way to London for the funeral, then surely he would have told her about Mamma drowning?

She said, 'She seemed quite upset. And then she just dashed off. I hope it wasn't anything I said. I wondered . . .'

A tap at the door; Jessie stuck her head in with an offer of tea and sandwiches.

'Not for me, thank you, Jessie,' said Rowan. 'What about you, Thea?'

'No thanks.'

As the maid closed the door, Rowan murmured, 'I'll scream if someone gives me another meat paste sandwich and cup of tepid tea. What did you wonder?'

Thea voiced her suspicion baldly. 'Whether Mrs Torrance was Dad's mistress. I wondered whether they'd met when Dad was at the London office and she was his lover, something like that.'

'What if she was? He deserved some happiness.'

The defensive note in Rowan's voice made Thea reluctant to pursue the subject further. Her gaze swung to the portrait of their mother that hung over the mantelpiece. Sigrid Craxton had been Swedish, raised in a cold, spare landscape of lake and forest. In the painting, Sigrid was wearing a white shirt and cream-coloured skirt. Her white-blonde hair fell loose to her waist and there was a touch of defiance in her blue gaze. Dappled sunlight falling through tall trees gave her the appearance of melting into the landscape, as if even then she had been fading out of sight.

Sigrid had died when Thea was six years old, in a sailing accident in which Thea, too, had almost drowned. Rowan, who had been thirteen years old at the time, had rescued her, swimming with her in her arms the half-mile from the site of the accident on a rocky outcrop off the coast of the Isle of Corran, to the Scottish mainland. The fact that Thea literally owed Rowan her life had made a bond between them that would tie them together for ever. Sisters were often close but the Craxton sisters were even closer than most. Even so, there were subjects Thea knew she must avoid with Rowan. Rowan never spoke fondly of their mother. She rarely spoke of her at all. When Thea tried to speak to her about Sigrid, Rowan became tight-lipped. Thea wondered whether they had clashed during Sigrid's lifetime, those two strong-willed, energetic females.

Though Thea, like Rowan, had loved their father very much, she had known he wasn't perfect. He liked to flirt with pretty women. There had been a holiday in the south of France where a dark, sulky creature he met on the beach had claimed much of his attention. Thea had spent a lot of that week trudging round sandy pine woods on her own, looking for wheatears and mistle thrushes. And she remembered another occasion at a hotel in Balmoral, where Hugh had enjoyed the company of a Mrs Vale. Thea, exploring

51

prehistoric sites in the nearby hills, hadn't minded, had only worried a little that her father might marry Mrs Vale, who had worn too much lipstick. Fortunately, he hadn't.

She changed the subject. 'I couldn't find an address for Malcolm Reid, either.'

'Who?'

'You know, Dad's friend.' Rowan still looked blank, so Thea explained, 'Dad was going to spend Christmas with him, remember, in the Highlands. He used to go hunting and fishing with Mr Reid.' Because she had not been able to find an address in her father's effects, she had not yet written to let Mr Reid know that her father had died. She must have another search. There must be letters, a phone number, something. She remembered how much her father had been looking forward to his fishing trip and dug her teeth into her lower lip.

'Ghastly Christmas for you, darling,' said Rowan gently.

'And for you.'

'Though at least it spared me the annual visit to the in-laws,' said Rowan, with black humour. 'I have that small consolation.' She glanced round the room. 'Oh dear, I suppose we'll have to sort everything out.'

All these familiar, beloved objects must be sold. Rowan and Patrick's house was too small to contain the Craxtons' furniture and ornaments. Thea felt a fresh pang of grief. It would be like parting with old friends.

Buck up, Thea, she admonished herself sternly. No use getting sentimental over tables and chairs. 'I'll go through Dad's paperwork,' she offered.

'Are you sure?'

'I've been through a lot of it already, to find people's addresses. And I know you hate that sort of thing.'

'I do, but you must give me things to do,' said Rowan firmly. 'I won't leave you with all the awful letter-writing.'

Thea wondered how Mrs Torrance had found out that Hugh Craxton was dead. Perhaps someone at the London office had told her. Had anyone from the London office come to the funeral? She did not know.

Patrick came into the room. 'May I get you girls anything? Sherry . . . tea . . . anything?'

They both declined. Patrick said, 'Before I leave tomorrow, Rowan, I'll give you some cash so that you can pay Jessie and Mrs Williams.' Mrs Williams came to the house daily to scrub floors and clean out grates. 'It's probably best if you give Mrs Williams her notice now, I'm afraid, but it will be worth hanging on to Jessie until the house is sold. You both looked whacked. Why don't you go up to bed?'

He put his hand on Rowan's shoulder. Rowan gave a little twitch and rearranged herself, brushing off the brief contact.

Thea rose and kissed them both, and then went upstairs to her bedroom. But though she lay in the darkness and conscientiously counted sheep, sleep would not come. Thoughts tumbled through her head. During the course of the afternoon, a treasured old ambition, that she would go to university and study history, had withered and died, scattered to nothingness like ashes in the wind, impossible now.

And yet she could not feel sorry for herself. Patrick would pay Jessie's and Mrs Williams' wages but he could not pay the wage bill for the entire firm. Everyone who worked at Craxton & Sons would shortly lose their jobs. They would not be paid their last week's wages.

Two mortgages, an empty bank account and a family business on the verge of bankruptcy. What else had her father kept to himself?

Thea's mind drifted to the last hike she and her father had taken, in the Yorkshire Dales, at autumn half-term. The patter of rain and the rush of papery brown leaves, hurled by the wind from the trees. The plash of their boots on the muddy path as they headed downhill to a farmhouse for tea. If she concentrated very, very hard she could still feel the weight of his arm round her shoulders. He must have known by then that the business was failing and he would lose everything. Was there valour in pretending cheerful optimism when you were on the brink of catastrophe, Thea wondered, or was it an act of folly? Had her father tried to keep the fact that his world was falling apart even from himself?

Sitting at the dressing table in what had once been her childhood bedroom, cold-creaming her face, Rowan wondered whether Thea was right, and that their father had had a mistress in London.

She brushed the thought away. It wasn't her business or Thea's. Downstairs, doors closed and Rowan heard footsteps on the stairs. Hastily, she wiped off the cold cream, and then, before Patrick came into the room, she climbed into bed, turned off the lamp and closed her eyes.

Sophie said, 'Where are you going?' and Duncan said, 'Out.' The slam of the front door reverberated through the house.

She found Stuart in the kitchen, scoffing a cold rasher of bacon.

'Did Duncan tell you where he was going?'

Stuart shook his head. Sophie looked out of the window. It was not yet properly light, a grey, wet early morning. Misery spread through her at the thought of poor Duncan wandering aimlessly round London in the cold.

'He's just angry about Dad,' said Stuart.

'I know, darling.' Duncan hadn't eaten any breakfast. Duncan was angry with Hugh, but he was also angry with her. Sophie did not say this to Stuart because Stuart might think it unreasonable of his brother. She could see how easily this small, reduced family of hers might split into factions if she wasn't very careful. And besides, she could perfectly understand why Duncan might blame her, too, why he might think her remiss and foolish for trusting Hugh, for letting him get away with it for so long.

Words escaped her, laced with tears. 'What if he doesn't come home?'

Stuart looked up. 'He will, Mum. He'll get hungry.'

'He might, I don't know, run away to sea or something!'

'He won't. Duncan doesn't like ships, he likes aeroplanes. Shall I wash up?'

'Thank you, darling, but it's all right.'

'I want to.' Stuart plunged all sorts of things into the sink: cutlery and glasses and bowls. Then he said, 'Mum, are you completely sure about Dad? That this isn't all a mistake?'

'Yes, I'm sure.' She put a comforting hand on his back. 'I wish there was a mistake, but I'm afraid there isn't.'

Stuart said nothing. The tap ran. When she had broken the news of their father's death to her sons the night before, after arriving home from her trip to Glasgow, their reactions had been predictable. Stuart had wept and Duncan had been suspicious. Why had he and Stuart not attended their father's funeral? Why had it been held in Glasgow, and not London? If Dad had died on Boxing Day, why hadn't they known about it? Or had she known and kept it from them?

In the answering of these questions, everything had been laid bare. Hugh's other family, the two daughters – Duncan and Stuart's *half-sisters*, for heaven's sake — and the illegality of her marriage: all had been exposed. *Christ*, Duncan had said softly, when she was through. And then he had gone upstairs — more door-slamming — and though, later, she had tapped on his door and said his name, he had not answered.

Stuart was washing up in the way of a teenage boy, swashing plates and bowls around so that water sloshed over the sink and dabbing ineffectually with the little mop. Sophie removed the remaining specks of food with the tea towel as she dried.

Stuart said suddenly, 'Mum, do you think . . . do you think it was an accident?'

'Your father marrying me, do you mean?'

'Yes.'

'It's hard to see how it could have been.' She saw that Stuart was trying hard not to cry again, and said gently, 'I think what you mean is that it might have been an impulse, that Hugh might have married me on the spur of the moment without thinking it through. And yes, I do think that's possible. We married in wartime. Plenty of couples made hasty marriages back then. Perhaps your father didn't believe that he would survive the war. Or perhaps his first marriage wasn't happy and he decided he deserved some happiness after all he'd been through. Yes, I can imagine him thinking that.'

'Do you miss him, Mum?'

He was gazing at her, yearning in his eyes. She knew he wanted her to say yes, to give Hugh permission, a let-out.

But she had promised to tell her boys the truth, so she said, 'At the moment . . . no, I'm too angry with him.' And too hurt. There were moments, many moments, when she hated Hugh, when she was glad that he had died, when she found herself hoping that Thea Craxton had lied and that he had suffered.

'I miss him, Mum.'

'Of course you do.' She put her arm round him. 'He was your dad.'

Later that day, when she was alone in the house, she burned Hugh's letters in the kitchen stove. Love letters he had written to her when he was in the army, on flimsy official paper, letters on blue bonded notepaper that he had posted to her when travelling on business. Postcards and birthday cards, treasured for years, and the little billets-doux he had sent to her daily when she was working at the hospital. Shoving them into the stove, she watched his words blacken and curl, every one of them a lie.

Chapter Four

April–June 1938

The was lying on her stomach on her bed in the Scotts' guest room, reading *The Voyage of the Beagle*. There was a tap on the door and Rowan came in.

Dragging herself away from the Galapagos Islands, Thea looked up. 'Gorgeous dress,' she said. The skirt of her sister's evening gown fell from the hips in folds of soft red. 'Is it new?'

'Quite.' Rowan looked evasive. 'I'm awfully sorry, but could you do me a favour?'

'Anything you like.'

'Could you take a letter to a friend of mine?'

'Now, d'you mean?'

'I'm afraid so. It's rather urgent.'

Thea took the letter Rowan held out to her and glanced at the address on the envelope. *Mr S. Pemberton . . . Charles Street.*

'Simon's an old friend of mine,' Rowan explained in a rush. 'He's very keen on antique furniture. I thought Daddy's little card table might be French and Simon might be interested, but apparently it isn't. I was going to speak to him tonight at the Charlburys', but I'd forgotten we're to dine with the Stanleys so I won't see him after all.'

'Can't you phone him?'

'He doesn't have a telephone.' A look of irritation crossed Rowan's face. 'He says they're intrusive and unpleasantly modern.'

'Jolly useful, though. Of course I'll take it. I could do with a walk.' Thea put on her bottle-green school mac and stuffed the letter into a pocket.

'Thank you, darling, so sweet of you.' Rowan hugged her. She handed Thea a ten-shilling note. 'You must take a taxi.'

'No need, I'll walk.'

'It's raining. And not at this time of night, not on your own. I insist.' Rowan frowned. 'You won't mention this to Patrick, will you? He'd only be cross with me for forgetting about this wretched dinner.'

'I won't say a thing.'

'Thea, your hat.'

Thea peered round the room. Her hat, a black felt thing, wasn't anywhere to be seen. She flicked up the hood of her mac, gave Rowan a smile and left the house.

She hadn't the slightest intention of taking a taxi. The drizzle was slight and she needed to stretch her legs. In the gardens that she passed, apple and pear blossom spilled, puffy and luminous, over brick walls and wooden fences. A magnolia raised its pale, ostentatious flowers to the dusky sky; she paused to admire the flush of pink on the waxy petals. Breathing in the heady scent of some shrub – she would look it up later – Thea jammed her hands into her pockets and walked towards Sloane Square.

She had been living with Rowan and Patrick in Mallord Street for the last fortnight. Not every brother-in-law would have accommodated a stray, impecunious sister-in-law, and she loved Patrick all the more for his generosity and kindness.

London was huge, unmanageable and confusing, a vast, bustling, soot-blackened mass of houses, government buildings, palaces, theatres, cinemas, factories, warehouses and offices. Thea was enjoying teaching herself to feel at ease with its sprawl. She wanted to be able to find her way around as instinctively as the girls of her own age who, in chic coats and little feathered hats perched on the sides of their head, lipstick and powder perfectly applied, travelled with a Londoner's slick facility, fitting themselves to the city's insistent, raucous rhythm.

Darting between traffic, she crossed Sloane Square. A silvery rain made the Tarmac and pavements gleam, blurring the new Peter Jones department building which was rising from the ground amid a cobweb of scaffolding. Cars and taxis flickered by, sheened with rain, with faces framed in their windows – a woman, her blonde hair the same drained, lifeless shade as her fur collar; a hard-faced man smoking a cigarette, his silk scarf a slash of white. On the pavement, a soggy double page from a newspaper, its headline blaring of the Sudetenland and Czechoslovakia, flapped wetly.

She walked past a sweep of tall, stately buildings, dodging out of the way of half a dozen loud-voiced gentlemen in black tie and tails, only to find herself almost tripping over an old woman, her hands and face covered in sores, crouched in a doorway. Thea fumbled in a pocket and dropped a couple of pennies in the tin mug. Ahead of her, an elderly couple walked hand in hand, sharing an umbrella.

Piccadilly was crowded and rainswept, a succession of bright lights and the mingling scents of wet pavements and *Shalimar* and the stale clothing of a one-legged war veteran, begging for coins. Thea admired the frocks and hats in the shop windows and peered into car showrooms where

Bentleys and Wolseleys were polished to a glacial shine. Couples spilled from taxis, hurrying through the rain to theatres and restaurants; half a dozen girls laughed and chattered as they emerged from a cinema, tying on scarves, splashing through puddles.

She turned into Half Moon Street, her hand brushing against the envelope in her pocket. Lamps glowed in the windows of tall, imposing houses. From the foot of a run of basement steps a dog barked at her; she clicked her tongue and it quietened.

She reached the four-storeyed building in which Mr Pemberton lived. The grace and antiquity of the house made her fleetingly regret not finding her hat and she made a half-hearted attempt at tidying her damp hair before ringing the bell. A doorman answered, Thea explained her errand and was let inside and directed up the graceful sweep of a central staircase.

A short, wiry man wearing a dark jacket and striped trousers opened the door to Mr Pemberton's flat.

Thea said, 'Mr Pemberton?'

'I am Mr Pemberton's manservant, madam. May I help you?'

Thea held out the letter. 'This is for Mr Pemberton.'

A voice called out in peevish tones, 'Is that you, Rowan? You're very late. I was expecting you half an hour ago.'

'It's not Rowan, Mr Pemberton,' Thea called back. 'I'm Thea Craxton, Rowan's sister.'

Simon Pemberton swept into view. He was tall and very handsome. 'So you're Rowan's sister.' He scrutinised her. 'You don't look like her.'

'People always say that.' She offered him the letter. 'Rowan asked me to deliver this.'

He thanked her but did not yet open the letter. Flicking it against his palm, he said, 'No doubt she's making some excuse.'

'She said the card table wasn't French, after all. She was going to tell you at the party but then she remembered that she had another engagement. I expect she's explained in her letter.'

'Do you? In my experience, Rowan rarely feels much need to explain.' Mr Pemberton frowned. 'Card table? Oh yes, the card table. You look rather wet. You had better come indoors.'

'That's very kind, but . . .'

Mr Pemberton spoke through her polite refusal. 'Give your coat to Leach, he will dry it for you.'

Thea did as she was told and gave her mackintosh to the manservant. Mr Pemberton said, 'You must join me in a cocktail.' Another hard glance at her. 'You're old enough for a cocktail, I assume?'

'Yes, I'm nineteen.'

She was seventeen. But this was London, and this was living, at last.

The hallway of the flat – oil paintings, statuary, and gilt and marble tables – promised splendours ahead, and the large, high-ceilinged drawing room she was shown into did not disappoint. Terracotta-and-gold curtains fell in sculpted swathes to either side of three tall windows that looked down over the street. The three large sofas, upholstered in cream and gold, were grouped round a marble fireplace. Arranged around the sides of the room were elegant, spindly chairs and settees and occasional tables and small, decorative cupboards. The room's grandeur and opulence was softened by the books and journals scattered on a low, central table.

'What a lovely room!' she exclaimed.

'So pleased you approve. Rowan tells me it's stuffy and over-furnished. Do sit down.'

Thea sat on a sofa, careful to keep her damp shoes away from the cream fabric. 'Rowan prefers modern things,' she said.

'Ah, here's Leach with our drinks. Leach makes the best pink gins in London.' Simon Pemberton added, 'Furnishing is one of the many topics on which Rowan and I disagree.'

Thea was trying to recover from having taken too large a mouthful of her bitter-tasting drink. She had been thirsty after her walk.

'She's awfully sorry,' she said. Rowan hadn't said she was sorry but it seemed tactful to say so.

'Hmm. Are you close?'

'Yes, very.'

'I have a sister, but we're not close at all. Would you forgive Rowan anything?'

Startled, she said, 'Yes, I expect so.'

'You have an understanding nature, then. I daresay that's fortunate with a sister like Rowan.'

'What do you mean?'

'One could never describe her as a *reliable* person, could one?'

'She's perfectly reliable about the things that matter,' Thea said crossly. 'Actually, I owe her my life. When I was a child, she saved me from drowning.'

'Did she? How admirable of her. One can picture it, Rowan ploughing through the waves, a child in her arms. She possesses physical courage, I've noticed that.' He made a placatory gesture. 'Forgive me, I've offended you. I'm afraid I'm in a foul mood today.'

He opened a gold cigarette case and offered it to her.

Thea took a cigarette and Simon lit it and his own, then snapped the case shut.

'Are you enjoying London, Miss Craxton?'

'Yes, thank you, it's tremendous fun.' The cigarette tasted foul, she thought, but in a different way to the gin. She added, 'I'm trying to find a job.'

'How fascinating. What had you in mind?'

'Office work, preferably. It's better paid than shop work or waitressing.' She wondered whether he thought her vulgar, talking about money. She suspected Simon Pemberton did not have to think much about money.

'Is that the height of your ambition, to work in an office?'

'No, I wanted to go to university, to study history, but my father died and I couldn't.'

'You're a bookish girl, then?' On his lips, the term sounded disparaging.

'I suppose I am.'

He made a loose gesture of the hand. 'I myself am completely without ambition.'

She wasn't sure whether he expected her to congratulate or commiserate with him, and so took refuge in the conventional. 'Have you and Rowan been friends for a long time, Mr Pemberton?'

'Simon. Do please call me Simon. No, not long. Though one saw her around. She's rather noticeable.'

He looked at her and frowned again. Thea wondered whether she had left a muddy footprint on the rug or had a smut on her face. But then he said, 'You have beautiful eyes, far finer than Rowan's.' Seeing her colour, he laughed. 'Poor Thea, I've embarrassed you. I'm sure that in the future a great many men will tell you the same thing. Tell me, which period of history are you interested in?'

They talked about ancient Egypt, and Simon showed her his collection of amulets in the shape of scarab beetles, which captivated her. After a while, she sensed his loss of interest in her, so she rose, saying that she must go. The butler, Leach, returned her mackintosh, now miraculously dry and deliciously warm – and the creases ironed out, she noticed.

She was relieved to escape both Simon Pemberton and his magnificent flat. The drizzle eased as she walked back to Piccadilly. Simon had made the comment about her eyes, which had been silly and untrue, to disconcert her. In teasing her, he had been amusing himself. Apart from their conversation about Egyptian history, no opinion of his had seemed genuine and every remark had come with a dash of mockery or provocation. But what annoyed Thea most had been the critical manner with which he had spoken of Rowan. *One could never describe her as a reliable person.* How dare he?

Uneasily, she made connections. The walls of the Mallord Street house were flimsy and at night she heard raised voices from Rowan and Patrick's bedroom, Rowan's voice mostly, along with discontented rumbles from Patrick. It felt uncomfortable, witnessing her sister's marriage at close quarters. It was a marriage that grated, neither seeming to find what they wanted in each other.

For much of the time, Rowan and Patrick lived separate lives. In the evening, Rowan would go out, a fox fur like a white cloud draped round her bare shoulders, clutching a little embroidered bag containing a purse, handkerchief, lipstick and compact. Patrick would return from chambers and plough alone through whatever plate of food the cook-general, Gwen, had left congealing in the oven. Afterwards, he worked at the dining-room table. He hadn't a study and there wasn't room for a desk in the bedroom. Much later, Rowan would come home, the fox askew, bringing with her friends who stayed, their loud voices and roars of laughter filling the house until the early hours of the morning. Sometimes some waif with nowhere to go ended up sleeping on the living-room sofa, and would still be there in the morning, wrapped in blankets, dead to the world, getting in Patrick's way as he got ready for work.

At weekends, there were always visitors at the Chelsea house. Rowan would invite people to a supper party or a dozen of her friends would drop by and Patrick would make cocktails. Rowan and Patrick were excellent hosts, Rowan sparkling and amusing and Patrick quietly charming, making sure no one felt left out. Guests always had a drink to hand and someone interesting to chat to.

Simon Pemberton had not only been critical of Rowan; he had been possessive. It was obvious that the story about the card table had been utter bunkum. He had hardly bothered even to pretend to lie. He was good-looking and cultured, both qualities that might appeal to Rowan. Thea had a horrible suspicion that Rowan might be in love with him.

She let herself into the Mallord Street house. The rooms were in darkness. She made herself a mug of cocoa and took it up to her bedroom. Stacked against one wall of the room were the files containing her father's papers, his correspondence, notebooks, address books and diaries, taken from the Glasgow house, which had been sold to pay creditors. The business had been wound up, too, though not before more uncomfortable surprises had been revealed. Craxton & Sons had no London office. There had never been a London office. Mr Ross, when Thea had asked him about it, had explained that all transactions were carried out in Glasgow, and that a team of sales representatives travelled round the country, drumming up business.

'But Dad often went away to the London office,' Thea had said, bewildered.

'Hugh often visited London.' There was sympathy – or perhaps pity – in Mr Ross's darting look. 'But it was unlikely to have been on Craxton's business. Your father's heart was never in his work, I'm afraid. He only inherited the business because Ralph, his elder brother, died in the war. Whatever he was doing in London, I don't think it had anything to do with Craxton's.'

So, then. Her father had travelled to London twice a month or so during Thea's school holidays to visit a London office that had been wholly fictional. Patrick had had a couple of suggestions. 'Hugh may have rented an office in London. Or he could have taken a desk in his club or in a library.' But Thea had found no record of her father making rental payments or ever having had membership of a club. And he hadn't been a library sort of man.

She sat on the bed, her gaze resting on the manila files. In the months since her father had died, she had been through every scrap of paper. She had found not a single reference, neither an address, phone number nor diary entry relating to her father's hunting-and-fishing companion, Malcolm Reid. No Malcolm Reid had contacted the house after Christmas to ask them why Hugh Craxton hadn't turned up at his bothy or castle or whatever in the Highlands. No Malcolm Reid had written to enquire after the health of his friend of many years. Thea had arranged for mail to be forwarded from Glasgow to London, but still, nothing. A suspicion was growing inside her, a voice that whispered to her that Malcolm Reid, like the London office, did not exist.

Why? Why had he done this? Why invent a business, a friend? All she could think was that the London trips and the jaunts in the Highlands had been convenient excuses, used by her father to disguise . . . something. A memory of Mrs Torrance, standing like a small, black-clad statue beside a snow-topped gravestone, drifted into her mind. She had, on the spur of the moment, nipped into a post office in South Kensington to check the telephone directory. But no Mrs Torrance had been listed. No Mr Torrance either. Torrance was not a very common name. Of course, it was possible that Mrs Torrance did not have a telephone.

Leafing through *The Voyage of the Beagle* to find her place, it occurred to Thea that there were vast tracts of her father's life – weeks and months, adding up to years – that she knew nothing about. It was as if she had thought she had finished reading a book and had only afterwards discovered that she had missed out entire chapters.

Thea's first job was as an assistant to a fortune-teller and psychic called Monsieur Pierre. Her duties were to answer the telephone and reply to correspondence. The pay was poor, twenty-one shillings a week. 'Monsieur Pierre's assistants don't tend to last long,' Miss Forrester at the employment agency had warned her, giving her a doubtful look. 'My last girl only managed a month. You could consider shop work. It's hard to suit girls without qualifications.'

She was referring to Thea's lack of shorthand and typing. Miss Forrester had recommended she take a course at Pitman's but Thea had resisted, preferring to plunge immediately into the world of work. She needed to earn money because she must escape from the situation in which she had found herself.

She was Rowan's messenger, the go-between who carried letters between Rowan and Simon Pemberton. Both maintained the pretence of being no more than friends. Thea knew that her complicity allowed them to keep up the pretence. Her shame in deceiving Patrick, in whose house she was a guest, and her guilt in facilitating a relationship which she suspected Rowan would one day regret, made her miserable. And yet she would never have refused her sister. They had always looked out for each other, she and Rowan.

Thea cherished the hope that if she said nothing Rowan might see sense or the affair with Simon Pemberton would fizzle out. But neither of those things had happened yet and the only way she could see of extricating herself from the part she was playing in the disintegration of Rowan and Patrick's marriage was to move out. She must find a home of her own. She could not live with Patrick and Rowan for ever; she had always intended to be independent. And for that she must save up money.

Monsieur Pierre and his wife were given to vicious, noisy quarrels; after an episode in which Monsieur Pierre was struck on the head by a butter dish, hurled by his wife, Thea resigned and went back to the agency.

Miss Forrester found her a job waitressing at the Ginger Cat teashop in Earl's Court. The café was in a cramped, dreary semi-basement but the pay was better – twenty-five shillings a week plus tips. On her half-days, Thea took the underground train to Russell Square and explored the British Museum. She spent a lot of time in the gallery where the finds from Ur were displayed, gazing into the cabinets that contained the small-eyed, bulky terracotta sow, the Royal Game and the silver lyre. She read how Leonard Woolley had excavated the game by placing a waxed cloth over the board and counters, and how he had constructed a wax facsimile to support the pegs and strings that were all that remained of the lyre. The artefacts were magical to her because they carried with them a memory of the long-forgotten people and places they had once belonged to. Sometimes she felt that if she only concentrated hard enough, the misty curtain dividing her from the ancient world would lift and she would be able to step back in time.

The Ginger Cat's proprietor, Mrs Woolfit, a widow in her sixties, baked the dispiriting scones and rock cakes that featured on the menu. The café's clientele was mostly female – middle-aged women with worn shoe-leather and darns in the cuffs of their cardigans and thick, wrinkled, gravy-coloured stockings. They liked to spin out a pot of tea and a rock cake to last an hour. Thea wasn't supposed to allow them to read novels or write postcards – 'Let them do that and they'll be here all day, dearie,' Mrs Woolfit explained with a sigh. 'And then where would we be?'

It was at the café that Thea met Peggy Garland. Peggy was studying art at the Slade and took her breakfast of coffee and a boiled egg there. She was tall, thin and talkative and wore green gingham smocks over dusty navy-blue cotton trousers, which she sewed herself. Her straight dark-blonde hair was cut into a blunt fringe framing her friendly hazel eyes. She lived in a basement room in a lodging-house in Bloomsbury, she told Thea, and had a boyfriend called Gerald, who was an explorer.

Thea and Peggy quickly became friends. Thea went to a party in Peggy's house. A dark, handsome Spaniard who'd had his right foot shot off at the Battle of Guadalajara played the guitar. They all danced and drank beer. Peggy's raucous laugh rose now and then over the wistful music.

One morning, arriving at the café, Thea found the front door locked and a handwritten note pinned up: *Closed until further notice*. Though Miss Forrester made enquiries, Mrs Woolfit was nowhere to be found. She had gone missing owing Thea a week's wages and the employment agency their fees.

'It's too bad of her. Too, too bad,' Miss Forrester complained with a sniff. She had a summer cold. 'And I thought we'd settled you, Miss Craxton. We don't have much at the moment, I'm afraid.' She ran a fingertip down a list. 'Dentist's assistant . . . lady's companion . . . trainee journalist – that won't do, I'm afraid, you'd need shorthand. Grocery deliveries, they'll want a boy . . . insurance clerk . . .'

'Why will they want a boy?'

Miss Forrester pushed her horn-rimmed spectacles up her nose as she focused on Thea. 'Bicycling. In all weathers. Delivering heavy bags of flour and boxes of biscuits.'

'I could do that.' Outside, the sun was shining. It would be delightful to speed through the London streets, delivering groceries. 'I'm a good cyclist.'

'If you're sure . . .' The doubtful glance attempted to change into an encouraging smile. 'Let's give it a try, shall we, dear?'

The man Sophie had fallen in love with and married, who had been the father of her sons and with whom she had lived for over nineteen years, had become unrecognisable to her. God knew what else Hugh had lied about. There might be other wives, scattered round the country, a battalion of them.

She was on guard all the time, braced against further shocks, and that was exhausting. It exhausted her, too, that her mind drifted continually towards Hugh and his daughters. In picturing Hugh with his Glasgow family she was tormenting herself, but she could not stop. It was an obsession to wonder whether Hugh had preferred his Glasgow life to his London life and to think that he might have loved his daughters more than his sons. If, indeed, he had loved any of them at all. She could muse for hours on how he had got round the practical problems of having two families. How had he explained his frequent absences? What excuses had he made for being away from the Glasgow home at Christmas, for heaven's sake? How had he kept track of the birthdays and school sports days and all the sudden emergencies that children fling up, without muddling them up and giving himself away?

She knew how. He would have invented business meetings, colleagues who must be spoken to. He would have had a flat tyre on the Great North Road or driven into a snowstorm coming over Shap. It occurred to her one afternoon, when she was mixing up cake batter, that he had not gone on his evening walks out of restlessness, as she had believed, but so that he could call his daughters from a public telephone box. He had disliked her going into his study because that was where he had written his letters to Rowan and Thea.

She was boxing up Hugh's books to sell to a second-hand shop when the thought popped into her mind that he must have sent his daughters to boarding school. That would have freed him up to travel to London during term time. On her hands and knees, angrily piling thrillers into boxes, she wondered whether Hugh had favoured the genre because he had seen his own life as a thriller. All those Erskine Childerses and John Buchans might have given him ideas.

She should consider herself lucky, she supposed, that Hugh had insisted she have her own bank account. It was not luck, she saw that now, but design. Hugh must have had at the back of his mind the possibility of some glitch in his complicated life – lives – because he had also put the deeds of the house in her name. He had given her a vague explanation, something to do with tax liabilities, which she hadn't listened to properly. She was so gullible. She should have known then that something was up.

Because Hugh had been away from home so often, she had dealt with their day-to-day household finances. So she was not one of those women who became flustered at the sight of a cheque book. Though she made economies, her savings were dwindling. Duncan had left school. He had refused to take up his place at Cambridge and now worked for an insurance house in Lime Street. Each week, he handed her a portion of his wages. Sophie resented bitterly that she should have become dependent on her son for money. Here she was, scrabbling around to pay the window-cleaner, while those two girls lived in luxury. The Craxton sisters wore beautifully cut clothes while her sons' shirts were patched and the collars turned. It was all so wrong. She felt she was owed something.

One day, she found herself walking through the streets of Chelsea. It was raining and she kept her eyes peeled, looking out for Hugh's red-haired elder daughter. Was that her, that tall woman in the long black coat? Did she live there, in that pretty cottage with the blue door and the window-boxes?

Rain dripped from the brim of her hat and the spokes

of her umbrella. She was shivering, and for an instant she seemed to see herself from the outside, standing on the pavement, drenched and cold. What on earth was she intending to do? Tell Hugh's daughter the truth? Demand a portion of her inheritance? Had she gone quite mad?

Chapter Five

July 1938

As Thea propped her bicycle against the back railings she caught sight of Patrick, standing in the scullery doorway. His hands were in the pockets of his cream linen trousers and a tanned V of skin showed in the open neck of his shirt.

He shaded his eyes, looking up at her. 'You're working late, Thea,' he said. It was past eight o'clock on a glorious July evening and the sky was sapphire blue and luminous. 'Or were you taking a message for Rowan?'

Her heart lurched. She couldn't lie to him, not even for Rowan. She nodded and came down the basement steps.

'Was the message to Simon Pemberton?'

'Yes.' She felt herself go scarlet.

'That swine. That idle, parasitical swine.'

He turned aside, but not before Thea glimpsed the expression on his face, a mixture of anger, guilt and regret.

But he said only, 'Do you know where she is now?'

She shook her head. 'No. Honestly, Patrick, I don't.'

He was silent, frowning. Then he said, 'Have you eaten?'

'Not yet.'

'Let's go out and get something, shall we? Gwen has left a stew in the oven but it looks pretty unpleasant.'

She sensed the effort he put into making his voice light, and it made her cringe. They went into the house. Patrick said, 'That damn tap,' and gave the scullery tap, which had a drip, a hard turn.

Upstairs, washing and changing into a clean frock, Thea dreaded the evening ahead. As they wandered along Mallord Street, even the sight of a buddleia alight with comma butterflies failed to distract her. And yet, Patrick did not speak of Rowan again. He had already, Thea concluded unhappily, found out everything he needed to know. Instead, he asked her about her job, delivering groceries to the smart set in Knightsbridge and Mayfair. She did her best to keep up the conversation but it was hard to speak when her heart had turned to an icy lump.

'I wish I could be seventeen again, like you, Thea,' he said, when they were sitting in the restaurant. 'Everything seemed so much simpler then. Sorry, I'm being a bit gloomy. You must forgive me for being such dull company. Rowan and I . . . well, you must have noticed that things aren't right between us.' Then he seemed to give himself a shake, and said again, 'Sorry. I don't mean to be a bore. I heard today that a friend of mine, Colin Slater, is leaving for Singapore. I'll miss him. Slater and I were at the same school. We were new boys together. I don't know how I'd have stood it without him. He's great fun, such a decent sort.'

Their food arrived on wide, porcelain plates that took up most of the small table. Patrick topped up their wine glasses as he talked about his friend. 'Slater was our best man. He came to dinner a few times when Rowan and I were first married, but they didn't hit it off. It's funny, I expected the two people I loved most in the world to get on like a house on fire.' Suddenly, he looked deeply unhappy. 'I hate to think of him living on the other side of the world. I hate how time seems to rush along and you end up neglecting the people you care about.'

'Patrick, I'm so sorry.' She was sympathising about Colin Slater, but she was also desperately ashamed of her role in Rowan's affair with Simon Pemberton.

And Patrick seemed to understand that, because he said, 'It's not your fault, Thea. You're not to blame at all.' He gave her a sad, tilted smile. 'It's my fault. I haven't made her happy. I've made a damnable mess of everything.'

After dinner, they walked back to the house, where Patrick fetched a hammer and wrench. There were noises from the scullery as he tried to fix the dripping tap and Thea heard several loud clangs, presumably Patrick hitting it with the hammer. But afterwards it went on dripping.

The following week, Rowan and Patrick gave a dinner party. Around midnight, after a flurry of farewells and kisses, the last of Rowan and Patrick's dinner guests left the house. Shortly afterwards Patrick went to bed, while Thea and Rowan kicked off their heeled shoes and set to clearing up discarded glasses and coffee cups so that Gwen wouldn't complain in the morning.

In the kitchen they washed up, then Thea put on the kettle. Rowan, in a tangerine silk backless gown, stood on a stool, putting clean glasses away in a high cupboard.

That afternoon, Peggy Garland had invited Thea to share her rented room. There was no easy way to begin the conversation they must have so Thea said bluntly, 'Peggy's room-mate is moving to Brighton and she's asked me to share with her.'

Rowan teetered, peering down at her. 'You won't, will you?'

'I've said yes.'

Rowan jumped off the stool. 'Thea, you mustn't go, really you mustn't.'

She had dreaded having this conversation, but having embarked on it could not go back. She tried to explain. 'I've saved up enough money. You and Patrick have been so marvellous and so kind. Please don't think I don't appreciate everything you've done for me – I do, so much. And please don't mind, I shall hate it if you mind. I need to have my own place, that's all. I can't live with you and Patrick for ever.'

'But I'll be so lonely without you!'

'You'll get your guest room back. And I'll visit you so often you'll get sick of me, honestly.'

Thea took the kettle off the stove. She put the mugs of cocoa on a tray, which she carried into the sitting room. Rowan padded in after her.

'It'll cost you a fortune, Thea. I can't see the point when we have a spare room. Won't you change your mind? Please?'

She had hoped to avoid mentioning her other reason for leaving but now saw that was cowardly of her. She set down the tray on the table.

'The thing is,' she said quietly, 'I can't bear this. I feel like the filling in a sandwich. Bitten down on from either side.'

'Thea . . .?'

'Simon.' The word was a whispered hiss because of Patrick, upstairs.

'Simon and I . . .' Rowan faltered.

'Please don't tell me you're just good friends. I'm not an idiot.'

Rowan sat down. 'Sorry,' she murmured. 'I should never have involved you. But I was desperate. It was wrong of me. Please forgive me.'

Thea dunked a biscuit in her cocoa. 'Patrick knows about Simon,' she said.

Rowan frowned. 'Thea, you're mistaken.'

'He told me.'

'Oh God. Are you sure?'

Thea nodded. A series of expressions flitted across Rowan's face: shame, fear, defiance. And now Rowan knew that Patrick knew, which meant she need play no further part in it. She should have been relieved but instead felt mean and wretched.

She said, 'Patrick told me you were one of the two people he loved most in the world.'

Rowan's head jerked up. Her eyes shone with tears. 'No. He can't have said that. It isn't fair!'

'Rowan, he loves you.'

Although everyone believed Rowan, who was beautiful and sparkling and capable, to be a self-confident person, Thea knew that deep in her heart, she wasn't at all. Thea hoped that if she could only accept that Patrick truly cared about her, they might be able to save their marriage.

But Rowan took a cigarette out of the case on the table. 'Patrick doesn't want me any more,' she said bluntly. 'I don't believe he ever did. I thought he did, when we married, but I was wrong.'

Thea felt out of her depth. She knew nothing about passion or about wanting. She had never even kissed a boy.

'I can't bear to live like this any longer.' Rowan struck

her lighter. 'I honestly think I'd have died if it hadn't been for Simon. I love him, Thea. I didn't mean to fall in love with him, but I have, and nothing can change that.'

Did a woman ever mean to fall in love with a man? Thea wondered. The word 'fall' suggested that love was an accidental, tumbling sort of process that came upon you unawares.

She wasn't sure whether she should ask her question but did so anyway. 'Simon feels the same, doesn't he?'

'I'm sure he does.' Rowan was crumpling her orange silk skirt into a knot while she took little puffs on the cigarette. 'You must think me so awful, cheating on Patrick. It's rotten of me, I know it is. I *wanted* to have a happy marriage. I never meant it to turn out like this. I wanted to do better than Mamma, and now look at me . . .'

Thea put her hand over Rowan's. 'You'll tear your frock,' she said gently. 'Dad and Mamma were happy, weren't they?'

'*He* was happy . . . or he would have been if . . . It was *her* fault!' The words burst out of her. 'I never meant to be like her!'

Thea had understood for a long time that Rowan blamed their mother for taking out the boat in the storm. If Sigrid had not been impetuous and rash then she would not have drowned and they themselves would not be motherless and their father would not have been devastated by the loss of his wife. Rowan was afraid that she had inherited their mother's heedlessness.

She gave Rowan's foot, with its scarlet-painted toenails, a consoling rub. Rowan tried to smile.

'Sorry. Don't take any notice of me. Ignore me. I'm upset.' The pins had fallen out of Rowan's hair and it fell over her face in a rippling copper curtain. 'It's all an utter mess, isn't it?' she said softly. 'D'you know, Thea, that for simply ages

I thought it must be me, that Patrick didn't love me properly because there was something wrong with me. But Simon loves me, so I know that can't be true.'

Rowan had intended to visit her dressmaker in Blandford Street merely to collect the tennis dress and skirts she had ordered. Feeling low and headachy, it had crossed her mind to cancel the appointment, but she had to get out of the house, so the grey crêpe for town, the light wool tweed for the country and the pastel-striped glazed cotton for the seaside were tried on in Edwina's peach-coloured changing room, the fit checked by Edwina herself and admired by Artemis Wilton, Rowan's friend, who was also a customer of Edwina.

'You never put on an inch, Rowan!' cried Artemis, who enjoyed her food and had grown quite stout round the waist. 'I'm so envious!'

The grey crêpe was especially flattering; studying her reflection in the mirror, Rowan's dark mood lifted a little.

Edwina rolled out lengths of fabric on to the table. 'These arrived only yesterday. Aren't they simply gorgeous? I've found a marvellous new man who gets his stuff directly from Paris.'

Rowan and Artemis admired the silks and satins. Their bright, roiling sheen made them seem almost alive.

'Irene Waterford is having a gown made up in the green shot silk with a lilac taffeta trim,' Edwina confided as she ran the fabric between finger and thumb. 'Strictly *entre nous*, the shade would suit you better, Rowan. Mrs Waterford struggles with a strong colour. But she won't listen to advice, so there you are. Isn't this chartreuse silk satin divine? Such a summery shade.'

Rowan imagined herself in green silk, dancing with Simon. Or the contrast of the chartreuse with her hair and her arm through his as they crossed a lawn at a garden party. Wear the right clothes and life might slot into place.

Edwina raised a finger. 'I've put aside a glorious little jacket for you, Rowan. Elsie, fetch the white velvet evening jacket I made up for Mrs de la Haye.' The assistant rushed off into a cupboard and Edwina lowered her voice. 'Poor Louise decided not to take it. Money troubles, I'm afraid. I can let you have it at a twenty per cent discount. It would look so sweet on you and it's such a useful little piece and works with simply anything.'

Rowan ended up ordering two evening gowns, one in the green silk and the other in chartreuse satin. She bought the jacket as well, in a rush of excitement and defiance. As Elsie checked measurements and wrapped up the velvet jacket in tissue paper, Edwina recounted the latest episode in the troubled saga of her affair with her married lover, Reynaud, who lived in the south of France.

Eventually Rowan and Artemis left Edwina's shop, brown paper packages in hand, with much kissing and can't waits.

'One can't help suspecting that the divine Reynaud is an utter rat,' remarked Artemis, once they were a suitable distance from the dressmaker's establishment. 'I wonder how many other mistresses he has, scattered round the Continent?'

Buoyed up by the shopping spree, they decided to lunch in Selfridges. Artemis hailed a taxi. In the restaurant, waiting for their food to be served, they talked about Artemis's daughter Elizabeth. When the waiter had been and gone and the subject of Elizabeth's clinginess seemed exhausted, Artemis gave Rowan a sympathetic look, and said, 'What is it, my dear? You seem upset. Has something happened?'

'Patrick has found out about Simon.'

Artemis widened her eyes. 'Oh, no.'

'He told me this morning, before he went to work.' Wretchedness washed over Rowan as she recalled Patrick's blatant misery. She had seen tears in his eyes.

'You poor thing,' said Artemis. 'How did he find out?'

'I suppose he'd seen us together at parties and things,' said Rowan vaguely. 'He must have noticed how we are with each other, how in tune.' She didn't mention Thea's role in Patrick's discovery of the affair because she felt ashamed of it. It had been shabby of her to have involved Thea.

'What are you going to do?'

'Do?' Rowan stared at her friend. 'I can't do anything. It's all such an awful, awful mess.'

After a silence Artemis said, 'You might promise Patrick you won't see Simon again. Perhaps he'd forgive you then.'

Rowan stabbed at her Russian salad. 'I can't. I simply can't.'

Another pause, then Artemis said carefully, 'Darling, there's a certain amount of choice involved in love, just as there is in most other things. It might hurt you to stop seeing Simon, and I'm sure it would be very difficult and painful, but it might be *wise*.'

Artemis was very keen on being wise. She disliked fuss and disruption and ran her life as she ran her houses in London and Hertfordshire, with smooth, unruffled competence. Though Artemis's marriage to wealthy financier Maurice Wilton was widely assumed to be one of convenience (Maurice was twenty years older than his wife and Artemis had a fondness for couture clothes, expensive jewellery and ocean cruises), Rowan knew the Wiltons to be very much in love.

'I can't give Simon up,' she said stubbornly. 'I love him. You understand, don't you? If it was Maurice . . .'

Affection settled on Artemis's strong, angular face. 'Poor darling.' She patted Rowan's hand. Witnessing the expressions that flickered across her friend's face, Rowan knew she was struggling for a way to say something unpalatable.

Artemis plunged in. 'Simon's my cousin and I've known him all my life and I hope you'll agree that gives me the right to speak out. I'm very fond of him, and of course he's utterly adorable, but he isn't . . . oh, I don't know, he isn't a *stayer*. He's thirty-six years old and he's never been engaged to a woman. Never anywhere *near* it.'

'He loves me.'

'Yes, I'm sure he does and I'm not for a moment suggesting otherwise.' Artemis fiddled with her lighter, then said, 'Simon must marry some day because of Ashleigh Place, but I've seen no indication that he's thinking of it yet. He's a man and men can afford to wait.' She gave Rowan a keen look, sighed, then broke off. 'I shouldn't interfere. What do I know about it? I just don't want to see you hurt.'

'Patrick and I haven't been happy for ages.' She couldn't bear to tell even Artemis, her closest friend, the truth about her marriage. During the very difficult conversation she and Patrick had had that morning, she had seen that Patrick, too, felt humiliated.

She said, 'I can't let things remain as they are, Artie, darling, it's not possible, I would die.'

'My dear . . .'

'I know Simon's not perfect, I know he can be a little

self-centred. But he loves me, he truly does, and at least with him I have a chance of happiness.'

Artemis had given up toying with her salad. She gave Rowan a careful look. 'Are you thinking of divorcing Patrick?'

'I don't know.' Rowan felt as if she might cry, here in Selfridges, among the rushing waiters and shopping bags and the lunch crowd in their best hats.

'Even if you're not, Patrick may decide to divorce you unless you promise not to see Simon again. Some husbands are happy to turn a blind eye but I don't imagine Patrick to be one of them.' Artemis took Rowan's hand. 'Please, please, promise me you'll think very hard before you take this step. Divorce is such an awful stain on one's reputation. Just think of poor Peony Deakin. No one speaks to her any more – not a soul. She lives in that ghastly little house in Wimbledon and has to look after Geoffrey's four children when they come to stay because they can't afford a nanny. Hilda Banister told me she's utterly worn out.'

A dislike of being lectured, even by someone she loved as much as Artemis, made Rowan murmur truculently, 'It's not the same at all. Simon isn't poor, like Geoffrey Deakin.'

'A woman's social standing never recovers from divorce. It would hurt you far more than it would hurt Patrick, even if he is a gentleman and takes the blame. That may not be fair, but it's how it is.' Artemis's tone softened. 'I'm only asking you to think very carefully, my love. I can see that things have been enormously difficult, and I sympathise, truly I do.'

They parted a quarter of an hour later – each feeling upset but claiming not to be – Artemis to go to a tennis lesson, Rowan to buy something for supper from the food hall. By the time she was on the bus home, the elation of her shopping spree had evaporated completely. She suspected that the chartreuse frock would make her look washed out and she regretted allowing herself to be persuaded by Edwina into buying the jacket. White velvet was such an impractical fabric. A single mark and it would be ruined.

That her friend had warned her off Simon with such seriousness disturbed her. Artemis had known Simon all her life. It could not be denied that Artemis had a point about the fate of divorced women. Both Artemis's remarks and this morning's conversation with Patrick troubled her deeply. And yet any pity she might have felt for Patrick had vanished when he had spoken of Simon.

'Do you seriously imagine that he cares for you?' he had said to her. 'Pemberton cares only for himself. He's a self-absorbed, affected ass, and incapable of thinking of anyone other than himself. Even if you were to be free, he wouldn't marry you.'

Rowan alighted from the bus before it turned off Piccadilly and made for Charles Street. She needed Simon to tell her that he loved her. She needed him to hold her in his arms and reassure her that everything was going to be all right.

The porter at the Charles Street house wished her good afternoon as she entered the vestibule. Upstairs, she rang the bell to Simon's flat. The butler answered the door. Hearing Simon's voice, Rowan rushed past Mr Leach into the drawing room.

On the threshold she stopped, the words she had intended to say frozen on her lips. Simon was not alone: an older woman wearing a maroon feathered hat was sitting on one of the ivory upholstered sofas. A slight, sulky-looking, pale child in a pink frock sat beside her. There was a tea tray on the table.

Seeing her, Simon's brows twitched into a frown. He stood up. 'Rowan.'

'I'm sorry . . .' She faltered, confused. 'I hadn't realised you were entertaining.'

He said crisply, 'Allow me to introduce you to Mrs Cecil and her daughter, Miss Francesca Cecil. Mary, Francesca, Mrs Scott is a friend of mine.'

Greetings were murmured and hands shaken, giving Rowan enough time to gather her wits. She was so sorry for intruding . . . had they come far?

Mrs Cecil said, 'Hertfordshire. We've motored from Steadings,' as if this should mean something to Rowan. The sulky girl, Francesca, was not as young as Rowan had first thought – eighteen or twenty rather than twelve. She was very fair, with straight, fine flaxen hair and a complexion of almost pearlescent whiteness. Mrs Cecil said in a tone that managed to be languid and bossy at the same time, 'Simon, I hope you remembered to book the theatre tickets.'

After a few more pleasantries, Simon took Rowan's elbow and steered her out of the room into the hall. She expected him to embrace her, to kiss and soothe her, but instead he hissed furiously, 'What are you doing here? You know how I loathe surprise calls.'

'I'm so sorry . . . I didn't realise.' He'd never been angry with her before. 'I needed to see you.'

'Your visit is very ill-timed,' he said coldly. 'The Cecils are old friends of mine.'

And what am I? she wanted to scream at him, but assembled sufficient dignity to whisper another apology and leave the flat. Out in the street, she struggled to hold back tears of humiliation. She did not dare take a bus, knowing that if she sat down quietly she would certainly cry, and so she walked home to Chelsea and Mallord Street, the weight of the parcels dragging on her arms.

Her headache had magnified into a pounding throb by the time she let herself into the house. There was a suitcase in the hall; in the sitting room, Patrick was taking books from a shelf.

Rowan put down her parcels. 'Why are you here? I thought you were in court.'

'The case collapsed. A key witness appears to have absconded.'

'What are you doing?'

'Packing my books.' For the first time, he looked at her properly. 'Rowan, I'm moving out.'

'Patrick, no.' Shocked, she stared at him.

'I think I must.'

'Please, Patrick – there's no need for this!'

He studied her. 'Where have you been?'

She was putting her door key in her handbag; she fumbled and dropped it on the floor. 'At my dressmaker's.'

'No, you weren't. I phoned Edwina and she told me you'd left before lunch.'

Rowan scooped up the key. She met Patrick's gaze. 'I went to see Simon. What did you expect after this morning?'

'Nothing.' He had blanched. 'I expect nothing of you, Rowan. And I ask nothing more of you. I know I have no right to.' He picked up another book. 'I only wish you would not throw yourself away on him.'

She collapsed into a chair. She felt exhausted, spent. To one side of her vision, lights flickered, the beginnings of a migraine. She said, 'I was unhappy and I thought it would make me feel better to see Simon. It didn't, if that's any comfort.'

'It isn't. I know that I drove you to him, and I take full responsibility for that. The least I can do is to leave you in peace and try not to make things worse.' Patrick clasped the holdall shut. 'You can stay in this house for as long as you wish. I'll have to sell it eventually, though, if we're to live separately.'

Separately. The word brought home the enormity of the moment. 'Oh, *Patrick*,' she murmured.

'I'll make financial arrangements for you, naturally, but you must decide whether you wish to go on living here.'

'I hate it,' she said. The house had proved, like her marriage, to be a disappointment.

He grimaced as he hoisted the holdall. 'Too many damn books.'

'Where will you stay? What will you do?'

'I'll be fine.' He produced a half-smile. 'A chap at my chambers is going abroad for a few months and has lent me his rooms. Will you want a divorce, Rowan, or will a formal separation do?'

'I don't know.' Her marriage had seemed a heavy burden but now a lump of misery threatened to choke her. 'I hadn't thought.'

'You must do so. Divorce isn't a simple process. These things take time.' At the door he paused and glanced back at her. 'I wish you well, truly I do. I hope one day that you'll forgive me.'

'Patrick, please, I can't bear it . . .' But the door closed behind him.

Rowan sat motionless. A few moments later, Gwen came into the room and asked her whether she should make coffee. Rowan shook her head and Gwen went back to the kitchen. There was a clattering of pots and pans.

She was all on her own now. Thea had gone and Patrick had gone and her father was gone, too. She had always hated being on her own. She thought of going to see Thea but it was only three o'clock and she would still be at work.

She went upstairs and lay down on the bed, hoping that by lying still she could quell the flickers of nausea. The new clothes remained in their packages, gathering creases. The memory of Simon's annoyance when she had turned up at his flat, and the thought that he might not love her, that she might have destroyed her marriage for nothing, preyed most powerfully on her mind at first. But after a while she felt only resignation. Her marriage was dead, she had known that for a long time. Whatever happened, it was not salvageable. Perhaps Patrick was right, and it was not her fault, and her failure had been in her reluctance to recognise the truth. She and Patrick should have remained friends; their mistake had been in trying to be lovers. It was different with Simon. If he did not love her then she did not know how she would go on.

She was splashing cold water on her brow to soothe her headache when the telephone rang. She dried her face and went downstairs.

'It's Mr Pemberton, madam,' said Gwen disapprovingly.

Rowan took the receiver. 'Simon? Where are you calling from?'

'My club. You know how I loathe these contraptions but I wanted to apologise for my bad temper this afternoon.'

'No, I was to blame, I shouldn't have come.'

'Do you forgive me?'

'There's nothing to forgive.' She wound the telephone cable round her forefinger. 'Do you still love me?'

'I adore you. I worship you.'

She let her suspicion that this was not quite the same

90

slide away and sat down, resting her head against the back of the chair. 'Patrick has left me,' she said. 'He found out about us.' She was beyond anticipating what Simon's response would be, beyond anticipating anything.

'I'm sorry to hear that,' he said.

'I suppose, in the end, it'll be for the best.'

'I expect you're right, although it may be disrupting.'

'Disrupting?' she cried. 'Disrupting? I feel as if I'm living in the middle of a tornado!'

'Yes, my love,' he said soothingly. 'I'm so sorry, you must be exhausted. Scenes are so exhausting.'

'I have the most fearful headache.'

'My poor darling. If only I could be with you, but I'm afraid I'm obliged to take Mrs Cecil and Francesca to the theatre. They have demanded a night out in the West End.'

'What are you seeing? A musical?' She imagined that the young girl, Francesca, might like musicals.

But he said, 'No, Shakespeare, and a tolerable one, The Tempest, thank goodness. Francesca's choice.'

'When shall I see you?'

'Not for a few days, I'm afraid. I've to leave for Ashleigh Place tomorrow.'

'Oh.' She felt desolate.

'Denzil has asked for me. I'm longing to take you there, Rowan.'

Her black mood lifted a little. Simon would not intend to take her to Ashleigh Place unless he was serious about her. She said, 'And I'd love to see it.'

'You'll adore it. And Denzil will adore you.'

'Tell me why you love it so.'

'I could say that it's because of its history. The ghosts you almost catch sight of as you enter a little-used room. Or the discoveries you make no matter how often you've been to the house, no matter how well you think you know it. Initials carved into a beam, a sherd of pottery dug up from a rose bed. Or perhaps it's because, when I was a child, Ashleigh Place seemed more of a home than my own.'

She pictured him as he spoke. Once, in the Charles Street flat, they had listened to a gramophone recording of *Così fan tutte*, and she had glimpsed on his face an expression of rapture. That he was capable of intense emotion was one of the reasons she loved him.

Chapter Six

September 1938

'I've joined the R.A.F.,' Duncan announced.

They were having Sunday lunch and had reached the pudding stage, a sultana sponge. Stuart said enviously, 'You jammy devil.'

Sophie dropped the cake slice. She stifled her impulse to squawk in panic, and said, 'Duncan, do you mean that you've *applied* to join the R.A.F.?'

He gave her a cool look. 'I'm most of the way through the application process. I had an interview at Adastral House a couple of days ago, on my afternoon off. They gave me a blue chit and sent me for a medical. A fellow told me they only give you a blue chit if they want you.'

You didn't tell me. You did all that without telling me. Fortunately, Stuart spoke before she could.

'Did you have to do maths and stuff? Will you fly Hurricanes?'

Duncan ignored him. 'They may write and ask your permission because I'm under twenty-one. You won't kick up a fuss, will you, Mum?'

She made a superhuman effort to answer him calmly. 'Not if you're sure this is what you want, Duncan, no.'

'I'm completely sure. Shall I serve?' He picked up the cake slice and plunged it into the sponge.

'When d'you leave?' Stuart asked.

'I don't know yet. They send you a letter saying you've been accepted for pilot training and then you go off somewhere, to a Training School.'

Stuart began to talk about Hurricanes again. Sophie poured custard on her pudding. It gave her something to do, though she knew she wouldn't eat it.

Stuart offered to help clear up after they had finished dinner, but Sophie said that Duncan should help instead and sent Stuart out to post her letters. Duncan was a far more efficient washer-upper and dryer than his younger brother. It wasn't hard to imagine him behind the controls of an aeroplane, composed and methodical. Except that it was terribly hard, unbearably hard, to picture her firstborn son doing something so horribly risky and dangerous as flying an aeroplane.

He said, 'I hope you haven't sent Stu out so you can lecture me, Mum. If you have, it's a waste of time.'

Sophie disliked his assumption of superiority, of having rumbled her. She said coolly, 'I sent Stuart out because I need my letters posted, but also because I wanted to speak to you in private. I want to be sure you're not doing this for the wrong reasons.'

A narrowing of his hazel eyes, Hugh's eyes. 'And what might the wrong reasons be?'

'Because you're angry with your father. Because you're angry with me.'

To her surprise and annoyance, he laughed. 'You have this extraordinary knack of putting yourself at the centre of everything. I've joined the R.A.F. because I wanted to join the R.A.F. I want to fly planes.'

'Then that's all right. This glass isn't clean.' She handed it back to him. Sulkily, he plunged it back into the sink. She said, 'So long as you haven't chosen to do the one thing that would upset me most *because* it's the one thing that would upset me most. As I said, if that's not so, then I respect your decision.'

'It's a career, Mum,' he said patronisingly. 'There's no need to get upset about it.'

Sophie busied herself with polishing the silver cutlery and putting it back in the case. Emotion swelled in her chest, a gathering tide. She said, 'My brother, Harold, died in the second month of the war, at the Battle of the Marne. He was my mother's favourite and she never got over it, never. I became an auxiliary nurse because of him, because I couldn't bear to sit around doing nothing after poor Harold died.' Duncan made to speak, but she silenced him with a sharp gesture, saying, 'A great many people believe that we'll be at war with Germany within a year or less. Have you considered that?'

'Yes, of course.' Yet she could tell by his failure to meet her eyes that he hadn't, much. And she regretted her harshness with him – he was a boy, a teenage boy who adored planes, and why shouldn't he want to learn to fly, and why shouldn't he feel excited and pleased at having achieved his ambition?

'I'm sorry,' she murmured. She put a hand on his sleeve. 'I'm not cross with you, honestly. I'm proud of you, Duncan, truly I am. And you should be very proud of yourself.'

This seemed to bother him more than anything else, because he scowled and concentrated on the washing-up. For several minutes, neither of them spoke.

Duncan put a saucepan on the draining board. 'Anyway,

it may not be for ages,' he said. 'Apparently they don't always tell you to report for training straight away.'

She recognised this as the nearest she would get to an olive branch, and patted his back. 'Then we must make the most of that time. I shall knit you some warm socks and gloves.'

Stuart came back from posting the letters. The boys headed off for the Fosters' house, to see if Michael and Thomas wanted a game of football. Sophie was making herself a cup of coffee when the doorbell rang.

Viola Foster was on the doorstep. She was carrying a basket. 'I hope you don't mind me interrupting your Sunday, Sophie.'

'Of course not. Come in.' Sundays had been deadly since Hugh had gone, the house too quiet, no shops to browse around to take her mind off things.

'I was having a clear-out and I wondered whether you could use these. Thomas has grown out of them.' Viola held out her basket. Inside was a stack of grey school shirts.

Sophie thanked her, though she suspected that Stuart, who was shooting up, would outgrow them in a month or two. She offered Viola a cup of coffee and Viola followed her into the kitchen.

'Duncan told us his news,' Viola said. 'I thought I'd come and see if you were all right.'

Duncan would have announced to the Fosters that he was joining the R.A.F., Viola would have said something like, *And what does your mother think?* And Duncan would have said, *Oh she's all right about it,* and Viola would have given him a look. Something like that.

Sophie said, 'I suppose it shouldn't have been a surprise. He's adored aeroplanes since he was about two years old.'

Viola, who was as slender as a wand, stirred three spoonfuls of sugar in her coffee, and said, 'He may not fly. He may end up as ground crew.'

'He wants to fly so I must want him to fly, too. It'll make him feel proud of himself, and he could do with that.'

'You're very wise, Sophie.'

Sophie stared at her friend. 'Me? Wise? Oh, Viola, if only you knew!' Her voice cracked.

Viola hugged her. She was tallish and boyish and bony and it was like being embraced by a bundle of twigs, made more so by the fact that Viola was a very brown sort of woman: straight brown hair, light-brown eyes, sallow skin and a tendency to wear brown- and cream-coloured clothes. Whenever she was with Viola, Sophie felt herself to be a collection of unconstrained, spilling curves.

'It's been so hard for you,' Viola said sympathetically. 'You've been so wonderfully brave since you lost Hugh. You must miss him dreadfully.'

'Not one jot.' The words came out without much prior consideration. She blamed Hugh for driving Duncan away from her. She held him responsible for her son's decision to join the R.A.F.

'Sophie?' Viola drew back.

'I don't miss him at all,' she said. 'I'm glad he's gone.' Too late to stop now, she thought fiercely. And if their friendship did not survive, then it was a poor thing.

'Viola, Hugh was married to someone else,' she said bluntly. 'I mean, he had married someone else before he married me. So we weren't ever really married at all, plainly. Do you have any of your cigarettes with you?'

Viola bent her narrow brown head as she rummaged in her bag. Sophie could not see her expression. She hadn't smoked for years. She had taken it up when she was an auxiliary nurse, in the war, but Hugh had disapproved of women who smoked so she had given it up when she married him. That memory made a fresh surge of rage race through her, that someone like Hugh, someone as dishonest and treacherous as Hugh, would presume to tell her off about anything. Would she ever stop feeling angry with Hugh? You would think you might run out of anger eventually.

Viola leaned forward to light Sophie's cigarette. 'You mean that he was widowed – or divorced – and he hadn't mentioned it? Don't you?'

'I mean that he was married to someone else, to a Swedish woman, and that he was still married to her when he married me.'

'Good Lord.' Viola wasn't given to displaying astonishment. She was a notably calm, still person, and Sophie had always assumed that she considered showing surprise or shock to be a sign of weakness. But she looked flummoxed now.

'I found out at the beginning of the year, when Hugh died. He was in Glasgow, you see, with his other family, when he fell ill. And then everything unravelled.'

'Good Lord,' said Viola again. Her light-brown eyes widened to saucers and her frown deepened. 'Hugh had another family. He had other children?'

'Yes, two daughters.'

'Oh, Sophie.'

'One of his daughters, the elder, lives in Chelsea. She's married. I don't know what her surname is but her Christian name is Rowan.'

'I don't know her. I don't know many people in Chelsea. They can be pretentious, don't you think, people who live in Chelsea?' Viola despised pretension. Then she said, 'I never thought Hugh was good enough for you. He was very handsome and charming, of course, but there was always something about him . . . not devious, exactly, more opaque. One could never tell what he was thinking. And he pushed you around.'

It was Sophie's turn to feel surprised. She said, 'He never raised his hand to me.' Though she couldn't think why she should defend Hugh, of all people.

'I meant that he was terribly good at getting you to do what he wanted. He was always good at getting his own way. With you, but with everyone else too. Doug, as well.' Doug was Viola's husband.

Sophie saw immediately that Viola was right. Why hadn't she realised that before? Hugh had always got his own way. If he didn't get it immediately he either wore away at you or went and did what he wanted to do anyway. She should have stood up to him more. Hugh had made all the decisions. He had decided where they should live and which school the boys should attend and where they should go on holiday and how many days a week they should employ Mrs Leonard, the cleaner. If she had demurred, he would have coaxed and wheedled but eventually he would have put his foot down. He had had a way of insisting that employed both charm and steel.

'I thought he was the love of my life, Vi,' she said. 'I feel such a fool.'

'He was an utter rotter,' said Viola fiercely. 'What he did was unspeakable. Don't you dare think you're to blame in any way.'

Viola's support lightened Sophie's heart. Lightness of heart was a feeling she had almost forgotten.

Viola said, 'Do the boys know?'

'I told them after Hugh died. Duncan's hardly spoken to me since.'

'I'd noticed that he's awfully sulky. I put it down to his age and missing his father. What about Hugh's daughters? Do they know about you?'

'I assume not.' When she thought back to that conversation she had had with Thea Craxton at Hugh's funeral, Sophie was slightly afraid that she hadn't been as careful as she should have been. She couldn't remember exactly what she had said; she hoped she hadn't given anything away.

She said, 'You're the first person I've told apart from Duncan and Stuart.'

'You should have told me *ages* ago! How frightful for you, to have gone through all this on your own!'

'I was afraid you'd be disgusted with me.'

'Oh, Sophie, that's so desperately sad. How could I be?'

'Hugh and I lived in sin for almost twenty years. A lot of people would be disgusted.'

Viola twisted her mouth to one side. Sophie assumed she was going to say something like, *Then they're not worth knowing.* To which she would point out that even if that were true, it was unpleasant to find oneself ostracised.

But instead, Viola said, 'I can hardly disapprove. I have a lover. Arnold's a wonderful man, we meet up a twice a month in a quiet hotel. It keeps me going, it helps me put up with Doug. I didn't tell you because I've always thought you were rather conventional.'

Viola talked on while Sophie attempted to make the necessary mental adjustments. Arnold made clocks. He lived in Bermondsey. He was unhappily married. It occurred to Sophie that there might often be a huge difference between how people appeared to be on the surface and how they were beneath. There was Viola, chest flat as a board, never a scrap of lipstick or face powder, telling her that Arnold was a wonderful lover, unlike Doug, who lacked imagination in bed. It was extraordinary, all of it, but she found there was some comfort in it.

Mr Ludgate, whose lecture in archaeology Thea attended one evening at Conway Hall, was a short, slight man who wore an old-fashioned frock coat and wing collar shirt, like Mr Chamberlain. Most of his students were men; the only two women were Thea and a yellow-haired girl who huddled in an enviably dashing black suede jacket at the back of the room. Sitting next to her was a tall man with curly copper hair. Thea heard the girl say to him, 'Honestly, Max, must you look so damnably bored? I went to your beastly boxing match.' Now and then Thea sneaked a look over her shoulder at the pair. In the first half of the lecture, while Mr Ludgate was expounding on current archaeological theories, Max read a newspaper; the headline, 'New British Defence Measures Likely Tomorrow', was ominous. The lecture moved from Flinders Petrie's discoveries in Egypt to Carl Blegen's excavations of Troy, and then to the settlement that Vere Gordon Childe had investigated at Skara Brae in Orkney. The newspaper was abandoned and Max folded his arms and slept. His snores were a percussive background to Mr Ludgate's voice.

Mr Ludgate addressed his audience as 'gentlemen'. It was as if Thea and the girl in the black jacket were invisible. When, at the end of the lecture, the students were invited to ask questions, Mr Ludgate responded to only the men's raised hands.

The girl in the black jacket approached Thea as they left

the building. 'Pompous old fool,' she said crossly. 'I wanted to throw something at him. Not one single mention of a woman archaeologist.'

'Are there any?'

The girl gave Thea a scornful look. 'Of course there are. My grandmother is an archaeologist. So is my mother. And haven't you heard of Dorothy Garrod? Or Mary Kitson Clark?' She reeled off several more names, then said, 'If you're interested, you should read this. I've finished with it.' She held out to Thea a book.

The title on the frayed front cover was *The Prehistoric Archaeology of Britain*, and the author was called Rana Hughes. 'Are you sure?' asked Thea.

'Oh yes, take it. I warn you, though, it's pretty dry.'

'Thanks awfully.' Thea was about to ask her name and address so that she could post back the book to her, but the girl had already turned away, saying to her escort, 'Hurry up, Max, or we'll be late.' The pair of them strode off to where a motorcycle was parked at the kerb. They climbed on to it and sped away.

Thea returned to the Bloomsbury lodging-house and let herself into the basement room. Peggy was out so she had the room to herself. By daytime they dressed up the two narrow beds with cushions and tartan blankets to make them look like sofas. The rest of their furniture comprised of a chest of drawers, a small table and two chairs. They hung their clothes and dried out their mackintoshes on hooks on the wall. Peggy's paints, sketchbooks, boards and canvases were stowed in one corner of the room and Thea's books stood in a tower beside her bed. They shared a kitchen and bathroom with the dozen other residents of the lodging-house. Sometimes they gave parties, noisy affairs that spilled out on to the basement area. Rowan's nickname for the room was 'the cupboard', but Thea loved it.

In the kitchen, she listened to the wireless while she searched for something to eat. The cycle of dread when she switched on the wireless, followed by relief when she found out they were not yet at war, was inevitably followed by a rising dread as the next news bulletin approached. The signal in the kitchen wasn't much good and often the news, which had been in that September of 1938 invariably gloomy and frightening, came through a fog of static and silences.

Tonight was no exception. The prime minister, Neville Chamberlain, had flown to Germany for further talks with the Chancellor, Adolf Hitler, on the future of Czechoslovakia. Hiss, crackle. Hitler was demanding that a sizeable chunk of Czechoslovakia be ceded to Germany. Another crackle, then the signal broke up.

There was no bread and Thea had forgotten to buy milk. As she made black tea she tried to imagine how she would feel if part of her country were to be suddenly given away to some other country. If Hampshire and Wiltshire, for instance, were to be handed over to France. It was inconceivable.

Another resident of the lodging-house, a tall, thin, ill-looking man called Miller, shuffled into the kitchen. He was wearing a grubby dressing gown and frayed slippers. The news report came to life again; he cocked his head to one side, listening.

'Christ, we'll be at war within the week,' he said.

'Do you think so?'

'Sounds like it.'

'Would you like some tea?'

'No, thanks. Have you any food?'

Thea shook her head. 'Sorry.'

'I haven't had anything to eat for three days.' Miller drew a glass of water and left the room, slippers slopping.

The voice of the B.B.C. announcer fractured into fragments once more. Thea switched off the wireless and took her mug down to the basement. Her appetite had gone and she felt sick inside. *We'll be at war within the week.* What if Miller was right? How pointless all her hopes and worries and ambitions would seem then. She recalled newspaper photos of Spanish towns that had undergone bombardment by German planes. In a week's time, London might be in flames. The lodging-house, and the room she and Peggy shared, might be ashes and rubble.

She couldn't think of anything useful she could do to prevent a war, and thinking about it kept her awake at night, so to take her mind off it she flicked through *The Prehistoric Archaeology of Britain* as she drank her tea. The name inked on the flyleaf, Helen Fainlight, must presumably belong to the girl in the black jacket, whose grandmother was an archaeologist. But as she ran her gaze down the chapter headings, she caught sight of another name, one so weighted with emotion for her that her heart seemed to skip a beat.

The Grey Dancers of Corran Island. One of the sites described in the book was on Corran. Her mother's boat, the *Iduna*, had foundered on the rocks off Corran, and her body had been washed up on its shore two days later. Sigrid Craxton had been buried on the island because it was, Thea's father had once told her, the place she had loved most in the world. Thea herself had no memory of the island.

She turned the pages to a pen-and-ink sketch of standing stones arranged in a rough circle – the Grey Dancers. Skimming through a folk tale of lovers, punished for breaking the Sabbath by being turned to stone, she settled to reading a description of the site. The thirteen menhirs of red sandstone were interspersed with smaller grey granite boulders. They stood on a flat, boggy plateau half a mile from the coast of the island. The tallest stone was twelve feet high. The writer described the circle as majestic and remarkable and dating back to the Neolithic Age.

An image prodded at Thea's consciousness of an immense stone standing proud against a shimmering blue sky. Green and ochre lichen was scrawled across its surface and beneath the palm of her hand she felt warm, sun-kissed granite. A distant sea sparkled in the sunshine. Was this memory or imagination? She had been six years old when her mother had died, six years old on that last, fateful visit to Corran. She wanted it to be a memory. She had so few recollections of the earliest part of her life and of her mother. A fall of wheat-fair hair, brushing against the bars of a cot. A high, pure voice, singing a song in a foreign language. A hand in hers as she ran across the sand, and the sound of laughter. Whenever she tried to look closely at these fragments they dissolved, like cocoa powder in hot milk.

Peggy and Gerald came into the room. 'We thought we'd go and see Ralph and Nancy,' Peggy said. 'Nancy has made soup. Are you coming, Thea?'

They went upstairs, banging on Miller's door on their way. Ralph and Nancy Wadham and their baby daughter, Mollie, occupied four rooms on the top floor of the house. Ralph, a thickset, bearded man in his thirties, was a set designer and lectured part-time at the Slade. His wife, Nancy, was younger and had once been his student.

There were around a dozen people in the room, sprawled on the chairs and rugs. Nancy was collecting up empty soup bowls. She had soft, handsome features, but tonight she looked tired and pale and her brown curly hair was scraped roughly back beneath a frayed mauve headscarf.

Peggy and Thea perched on a windowsill; Gerald sat on the floor at Nancy's feet. They had arrived in the middle of a heated discussion and the tension in the room was palpable.

Ralph Wadham was saying loudly, 'We need to find a civilised solution to disputes between countries, rather than leaping in, all guns blazing.'

'Chamberlain's solution may not seem especially civilised to the Czechs.' This from a pale, clever-looking boy called Leo, whom Thea had met before at the Wadhams'.

'Czechoslovakia didn't exist a quarter of a century ago. It's the product of a deeply flawed peace treaty.'

'I don't think I'd be awfully keen on it if I were a Czech,' a girl with flaxen plaits said. 'Suddenly finding myself in a different country on the whim of a bunch of old men.'

'It's hardly a whim. It's a way of achieving change without violence, do you understand? What would you prefer us to do? Invade Germany because it doesn't agree with us?'

'I didn't say *invade*, I meant—'

'To use force would be inconceivable, both practically and morally.'

'But if we sit back, let Hitler do what he wants . . .'

'Using military might would make us as bad as them, surely that's obvious.' Ralph spoke with authority and the girl with the plaits subsided.

Peggy said to Nancy, 'Sit down. You look done in.' They shuffled up the windowsill to make room for her.

'Thanks.' With a sigh, Nancy sat down. 'Mollie was up half the night. Teeth.'

Ralph said, 'Where's the pudding, Nance?'

Nancy rose and went to the kitchen. Thea and Peggy followed her. The small wooden table and draining board were piled high with mixing-bowls and utensils. Dirty saucepans steeped in grey water in the sink.

Nancy quickly washed bowls under the tap while Thea and Peggy dried them. 'We only have six,' she said. 'Don't give Ralph the chipped one, he'll make a fuss. We'll have to use tea plates. Oh no.' Another exasperated sigh. 'They're dirty too.'

'What about saucers?' suggested Thea.

'Saucers, yes.'

Back in the sitting room, a boy called Gwyn offered to serve the pie. Thea noticed how the evening sun filtering through the windows cast a sheen on his loose dark curls. She liked looking at him but found it hard to say exactly why. What was it in the angle of a cheekbone or the dipped curve of an eyelid that made you want to look and look and look?

Gwyn glanced up and caught her gaze. Mortified, Thea turned away.

'Shush,' said Nancy urgently, putting her head to one side. 'Is that Mollie?'

'I'll go and have a listen, Nancy.' A tall girl called Roma, who was dressed in navy dungarees over a white shirt and who worked as a model at the Slade, stood up.

'If you rock the pram she might go back, Ro.' Roma left the room.

'Britain has cravenly accepted German and Italian aggression,' Leo was saying. 'By refusing to arm the Spanish Republic we're helping to ensure Franco's victory. As for the Italians, they used poison gas in Abyssinia, for God's sake, and still we did nothing. I despair.'

'The choice of weapons hardly makes much difference,' said a girl called Amy, who had a room on the ground floor. 'It's all vile.'

'You don't think there's something particularly vile about poison gas?'

'If you make it out to be a special case, aren't you saying that it's perfectly fine to use conventional weapons?'

'No. That's rot, utter tommyrot.'

Someone mentioned the Peace Pledge Union. 'Chatter,' Leo said. 'Pointless, self-serving chatter. Pacifism's a way of dressing up appeasement, making it sound acceptable.'

Suddenly Ralph roared, 'Good God, you warmonger!'

'*Warmonger*,' repeated Leo, clearly affronted.

But Ralph was peering into the jug. 'There's no custard left. Poor old Jakob hasn't got any.'

'That doesn't matter, Ralph,' said Jakob, who was an academic and a German Jewish refugee. 'The apple pie is perfectly delicious on its own.'

'You'd better make some more, Nance.'

'There isn't enough milk. I need the rest for Mollie.'

'We can't have apple pie without custard.'

They all heard the wail of the baby, a despairing sound. Nancy pressed her lips together as she took the jug and went into the kitchen.

Jakob spoke again. 'Ralph, you speak as if we're *waiting* for something to happen. But it has already happened, and it's happening more and more each day. The ambitions of the men of power are not just hypothetical problems, the horrors are already there. They are just not here, in England, not yet. But even here, in comfortable London, there are those who have sympathy with Hitler's aims.'

Roma came back into the room. 'Mollie's wide awake,'

she said. 'Nancy's trying to settle her. She thinks it's her teeth.' She sat down beside Gwyn, who ran his fingers up and down her spine. Thea looked away.

Ralph was speaking again. 'My father's been in an asylum since the Great War ended. Twenty years. My mother and I visit him once a month. He can barely get a sentence out. He doesn't know who I am. All my life, I've had a pretty good reminder of what war does to people.'

Peggy touched Thea's elbow and together they went into the kitchen. They took turns soothing the baby. Mollie felt plump and warm in Thea's arms; when she breathed in the scent of the infant's velvety skin she felt better, her worries fading away. Then Nancy took Mollie and sang to her softly and Peggy and Thea made cups of tea and coffee for everyone. Ralph seemed to have forgotten about the custard. The argument about Munich went on, drifting into the kitchen.

'One should never give up talking.'

'It's worked well with Franco, hasn't it? And, my God, it's getting the right results with Hitler.'

'Now you're being facetious.'

Nancy was gently rocking Mollie. The child's eyelids drooped and her head rested against her mother's shoulder, and there were longer gaps between the sobs. Thea thought of the book and the pen-and-ink sketch of the stones on Corran. Had they gone there, she and her mother? Might they have wandered among the stones – might her mother have held her in her arms when she grew tired, dropping kisses on the top of her head, as Nancy was kissing Mollie?

Shortly afterwards, they left. Gerald wanted to stay so Peggy and Thea went downstairs on their own.

Peggy murmured to Thea, 'Nancy told me she's pregnant again. She can't eat a thing. She can't keep anything down.'

'How awful.'

In their room a greenish light, the last of the evening sun, tumbled between the dusty, dusky leaves of the London plane outside the window on to the cracked lino floor.

'Nancy's a frightfully good painter,' said Peggy. 'Her tutors at the Slade thought she was frightfully good.'

'What did she do?'

'Oils, mostly. She painted flowers. Huge canvases, the most brilliant colours, utterly gorgeous.'

'I don't suppose she gets much chance to paint now.'

'Never. Not since she had Mollie.'

'Do you think you can still call yourself an artist if you don't paint any more?'

'Nancy'll get back to it one day.'

Thea wondered whether she would. She remembered how weary and resigned Nancy had sounded when she had told her not to give Ralph the chipped bowl. *He'll only make a fuss.* As if it was her role to soothe her husband, much as she soothed her baby daughter.

'You'd think Ralph would have helped more,' she said. 'He must know how tired Nancy is.'

Peggy snorted. 'Ralph never helps, hadn't you noticed? He thinks all that, cooking and serving food, is women's work. None of the men helped.'

'Gwyn did, a bit.'

'Gerald didn't.'

'Are you going to marry him, Peggy?'

'I don't know. Anyway, he's going away soon.'

'Where?'

'To South America, to Brazil. A friend of his is setting up an expedition and has asked him along. They're hoping to find a lost tribe.'

'How exciting.' Thea felt a stab of envy. How she would love to travel, like Gerald! Her gaze drifted to *The Prehistoric Archaeology of Britain*, lying on her bed. Although she enjoyed her London life, she had lately found herself longing for open spaces, for mountains and sea. There was talk at the grocery shop where she worked of replacing the bicycle deliveries with a van, so she might be out of a job soon. It occurred to her that she could travel to Corran and see the standing stones for herself. She had saved up enough money.

Peggy dug her hands into the pockets of her green cotton skirt. 'Gerald says he loves me but then he goes away for months and never writes,' she said.

'I expect it's difficult, if you're in the jungle.'

'He went to Scotland for three months and only sent me one mouldy postcard. They have post boxes in Scotland, wouldn't you think?'

'They do, yes, loads of them.' Thea felt gloomy about her own romantic prospects; she hadn't yet had a steady boyfriend. The boys she was attracted to, boys like Gwyn, were already spoken for, and those who expressed interest in her she had so far found unappealing.

She said, 'I wish I could meet someone. I'm afraid I put them off.' She was too *bookish*, perhaps: she remembered Simon Pemberton's choice of word.

'Of course you don't. You just haven't met The One.' Peggy mimed a swoon and Thea laughed.

That September, Simon took Rowan to Ashleigh Place. Lush hedgerows barricaded the narrow, winding Suffolk roads and early autumn sunlight filtering through beech leaves dappled the verge where he stopped the car to kiss her. The house lay a few miles from the village of Hawkedon, among parkland in which ancient oaks and horse chestnuts cast deep shadows on the grass. Simon's enjoyment in her delighted exclamation at her first sight of Ashleigh Place was evident. The house lay on the far side of a shallow rise, a sudden vista that supplied a subtle drama. The air, scented with lavender and box, and the faded, earthy shades of the house's timber beams and redbrick walls, and the front garden with its yew topiary chess pieces: all these combined to make a delicious assault on the senses.

Simon's uncle, Denzil Pollington, was full of bonhomie and compliments as he greeted them. A sparse fringe of fluffy white hair showed beneath Denzil's maroon embroidered and tasselled Turkish cap. Buried beneath folds and pouches of skin, his pale-blue eyes were sharp and alert. Nothing that could make her comfortable was too much trouble for him. At dinner time, he arranged a tartan rug over his knees and suggested the maid bring Rowan a rug, too: the old house was cold and had no electricity, relying on oil lamps, candles and open fires. Denzil chided Simon for not having brought her to visit him before and coaxed her to eat morsels of food and to try a glass of Sauternes from Ashleigh Place's cellar.

In his early seventies and complaining of ill health, Denzil excused himself from the dinner table early and went to bed. Rowan and Simon were the only guests; when his uncle was out of earshot, Simon smiled gleefully. 'He adored you, darling,' he said. 'Well done.'

The following morning, rising early, Rowan went out alone to explore the garden at the back of the house. The air was cool and fresh, the sun white and low. Her gaze was diverted by clouds of purple salvias and small pink-and-white daisies that sprang from crevices in the walls and between the flagstones on the path. To one side of a pond in which goldfish darted, a stone nymph stood, water dripping from her upturned urn.

She reached the limits of the garden, then looked back. She had wondered whether Simon would wake and come after her. She cherished the hope that he might propose to her that day, that he had brought her to Ashleigh Place to see the house in which they might eventually live. She thought it was his purpose in asking her there. She was not yet free to marry but she imagined Simon telling her he would wait for her.

But there was no sign of him. She headed across a meadow of rough grass. A red cow looked at her with long-lashed brown eyes and the leaves on the trees and hedges were pressingly green. She passed a barn, a stables and a timbered cottage where a man weeding his vegetable patch tipped his hat to her. In a coppice of alder and elm a green wood-pecker laughed raucously as she stood beside a stream and watched a kingfisher's orange-and-sapphire dive.

She walked back through the wood and the meadow. Simon met her in the garden.

'Where were you?' He sounded cross. 'You're late for breakfast. Denzil has been asking where you are. He has an engagement so we won't stay for lunch.'

She kissed him, putting aside her disappointment that they were to leave so soon. That Simon had taken her to Ashleigh Place was in itself a declaration of love. She linked her arm through his. 'What a perfect place, darling,' she said. 'You were right, this is the most perfect house in the world.'

*

The Friday evening that Rowan spent with Nicky Olivier coincided with Neville Chamberlain's return to London after his third trip to Germany. In his rooms in Belgravia, Nicky uncorked a bottle of champagne and switched on the wireless. Together they listened to the broadcast from Heston airport, to the commentator's description of the Prime Minister alighting from the aeroplane and brandishing to the cheering crowds the piece of paper, signed both by himself and Hitler, that was his reward for his labours. It was a guarantee, Chamberlain claimed, that the two countries would never go to war again.

'Peace for our time,' quoted Nicky, after turning off the wireless. He chinked his glass against Rowan's, then returned to the sofa. A cynical smile spread across his dark, saturnine face. 'So I don't have to become a soldier quite yet. Such a relief.'

Chapter Seven

November 1938

Thea travelled north by a circuitous route, taking in the
Lake District, where she visited the Castlerigg standing
stones. A succession of trains carried her on to Ardrossan
on the Firth of Clyde, and from there she hitched a lift in
a delivery van along a winding coastal road to a tiny, windswept port. The ferry sailed to Corran twice a day, carrying
mail and supplies.

As she sat in the small boat, crossing the strait, she felt a
wave of nausea sweep through her, drenching her with sweat
as she tried to focus on the grey bulk of the approaching
island. Alighting at Portmore and collapsing on to a low
stone harbour wall, she was wretchedly aware of her hope-
lessness. She should be feeling moved or unnerved or
overwhelmed to find herself here on Corran, the island where
the Craxtons had once owned a holiday home and where
her mother was buried. Yet all she could feel was relief at
having got through the voyage without actually being sick.

Eventually she was able to take an interest in her surround-
ings. A steep street led away from the cluster of stone houses
round the harbour; she headed up it, passing a pub, a shop

and a simple, whitewashed church. Then the small settlement fizzled out and she found herself among fields and meadows.

She dropped her rucksack over a five-bar gate and clambered after it. After pitching her tent in the field she felt ravenous. She made herself a supper of tomato soup and oatcakes and read until the light faded, then curled up in her sleeping bag and fell profoundly asleep.

The next morning, Thea set off for the standing stones. A walk of a couple of miles took her to a footpath that led off from the road. And then she was climbing steadily uphill, into the interior of the island. A stream forded by stepping stones washed across her route before the woodland gave way to open ground and the track narrowed to a thread of beaten-down grass and flattened earth. Her boots squelched mud and her gaze darted, entranced, from a clump of bright orange fungi – *aleuria aurantia*, she thought – to green ferns like knife blades, and, improbably in November, a lone harebell, bobbing on a sheltered tussock of grass.

The path became sketchier, mislaying itself among rocks and clumps of gorse, looping round boulders velvety with moss. And there, suddenly, ahead of her, were the Grey Dancers in their grassy clearing. She stood still, awed. The majesty and huge scale of the monument took her breath away. *The stones are in the shape of a flattened circle . . . as at many Neolithic sites an entrance is formed by two large menhirs:* the words of Helen Fainlight's book, which was in her rucksack, returned to her. She placed a palm against the surface of one of the thirteen red sandstones; warmed by the sunlight, it felt almost alive.

She made a sketch of the site and took photographs, and then ate the bar of chocolate and apple she had purchased earlier in Portmore's shop. Had the ancient people lived near the stone circle, or had it been used purely for ceremonial purposes? Perhaps they had chosen this site because it was a flattish expanse on an island that was little more than a rocky peak. How hard life must have been when everything you ate must be hunted or picked or cultivated in the stony earth. How hard it must have been to keep warm in the long, dark winters.

Raindrops made black spots on the stones and charcoal clouds obliterated that morning's cornflower-blue sky. As a flurry of rain drew a silver-grey curtain over the stone circle, Thea took the downhill, wooded path from the far side of the clearing. Beneath the rust-coloured columns of the tree trunks she found shelter and the cold solemnity of a cathedral. Here, again, was profusion: there was fly agaric, the red-and-white toadstool of fairy tales, and over there a gleaming, sticky brown fungus she was unable to identify, which seemed on the verge of deliquescing back into the earth. And there another, jelly-like and translucent, which if she touched her fingers might slip right through. *Auricularia auricula*, and a particularly fine example. She knelt in the pine needles to draw it.

The rain blew itself out as she emerged back into open ground. A path meandered downhill among rowan and birch. The sea was a distant, sparkling blue triangle; in the sky above, a buzzard circled.

The lettering on the older headstones in Portmore's graveyard was worn away by rain, wind and time. Men had died at sea, mothers had perished with their newborn infants, and children, much loved, had succumbed to fevers. Thea found her mother's grave marked by a simple white marble headstone in a corner of the plot, in the shadow of a yew tree.

She read the inscription. *Sigrid Margareta Craxton, 1892–1927, beloved wife of Hugh Craxton. Rest in peace.*

She brushed away fallen leaves from the grave and placed on it the spray of autumn berries she had gathered that morning. A breeze tasting of salt and sea and the cold coming of winter looped and danced round the churchyard. Rowan had told her that the three of them – herself and Rowan and their mother – had come to Corran most weekends during the summer of 1927. What had brought Sigrid Craxton to this isolated place, over and over again, that summer? She might have pined for the chilly countryside of rural Sweden, the land of her birth and upbringing, and found some of that remoteness in Corran. It was easy to see why it must have captivated her. Thea, too, had fallen in love with the island.

And yet something sat uneasily with her. *The three of them.* Sigrid and her daughters had visited the island repeatedly during that summer of 1927. Sigrid and her daughters, but not Hugh. Sigrid, who had loved to swim and sail, had been like Rowan, perhaps, a restless woman with an energy she needed to work off. Rowan couldn't sit still – perhaps Sigrid had been the same. Beneath her vitality and busyness, Rowan was unhappy. Perhaps Sigrid had been unhappy too, and that was why she had come here so often that last summer. Would Sigrid have spent so much time away from home if she had been happily married? An image of a woman in black, standing by a gravestone, drifted into Thea's mind.

It was plausible, wasn't it, that during those weekends when Sigrid had been at Corran with her daughters, sailing the *Iduna*, Hugh Craxton, too, had been away from the family home. It was plausible that her father had been visiting his

118

fictitious friend, Malcolm Reid, and his possible mistress, Mrs Torrance, even then.

Duncan had been ordered to report to a Flying Training School in Desford, in Leicestershire. The days before his leaving home passed in a flurry of preparations. Sophie tried to hide the constant ache in her heart. All too soon, the morning of his departure arrived. They breakfasted together, then Duncan put on his coat in the hall. They embraced and said their farewells, and he left the house. At the gate he looked back and gave a smile and a wave.

From an upstairs window Sophie watched him. She could read in the way he walked both optimism and apprehension. The thought tugged at her heart that he was a man now, that the boy was gone for ever, but she held back her tears so that she could keep him in her sight for as long as possible. Then he was swallowed up in the crowds; though she strained to see him she could not, he was gone.

It was washing day, so she and Mrs Leonard stripped the beds and laundered the linen. In the afternoon, Sophie was clearing out the spare room when Stuart came home from school. She heard him bound upstairs.

'Hello, Mum.'

'Hello, darling.' She kissed him. 'How was school?'

'Fine. What are you doing?'

'Measuring the windows. Would you hold the other end of the tape?' He did so. 'I need to earn some money to pay the bills,' she said. 'I thought we could rent out the spare room to a lodger.'

'Good idea.'

She glanced at him. 'You don't mind?'

He shook his head. 'Why should I?'

'Five foot six,' she said, noting the measurement down. 'These curtains have been up since we bought the house. The room needs a coat of paint as well.'

'I'll give you a hand, Mum.'

'Thank you, darling.'

Stuart went downstairs to get something to eat. Sophie's mind drifted to the Glasgow house in which Hugh's daughters lived. She imagined it to be decorated with wallpaper from Sanderson and hung with Liberty curtains. Meanwhile, she and her boys would make do with cheap distemper and glazed cotton from the Army & Navy.

Taking a lodger seemed the best solution to her pressing financial problems. The only alternative was to sell the house and move into a smaller house or flat, and she was reluctant to do that. She looked out of the window, remembering how Duncan had grown smaller and smaller and then had been lost in the crowds. In a couple of years' time, Stuart too might leave home, and then she would be alone in the house. A lodger might provide some companionship. Looking after someone would at least give her something to do.

She wondered whether she would ever find love again. She did not know how she could ever trust a man enough to allow even the possibility of love. And yet she still needed love and warmth and friendship and companionship. These things, surely, were as essential to happiness as food in the belly and a fire in the grate. She was forty-two years old, and when she caught sight of her reflection in the mirror she thought she was still pretty enough. In the street, men still gave her admiring glances. It was hard to give up on that part of herself.

*

A narrow footpath, lush with rust-coloured ferns, wound down the cliff to a shoreline strewn with rocks and pebbles. From the cliff-top, the choppy Prussian-blue sea had a diamond glitter. As Thea headed down the path, ferns and brambles brushed against her legs. The grey shards of other islands, smaller than Corran, rose from the bay. Hundreds of islands were clustered along the west coast of Scotland like beads spilled from a broken necklace.

On the beach, the rush and scrape of water on sand and the slap of sea against rock accompanied her walk. She climbed on to a boulder that jutted out into the sea. When the biggest waves struck, their fine spray reached her. She sat for a long time, watching the gannets that dived with the clean exultant flight of an arrow.

She set off again, rounding the headland. Glistening brown ribbons of seaweed and the transparent, glutinous remains of jellyfish were scattered along the shore. Her boots crunched over rocks and pebbles. In a cave hollowed out of the cliff face, the sound of the sea retreated and was replaced by an echoing drip of water. The cavern dug deep into the cliff, its furthest point obliterated by darkness. Had the Neolithic people who had made the stone circle inhabited these caves? Thea pictured fires burning, throwing shadows on the stone.

The rain set in; she put up the hood of her mackintosh as she headed up a steep path that snaked back up the cliff. When she looked round, she saw that the sea was blanketed by a grey haze. The cliff-top along which she walked was exposed, with no trees to offer shelter from the squall. Thea was not lost, exactly, but neither was she sure entirely where she was. She caught sight of a small, low, whitewashed house and made her way towards it.

The sky cleared again and the sun came out. In the distance, a rainbow shimmered over the sea. There was the scent of rain-swept grass and the wet-dog smell of her mackintosh. The garden of the house was surrounded by a wall, presumably to protect crops from fierce sea winds. Reaching it, she saw that it was neatly laid out in a pattern of paths and raised beds. Branches outstretched their gnarled fingers from the stunted trees. Willow had been pleated into a tunnel over a curving path and a tree trunk carved into the form of leaping fish. A stone bird, perched on the wall, seemed about to soar and spear the waves like the gannets she had watched on the beach.

A man came out of the house. He was middle-aged and wearing corduroy trousers, worn at the knees, and a plaid shirt.

He gave her a cheerful wave. 'Good morning to you!'

'Good morning.'

'It's a fine day for a ramble.' He came to stand at the gate.

She agreed that it was, then asked directions to Portmore. She was only a couple of miles from the town, he told her, sketching out her route with quick gestures of the hand.

She said, 'Are you a sculptor?'

There was a strength in his features, and his dark eyes had the clarity and sharpness of a hawk's. His straight black hair was run through with grey. 'No,' he said. 'My sister, Eilidh, is the sculptor. I'm a gardener and a writer of stories and poems. And you? What are you?'

'I'm nothing much,' she said frankly. 'I'm out of work at the moment. I used to deliver groceries on my bike but now they're using a van instead.'

'Ah, the march of progress.'

'When I go back to London, I'll look for another job. I thought I'd come to Corran first. I wanted to see the standing stones.'

122

'And have you been there?'

'Oh yes, it was magical.'

He gave her a warm smile. 'It's one of my favourite places on the island. On the earth, I think. Wait there, I've something to show you.'

He went into the house, emerging shortly afterwards with an object cradled in his palm. When he opened his hand, Thea saw that he was holding a stone axe-head.

She gasped. 'It's beautiful. May I hold it?'

'Of course.' He passed it to her. 'The Grey Dancers gave it to me. I've come across several of them there.'

Made of grey granite, it was something between an oval and a triangle in shape. Thea ran her thumb over the smooth curves. The axe-head settled into her palm as if it belonged there, a thing of elegance and purpose.

A woman's voice called from inside the house, 'Lorcan! Your dinner's ready!'

'I should go.' Thea made to give him back the axe-head, but Lorcan said, 'No, keep it.'

Startled, she said, 'I couldn't possibly.'

'I'd like you to. Take it back to London with you. Then you'll always have a part of Corran with you.' Looking at her, he frowned. 'In fact . . . wait a moment.'

He went back inside the house. A few moments later he returned, holding a book, which he offered to her. 'I'd like you to have this,' he said.

'Thank you.' She saw that it was a volume of poetry called *Leaving the Island*, written by Lorcan Richardson. 'That's so kind of you,' she said.

Thea put the axe-head and the book inside her rucksack, said goodbye to Lorcan and set off for Portmore.

*

A storm got up during the night, howling between the trees and whipping through the gaps between the tent flaps. It was still raining in the morning, but the wind had dropped a little. Thea walked down the slope of the meadow. The sea was ridged like a dragon's back, the water sometimes smooth, black and shiny like flint, and at other times mottled and dancing and alive with peaks of white foam. Among a maelstrom of grey and white, she thought she glimpsed a reef of rocks.

Perhaps those were the rocks on which her mother's sailing boat had foundered. *It was a stormy day*, Rowan had said to her when she had asked her about the accident. A day much like today, perhaps. What else had Rowan said? *That little voyage between the island and the mainland, it was nothing to Mamma, it was like crossing a road. Afterwards, they wondered whether she hadn't realised the wind was so strong. Or maybe the visibility was poor because of the rain and she didn't see the rocks until it was too late. Maybe when she saw what was happening she tried to turn the boat too fast. That's what Dad thought, that she must have broached and hit the rocks and taken on water and capsized.*

Thea shivered. What sort of woman would risk her children's lives by taking them out to sea in a small boat in a storm? A reckless woman, she thought, as she headed back to the tent. Or a desperate one.

Once her belongings were stowed, she headed for Portmore. The sea had calmed, allowing the mail boat to take her back to the Mull of Kintyre. After she had recovered from the voyage, Thea trudged up to the Ardrossan road and hitched a lift with a woman driving a truck of sheep, which baaed and bleated throughout the journey. From Ardrossan, she took a train to Glasgow, and from there another train to London. She fell asleep in the carriage reading Helen

Fainlight's book and did not wake until the train was passing through the London suburbs. She had almost run out of money, she thought. She must find a job. She must find a purpose to her life.

First, though, she must trace Helen Fainlight and give her back her book. The next morning, she went to Kensington library. Fainlight was an uncommon name and only two were listed in the London telephone directory. Mr W. Fainlight lived in Earl's Court, a bit of a trek, but Professor M. Fainlight's address was in Gordon Square, not far from the British Museum, which meant they were practically neighbours. Thea decided to try Professor Fainlight first.

A parcel wrapped in brown paper had been left on the top step of the house in Gordon Square. Thea rang the bell.

A girl in a tartan skirt and handknit mauve sweater answered the door. 'Hello. May I help you?'

'Someone left this for you,' said Thea, giving the girl the package. 'I'm trying to find a Helen Fainlight. I wondered whether she might live here.'

A voice from along the hall called out, 'Who is it, Lucy? Is it Stafford?'

'No, Grace, it's a friend of Helen's. Sorry, what's your name?'

'Thea Craxton.'

A second, older woman – Grace, Thea surmised – appeared. 'Do come in, please,' Grace said. 'Helen isn't here but we're expecting her at any moment.'

Thea followed her down the hallway. Grace was tiny, a head shorter than Thea, and her silver hair was piled up in a messy bun at the back of her head. She walked with a limp.

The shelves and glass-fronted bookcases that lined the walls of the hallway contained hundreds of fascinating objects – fossils and sherds of pottery and clay beads and bones. There were books in double rows and the spaces above them were filled by more books lying on their sides. Thea's gaze moved to the opposite wall, where photographs of pyramids and archaeological trenches outnumbered the conventional family portraits.

Grace said, 'Are you a Dorothea or an Althea? Or perhaps even a Theodora?'

'None of those. I'm just Thea.'

Grace led the way into a room containing an apple-green sofa, several chairs and a desk whose surface was almost lost beneath a typewriter, papers and journals. A fire burned in the grate. Grace took an upright chair and Thea sat down on the sofa. Somewhere in the house the telephone rang and a dog barked and music and distant voices murmured.

'This modern fashion for short names is very sensible,' said Grace. 'My parents saw fit to christen me Wilhelmina Hiltraud Grace. Naturally I disburdened myself of the first two as quickly as possible. I see you have a copy of Rana's book.'

Thea was clutching The Prehistoric Archaeology of Britain. 'It isn't mine,' she explained. 'It belongs to Helen Fainlight. I need to give it back to her.'

'Helen is my granddaughter.' Grace beamed. 'It's always a pleasure to meet one of her friends.'

The girl in the tartan skirt, Lucy, put her head round the door. 'Shall I make us all some tea?'

'That would be very kind.'

'I'd better rescue Sylvia and Russell from Monty. I don't think he's let them have any lunch.' Lucy went off.

An old spaniel trotted into the room and lay down panting on the floor beside Grace's chair. 'Monty is my husband,' explained Grace. 'Did you enjoy the book, Thea?'

'Tremendously.'

'Rana is a great friend of mine. She writes wonderfully of the Neolithic era. Of course, she wrote the Orkney chapter before Vere Gordon Childe did his marvellous work there. An archaeologist has constantly to adapt to new knowledge. It's no good being miffed when one's theories are super-seded. We live in an age when so many new and exciting sites and artefacts are being discovered. Have you been to Skara Brae, Thea?'

'No, not yet. But I've seen the Grey Dancers, on Corran, and Stonehenge and Avebury.'

'So you're interested in archaeology?'

'Very.'

'There are people who look at a Neolithic circle and see only a heap of old stones. And there are those of us who see such places as doorways into another time. You don't work in the field?'

'I'm afraid not. I'd love to, though.'

'Would you, indeed?' Grace smiled. 'Are you good at drawing, Thea?'

Startled at the change of subject, Thea said, 'Yes, I think so.'

'Which school did you go to? Did you take your Higher School Certificate? What were your favourite subjects?'

Thea answered Grace's questions as best she could. The telephone rang again, a door opened. In the corridor, someone squealed, 'Joan! Russell's here! He's awfully tanned.'

A handsome, white-haired older man in worn and baggy tweeds ambled into the room. 'There you are, Monty,' said

Grace. 'You must meet Thea Craxton. She's a friend of Helen's. Thea, this is my husband, Monty Fainlight.'

They shook hands. Monty said, 'Stafford's on the telephone, Gracie. He wants to speak to you. Is no one making any tea?'

'Lucy is. It'll be here in a tick.'

'Thank God for that. I'm parched.' He wandered off.

'Forgive me, Thea, I must take this call.' Grace, too, left the room.

Thea liked sitting in Grace Fainlight's study. She liked the way the winter sunlight spilled through the French windows and washed in watery flickers over the polished wood floor. She liked the fact that you would never run out of interesting things to look at or books to read. And she liked Grace herself, and felt straight away at ease with her. Grace cared about the things she cared about. But she knew she must be straight with her. Helen might not even remember her.

Grace returned. Before there could be another interruption, Thea said, 'Helen's not really a friend of mine. I mean, I liked her awfully when we met, but it was just once. It was so generous of her to lend me the book but I didn't manage to get her name. I only know it because she wrote it in the book.'

Grace smiled fondly. 'That's sounds like my Helen.'

Lucy came in, carrying a tea tray. Half a dozen men and women drifted in after her. Lucy poured out tea while the others spread themselves around the sofa and chairs or sprawled on the floor. Their conversation, about a lecture by Mortimer Wheeler, died down long enough for Grace to introduce Thea and then whirled off in another direction. Monty stood in the centre of the room, a cup of tea in hand. When his tea spilled into the saucer, he drank from it. Cakes were sliced, and scones and strawberry jam offered round.

At the sound of the front door opening, Grace looked up expectantly. A few moments later Helen and Max appeared. Helen's fair hair was windswept and she was wearing the black suede jacket that Thea remembered from the lecture room.

'Are we frightfully late, Granny?' Helen stooped to kiss Grace. 'The wretched motorbike wouldn't start. Hello, Grandad.' She hugged Monty. 'I'm starving.'

'Darlings, so lovely that you could come,' said Grace. 'If you move those papers, Max, you could sit on the desk. Thea is here, Helen. You remember Thea.'

Helen dropped her jacket on the floor and stuffed a scone into her mouth. 'Oh yes. That awful lecture by that awful man. How are you, Thea?' She sank down on the rug by her grandmother's chair and ran the spaniel's long, silky ears through her fingers.

Monty began to talk about an archaeological site in Switzerland, near Basel. Russell passed round a handful of photographs.

'Amazing amphitheatre,' someone said.

'Romans, though.' Helen made a face. 'What? Don't tell me you don't agree with me. You must admit there's something unutterably dreary about Romans.'

Max snorted. Monty said, 'Can one write off an entire civilisation?'

'I don't see why not.'

'Helen has very strong opinions,' said Max.

'I should hope so. People without opinions are as dull as ditchwater. You're very opinionated, Max.'

'So I am.' He blew her a kiss.

'Have you heard from your father, Helen?'

'I had a letter this morning.'

'We should send Tobias copies of these. Have you an address for him in Sweden?'

Helen fished an envelope out of a pocket and passed it to Grace. 'Here, Granny.'

'I'll post them to him,' volunteered Lucy.

'Fascistic, in fact,' said Helen, spraying scone crumbs. 'The Romans. You know what I mean. Whenever I think of Romans I always think of the worst kind of repressive masculinity. Even worse than Max.'

'Thank you, sweetheart.' He gave a little bow.

'My darling girl, they were different times,' said Grace. 'Thea has brought you back your book, Helen.'

'What book?'

'Rana's book.'

Helen dropped a spoonful of jam on another scone. 'You can keep it, if you want. Stop it, Max, this is my scone. Get one of your own.'

'Thea is interested in pursuing a career in archaeology,' said Grace.

'Why doesn't Thea fill in for Rosemary?' asked Helen.

'Just what I was thinking.' Grace's gaze moved to Thea. 'I need someone who can draw and take notes for me. My wretched hip makes it hard for me to get about so I need a reliable assistant. Do you type?'

'Yes.' Suddenly, Thea's heart was beating very fast. She felt as if she was teetering on the edge of something wonderful, but added honestly, 'Though not terribly fast.'

'That doesn't matter. I take it you don't mind getting your hands dirty?'

'Not at all. I enjoy it.'

'And your domestic situation . . . there's no husband and babies?'

'Good Lord, no, I'm as free as a bird.'

'Excellent.' Grace looked pleased. 'So then, would you consider working for me, Thea?'

Chapter Eight

December 1938

Though they were now free to make what arrangements they chose, Rowan sensed that she still occupied only a compartment of Simon's life. Days passed in which she did not see him. He introduced her to some of his friends but not others. He had set up a charitable club in Dean Street for impecunious artists, to provide them with a comfortable refuge and a square meal, and now and then made vague promises to take her there which never came to anything. She had assumed that their visits to Ashleigh Place would become a regular occurrence, yet though Simon had visited Denzil several times since September, he had not asked her to accompany him again. Rowan was afraid that some of the heat was cooling out of the affair.

Artemis had warned her that people might cold-shoulder her if she divorced Patrick, and she had been right. Rowan was not even yet divorced, was still stranded in the social desert of the separated woman, and yet a number of friends, one or two of whom she had thought intimates, had dropped her. One day, in Selfridges, she caught sight of a friend at a table. Rowan offered to join her but the woman turned aside and took a compact from her bag. 'I don't think so, Rowan,' she said as she checked her face. That was all. *I don't think so,* but the incident cut deep.

On a Friday afternoon in December, the porter handed Rowan a letter as she and Dora Mottram, an old school friend who had fallen on hard times, returned after lunch to Rowan's flat in Macklin Street. Patrick had bought the flat for her after selling the Chelsea house. Recognising Simon's strong black handwriting, Rowan slipped the letter into her pocket and made Dora tea before opening it.

With a thrill of optimism and pleasure she saw that Simon had invited her to Suffolk again. *My dear Rowan,* he wrote, *are you free to come to Ashleigh Place tomorrow? Denzil complains that he hasn't seen you for an age. I will call for you at one o'clock sharp.*

The Bentley headed along roads where factories and warehouses were squashed together like dog-eared cards in a pack. Spider's webs of rusty fire-escapes clung to the walls of soot-blackened terraced houses and tall, drum-shaped gasworks dwarfed the shops and railway stations. Then they were in the north London suburbs, where rows of paired villas with whitewashed pebble-dashed walls and half-timbered gable fronts punctuated garages, roadhouses and municipal parks.

'It's all so appallingly *polite*,' said Simon, who was in a bad mood. 'If I were forced to choose between living in the suburbs or the slums, I believe I would choose the slums. At least there's *life* there.'

'There's a dear little pub,' Rowan pointed out, in an attempt to cheer him up. A crudely painted inn sign showing a retriever with a dead pheasant at its feet swung outside a small whitewashed building. 'Shall we stop for a drink?'

'We haven't time. There's tea in the flask if you're thirsty. Did you see the name of that inn, the Dog and Gun? Twenty, thirty years ago, this would have been countryside. A hundred years ago, before the common land was enclosed, it would have been a marshy wilderness. How we have desecrated our land.'

His handsome features settled into an expression of disapproval. The roads narrowed as they left Braintree, plunging into a countryside of ploughed field and copse.

Beyond Castle Hedingham, the car had a puncture and they had to pull into the side of the road. Simon wrestled bad-temperedly with the tyre, refusing Rowan's offers of help. She sat on a five-bar gate, eating a slice of the lemon drizzle cake that Leach, Simon's man, had packed.

At last they arrived at Ashleigh Place, where Simon parked on the forecourt with a scrunch of gravel. They were welcomed to the house by Mrs Frostick, Denzil's housekeeper, who showed them to their rooms. Mr Pollington was resting, she told them; he expected them for drinks in the great hall at six o'clock.

A housemaid helped Rowan into her chartreuse silk satin evening gown and she was ready and waiting when Simon knocked on her door.

'You look magnificent,' he said, and kissed her.

As they descended the stairs, they heard voices issuing from the great hall, Denzil's and a woman's. Simon stopped suddenly, frowning.

'Oh, no.'

'What is it?'

'She is here. It's too much.'

'Who?' She tugged at his sleeve. 'What is it, Simon?'

Turning towards her, he hissed, 'Mrs Farmer. She's a widow, she lives locally. She's the most appallingly vulgar woman. I hope Denzil has only invited her for drinks.'

They went into the great hall. Simon's uncle was sitting in a chair beside a huge stone fireplace. Denzil was in evening dress, a rug arranged over his knees. A woman in a black evening gown stood beside him, a sherry glass in her hand. At her feet, a Pekinese dog slumbered.

'You must forgive me,' Denzil said, as he shook hands with Simon and pressed a kiss on Rowan's fingers, 'for not rising to greet you, but I am appallingly unwell, simply plagued by rheumatism. Simon, you have met Mrs Farmer. Mrs Scott, let me introduce you to my dear friend, companion and solace in my old age, Mrs Clarice Farmer.'

The two women shook hands. 'Ever so pleased to meet you, dear,' said Mrs Farmer. 'You must call me Clarice.'

Rowan supplied her Christian name and Clarice Farmer said with an expression of satisfaction, 'There! Now we're all friends together, aren't we, Pooky?'

Mrs Farmer was addressing Denzil, not the Pekinese. Though Simon visibly winced, Denzil did not appear to take offence at the nickname, but gave an indulgent smile.

'Please do sit down,' Clarice invited them. As if Ashleigh Place were her home, thought Rowan. Simon bristled.

Drinks were served, giving Rowan the opportunity to observe Mrs Farmer. She was neither all that young – forty-five or so – nor all that pretty. Her figure was plump and voluptuous; that and her dark-brown hair, which fell in soft waves, compensated for a coarse complexion and heavy features. Her gown, which Rowan surveyed with an experienced eye, was undoubtedly expensive, but strained too tightly round the bust and hips.

Clarice Farmer related to them at length a series of unfortunate events that had recently taken place – a nest of mice discovered in the larder of her home, a friend who lived with her having to rush off to nurse a cousin through a serious illness, her housekeeper falling off her bicycle and spraining her wrist.

She finished, 'If Denzil hadn't so kindly invited me to dinner, I'd have found myself all on my own with a plate of bread and cold ham!'

Simon shot her a poisoned glance. 'It was good of you, Denzil, to take on another guest at such short notice.'

'I'm afraid you misunderstand.' Denzil eyed Simon coldly. 'I invited dear Clarice some days ago. You are the afterthought, Simon. By the way, you were very late. I expected you much earlier. I had hoped to talk to you about Priest's Field.'

'I'm sorry. My motor car had a puncture.'

'I can't bear unpunctuality,' said Denzil. 'It's a pet hate of mine. It has always been so.'

Simon said, 'Has Richards made an offer for the field?'

Denzil made a peevish gesture. 'Yes, but it's most disappointing.'

'Then you must refuse it.'

'And be obliged to drain those acres throughout another winter?' Denzil gave a wintry cackle of laughter. 'There speaks the town dweller.'

'Denzil, I assure you, I'm as concerned as you are.'

'In my present state of health, such a worry could be the last straw.'

They were spared attempting to find a suitable response by the maid announcing that dinner was served. They moved into the dining room, a cold, cavernous expanse made dark by wood panelling, where the oil lamps and candles struggled to relieve the gloom.

The first course was a beef consommé, delicately flavoured and perfectly strained. Denzil employed a skilled cook. Claret was poured and there was a moment when it seemed as though everyone might put their nerves and resentments behind them, but then Denzil spoke again.

'Such an age since you last visited me, Simon. I daresay you find more exciting occupations than calling on a sick old man.'

He seemed, Rowan observed to herself, determined to punish poor Simon, who looked startled and wounded at the remark. Sorry for him, and in the hope of lightening the conversation, she said with a smile, 'Goodness, Denzil, he was here only a fortnight ago. Sometimes I hardly seem to see him.'

Denzil's small, tapered pink fingers tore at a piece of bread. 'I don't suppose a woman like yourself, Mrs Scott, finds herself short of *male followers*.'

It took Rowan a moment to absorb the remark, and to recognise the depth of the insult. She waited for Simon to spring to her defence, but when he said nothing she disguised her shock and said lightly, 'You're right, I'm fortunate in having a great many friends.'

Clarice weighed in. 'I have more friends than I have time for! There are my London friends, that I made when poor Ronald and I lived in Highgate, and all my Lavenham friends. Do you know, hardly a day passes in which someone does not invite me to lunch! I'm forever writing letters or talking on the telephone to my old school friends. Of course, I always make sure to spend time with my *special* friends.' She touched Denzil's sleeve.

Clarice Farmer's inane, self-obsessed monologue was a blessing, because it gave Rowan's anger the chance to cool. She tried to catch Simon's eye, but he was studiously looking in another direction. Though she attempted to explain away his lack of support by telling herself that he was simply being good-mannered – they were, after all, at Denzil's dinner table, in Denzil's house – it hurt.

After that, Rowan made little effort to take further part in the conversation. Denzil largely ignored her; all his attention was on Mrs Farmer, all his compliments and little stories directed towards her. It was at Simon that he aimed the majority of his jibes. Simon allowed his hurt and irritation to show only in the frowns that flickered across his face and the tension in his shoulders, but Rowan suspected that he was loathing the occasion as much as she.

The two men fell to discussing the purchase of a copse adjoining Denzil's property. The farmer who owned it was struggling in the agricultural depression; Denzil wished to buy it because the land acted as a barrier between Ashleigh Place and the road. Simon agreed with Denzil that the farmer was asking too high a price.

'I wrote to Martin myself,' said Denzil, 'in my own hand. I felt sure he would agree to sell but he sent back a vulgar, illiterate scrawl by return of post, turning down my offer.'

'The Martins have owned Owlstone Wood for more than a century,' Simon pointed out. The maid was serving a plum frangipane with cream and custard. 'All you need do, Denzil, is wait. When he's facing bankruptcy, he'll be forced to sell.'

'Wait?' cried Denzil, outraged. 'While motor cars and pantechnicons thunder past my gates?'

'Now, now, Pooky,' said Clarice unwisely. 'You mustn't be cross. You must think of your heart.'

'Please don't use that ridiculous nickname,' Denzil snarled nastily, and Clarice blenched.

'I only meant . . . I worry about you.'

'As do I,' said Simon. 'You must take care of your health, Denzil.'

But Denzil's vicious mood was not to be soothed. With a sly gleam in his sharp blue eyes, he said, 'I must have been mistaken, then. I was under the impression that you were counting off the days until I shuffle off this mortal coil and Ashleigh Place is yours. I thought that was the purpose of your fawning, Simon. If so, you may be in for a disappointment. I intend to live a good few years yet. I may alter my will. I may even marry, if I find the right woman.'

He put his hand on Clarice Farmer's small, plump one. She brightened visibly.

Simon had whitened. 'Denzil, I assure you that has never crossed my mind . . .' He subsided, beaten and miserable.

Shortly afterwards, Rowan and Clarice rose from the table, leaving the men to their port and cigars. In the great hall, Clarice poured out coffee and chattered about inconsequentialities. Quarter of an hour or so passed, and then Simon came into the room and told them that Denzil had gone to bed.

'Oh, the poor love!' fluttered Clarice. 'I'll go and make sure he has everything he needs.'

Simon's cynical gaze followed her as she left the room. He barely waited until Clarice was out of earshot before muttering to Rowan, 'Dear God. I suppose she intends to tuck Pooky up for the night.'

'Or something like that.'

His brows snapped together in a frown. 'You don't think they're lovers?'

'Simon. I should be very surprised if they aren't.'

'I assumed he was past all that.'

'I'm sure she makes it her business that he is not.'

'Damn her.' Simon sat down, tugging at his collar and tie. 'Her nerve, her utter, arrogant nerve! She already sees herself as chatelaine of Ashleigh Place! He wouldn't marry her, surely? No, he's not that much of a fool.'

Rowan stifled a sigh. 'Darling, Mrs Farmer has a fine figure and appears to find Denzil's every utterance amusing. Men have married for a great deal less. But I'd rather not talk about them any more. I've seen enough displays of self-indulgence for one evening. I'd like a brandy, please. A large one.'

Clarice Farmer did not return downstairs. The maid bobbed in now and then to empty the ashtrays and offer more drinks and coffee. At around midnight, Rowan and Simon went to bed. In her room he made love to her, a brief, energetic tussle that seemed to relieve him of some of his more violent emotions before he returned to his own chamber.

Neither Mrs Farmer nor Denzil were at breakfast in the morning. Afterwards, Simon went upstairs to enquire after Denzil's health. When he did not return, Rowan put on a coat and went outside. But the garden lacked the magic of earlier in the year; the blackened heads of Michaelmas daisies drooped wetly in the rain and the birdsong had been replaced by a chilly, dripping silence. After walking for half an hour, she went back to her room, where she packed.

At length, Simon knocked on her door. 'Denzil is ill,' he told her. 'Dr Paxman came during the night and he has insisted he keep to his bed. That woman was all for looking after him but I had a word with Paxman and managed to convince him that Denzil needs a professional nurse. There's little point in us staying on.'

There was no sign of Mrs Farmer and Simon did not suggest that Rowan say goodbye to Denzil. As they headed down the drive, he was silent. It was not until they were threading through the damp brown countryside that the words burst out of him.

'What if he should marry her?' The possibility must have been preying on his mind. 'What if they should have a child?'

Rowan, who was bored with the subject, said, 'I don't expect he will marry her. He claims to loathe vulgarity, after all. And she may be too old to bear a child. But if he did choose to marry her and if they were to have a child, then you would have to grit your teeth and congratulate him.' She studied him thoughtfully. 'Has it occurred to you that marrying her might make him happy?'

'Happy?' he said scornfully. 'How can you possibly think that?'

'It must be lonely, living in that big old house, so far away from anywhere. If you love him, then you must presumably care about his happiness. I can only assume you must love him a great deal to tolerate the way he treats you.'

He shot her a glance. 'What do you mean?'

'You are forever at his beck and call, like Clarice's wretched little lapdog.'

'Rowan, don't.'

There was an edge to his voice but she disregarded it. 'Last night, he was vile to you.'

'It's his way. It doesn't mean anything.'

'If you choose to tolerate his insults, that's not my affair. But it is when he insults me and you say nothing to defend me.'

An expression glanced across his face and then was gone. Irritation? Guilt? She was unsure.

'Denzil was unwell,' he muttered. 'He was in pain.'

'He was well enough to eat a four-course dinner, with second helpings. Well enough to drink a half a dozen glasses of claret.'

'I didn't realise you were counting.'

'He's a hypochondriac, surely you can see that? He has you and Mrs Farmer twisted round his little finger.'

'Please don't class me with that appalling woman.'

'Why not, when you both allow him to get away with rudeness and selfishness? Last night, I found myself wondering whether you cared more for Denzil's good opinion than mine.'

'That's utter rot. You don't understand.'

'You're right, I didn't understand till now. It's because of the house. You may love Denzil but you love the house more. I didn't realise you wanted it so much. A house is just a house.'

'Ashleigh Place is an exceptional house.'

'And Denzil is a spoiled and exceptionally unpleasant man.'

'He's my uncle,' said Simon angrily, pointedly.

They were driving through a low, wooded valley where a mist rolled out of the trees, encroaching on the road. Rowan had felt no particular attachment to any of the houses in which she had lived. 'People are more important than houses,' she said. 'I'd never put a house before a friendship.'

His expression thunderous, Simon jabbed his foot hard on the accelerator. 'Something you may consider, my dear, is that I've known Denzil far longer than I've known you. And after all, he had a point. We *were* late.'

'The car had a puncture. It was no one's fault. A true friend would understand that. As for that poor farmer . . .'

'What farmer? What on earth are you talking about?'

'The man whose land Denzil is trying to buy.'

'We were talking business. Women are incapable of understanding business.'

'I'm perfectly capable of recognising greed and meanness when I see it.'

'Meanness? I'd call it carefulness. You are foolish with money, Rowan. You spend it like water, I've seen you. You surround yourself with scroungers and spongers.'

'That's not true!'

'That friend of yours, that dowdy woman . . .'

'Are you speaking of Dora Mottram? Her husband died young of some frightful illness, leaving her with nothing.'

'She's a leech. You treat her to lunch, you buy her gifts. No wonder she's forever toadying around you.'

'Dora has been unlucky,' she said hotly. 'You— you, who've always been so fortunate, what would you know of hardship?'

'I've made my own good fortune. I'm not wasteful and extravagant, like you.'

'I'd rather be wasteful than mean!' Rowan cried. She was by now breathless with rage. 'I'd rather be extravagant than forever kow-towing to some vile old man! I could never marry a man who was incapable of generosity!'

His eyes widened and his gaze darted to her. There was a heavily weighted pause as she registered the surprise, even bewilderment, in his expression.

'Oh,' she said, and her voice seemed to shrink. 'Oh, I see.'

It was as if she was viewing him clearly for the first time. Before, she had looked through a veil, a pleasant filter of her own making. Slowly and painfully, she said, 'You've never thought about marrying me at all, have you, Simon?'

He made a conciliatory sound. 'Darling, please. It's not as though you're free.'

'No, I can see that marriage has never even crossed your mind. You don't love me, not really, do you? You're incapable of it. You'll only ever love yourself . . . and that wretched house. Do slow down, for pity's sake, or you'll kill the pair of us!'

He braked, then said coldly, 'You're right, I would never marry you, Rowan. Money would run through your fingers like sand. And besides, Denzil disapproves of divorced women and would never contemplate having one in the family.'

The countryside hurried by, trees and hedges blurred by her tears. 'Oh, why are you men always such a disappointment?' she cried out. 'First Patrick – and now you!'

A glint of cruelty came into his eyes. 'You do know, surely, Rowan,' he said, 'that your marriage could never have been a success? After all, Patrick prefers boys.'

A part of her had suspected this for a long time. Patrick's lack of interest in her in bed and his powerful affection for his friend Colin Slater had eventually led her to question his sexuality. She had got tiddly one night with Nicky Olivier, who also loved men, and they had talked about it. To Patrick, she had so far said nothing.

She hated that Simon should speak in such a cold and brutal way of such a painful matter. 'Shut up, Simon,' she said furiously.

'Everyone knows.'

'I said, shut up.' She grabbed the handle of the passenger door.

'What are you doing?'

'Getting out.'

'Don't be ridiculous.'

'I can't bear to be in this car with you any longer!'

'Rowan, you're being hysterical. Leave the door alone, you'll hurt yourself. There, have a drink of tea and calm down.' He passed her the Thermos.

It infuriated her that he should tell her to calm down when he was responsible for her misery and anger, but she had no idea where they were, there was not a bus stop, railway station or even a house in sight, and her heart was pounding and she felt desperately upset. She wrenched the stopper from the Thermos, took a long draught of tea and stared out of the window, and they did not say another word to each other for the remainder of the journey.

'I'd like to meet them.'

From across the dining table, Duncan, who was home on leave from the R.A.F., stared at Stuart. 'You're not serious.'

'I am. I would.'

Stuart was talking about Hugh's daughters. It was Boxing Day, the first anniversary of Hugh's death, and Stuart had said as Sophie had served the cold gammon, *I expect Dad's daughters are thinking about him today, too, don't you, Mum?* And then, before she could reply or Duncan could tell him to shut up, he had dropped his bombshell.

I'd like to meet them.

Duncan said, 'They're nothing to do with us.'

'They're our half-sisters.'

'Don't try to pretend there's some sort of a relationship between us, because there isn't,' said Duncan, coldly furious. 'You're talking rubbish, as usual.'

'*Duncan,*' said Sophie.

She could tell that Stuart was upset by the frown that pleated his forehead. But he persevered. 'I've been thinking about it for ages. You may not like the fact that we're related to them, but we are, and I think the stupid thing is trying to pretend we're not.'

Duncan put his head to one side and gave a disbelieving laugh. 'Stuart, this is not going to happen. Forget it.'

Stuart turned to Sophie. 'Is that what you think too, Mum? That I should forget it?'

Yes, she wanted to say. But, recognising how important this was to him, she chose her words carefully. 'Stuart, it's very likely they know nothing of your existence.'

'*We* worked it out. They may have too.'

'It's possible. But if they haven't, mightn't it be cruel to tell them?'

Stuart's frown deepened. 'I bet you they know *something's* off. And if it were me, I'd rather know.'

'Not everyone's as crashingly naive as you.' Duncan rose from the table. 'What do you imagine will happen? That you'll be welcomed with open arms? The long-lost relative, the prodigal brother? You still don't get it, do you? *We're* the interlopers. *We're* the bastards.'

He left the room. His final word seemed to reverberate. Seconds later, Stuart, white-faced, followed him.

From the hall, the boys' raised voices continued. She should go and sort it out, Sophie thought wearily, but she remained at the table surrounded by the abandoned Boxing Day lunch. Eventually there was the sound of the front door closing, then silence.

She knew that she should have spoken to Stuart about Rowan and Thea Craxton before. Stuart liked to reason things out over time. He didn't bury difficult subjects, as Duncan

146

did. Stuart would have thought about those girls and would have recognised that they had a relationship, however awkward, however unwanted. She knew her Stuart, and she should have encouraged him to ask her questions instead of wallowing in her own anger and misery. They each had their own way of confronting – or evading – the disaster that had befallen the family.

Stuart had every right to meet his half-sisters . . . and yet the idea horrified her. Another Christmas ruined by bloody Hugh, Sophie thought as she stacked up plates.

It was almost eight o'clock in the evening by the time Stuart returned alone to the house.

'Where's Duncan?' Sophie asked anxiously, as she went to meet him in the hall. 'Is he all right?'

'He's fine. He just needed to let off steam. We went for a walk and then we went to the pub.'

The pub. She was about to point out that he was only sixteen when Stuart added, as he prised off his shoes, 'He's at Sally's now.'

'Sally?'

'His girlfriend. Is there any food, Mum? I'm starving.'

'I didn't know Duncan had a girlfriend.' She heard her voice squeaking frantically as she followed Stuart to the kitchen.

'They've been going out for ages.'

Well, she thought, as he opened the breadbin. Did she know anything about her sons any more?

'What's Sally like?'

'She's jolly decent.' Stuart sawed a doorstep of bread and slapped a slice of leftover ham on it. Then a tablespoon of piccalilli. 'And she's a looker. Shall I make you a sandwich, Mum?'

'Yes, please.' She, like the boys, had left most of her lunch and she was hungry. She sat down at the kitchen table and attempted to digest the information that Duncan had a steady girlfriend. Stuart cut two uneven slices of bread.

She said, 'Stuart, if you want to contact Rowan and Thea—'

He interrupted, 'It doesn't matter.'

'I should have talked to you about them before.'

'Duncan thought you wouldn't want to.'

She didn't. But she said, 'I spoke to Thea, the younger girl, at the funeral. I didn't speak to her elder sister, Rowan, who is married, but I saw her.'

'What were they like?'

'They seemed pleasant enough,' she said reluctantly. 'Thea's about your age. She came to talk to me after the service. I think she noticed that I was on my own.'

'They didn't know who you were?'

She shook her head. 'I told her I was a friend of Hugh's. I gave her my maiden name.' She gave a rather strangled laugh. 'I remember that it crossed my mind that she was finding the occasion as ghastly as I was.'

She was surprised to find it a relief to acknowledge that Hugh's daughters were ordinary girls and not rapacious monsters. And maybe Stuart was right. Maybe Rowan and Thea Craxton did suspect, as he had put it, that something was off.

But she found herself saying, her voice rough, 'The thing is that if you talk to them, they might want to talk to me. And I don't think I can face that, not at the moment. For one thing, they might hate me. If you look at it from their point of view, they'd have every reason to hate me. And I can't cope with that on top of everything else.'

Stuart, who was taller than her, patted her head – much, she thought, as a father might pat the head of a toddler who was having a temper tantrum.

'It's okay, Mum. Don't worry about it. It was just an idea. Forget it.'

The final break-up took place in the bar at the Ritz. It was between Christmas and the new year. There was no suggestion of dinner, and afterwards it occurred to Rowan that Simon had proposed meeting her there because she was unlikely to make a scene in such an august and splendid a setting.

Not that she would have made a scene, anyway. In the days that had passed since they had returned from Ashleigh Place, Rowan had had plenty of time to think about their quarrel. Simon would never have married her; he had no interest in marriage. She had been a pastime, another lovely acquisition, like the ormolu tables and Louis Quinze chairs in his flat.

He did not put it like that, of course. She was a beautiful and magnetic woman and he wished her every happiness. He was going away for a few months – she understood, didn't she?

She did, perfectly, she reflected in the taxi home. Rain flung itself at the window. The rain, and her tears, blurred the lights of Piccadilly and distorted the features of the people on the pavements. She had always recognised that Simon was self-centred; what she had failed to realise was how deeply the pursuit of his own interests and pleasure was ingrained in him. His life suited him admirably. So why should he change it?

Chapter Nine

Thea's desk was in a small room opposite Grace's study. Like the other rooms in the Fainlights' house, this one was crammed with books and cases containing sherds of pot and coloured clay beads. A stone image of Bastet, the Egyptian goddess in the form of a cat, gazed haughtily at her from a corner cupboard.

To begin with, she spent her time answering the telephone, typing letters for Grace and filing documents. After she had been working for six weeks Grace gave her more interesting tasks: the transcription of field notes, a huge box of photographs from an expedition to organise and label. She got to know her way round the big, sprawling house and became familiar with its inhabitants. The house was always full of people. Monty's students and Grace's colleagues and friends would drop in for lunch with tales of travel somewhere exotic or for coffee and a chat about the latest archaeological theories.

Monty and Grace had one son, Tobias, who lived in Sweden, where he had a position at the Museum of History in Stockholm. Tobias was separated from his wife, Helen's mother, who lived in the United States. Helen, who was twenty-one years old, lived with her grandparents at Gordon Square. She and Thea quickly became friends. Grace was trying to coax Helen to study archaeology at university; Helen so far was resisting. 'I don't mind coming along to a dig. That's always good fun,' she said to Thea one lunchtime when, unusually, only she and Thea and Lucy, Grace's house-keeper, were in the house. 'But devote my life to digging up old tombs? No, thank you. There are far too many archaeologists in this family already.'

Helen's boyfriend, Max, had asked her to marry him, Helen told Thea. She was trying to make up her mind whether to do so or whether it would be a terrible mistake. 'But do you love him?' Thea asked, and Helen looked up from the book she was leafing through and said casually, 'Oh, yes, madly, though he's a silly old thing sometimes.' It was obvious to Thea that Max, who did something financial in the City, adored Helen, though he teased her a lot.

Grace had a habit of giving Thea a book or article to read as she left work at the end of the day. 'You might find this rather interesting,' she would say, handing Thea Hilda Petrie's 'Egyptian Hieroglyphs of the First and Second Dynasties' as she buttoned her coat. Or, unearthing a copy of the proceedings of the Prehistoric Society, 'There are a couple of excellent articles on the Neolithic, Thea. I'm sure you'll enjoy them.' When Thea later returned them, Grace always found time to talk to her about their contents.

There was an ease between Monty, Grace and Helen that delighted Thea. Beneath the liveliness and the appearance of chaos in the Gordon Square household there was always order. Thea was blissfully happy, working for Grace. She knew that she had fallen on her feet in the most remarkably fortunate way.

But it struck her how different the Fainlights' family life was to how her own had been. There were no unpredictable absences or sudden mysterious journeys. You could ask what questions you wanted without fear of upsetting anyone. There were no silences and no secrets.

Helen was perched on Thea's desk, eating an apple and talking about her recent visit to her father.

'Stockholm was perishing,' she said. 'Dad loves snow but I can't stand it. We had pickled fish for breakfast.' Crunch, crunch. 'I'd prefer to live somewhere hot, on a Greek island or somewhere, wouldn't you, Thea?'

'I like cold places.' Thea fitted a fresh sheet of paper into the typewriter.

'That's because you're Scottish.'

'My mother was Swedish, so I'm half-Scottish, half-Swedish.'

'You'd probably like pickled fish for breakfast, then. Dad's coming here in a few weeks. He has a month's sabbatical from the museum. He's going to come to Barbury Hill with us.'

'Is he? I bet Grace is pleased.'

Helen dropped the apple core in the bin and went in search of coffee. Thea began to type again. In May, Grace was to lead a dig at Barbury Hill, a causewayed camp in Wiltshire. The entire household, from Monty to Lucy the housekeeper, had been roped in to make preparations for the dig. Permissions had been gained, sponsors secured, budgets drawn up. The equipment was being assembled – picks, trowels, wheelbarrows, ropes, shovels, tents and storage for any finds. Thea was helping to organise the transport of these items to an out-of-the-way site on the Wiltshire downs.

She finished the letter and took it to Grace to sign. Grace put down the phone as she came into the room.

'That was Russell. He and Sylvia have decided to go to Crete this year.' Grace steepled her hands, pressing her palms together. 'He's sure the government will bring in conscription soon. He said he's going abroad while he still can. I've told him that I quite understand.' She took off her glasses and polished them with her silk scarf. 'There is the temptation, don't you agree, Thea,' she said quietly, 'to lose ourselves in the past and try to put the present and, God help us, the future, out of our minds?' She sighed and looked back at the list on her desk. 'It's rather a blow. I was counting on Russell and Sylvia. This leaves us short-handed.'

'Helen told me that Tobias is coming back for a while.'

Grace's face brightened. 'Isn't it wonderful news?'

'If you gave me a list of possibles,' Thea offered, 'I could phone round for you now.'

'You don't have to dash off, then?'

It was half past six. She and Peggy were staying in Rowan's Covent Garden flat because Rowan was in New York with her latest boyfriend, a man called Bobbie Wharton. Rowan had insisted Thea and Peggy borrow the flat while she was away and Thea had accepted gratefully. The flat was much nicer than the basement room, which in winter grew black mould.

'Not at all,' she said.

'Then, let me see.' Grace opened her address book, a large and battered leather-covered volume, from which scraps of paper floated now and then to the floor like flakes of snow.

'Nina, you might try Nina . . . no, on second thoughts, she mentioned that she was working for Mortimer this summer. What about Geoffrey, Geoffrey King? One-handed, poor man, but he did the most marvellous work in the Somerset Levels.'

Pages were turned, names added to the list. Lucy came in with a tray of coffee and biscuits.

'Will Towler,' said Grace. 'I have his number. He may know of one or two others. Eva . . . it would be wonderful to have Eva. She is so meticulous. She took her lover's name, though they never married. What was it? Harper, that's it. He died some years ago, sadly. Laurence . . . I shall speak to him when he comes to dinner tonight. Tell them the pay will be a pound a week all found. It's a pittance but we'll have a marvellous time. You'll stay for dinner, won't you, Thea?'

'Yes, please.'

The phone rang, a door slammed. Monty came into the room, talking of antler picks, and Thea retrieved the telephone directory from the hall. She worked through the list, ticking off those people she had managed to get through to and underlining the numbers she must call again in the morning.

When she reached Eva Harper's name something occurred to her. *She took her lover's name, though they never married.* She ate a fruit gum while she flipped through the pages of the telephone directory to the Cs.

Ca . . . Ch . . . Cr . . . And there it was, at the foot of the page, one solitary Craxton. Mrs S. Craxton, in fact, of 17 Gilbert St, South Kensington.

Though Bobbie Wharton was a wonderful dancer he had no conversation and his sense of humour was puerile. His idea of a joke was to drop an ice cube down the back of a waiter's shirt. New York was thrilling, but by the time Rowan sailed back to England on the *Queen Mary*, the affair was over.

The crossing was cold and stormy. Even if they hadn't stopped speaking to each other by then, she would have seen little of Bobbie as, horribly ill, he was confined to his cabin. Rowan, who was never seasick, spent much of the voyage wrapped up in furs and blankets, sitting on the promenade deck, watching the implacable force and energy of the waves. The liner raked back and forth on the heavy seas; now and then a granite-grey wave drew itself up as high as a cliff before plunging down with a furious roar. Stewards came round offering hot drinks, a few other hardy souls paced the decks, but most of the time she was on her own and so had plenty of time to think.

The storm intensified. Rain drove against the deck and the wind screamed. A bulky wave reared up and crashed against the bows of the ship. Looking round, Rowan saw that she was the only passenger on the first-class deck. From a doorway, a steward raised a hand, beckoning her to take refuge inside the ship, but she hardly registered him. She was remembering Corran and the wild sea in the Firth of Clyde, the slap of waves against the *Iduna* and the resistance of the water as she struggled to swim to shore with Thea in her arms. She blinked as if to wipe the image away.

A hand touched her shoulder. 'Mrs Scott!' the steward shouted over the clamour of the storm. 'You must come inside! It's not safe out here.' Rowan jerked out of her trance and made her way to the cocktail bar.

Two days later, the liner docked at Southampton. Rowan declined an offer of a lift to London from a still-greenish Bobbie and took the train instead. It was evening by the time she reached the Covent Garden flat. Thea and Peggy were away. Peggy was in Wales with her boyfriend, Gerald, and Thea was in Wiltshire, preparing for an archaeological dig.

From the heap of post on the doormat Rowan retrieved a handwritten note from Artemis, asking her to telephone as soon as she arrived home.

Rowan called her friend. 'Darling!' cried Artemis. 'You're back! How are you? Didn't you simply adore New York? I've missed you awfully. May I pop round to see you?'

Rowan was disentangling a heap of stockings when Artemis rang the doorbell. They embraced. The flat was cold and Artemis kept her fur coat on while Rowan asked after Maurice and Elizabeth.

While Rowan was making them both a gin and it, Artemis said, 'Have you heard that Denzil has died?'

Rowan, pouring sweet vermouth, looked up. 'No, I hadn't.' She thought of the sour old man, playing his games, weaving his webs. So he had been ill after all.

'He's left Ashleigh Place to Simon.'

'Simon must be delighted. But how disappointing for Clarice Farmer.'

Artemis smiled, then hesitated. It was this that made Rowan suspect that the death of Denzil Pollington was not the only news she had come to impart. She shook a dash of orange bitters into the glasses, then offered one to her friend.

'Thank you, darling. Mmm, glorious.' Artemis put down her glass and gave a little sigh. 'I hate having to tell you this, but I thought it better you hear it from me than from anyone else. Simon is engaged to be married.'

Rowan stared at her. 'Simon? *Engaged?*'

'Yes. I'm sorry, I know it must be a frightful shock.'

Shock could not begin to encompass the emotions that rolled through her. Disbelief, first. 'Artemis, are you sure?'

'I'm afraid so. The Cecils put the announcement in *The Times* last week.'

'The Cecils?' Rowan remembered the whey-faced girl she had met in Simon's flat. 'Simon is engaged to Francesca Cecil?'

'Yes.'

She managed, just, to stop herself saying, *But he can't marry her, she's little more than a child,* or worse, *But he told me he would never marry.* What Simon had actually said was, *I've never been tempted by the institution of marriage.* As her disbelief faded and was replaced by misery, she saw that what Simon had meant was that he had never been tempted to marry *her*.

'Darling, you've gone as white as a sheet. Sit down.' Artemis steered her into a chair and put the glass in her hand. 'Drink up.'

Obediently, she took a swallow. 'I thought I was over him,' she murmured.

Artemis sat down beside her. 'The Cecils are distant cousins of the Pembertons,' she explained, gently. 'Simon's mother was a Cecil. I believe there was an understanding that Simon and Francesca would marry one day. And Ashleigh Place eats up money and Francesca is an heiress, so, you see . . .' Artemis patted Rowan's hand. 'Simon has always been mercenary. I've told him how appalling he is. One wonders how that infant will cope in that freezing cold house. Whenever I've visited, I've felt almost dead with cold. And the plumbing – well, my dear! One hardly dares take a bath. Don't you think Francesca looks tubercular?'

Rowan didn't respond. She could summon up neither anger at Simon nor resentment of Francesca. What she felt instead was deep dejection as she understood how little she had meant to him. Humiliation piled on humiliation as it occurred to her that it was highly likely that Simon had been seeing Francesca at the same time as their affair. There may well have been an understanding between Simon's mother and Francesca's, but there must also be affection and attraction between fiancé and fiancée. Rowan knew Simon well. The engagement would not only be a financial transaction. A man as fastidious as Simon would expect certain things from marriage. He would expect his wife to be beautiful, elegant and cultured. He would expect to feel regard for her, at least.

Rowan finished her drink quickly, then stood up. 'We should go out,' she said. 'It's weeks since I've seen anyone.'

Artemis gave her a doubtful look. 'Rowan, are you quite sure?'

She was; they took a taxi to the Savoy. All her friends were in the American Bar: the Manninghams, the Vaughans and the Charlburys. Rowan talked and drank, telling stories about the liner and New York, making them laugh.

She thought she was having a good time until, in the early hours of the morning, she caught sight of her reflection in the mirror behind the bar. It seemed to her then that she looked grotesque. Pallor made her face as greenish as Bobbie's had been on the ship and her smile had something of a grimace. Her vivacity fell away and though she remained sitting at the table she no longer took part in the conversation. It was as if she was acting in a play and had forgotten her lines.

A feeling of devastation sank through her. She had been mistaken about so much. She was aghast to recall that she had, if only fleetingly, believed herself to be in love with

Bobbie Wharton. She found it doubly mortifying to recall how deeply she had loved Simon. Neither man had proved worthy of her love. And it was not as though she had not been warned. Artemis had tried to warn her, Simon himself could not have been plainer. So she had only herself to blame. How could she have got it so wrong? She felt very stupid.

As for Patrick, since they had separated they had met several times to discuss the arrangements for the divorce. Their chilly, well-bred exchanges failed to disguise a deep chasm of hurt. Neither Simon nor Patrick had loved her as she longed to be loved. Patrick had loved her but had not desired her. As for Simon, he had desired her but had never loved her. She was afraid she might never find the love she yearned for, a love that was passionate and true and selfless.

'Time to go.' Artemis was at her side.

'I'm not tired.'

'Darling, you're exhausted.'

'I won't be able to sleep,' Rowan said mulishly.

'Then come back with me to Belgravia Square and we'll stay up all night and have a good chat.' Artemis patted her elbow, coaxing her to stand.

As the doorman tipped his hat to them and they left the hotel, Rowan felt a surge of panic. She half-expected the weather to have changed while she was in the American Bar, for unseasonal ice to have glazed the streets and solidified the Thames.

But outside everything was as before. A few cabs ran along the Embankment and the air was scented by the murky coolness of the nearby river and the sweet spring scent of winter hazel. After all, she thought, it was only she who had altered.

*

The early morning was Thea's favourite part of the day. The birds, singing their joyful morning chorus, woke her. She dressed and washed quietly so as not to disturb Helen, who was not an early riser. Leaving the tent, she stuffed a handful of raisins into the pockets of her shorts and headed up to the site.

The sun lifted itself through the shimmering sky behind Barbury Hill, making the dew on the grass sparkle. The liquid, tumbling song of skylarks was as bright as quicksilver and her feet trod a path of bone-pale chalk. At the top of the hill she turned slowly, taking in the panorama, seeing how the hazy green Wiltshire downlands melted at their furthest reaches into a bruised violet horizon.

That morning, she was the first to arrive at the site. Barbury Hill was a series of vast concentric ditches, punctuated by causeways. During the first week of the dig they had opened up the three archaeological trenches that now sliced through the causeways and the ditches behind them. The men shovelled the soil and barrowed it to one side of the site and then the women began to work at the gashes made in the field, carefully scraping away fragments of chalk and soil. It was like turning a page in a book. You removed another layer of earth and glimpsed the gleam of a flint arrow-head. The previous day the points of an antler pick had showed in the section of trench Thea was working on. Soil was permanently embedded beneath her fingernails and her knees were scratched and grazed.

She felt a stirring of regret at their despoliation of the perfection of the Wiltshire countryside. She had to remind herself that the causewayed camp itself was man-made, that Grace believed the ditches to have been added over a considerable period of time, and that this ancient landscape had endured change for five thousand years or more and could withstand a little more. When the dig came to an end in late summer they would pack away their tools and the finds, backfill the trenches and replace the turf. Within a few years nature would have erased the marks on Barbury Hill.

She ate the raisins, then took out her trowel and knelt down by the trench. She began to scrape away at the soil that covered the antler pick. She breathed in the damp, decaying, loamy smell of the earth and heard distant voices. Her colleagues were heading up the hill. The sun beat down on her head; it was going to be another hot day.

At twelve they broke for lunch. They ate it in the shelter of a clump of oaks at the foot of the hill. Lucy distributed the mail; her back against a tree trunk, Thea ate a sandwich and read Rowan's letter.

Disaster, Rowan wrote. *We were having supper in a perfectly charming inn in the Black Forest when Christopher announced that he had fallen in love with me.* Thea shifted to escape the glaring sunlight. *He's gone back to England in a huff*, Rowan went on. *I'm travelling on my own now. I can't go home yet, Thea. I simply can't face it.*

Lucy came round with a Thermos of coffee. Thea tucked the letter into her pocket. People ate and chatted and dozed and then at two o'clock they went back to work. Though she was wearing a wide-brimmed straw hat, sweat trailed down the back of her neck. All her energies should be concentrated on this, the unearthing of the archaeological find, but her mind kept drifting to Rowan's letter.

I can't go home yet, Thea. I simply can't face it. Rowan had been deeply wounded by wretched Simon Pemberton's engagement. They had talked at length about it, and Thea had understood that Rowan was unable to think of anything

161

else. She would go round and round in circles, always coming up against the same buffers: that Simon hadn't loved her, that she was the sort of woman men slept with but did not marry. That it was all her fault.

Then, suddenly, Rowan had announced that she was planning to tour Europe with a friend, Christopher Page. *I've been feeling awfully blue*, she had admitted to Thea. *I have to get away*. There had been a flurry of packing and seat-reservations and then Thea had waved her off on the boat train.

The tip of the antler was free. Thea took a pastry brush from her pocket and eased the white dust from it. One of the boys, Will, a few years older than her and a veteran of several summers' digging, crouched beside her.

'That's some antler you've got there, Thea,' he said.

The sun was scorching her shoulders but she kept on working away. She scraped at the soil that clung to the other end of the antler, where its owner would have gripped the handle. *I've made such a mess of everything*, Rowan had said to her. *I always make a mess of everything*. Rowan blamed herself, and no matter what Thea said, no matter how often she pointed out that Simon Pemberton was a self-centred pig, she couldn't seem to get through to her. Rowan blamed herself for marrying Patrick too. That she also blamed Sigrid for the accident off Corran made Thea think that the pattern had been established a long time ago, in Rowan's childhood. The loss of the *Iduna* and Sigrid's drowning had affected Rowan badly. She, Thea, had no recollection of the accident, but she found it painful even to imagine how traumatic Rowan's memories of that day must be. Rowan disliked herself. Rowan seemed to dislike their mother too, but she refused to talk about that.

'Nearly there,' said Will. He stood up and hailed Grace.

'There we are,' murmured Grace. 'Nicely done, The

In the tent where they stored the finds, Thea wrote a

for the antler pick and noted it in the finds book. Then she
took some photos and made a pencil drawing in her notebook. The thought that she had been the first person to
touch the artefact in four thousand years or so filled her
with awe. There was an assumption that picks such as these
had been used by men, but as Thea began another sketch
she found that she was drawing a woman, sturdy and squat
and clad in animal skin. Her black hair tumbled down her
back as she raised her arms above her head to wield the
pick.

The tone of Rowan's letter worried Thea. *I can't go home yet.
I can't face it.* Maybe going to Europe hadn't worked for
Rowan. She had been in a downward spiral for some time
now, since the death of their father. She, Thea, must find
some way of helping her. There was a step she was thinking
of taking, that she had been mulling over for weeks. Her
instinct was to break the silence, to force the secrets into
the open. Secrets were poisonous and pernicious, they
choked off the light.

Might the Mrs Torrance she had spoken to at her father's
funeral be Mrs S. Craxton of Gilbert Street? Should she try
to find out whether they were one and the same, or should
she leave well alone?

But it was already too late for that. She couldn't leave well
alone because things weren't going well. Thea was afraid
for Rowan. She should have been blissfully happy here, doing
what she had always wanted to do in this most glorious
place, but a part of her ached all the time for Rowan. The
person she most loved in the world was not happy. And that
meant she could not be happy either.

She needed to find out the truth for Rowan's sake and her own. She had a last peek at the antler before putting the lid on the box. To have a rational view of the present you had to see the past clearly. She was going to peel away the veil that covered that past.

Rowan and her companions, an English couple called Fay and George Winchester and their friend Lucian Cardew, an American, were dining in a trattoria in a village between Fiesole and Monte Ceceri. Rowan had met Lucian and the Winchesters a fortnight before on the train from Milan to Florence. In the evenings the four of them went out to dinner together. Afterwards, Rowan and Lucian returned to their hotel in the Via degli Strozzi, where they made love.

Lucian was thirty-nine, tall, dark and saturnine; he had been married, once. He disliked the hot weather and spent his days immured in gloomy, marble-floored salons, reading and drinking. Rowan felt obliged to see Florence's sights, though she too had tired of the heat and the dust and flies and the men who trailed round after her, crying 'Bella, bella', pestering her with invitations to dinner in their nonna's restaurant.

The terrace overlooked a steep incline where inky cypresses melted into a sky of apricot and violet. Though they had driven out of the city to escape the heat, it seemed to Rowan that they had brought it with them, heavy and suffocating. It was late, and the tables were emptying. They had reached the coffee and liqueurs stage of the meal and a languor had fallen over the party. The men, who were rather drunk, had taken to hurling the sweet biscuits the waiter had brought to accompany their brandies over the stone balustrade, competing with each other to see who could throw them furthest.

'They are so awful, aren't they?' Fay Winchester said to Rowan. 'George, Lucian, you're behaving like schoolboys.'

'Bet you five quid you can't hit that rock.'

'George, honestly.' Fay's small blue eyes gleamed avidly.

'We're out of damned biscuits. Waiter!' George – portly, pink-skinned and round-faced – flapped a hand in the air. 'Bring us more biscuits.'

'So childish,' murmured Fay. She rose from her seat and went to stand beside Lucian, resting her forearms on the balustrade as he took aim.

Rowan remained where she was. Tonight, she felt separate from the others in the group. Though she should be enjoying herself, she wasn't, but the thought of returning to Florence gave her no pleasure either. Her dusty trudges round the Boboli Gardens, searching for a scrap of grass that was not parched, and her headache-inducing tours of the Duomo had long since palled. She was tired of Florence, she would have to move on. Where to, though? She was running out of money.

A curse from George and a burst of applause from Fay made her look up.

'Five pounds, if you please, Winchester,' said Lucian.

George leafed through his wallet. 'I've only damned lira.'

'Then you must give me a pledge in lieu. What shall it be? I know, I'll have a lock of your wife's hair.'

Fay shrieked and made show of cowering as Lucian took a penknife out of his pocket. *Lucian, you're a monster!* The other diners were staring at them.

In a single, neat stroke Lucian cut a long lock of Fay's platinum-fair hair, then held it up like a trophy. It gleamed, a silver ribbon in the moonlight.

Fay gasped and put a hand to her head. 'My hair . . .' This time, she looked genuinely upset.

'It doesn't show,' Rowan said, attempting comfort, though it did.

'Damned nerve,' said George angrily.

Lucian's black eyes flickered. 'No need to take offence, dear fellow.'

The head waiter was marching purposefully across the terrace towards their table. 'We should go.' Rowan stood up. 'Before they throw us out.'

The women gathered up their silk shawls and bags; Lucian dropped a bundle of notes on to the table. As they left the restaurant, George said, 'Race you back to Florence, Cardew. A tenner, this time. And I'll have that lock of hair back.'

Lucian gave his lazy smile. 'Sure.'

He took Rowan's hand in his as they walked down the hill to the cars. The Winchesters went ahead of them, Fay's high heels clacking on the narrow, paved street.

Lucian said, 'Are you having a wonderful time, Rowan?'

'Not really.'

Again, he smiled. 'You should do as I do. Make the most of whatever amusement you can find and accept disillusion as inevitable. Most men are pretty average, by the nature of things. Damn it, he's off.'

The Winchesters' green Jaguar Roadster headed in clouds of dust out of the square. Lucian opened the door of his open-top Alfa Romeo and Rowan climbed in. A full moon illuminated their drive through the village. She felt her remoteness from her companion as they gained the open road that led through the countryside to Fiesole. The ancient Tuscan landscape, washed by silvery moonlight, was heartbreakingly beautiful, and yet as she gazed at it she felt nothing. She had travelled to Europe to escape her unhappiness but it seemed to her that she carted it about with her, a heavy, cumbersome piece of luggage.

Driving along a straight section of road, they caught sight of the Jaguar, a short distance in front of them. Lucian stabbed his foot on the accelerator and the Alfa's engine growled as it gathered speed. A part of Rowan welcomed the distraction of danger. Speed transformed the cypress trees into mere flickers of a zoetrope. The darkness to either side of the narrow beams might have contained anything at all.

As they hurtled round a corner Rowan caught sight of a motor vehicle heading towards them. 'Lucian, look out!' she cried.

He swung the Alfa on to the verge, avoiding the clash of wheels by a whisker. 'This is fun, isn't it?' he yelled, over the roar of the engine. 'Don't you think this is fun?'

Now she was frightened. 'Slow down,' she pleaded. 'Lucian, please slow down.'

Rounding another bend in the road, they saw the Jaguar.

'Got the bastard,' Lucian murmured.

A deep pothole loomed to their side of the road. Lucian flicked the steering-wheel to avoid it and Rowan felt the sideways tug of the back wheels. Lucian swore as he fought to control the skid, but it was as if they were spun round in a whirlpool. Rowan screamed as the car streaked off the road and was propelled over the verge and a ditch. She was flung forward violently; there was the whump of crumpling metal. The force of the collision knocked the air from her lungs. Drawing in a rasping breath, she heard the whirr of wheels and the whine of the engine.

Rowan opened her eyes. She had been thrown into the footwell and something was jabbing into her face. She

167

brushed away some twigs. She couldn't work out why there were twigs in the car. The headlamps were out and it was dark.

'Lucian,' she croaked.

There was no answer. She shuffled back up into the seat. The car was lying at a sloping angle. The thought came to her that he had been thrown out of the vehicle, that he was dead. 'Lucian.' Her voice trembled. She reached out to him.

Her fingers brushed against the sleeve of his jacket. He moaned. Rowan gave a desperate glance back to the road, hoping to see George Winchester's Jaguar heading towards them. But there was only darkness.

Scrabbling in the glove box she found a torch. The beam of light illuminated the interior of the car, which was scattered with leaves and branches. The Alfa's bonnet had concertinaed into the trunk of a tree. Any thought she had had of driving to get help for Lucian faded; the car was a wreck.

Lucian was slumped against the steering-wheel. When Rowan touched his forehead her fingertips came away damp with blood. Reaching across, she turned off the ignition. The movement made him groan again.

'I'm here, Lucian,' she said. She tried to sound calm. 'Don't worry, it's going to be all right.'

'Sorry,' he whispered. 'What a damn fool. Sorry.'

'Sweetie, it's going to be all right.'

Slowly he straightened and sat back against the seat, his features contorted with pain. The jagged gash across his forehead was bleeding copiously. Rowan had been a Girl Guide once, an age ago, and had learned first aid. She bit the hem of her silk wrap to tear it, ripped off a strip and bound it round his forehead. She felt the fast pounding of his pulse. He was shivering so she spread the travelling rug over him.

Fear rushed through her. He might have broken his skull. The steering wheel could have crushed his ribs or punctured a lung. He could be bleeding internally, bleeding to death. She made a decision.

'Lucian, I think I should try and get help,' she said. 'I won't be long, I promise. Is there anything I can do for you?'

'My head hurts . . .' he whispered. 'And my shoulder . . .'

'I know, darling. Look, I'll try and make you more comfortable.' Very carefully, she picked off the twigs that were scattered over him, and then, kneeling on the passenger seat, tried to adjust his position.

'Is that any better?'

'Yes.' Another gasp. His eyes were closed. 'You're a great girl, Rowan.'

'I'm going to go now, but I'll be back very soon.'

She climbed out of the car and walked up the road, swinging the torch from side to side, hoping that it might illuminate a farmhouse or other dwelling. But there were only fields and copses and the cypress trees, like black tombstones, and though she jogged on to the next bend in the road and peered out over more fields, praying that she might see a lit window, there was nothing.

She went back to the car. 'Lucian, sweetie, how are you doing?'

He had slumped down in the seat again. His eyelids fluttered and he made murmuring noises.

'Someone will come along soon, I'm sure,' she said, trying to sound confident. 'And then we'll get you to a doctor who can patch you up.'

The makeshift bandage was soaked in blood; she tore off another strip of her scarf. The car smelled of petrol and blood. Though the night air was warm, Lucian's skin felt cold to touch. She put her arm round him so that she could share her body heat. When she said his name again, there was no response and she saw that his eyes had closed.

She was alone. An image bobbed into her mind's eye of Thea, flung about by the waves near Corran, her skin white, eyes shut. All the time Rowan had been swimming to shore with her she had been afraid that Thea was already dead. She shook the memory away. Start thinking about Corran and she'd fall apart, and then what good would she be to Lucian? She knelt up on the seat and checked the bandage again. The bleeding seemed to have lessened.

She heard something and looked up. At first she could see nothing, but then, as the sound grew louder, she realised with a huge rush of relief that she was hearing the gentle clopping of a horse.

She shouted, 'Help! Please help me!' and scrambled out of the car, swinging the torchlight up the road.

A horse and cart was coming along the road towards them, the cart's flat bed bearing wooden barrels. It drew up beside them. The driver, a broad-shouldered man with shaggy black hair, looked across at the wrecked motor car. He said a few words of Italian to Rowan, out of which she picked out, 'morto'.

'No, no, he's not dead! I have to get him to a doctor.' She fumbled for the word. 'Dottore! Per favore! Please, you must help me!'

The barrels were pushed aside; together Rowan and the carter hauled Lucian out of the Alfa. He screamed as they moved him, a terrible sound, but slipped into unconsciousness again as they laid him on the back of the cart. Rowan tucked the travelling rug over him and knelt down beside him.

The journey felt interminable, the cart slowly lunging and jerking the couple of miles to Fiesole. She was thankful that Lucian was unconscious so that he could not feel the movement of the vehicle. In Fiesole, the driver came to a halt outside a villa. He hammered on the door and eventually someone – a manservant, Rowan assumed – came out.

The manservant and the carter carried Lucian indoors, through tiled passageways to a kitchen, where they laid him on the table. A woman, in her sixties perhaps, wrapped in a velvet robe and her hair in pins, came into the kitchen and said in heavily accented English to Rowan, 'The doctor will come soon.' Then she wandered away. The manservant too, went out of the room, leaving Rowan with Lucian.

She sat down in a chair beside the table. The kitchen was large and sparsely furnished and the light came from oil lamps. The bleeding had started up again; Rowan folded a tea towel and pressed it against Lucian's head wound.

The manservant returned, this time accompanied by the doctor, a short, rotund man in dusty black. Glancing at Lucian, he tutted, slowly shaking his head, and then opened his leather bag.

'You will stay.' He pointed at Rowan. 'You will be my nurse. You will not . . .' He mimed a faint.

'Of course not,' she said.

'You are not hurt, signora?' He was taking a stethoscope out of the bag.

'No, I don't think so.'

The doctor had some English, Rowan had a little Italian and they both spoke passable French. The manservant hovered, shining an oil lamp on to the table. Rowan held Lucian's head as the doctor stitched the wound. He groaned as his smashed shoulder was bound to his body in a sling.

Eventually it was done and the doctor and the manservant carried Lucian to another room and put him to bed. The doctor came back to Rowan.

'Gennaro will sit with Signor Cardew. I will return in the morning and we will see how he does. There may be injuries inside.' He gestured to his stomach and chest. 'If he does not do so well, I will arrange for him to be taken to the hospital in Florence. But he is young and strong and let us pray that he recovers. He has been fortunate, he could easily have been killed.' He smiled at her. 'You are a good nurse, madame. You did well. But now you must rest.'

Gennaro showed Rowan to a small room on the first floor. She thanked him and then shut the door and sat down on the bed. She ached with fatigue and reaction. A glance in the oval mirror above a set of drawers showed her that her face was badly scratched.

Someone had left on top of the bedside table a tray bearing a glass of red wine and a plate of biscuits. A towel and nightdress had been placed at the foot of the bed. Rowan dabbed the towel in the washstand and dabbed at her face, trying to clean it up; the deep grazes hurt now. She drank the red wine and nibbled a biscuit. The biscuits made her think of Lucian and George at the trattoria and their stupid game. Her shaking hands struggled to undo the zip of her evening gown, which was torn and filthy, but she managed it at last and pulled the nightdress over her head.

She lay down on the bed. Though she was exhausted beyond endurance sleep would not come. The chill had reached inside her, and though the night was warm and she drew the blankets up to her chin, she could not stop shaking.

Now she could not hold back the memories. They rushed in at her, like the current that poured through the strait between Corran and the mainland. She was thirteen years old again, and she was on the island and screaming at her mother. 'I saw you with that man! I heard what he said! I hate you! I hate this place!' Her words were indelible, and she knew she would remember them for the rest of her life.

And then they were on the shore and Mamma was pulling on her oilskin and telling her and Thea to get in the *Iduna*. And the rain was falling hard and the sea was mottled and dancing and the waves had white tops as the sailing boat pulled away from Portmore. Sigrid's long, pale hair was whipped by the wind as she worked the sails and rudder, and her beautiful features were distorted by effort and grief.

Everything had happened so quickly. She was in the sea and waves were washing over her head and the shock of the icy water washed away everything but terror. There was water in her mouth and her nose and she couldn't breathe and she couldn't see Mamma or Thea and couldn't tell which way up she should swim to reach the air. She was drowning, and while she drowned her own words echoed in her ears.

I hate you, I hate you.

Chapter Ten

July–August 1939

Sophie's lodger, a young man called Roland Toft, had been called up for military training. Stuart was helping Sophie sort out the room for its next inhabitant, a middle-aged woman.

They had stripped the bed and swept the floor. Stuart was scrubbing a patch on the rug where Mr Toft had spilled a cup of coffee. Sophie started on the window-panes.

Her eye was caught by a figure standing on the far side of the road. Her heart gave an odd little squeeze and her hand, gripping the chamois leather, paused. Could it be her? No, she was imagining it, surely. But then the girl moved a little, and she knew it was her.

She must have made a sound because Stuart came to stand beside her. 'What is it, Mum?'

She gave her head a little shake but could not look away. 'There,' she whispered.

Stuart followed her gaze. 'I don't see . . .'

But then he did, she thought, because he frowned and said, 'Mum?' and his gaze swung from the pavement outside before returning to her. Sophie remained mute, frozen, as Stuart put down the scrubbing brush and left the room.

She heard the front door open and close and went on watching through the window as Stuart crossed the road to where the girl stood. They seemed to talk for a while. And then Stuart and Thea Craxton walked away together.

Later, Thea, walking through Covent Garden, thought over what Stuart had told her, and then she thought how nice he had been, and then some more about the fact that Stuart's mother, Sophie Craxton or Sophie Torrance, depending on how you looked at it, had been married — sort of — to her father, to hers and Stuart's father, for more than nineteen years. The marriage was invalid because Hugh had been married to Sigrid for some of that time, until she died. And now Hugh was dead too. Which meant that Stuart's mother wasn't really Sophie Craxton, but had remained, unknown to her, Sophie Torrance all along.

Stuart was a person who liked a bit of clarity, as Thea did. They had that in common, as well as the other thing. So they had spent a long time sitting in a café, exchanging times and dates and working everything out. Hugh had married Sigrid in 1912. And then he had married Stuart's mother, Sophie, in 1918. Rowan had been born the year the war had broken out, Duncan the year after it ended. As for her and Stuart, there was only a year between them.

'Two babies,' Stuart had said, widening his blue eyes. 'He must have done a lot of dashing about.'

Momentarily they had wondered why, after Sigrid had died in 1927, Hugh hadn't married Sophie and sorted out his life, but of course the answer was obvious. Hugh couldn't have married Sophie again without telling her that he hadn't married her properly before. They both agreed that Hugh Craxton had been a man who never liked to admit being in the wrong. And perhaps these things had an impetus of their own. Once you started lying you went on lying. You forgot to mention your wife and child to the pretty hospital nurse you fell in love with, and somehow that led to you inventing a London office, a convenient friend in the Highlands, and hiding your financial troubles and all sorts of other things.

'We used to play this game, Dad and I, when I was little,' Stuart had said, before they parted. 'I'd watch while he hid something – a coin, a dice, a reel of cotton – in the sitting room. I'd have to guess where it was and I always got it wrong. I'd be sure it was on a shelf but it would turn out to be in his pocket, something like that. Sleight of hand, Dad called it. He was good at that, sleight of hand. I wonder whether it all was a game to him, Thea, a great, complicated game that kept his mind off all the things he didn't want to think about.'

Thea let herself into Rowan's flat. Peggy was away, which was just as well, because she wouldn't have known what to say to her. She had forgotten to buy the eggs she had meant to purchase for her supper; well, that was the sort of thing that happened when you ended up talking for hours to the half-brother you'd never known you had.

She was peering into the larder, which was almost empty, when she heard footsteps on the stairs. She'd have known those footsteps anywhere.

Thea opened the door. Rowan was standing on the threshold, fumbling in her bag. She was wearing a crumpled cream linen skirt and jacket and she had put her suitcase down beside her. One side of her face was criss-crossed with scratches that had healed to pink lines across her cheek and forehead.

'Rowan,' she said, at the same time as Rowan said, 'Oh, Thea.' And they fell into each other's arms.

'Your face,' Thea said. 'Oh, Rowan, your poor face.'

She made coffee. There was no milk so she borrowed a jug from a neighbour.

Rowan said, 'I was in a motor accident, in Italy. The man I was with, Lucian, who was driving, was hurt quite badly. I stayed with him until his sister, who lives in Paris, was able to travel to Fiesole. He's going to recover, but it'll take a while.' She ran her fingertips over the right side of her face. 'This, it's nothing. I may have a little scar or two. Anyway, as soon as Patricia, Lucian's sister, was able to take over, I left. I was running out of money and besides, I was longing to come home.' She gave a wry smile. 'I was so sick of being abroad, Thea. You can't believe how sick of it I was. So I bought a train ticket to London. I planned to sleep for hours in the wagon lit. I wasn't able to sleep at all while Lucian was so ill, I was so worried about him, and I was so tired. But then, at Milan station, while I was changing platforms, someone stole my purse. So there I was, in the railway station, going through my bag and my suitcase. I just couldn't believe my purse wasn't there. In the end, I emptied everything out on to the platform, all my clothes, everything. All my money was gone, and my train ticket too. It was simply the last straw.'

Thea said, 'What did you do?'

'I cried.' Rowan poured out the coffee and handed a cup to Thea. 'I sat down on the platform beside my case and simply howled and howled.'

'Oh, Rowan.'

'And then a nice woman saw me and asked if she could help. She was English, older than me, and I'm afraid I just wept over her. It wasn't only losing my purse, it was the car crash too, and, oh, everything else that's gone wrong – Patrick . . . Simon . . . everything.'

'Poor Rowan. Thank goodness you're home now.'

Stirring sugar into her coffee, Rowan said quietly, 'A lot of it has been my own fault. I've made such a mess of things. I don't know what I'd have done if Genevieve – that was her name – hadn't helped me. I was afraid I'd have to go to the British Consulate. I was picturing myself trudging through Milan with my suitcase, trying to follow directions with my hopeless Italian. And it was so hot. I've realised that I detest hot weather, Thea, I'm not made for it. Anyway, Gen offered to lend me the money to buy another train ticket. She told me she was travelling back to London that afternoon and suggested we travel together.'

'How kind of her.'

'It was so kind, and I was so relieved and grateful.'

Strangers could be so unexpectedly generous. Tears stung Thea's eyes as she thought of Stuart, crossing the road to talk to her, and how sweet and thoughtful he had been. And how, although finding out that their father was a bigamist must have been in a way even more awful for him than for her – it was Stuart and his brother who were illegitimate, not her and Rowan – he had taken the time to be kind to her. *I know this must be an awful shock finding you have a stray brother or two. There's a café down the road – why don't I buy us a cup of tea?*

Rowan took up her story. 'It's a long journey from Milan to London. Gen and I talked a lot and I had plenty time to think. I thought about Lucian, of course, and how I'd been wasting my time on men I didn't love a bit. I'm not sure I even liked him very much. And I thought about Simon. If I hadn't been looking for someone to love me, then Simon might have been fun. But I was, and I think I always will be, and he broke my heart. As for Patrick, I should never have married him. He's a good man, but we weren't right for each other. I was very young and I thought marriage might settle me down, but I'm far too fidgety for someone like him. And anyway, he couldn't love me how I need to be loved.' Rowan smoothed the creases out of her skirt. 'And I thought about Mamma, too. How everything, always, for me, in the end comes back to Mamma, and to what happened on Corran.'

'Rowan,' Thea said gently. 'You don't have to talk about this now.'

'I do.' Rowan gave her a hard stare. 'If I don't do it now I'll lose my nerve. I should have found a way of telling you ages ago.'

'Telling me what?'

'About Mamma and Corran. And about you. The truth. You have the right to know.'

As she sifted Rowan's words, Thea felt a stirring of apprehension. The events of the day had knocked the capacity for curiosity out of her. She wondered, in a confused way, whether Rowan knew about Sophie, knew about her father having had another family all along – but no, it couldn't be that, it didn't fit.

Rowan was saying, 'I've been angry with Mamma for so long. I think I'm like her and knowing that made me feel even angrier. I'm restless and impatient, like she was, and I can't seem to settle to one man. But maybe I understand her better now. Maybe I can see why she did what she did. Mamma was having a love affair, Thea, with a man who lived on the island.'

Thea tried to say something but couldn't. She had been

given far too many shocks to digest in one day and there was a limit to how much you could take in. Mutely, she stared at her sister.

'I overheard Mamma talking to her lover, that last day on Corran,' said Rowan. 'It had started to rain so I left you playing on the beach with the other children while I ran up to get our macs. Mamma wasn't in the house so I went to look for her. I saw her in the garden, talking to a man. She was crying. The rain was pouring down and they were shouting at each other and she was crying. He was telling her to leave Dad. He was *begging* her to leave Dad. And she was telling him that she couldn't, because of us, because of you and me.'

Thea said, 'It doesn't matter now. It was a long time ago. None of that matters any more.'

'It does, I'm afraid. It matters to *you*.'

Did she even care that her mother had, according to Rowan, taken a lover on Corran? She didn't think she did, much. It was a long time ago. Only a couple of hours had passed since Stuart had told her that their father had married his mother, Sophie, in 1918. So by the time she bought the holiday home on Corran Sigrid's marriage can't have been good, to put it mildly. Sigrid had had a short life. It would seem a shame if she hadn't found some happiness.

But then Rowan repeated, 'It matters to you, Thea. More, you see, than it does to me.' And she began to have an inkling of what Rowan was trying to tell her.

'Mamma said she couldn't leave Dad because of you and me. And *he* said, her lover said, "But Thea is my daughter, not Hugh's."'

Rowan said something else but Thea hardly heard her. *Thea is my daughter, not Hugh's.* She walked to the window and looked out at the little square of garden, at the washing hanging on the line and the black cat winding between the pots of pinks. She was reminding herself that the everyday world was ticking on, and that not all days would be like this one.

Thea is my daughter, not Hugh's. She wanted to tell Rowan that she must be mistaken, that she had been a child, that the tragedy at Corran had taken place more than a decade ago and that memory plays tricks on you. But a moment's thought plunged her into doubt. There was Rowan, tall and red-haired like Hugh, and there she was, small and slight and dark. There was Rowan, a whizz at skiing and tennis and always in demand at social events, and there she was, loathing parties and never picked for a school team in her life. People encountering her after they had met Rowan first tended to say in a disappointed way, 'You don't look like your sister.' Even blasted Simon Pemberton had said that.

She heard Rowan say in a small, frightened voice, 'I couldn't tell you before, when Dad was alive. It would have hurt him so much. You do see that, don't you?' And then, 'She betrayed him. He was a good man and she betrayed him.'

Thea turned round. Rowan was sitting on the sofa. The scars on her face stood out like pink crayon marks against her white skin. Thea thought of the burden secrets imposed and her heart overflowed with pity and love for her sister.

No more, then. 'Well,' she said. 'Maybe not.'

On Monday, Thea went back to Wiltshire. She needed the routine and distraction of her work and the timelessness of the landscape. She needed the Fainlights and the others on the dig, who were both her colleagues and her friends. And she craved something to get her teeth into, civilisations that she could learn about and discover, which would take up that part of her mind in which thoughts had whirred ceaselessly since her conversation with Rowan.

In her absence, they had dug another trench in one of the causeways. Bones, both human and animal, were emerging, as if the chalk was spitting them out. The thigh bone of a warrior, the finger bones of a woman who had picked seeds and berries to make food, and the remains of an infant, her foot bones like tiny, pearly beads.

At midday, they always downed tools to sit in the oak copse and eat their lunch. Often, this summer of 1939, the talk was of the coming of war. In March, Hitler's armies had occupied the dismembered remains of Czechoslovakia. In May, Germany had formed a military alliance, the Pact of Steel, with Mussolini's Italy.

One of the archaeologists, Geoffrey, had lost an arm in the Great War. He never talked much and Thea had noticed that there were conversations he turned away from. One lunchtime, they were speaking of Hitler's claim to the Danzig corridor, the strip of land that was Poland's access to the Baltic Sea and which divided the bulk of Germany from its territories in East Prussia.

'He'll never be satisfied,' Geoffrey said suddenly. 'People like that never are. You give them one thing and they demand another. When we're tearing each other to pieces in the trenches again, Hitler will still want more.' He rose and walked away, back up the hill to the dig.

Lying awake in the tent that night, Thea thought about her mother. Sigrid had bought the house on the island and the sailing boat, the Iduna, shortly after the end of the Great War. She must have been upset by her husband's frequent absences; she may even have accused him of infidelity, which Hugh, a practised liar, would have denied. On the island, sailing the boat she loved, Sigrid had found pleasure, distraction and consolation.

And unexpectedly, she had fallen in love. After that, she had returned frequently to Corran. If she, Thea, was the daughter of Sigrid and her lover, then the affair must have gone on for at least seven years.

And then matters had come to a head. Perhaps Sigrid's lover had had enough of secrecy or perhaps he had wanted to be openly acknowledged as the father of his daughter. Whatever, they had quarrelled and, disastrously, Rowan had overheard.

Sigrid would have tried to comfort her daughter, to explain. But Rowan had understood only her mother's betrayal. *I hate you*, she had said. *I hate this place. I want to go home.* And so Sigrid had taken the fateful decision to leave the island that day.

'We left Corran that morning,' Rowan had told her. 'After the accident, no one could understand why the boat had ended up on the rocks – why, when Mamma was such an experienced sailor, she'd made such a stupid mistake. But I knew. It was because of what happened. It was because she hadn't got her mind on it. She was upset because she had quarrelled, with her lover and with me.'

Poor Rowan. What a memory to carry with her for years, of betrayal, regret and tragedy. Thinking about that, Thea could have wept.

One evening on the dig, she was searching for a clean pair of socks when she came across her father's cashmere scarf, rolled up in the bottom of her rucksack. Hugh Craxton hadn't been a good man and she wasn't really his daughter.

183

Yet she took out the scarf and pressed it against her face, feeling its soft caress, breathing in scents so faint they had become little more than a memory of scent: Blenheim Bouquet and Turkish tobacco, fragrances that still, in spite of everything, conjured up his smile and his hand in hers as they walked in the hills above Loch Lomond.

It was a fine August evening. As the country teetered on the brink of war, ordinary things had become imbued with a heightened loveliness. Rowan and Thea were making their way to Sophie's house in Gilbert Street. Rowan was telling Thea about the interview she had had that morning at St Anne's hospital.

'I think it went all right. It's hard to tell. The matron said she'd let me know.'

Rowan had decided to train to be a nurse. She had written letters of application to half a dozen London schools of nursing and St Anne's had replied, offering her an interview. She felt cheerful, sensing a new direction for herself.

The doctor in Fiesole had given her the idea. *You are a good nurse*, he had said to her, that evening Lucian had almost died. *You did well.* Though she suspected him of being kind, she needed to do something useful with her life. Anything other, in fact, than run round after hopeless men. Nursing would be useful, especially if, as now seemed inevitable, there was a war. She had decided to give it a go.

Rowan and Thea linked arms. Thea had an *A–Z* with her and Stuart had scribbled directions on the letter he had sent to her, telling them that his mother would like to meet them. They had nothing in common with Sophie Craxton, Rowan thought, and yet they had everything in common.

They turned into Gilbert Street. Number 17 was a neat

redbrick villa with a pot of white geraniums by the front door.

'If she's utterly ghastly,' Rowan murmured as Thea pressed the bell, 'I shall invent a headache so we can escape.'

Stuart answered the door. Thea introduced him to Rowan and they followed him into the house.

A woman came into the corridor. Sophie Craxton was wearing a cotton summer frock of striped cream and apple green, and she was smiling. And Rowan, catching a first glimpse of her, was surprised to find that she liked her immediately.

PART TWO

WE'LL WAIT FOR TOMORROW
1940–1944

Chapter Eleven

June 1940

You've left it too late. The words ran through Thea's head over and over again as the train rattled to a halt at a station somewhere in France. She couldn't see which station it was because she was standing jammed in the corridor between a portly woman in a yellow dress and an old man smoking a pipe and she couldn't move.

The other passengers in the train were, like her, fleeing France. Thea had taken the train unsure where it was heading to. No destination had been announced but a rumour had sprung up that it was making for Cherbourg or one of the other Channel ports, and so she had squeezed herself into a carriage. At least, she had told herself, it would take her away from the swiftly advancing German front line. The train's progress had been frustratingly slow, given to sudden long stops in sidings or at deserted stations. Through a scrap of window Thea had seen the glint of aeroplanes, high in the bland blue summer sky. Halfway through her journey, someone had claimed they could hear gunfire and a ripple of horror had run through the carriage.

Through the window, she glimpsed a station platform,

with crowds of men, women and children and their suitcases and bags and birdcages. It looked much the same as all the other stations she had passed through, and for a horrible moment Thea wondered whether she had spent the intervening hours going round in a circle and was back in Paris. She craned to see where they were.

A guard thumped on the window, telling them they had reached the end of the line. There was a groan from the passengers and a man started to protest loudly, a frantic edge to his voice. A door was flung open, letting some air into the hot carriage. The passengers spilled out and Thea found herself on the platform. A sign told her that she was in Alençon, in Normandy, a hundred miles or so to the west of Paris.

So that was all right, she told herself encouragingly as she made her way along the platform. At least she was substantially closer to the Channel coast and a boat that would take her to England than she had been that morning. She wound in and out of the crowds, hoping to find a train that would take her to Cherbourg or St Malo. It was hard to get anywhere in the dense crowds. The platforms were so closely packed she carried her rucksack in front of her, gripping it tightly. Babies howled and children dashed round the benches and heaps of luggage while their parents scolded them. When Thea asked a porter to direct her to a train to one of the Channel ports he spread out his hands, palms up, and shrugged.

She came across a man shouting through a megaphone. He wore the uniform of a French railway official and was telling everyone that there would be no more trains that day. A sigh rose from the multitude but most remained where they were, staring at the destination boards. Perhaps they didn't believe him, or perhaps, having found somewhere to stand, they were determined to hold their place and wait for tomorrow.

She made her way out of the station. A great mass of people thronged round the building, spreading across the forecourt and roads. It was a warm June day and it felt better to be walking away from the crowds. Thea slipped off her rucksack and took out her water bottle and drank deeply, then pressed on. Passing a row of shops, she bought apples and cheese and bread. Then she went into a *tabac*, hoping to purchase a map, but the proprietor told her that he had no maps of France or Normandy left. He had hardly any newspapers either; the few scattered on the counter blared of the rapid advance of the German army through northern France. The enemy was on the Dieppe–Paris road. There were tanks in Rouen.

The proprietor gave Thea directions westwards, out of town, but she didn't need them, not really, because she had only to follow in the direction that everyone, it seemed, was heading. The whole of France appeared to be taking to the roads. All, like Thea, were travelling as fast as they could away from the battleground that the country had turned into.

She found herself among a column of refugees so vast it could move only at a glacial pace. People moaned about the trains, the roads, some relative who had held them up and the inconsiderateness of their fellow travellers. Oddly, they didn't talk much about the two armies locked in a struggle to the death somewhere to the north. Carthorses jostled against expensive motor cars, whose polished chrome and black metal were already dulled by dust. The weather was hot and dry and tempers flared. Cyclists wound between those on foot, imperiously ringing their bells and calling to the pedestrians to get out of their way. Babies were pushed in prams and old grandmothers, swathed in black, in wheelbarrows. Along the roadside lay the detritus abandoned by the exodus – a gaggle of geese, a set of encyclopaedias, a flowered china tea-set, treasures that had turned into burdens as their owners' journeys had lengthened. More than once Thea saw, heartbreakingly, a small child standing alone at the side of the road, sobbing for its mother.

You've left it too late, the voice in Thea's head repeated in time with her footsteps. *You've left it too late.*

For the past four months she had been living in Switzerland. She and Grace Fainlight had travelled there earlier in the year to make preparations for the dig that summer at the Roman amphitheatre outside Basel. Monty had joined them in April. She had felt as if her life was opening out. Back then, she had imagined that her life would go on like this, that the years would pass and she would work on archaeological digs and travel to all sorts of wonderful places, to Greece and Italy and Persia. She hadn't foreseen that the window would so suddenly slam shut, leaving her desperately hurtling back to safety and the narrower life she thought she had left behind.

The news on 10th May of the German assault on the Netherlands, Belgium and Luxembourg had come as a body blow. You knew it might happen but still somehow wouldn't really bring yourself to believe that it would. With dismaying rapidity the battle for France had followed. Even then they had assumed for a long time – for too long a time – that it would be all right, that the French army would repel the invasion. They had imagined that this war would be a repeat of the Great War, that the conflict would take place to the north, in Flanders fields, as it had in 1914. Instead, German tanks and infantry had poured with lightning speed through and around the French defences, like water squirting out of holes in a rusty pipe.

Thea wondered whether it had taken them so long to react because the enormity of the disaster was too terrible to take in. For herself, there was a dash of selfishness, too. She was doing the work she loved with the people she loved, and how could she possibly accept that she might lose all that on the whim of a mad dictator? And so it had not been until towards the end of May, by which time the British Expeditionary Forces were in full retreat from the beaches of Dunkirk, that she had decided to make her way home, back to England.

Though it seemed an age, less than a fortnight had passed since the evening when Grace had told her that she and Monty had decided to remain in Switzerland.

'We've lived through one war and neither of us can bear to live through another,' she added. 'Tobias fought in the trenches and I saw what it did to him. I can only be thankful that he's decided to stay in Sweden.' Sweden, like Switzerland, was a neutral country.

They were sitting on the balcony of the apartment the Fainlights had rented on the outskirts of Basel. A rosy sunset filtered on to Grace's pots of herbs.

Grace said, 'Won't you change your mind and stay with us, Thea? Monty and I would love you to stay.'

'I can't,' she said, 'because of Rowan. I need to go home to Rowan.'

'Of course.' Grace's features were seamed with anxiety. 'Thea,' she said, 'I'm worried about Helen. It's three weeks since I had a letter from her. I've written more than a dozen times but she hasn't replied. The last time I heard from her, she was staying in Paris. She'll be safe there, I'm sure, Hitler won't reach Paris, but nevertheless . . . Would you do something for me, when you get there? Would you go and see her and tell her to come here, to Basel, to me? Or, if she prefers, to her father in Sweden.'

Thea promised to speak to Helen. She kept to herself the thought that no one could persuade Helen to do something she didn't want to do.

'Thank you, my dear.' Grace sighed. 'It worries me, not knowing what her plans are. She can be so headstrong.' She put her hand over Thea's. 'We'll miss you. What do you plan to do, when you return to London? We all may have to start from scratch, I'm afraid, and find something useful to do.'

'I'll think of something,' said Thea.

Grace rose from her seat and left the balcony, returning shortly afterwards with an envelope, which she handed to Thea.

'Nicholas Grey is a friend of mine,' Grace said. 'He's a junior minister in the government. Give him this letter. He may be able to find you something.'

Thea and the Fainlights said their farewells at the railway station the following morning. There was the silent, mutual pretence that the war might end soon, that the invader would quickly be repelled. Afterwards, Thea wondered if it would have been braver, perhaps, to acknowledge the catastrophe that was about to take over all their lives.

Arriving in Paris, she booked into an inexpensive *pension*. That first afternoon she discovered that Helen had already left the address that Grace had given her. The concièrge thought she might have gone to stay with a friend on the

Left Bank. The friend, a girl called Annette, was hard to find and when, eventually, Thea traced her, she told Thea that it had been a month since she had last seen Helen.

Annette wrote down the names of Helen's other Paris friends. Thea made phone calls and wandered round, leaving notes. The restaurants went on serving their fine food, the gardens at the Tuileries looked glorious, and the boats continued to glide up and down the Seine. And yet Paris was subdued and quiet. Even the city's notorious traffic seemed muffled. Behind a façade of normality, people were making phone calls and studying maps, making plans, wandering round those elegant apartments in the sixth arrondissement, perhaps, trying to decide what to take and what to leave behind.

Helen was nowhere to be found. Someone told Thea that she had already gone back to London. She sent a postcard to Grace.

In an acknowledgement of defeat, hundreds of thousands of British and French troops had been evacuated from the Channel ports to the south of England. Hitler's armies were rushing like a black tide closer and closer to Paris, and what had previously seemed unimaginable, the stuff of nightmares, became frighteningly real. Belatedly, Thea realised that if she left it any longer she might not be able to go home. And suddenly she, like everyone else, was packing her bag and heading for the railway station.

The bonnet of a motor car nudged her. A woman stuck her head out of the window.

'Awfully sorry!' An English voice.

Thea rubbed her hip. 'It's all right.'

'Oh Lord, I'm so sorry, but these roads . . .'

'Honestly, I'm not hurt at all.'

A man's voice said, 'Scottish, are you?'

'Yes.'

'Hop in the back, why don't you?'

Two days had passed since Thea had left Alençon, two days of maddeningly slow progress. She thanked the English couple and climbed into the car. Three people were squashed into the rear of the small Citroën, a man and two women. The only way Thea could fit in was to sit on the lap of one of the women.

'Good thing you're tiny,' said the woman. 'Good thing I've plenty of padding.' She shrieked with laughter.

They introduced themselves. The driver was called Richard Collins and the dark, pretty woman in a cherry-coloured silk frock, sitting in the front seat beside him, was his wife, Mary. The rear passengers were plump Charlotte King and her husband, Jim, and another woman, Joan, older than the others. They were all teachers at an English-language school in Paris.

The Citroën was able to move little faster than the crawling column of refugees. The roads became more and more choked with abandoned vehicles and livestock as they pressed on; often they ground to a halt in a queue of motor cars, all hooting their horns. But it was nice to be able to sit for a while. Richard and Mary were discussing whether they should keep heading west or make for the south. They'd be able to get home, Richard said, through Spain or Portugal or even North Africa.

They diverted off the main road and then drove at speed between meadows and copses. Here, deep in the French countryside, only her blisters and the dust on her legs reminded Thea that she was heading through a country at war. In the evening, they stopped outside a village and picnicked on a meadow starred with daisies. She must have dozed a little, lying on the grass, because Mary woke her up and told her that they had decided to drive south after all.

'Joan knows of a villa near Montpellier that we should be able to use. It'll be a longer journey but Richard doesn't think the roads will be so bad. Someone said that some of the Channel ports are already in German hands. You can come with us if you like, Thea.'

She thanked Mary but said that she would try her luck going west. Before they parted, Mary gave her a bag of biscuits and Richard drew her a map, balancing his notebook on the Citroën's bonnet, France reduced to a hexagon, a big scribbled ink dot for Paris and a smaller one for Alençon, where her train had come to a halt. Other dots on the coastline marked the ports: Le Havre, Cherbourg, St Malo, St Nazaire. She had known Richard and Mary Collins for only a couple of hours but, walking away from them felt as if she were leaving her last old friends.

Thea was back in the long procession of refugees when a sound made everyone look up to the sky. 'Stuka!' someone called out, and there were screams as people ran for cover.

The aeroplane shrieked low over the road. Lights flashed and there was a deafening clatter of machine guns.

The noise diminished and Thea, trembling, picked herself out of a ditch. She heard screams and a terrible squealing sound. It took her a second or two to understand that the squeals were coming from a horse, which was lying on its side, its chestnut coat smeared with blood. A woman was sprawled motionless on the road, her skirt rucked up to her hips, revealing long beige knickers, and a child's white smock was turning red. A pram had toppled over, spilling its contents, and a woman was scrabbling through blankets, her eyes wide, her mouth open in a silent scream. A young man grabbed a bicycle from the verge and cycled away and a grey-haired man yelled and stumbled after him.

Thea walked on, skirting round a twitching body at the roadside, what had once been a man reduced to a heap of bloodied clothing, the injuries too gross to survive. When she saw a gap in the hedge she slipped through it, then crossed a couple of fields before heading into woodland. Beneath the canopy of leaves and branches all was still, shady and silent. She headed deep into the forest until she couldn't see the fields any more, then sat down on a log, closed her eyes tightly and pressed her fists against her forehead. She heard the squeals of the dying horse and saw the man's mutilated body. She should have stayed and helped and yet she had walked away. She felt stronger alone, free of all those complaining, frightened men and women, but it had been wrong of her to walk away, she knew that. She should have done something. But every impulse had told her to escape.

Though the woodland calmed her she couldn't stop shivering. Eventually she shouldered her rucksack and set off again. She did so carrying a burden of guilt and a troubling awareness of her own shortcomings. She was the wrong sort of person for war, she thought. She lacked heroism.

She had the map that Richard Collins had drawn for her and a compass. She kept heading west, over slopes and low escarpments and beside streams, from which she filled her water bottle. She preferred the forest, she felt more at home in the forest, and it was a relief to be on her own, but since the Stuka she found it impossible to clamp down her fears.

198

Britain was at war with Germany. If she didn't make it back to England in the next week or so, she would be interned. She was making for the ports but didn't know whether they remained open. Mary Collins had said that some were already in German hands. If she was interned, she might not see her home again for years. She might not see Rowan for years. She wished Rowan was here with her, striding along beside her, keeping her spirits up. And then she was thankful that Rowan was safe in London at St Anne's hospital, training to be a nurse.

She walked until the sun had turned into columns of gold between the tree trunks and a barn owl flew low across her path, a pale ghost. By the time she stopped, at least part of her mind was occupied by her aching legs and the pain of her blisters instead of the screaming horse and the woman scrabbling through the pram blankets.

She hadn't a tent because she hadn't thought, little more than two weeks ago, packing her rucksack to take a train from Basel to Paris, that she would need one. She ate an apple and the last of her biscuits and attended to her sore feet. Then she dozed fitfully out in the open air, rolled up in her mackintosh. She wanted to stay in the forest for ever, and never come out. She felt safe there.

She emerged into rolling countryside. The sun beat down and the fields and the meadows were divided by lush hedge-rows festooned with honeysuckle and dog-rose. Tall poplars cast violet shadows over the golden wheat and maize.

Thea took the road until, shading her eyes against the sun, she saw in the distance a formation of tanks lumbering across a field, giant metal insects creeping closer and closer. After that, she kept to the footpaths and farm tracks. Now and again she heard the sound of battle, the rumble of guns and the terrible but by now horribly familiar shriek of dive-bombing warplanes. She was unsure whether she had gone further north than she had intended or whether the enemy had penetrated further south. Neither thought was comforting.

She was worried about her feet. Stupidly, she had left her walking boots behind in Basel and had taken only leather sandals. She had two pairs of socks, which she alternated, washing them out in streams when she had the chance. The socks were full of holes and stuck to her blistered, bloody feet. She had used up her supply of plasters and ripped up handkerchieves to bind up the worst of the blisters. But her feet hurt a lot, and though she tried to ignore the pain, she knew she was walking more slowly each day, and that alarmed her.

Her journey took her through villages and hamlets where she was able to buy food. Some of the villages were deserted, but in others, people went about their business, seemingly untouched by the war. On a late afternoon, she came across a dozen exhausted French soldiers sleeping beneath the plane trees that surrounded a square. Thea was bare-legged and wearing shorts. Ordinarily, that would have incited a barrage of wolf whistles and comments, but from these young men, nothing, not a flicker of interest. Her legs were streaked with dust and it was a struggle to drag a comb through her hair, so the men's lack of reaction was understandable, she felt. But as she approached them, her map in hand, she saw the dull, dead expression in their eyes.

One of the soldiers pointed to a spot on her map between Rennes and Fougères, about forty-five miles from St Malo. Then he told her that Paris had fallen. At first, she thought she must have misunderstood him, but he repeated it. The

Wehrmacht had entered Paris. The French capital, that glorious, graceful city, was in German hands.

The ache in her heart as she walked on seemed to spill into her bones and lungs. She hadn't prayed since she had been obliged to at Assembly at her boarding school, but she prayed now, that Helen was safely in England, that everyone she loved would be all right, that she would get home.

She was the first person to reach a tiny, isolated hamlet, and so it was she who passed on to the village the news of the fall of Paris. She was in a boulangerie, and the woman serving her looked at her as if she was mad or wicked and refused to take any money for the bread she bought, waving her away as if she was infectious.

Whenever she reached the top of a hill or rise, she searched the horizon, praying that she would catch sight of the distant glitter of the sea. The sea might be just over that next hill or it might be miles and miles away. She hadn't slept properly for more than a week and all the little villages had started to look the same, the same shuttered houses and tree-lined squares and small, dark bakeries. She tried to damp down her fear that she had lost her way, that though her sense of direction was good the paths had been so winding and the days and nights so disorientating she could easily have veered off course. She might be heading into the vast, rocky bulk of the Breton peninsula rather than towards the coast. She might be wandering round in circles, a hellish and exhausting journey that would end only when she stumbled into the hands of the enemy and was interned. Or she might reach St Malo only to find that it was already occupied, or there were no boats to ferry her across the Channel.

Her shoulders were sunburned and her eyes were gritty with dust. She had a headache all the time, because of the heat, she supposed. But it was her feet that worried her most. After so many days of walking they were a mass of bleeding sores and blisters. The worst of the blisters had burst; a large one on the side of her right foot, more than three inches across, was oozing yellowish stuff. The blisters on the soles of her feet were particularly painful and made every step an ordeal.

She had told Grace she was leaving Switzerland because she wanted to be with Rowan, but that was not the only reason she longed to go home. Having conquered northern Europe, Hitler's attention would turn to Great Britain. Thea wanted to be of some help to her country. The incident with the Stuka had shown her the limits of her courage and she suspected that whatever she was able to contribute would be insignificant. But still. To play her part she needed to get back to England, and yet the state of her feet meant that she was covering fewer and fewer miles each day. The thought that eventually she might not be able to go on at all was a terrifying possibility.

She sat down on the grass beneath a stand of scrappy willows and had a drink of water. No use thinking like that, she scolded herself. She looked out at the bowl-shaped valley in front of her, which was bisected by a winding, stony track. Chin up, Thea. Perhaps, when she climbed up the slope on the far side of the valley, she would look out and see the sea.

She unbuckled her sandals, then gritted her teeth as she peeled off her socks. She folded up her last handkerchief, grimacing as she tied it round her foot. She couldn't imagine walking another mile, let alone twenty or thirty. She wasn't sure she had it in her. But it was nice to sit for a while and the cool, shady air felt pleasant on her sore feet. She tried to brush away dark thoughts by focusing on the landscape.

She drank a few more mouthfuls of water and ate the heel of a baguette. She set her compass on a stone and watched as the needle quivered and stilled, confirming her direction. She should walk on – and yet the impulse to rest was overwhelming. Her eyelids grew heavy; she let them close.

A loud chug-chug-chug broke through the chatter of the birds, jerking her awake. She saw a khaki-coloured motor-cycle heading towards her, down the track through the field. Fear lent her speed and she pulled on her socks and stuffed her belongings into her rucksack and tried to hide behind a tree trunk. But then, peering out cautiously, she saw the front wheel of the motorbike strike a large stone. It skidded off the track and toppled on to its side, flinging the rider to the ground.

Thea stood up. Sunlight glittered on the motorcycle's chrome handlebars and its wheels spun frantically. The rider, who was now lying motionless at the edge of the field, was wearing the khaki uniform of the British Expeditionary Force, not the field grey of the Wehrmacht.

She loped down the incline, calling out, 'Are you all right? Hello?'

Kneeling down beside him, she looked at the soldier closely. He was young and his clothing was, like hers, torn and grubby. Beneath his jaw she saw to her relief the beat of a pulse. Tanned skin, whitened with dust, a firm mouth, straight black brows over closed and long-lashed eyes. An ear that was a perfect sculpting of fold and whorl. She thought him beautiful and had a sudden impulse to reach out and stroke his black curls, to touch that hollow at the corner of his mouth.

'Hello?' she said again. She patted his shoulder. 'Are you okay?'

He groaned. Thea sat back. When he opened his eyes she saw that they were the deep blue of the cornflowers in the fields.

She said, 'Are you hurt?'

'Don't know.' Another groan. 'What an idiot. What a damned idiot.'

'Your front wheel hit a stone.'

He sat up. 'You *are* hurt,' she said. Blood oozed from a cut at his temple and his palms had been scraped raw by his skid across the track. 'Here.' She untied the cotton square she wore round her neck, folded it and handed it to him. 'Use that to staunch the blood.'

'Thanks.' He pressed it against the head wound, then gave the motorcycle an affectionate pat. 'It was almost out of fuel anyway,' he said. He looked at her. 'You're British, aren't you?'

'Yes. My name's Thea Craxton.'

'Cormac Jamieson. What are you doing here?'

'Much the same as you, I should think. Trying to get home.'

A sound made Thea look up to where ominous silver glints sprinkled the sky. 'Planes,' she said, scrambling to her feet. 'I can't tell whose they are and we'd better not wait around to find out. Come on.'

She hooked a hand under his arm to help him stand up and they limped and shuffled uphill to a thicket that offered some cover. They stood side by side beneath the trees as the warplanes circled above them. Cormac Jamieson was more than a head taller than her. He narrowed his eyes, peering up through the trees. The whine of the dive-bombing Stukas as they rose into the air and then swooped down made fear gnaw at her belly. And there it was again, that strange, unsettling longing to bury her head in this stranger's chest, for him to wrap his arms round her and hold her close so that she could no longer hear that hideous nasal roar.

'They're going,' he said.

The two aeroplanes wheeled in a wide arc and then headed back in the direction from which they had come. Thea let out a breath.

Cormac said, 'Where are you making for?'

'St Malo.'

'Looks like we're heading in the same direction, then. We were told there'd be transport from St Malo.' He flicked open a map, then pointed to a fold. 'I think we're somewhere round here. So another eight, ten miles at the most.'

Eight miles. Maybe she'd be able to walk another eight miles. Was it possible?

Cormac dusted the grit and earth from his uniform and shouldered his kitbag. 'We should head off,' he said. 'The sooner we get there, the more likely there is to be a ship.'

Beyond the thicket, more fields and more hedgerows. They had walked a short distance when he said, 'You're limping.'

'It's just blisters.'

'Let's have a look.'

She sat down on the verge and peeled off her socks. She heard his indrawn breath. He had a tin of plasters and a small bottle of iodine in his kitbag. They shared the iodine, a few drops for his head wound, a few drops more for her feet.

He offered her a pair of khaki socks. 'They'll be far too big,' he said 'but at least there aren't any holes in them. How far have you walked?'

'Since Alençon, pretty much.'

He whistled. 'That's quite a distance.'

Thea sorted out her feet and Cormac checked the map again. Once she had buckled up her sandals, he picked up her rucksack and slung it over his shoulder, ignoring her bleats that she could manage perfectly well.

As they walked, he told her his story. He had been part of the British lines-of-communication troops. When his superior officer had told them that it was every man for himself, he and some of the soldiers in his unit had decided to make for Cherbourg. One evening, somewhere near Rouen, they had dozed off only to be woken after a short time by the sight of half a dozen tanks heading towards them. Cormac and his friends had had only moments to grab their bikes and had sped away, leaving behind their helmets and gauntlets. The following day they had met up with another British soldier who, like them, was making for the Channel coast. He had told them that the route to Cherbourg was blocked off by the enemy and so they had turned south, for St Malo.

'And then, I can't remember when it was, a day, a couple of days ago, we came round a corner and there were the Wehrmacht, dozens of them swarming around.' Cormac wiped away the dust and sweat from his eyes. 'I went one way and the rest of my unit went another. Afterwards, I tried to find them but they'd gone. I don't know if they were captured or what. There are Germans everywhere, behind every tree. You take a bend in the road and there's a tank.'

As they walked, the sound of gunfire was a low, repetitive murmur, taunting them, reminding them how easily they might succumb to disaster. Thea had hoped her feet would feel better with the plasters and new socks but they hurt even more. Every step was like treading on broken glass. She sensed Cormac slowing his pace to match hers. He had been kind to her but she was steeling herself for the moment when he'd decide to go ahead on his own. He'd be able to make far quicker progress without her.

Another dip in the road, then she was stumbling up the rise towards the summit. Her longing to see the sea was intense. She'd be able to keep going if the sea was at last in sight. When, looking out, she saw only the same fields, the same hedgerows, her sense of disappointment was so acute she could have wept.

The words burst out of her. 'I'm holding you up. You don't have to wait for me. I wouldn't blame you.'

Cormac scanned the roadside, then cut with his knife a straight branch from an ash tree. 'Lean on that,' he said. 'Thea, I'm not going to leave you. We're doing this together, okay?'

She bowed her head, mumbling, 'I'm not sure I can.'

'One step at a time. That's all you have to do.'

'If they lock me up at least I won't have to walk any more.'

'Rot. You don't really think that, I know you don't. We're nearly there. You've almost done it. This time tomorrow you'll be home.'

You can't know that. But she didn't say it, afraid he'd get sick of her whining and leave her at the roadside. She was tired of being alone and his optimism reassured her, and so, less rationally, so did his northern accent. To be in the company of a practical, sensible British person made this awful, endless journey so much more bearable. That he had a proper map, that he was the kind of man who could ride a motorbike and dodge enemy troops encouraged her. *This time tomorrow you'll be home.* Unexpectedly, in spite of her sore feet and her exhaustion, his words ignited in her a flicker of hope.

They set off, Thea leaning on the stick. *One step at a time.*

He said, 'What were you doing in Alençon?'

'I was only there for a few hours. I was in Paris before that, and before Paris in Basel. I'm an archaeologist.'

'An archaeologist? Impressive.'

'I'm very lowly. Mostly, I make notes and label things. But I love it,' she added frankly.

She told him about the Fainlights and the dig at Barbury Hill. He was talking to her to keep her spirits up, she knew that. A lot of people thought archaeology as dull as ditch-water. But if he was pretending, he was making a convincing job of it.

She explained about her decision to go to Paris and her search for Helen. 'I hope I didn't miss her,' she said. 'I hope she's back in England, or in Sweden, with her father.' Then, aware that she been chattering on about herself for ages, she said, 'What do you do when you're not in the army, Cormac? Or are you a regular soldier?'

'I joined up in nineteen thirty-eight.' They paused at the roadside to check the map. Folding it, he said, 'You okay to continue? Top of that next incline, we'll have a longer break.'

Again, they set off. He said, 'I'd had an almighty argument with my father and couldn't go back home. The army seemed a good idea.'

'Don't you and he get on?'

'He's a difficult old devil. Most of the Jamiesons are capable of blowing their tops at the slightest thing, but Dad has a temper like a powder keg. We fell out over something and I needed to cool off.'

'Maybe it's good to have your disagreements out in the open air. Better than keeping secrets.'

'Maybe.' A flash of a smile. 'Me, though, I'm as peaceful as a lamb.'

She laughed. 'Glad to hear it. Where do you come from?'

'A place called Crawburn, in Northumberland. It's the finest place on earth.' He said this simply, as if it was an inarguable fact. 'What about you? You're Scottish, aren't you? Have you family back home?'

'None at all in Glasgow now. Both my parents are dead. I have an elder sister, Rowan, who lives in London.'

'I have a younger sister, Nicola. My mother died when I was twelve. I don't blame Dad for being as he is, he's had a rough time.'

They reached the top of the shallow slope. Thea sank down gratefully on the grass and Cormac sat beside her. She saw him wince.

'Does your head hurt a lot?'

'A bit.' He pressed his fingertips against his forehead and screwed up his face. 'I might have to rest for five minutes, Thea. Just five minutes. Wake me up if I sleep any longer. Promise me.'

'I promise.'

She noticed how he fell asleep instantly, the moment his eyes closed. Beneath the dust and the tan his skin had a bluish tinge. A fly buzzed over his face; she brushed it away.

He woke on the dot five minutes later and she shared with him the last of her food. Afterwards, he strolled ahead to recce the fields and paths. She watched his long stride and the way he shaded his eyes to scan the sky. She could tell from the way he held himself that his head hurt a lot.

They set off again. The rattle of gunfire grew louder as they approached the coast. They decided to take the road rather than keeping to the tracks and footpaths, as they had been doing so far. It would be riskier but quicker. Thea suspected that Cormac, too, knew that they were both reaching the end of their tethers. Added to the strain of the past days and weeks was the need constantly to scan the next field and the next hedgerow for troops and to search the sky for aeroplanes. The Wehrmacht and the Luftwaffe would advance south and west through France with the aim of cutting off the Channel ports and so preventing the embarkation of any further Allied soldiers. She and Cormac needed to reach St Malo before the enemy did.

By early evening they found themselves in a village of whitewashed houses and roses spilling over stone walls. English families were piled into motor cars or on to horse-drawn carts, making for St Malo. Young men on touring bicycles studied maps and passed water bottles between them. The uniforms of the soldiers of the B.E.F. were as ragged and grubby as Cormac's and their faces were streaked with dust and hollowed and shadowed with tiredness.

The houses thinned; a row of little cottages, an old woman hoeing an allotment, a dog chasing a rabbit through a field.

Cormac said, 'Look.'

In the distance, beyond fields scattered with villages and hamlets, was a wide strip of turquoise and azure sea. Chips of light sparkled where the sun danced on it.

Her heart lifted. 'Oh, Cormac,' she said.

He was leaning against a tree trunk. Blue shadows beneath bluer eyes. 'Told you,' he said, with the ghost of a grin.

'Do you need a rest?'

'No, I'm okay. We should get on. You?'

'I'm all right.'

They walked on. Thea felt lightheaded: the heat, the brightness of the sun. They no longer talked and she sensed the effort of putting one foot in front of the other was as great for Cormac as it was for her.

As they approached the port the paved roads, edged with tall houses, were clogged with traffic and pedestrians. Crowds jostled against them, everyone heading in the same direction, for the harbour. Cormac gave her his hand as they threaded between the multitudes and she felt the warmth of his fingers in her palm. People were abandoning their motor vehicles and carts, hauling bags and cases and babies out of back seats and boots and making the remainder of their journey on foot.

Cormac said, 'Thea, there's a ship!'

And then they were hugging each other, and he was laughing and she was crying and he was holding her tightly and she could smell the scent of his skin and feel the warmth of his arms. And then, his grip slackened and he dipped his head and his lips brushed against hers, dry and salty and warm, and her heart was so full she couldn't speak.

They walked on, Cormac holding her hand tightly as he carved a path through the surging masses of people. Someone gave them directions to the British Consulate, where Thea queued up to present her passport so that she could obtain a permit to board ship. Now and then, standing in the queue, she glanced back at Cormac. He had propped himself against a wall; beneath the tan and the dirt his skin was pallid and filmed with sweat.

All round them, women were weeping and men muttering

curses under their breath as French citizens, refused permits to sail to England, were divided from their British relatives. When her own permit was issued, Thea felt faint with relief. She pressed through the crowds to Cormac's side. His eyes were closed.

She touched his hand. 'Are you all right?'

His eyelids flickered. 'I'm fine.'

'How's your head?'

'Sore.' He put a hand to his forehead.

They left the building and made for the quayside. Now it was she who was supporting him. She felt his weight against her and a couple of times he stumbled.

As they approached the ship, a voice called out, 'Jamieson!' A soldier, fair-haired and with a friendly, open smile, was making his way through the river of khaki towards them. 'I thought you'd been captured,' he said. 'Am I glad to see you!'

'Coleman,' said Cormac. 'Thank God.'

'The others are all here,' the fair-haired man said. 'Come on.'

'Give me a moment. Thea, you must go on board.'

'Cormac . . .'

'I'll have to join the rest of my unit.' He smiled at her. 'Go on, Thea. God bless and have a safe journey home.'

The sailor at the foot of the gangway impatiently demanded her papers and she was hurried on board. On the deck, she looked back. Cormac raised a hand in salute. 'I'll write to you!' he called out. 'Where do you live?'

'My sister's flat is in Macklin Street!' And then she was pushed aside as the last of the passengers climbed on deck and the gangway was drawn up. When she looked down to the quayside she could no longer see Cormac and she felt bereft.

She felt the rumbling of the ship's engines beneath her feet as the vessel pulled out of the port. People said you wouldn't be seasick if you stayed on deck and people said you wouldn't be seasick if you kept your gaze on the horizon. And to begin with Thea hoped they might be right. But as the ship emerged out of the bay into open sea and the hull rose and plummeted with the movement of the waves, the familiar nausea coiled restlessly in her belly. At least, she thought, as she pressed through the crowds, searching for a space by the gunwale, feeling sick distracted her from the bombers circling like raptors overhead. Just in time, she found a gap and was horribly ill into the churning waves below. In the moments of relief that followed, she thought of Cormac, of his embrace and his kiss, and in spite of exhaustion, sunburn, blisters and sickness, delight washed through her. And then with horrible inevitability the nausea returned, until at last she slumped down beside the gunwale and fell into an exhausted sleep.

Chapter Twelve

June 1940

He was very young, just twenty years old. He was a soldier, a private, and his name was Alfred Claybourn. He lay motionless on the bed beneath blue hospital blankets, and Rowan, who had been assigned to special nurse him, was able to see only his tuft of light-brown hair the colour of a sparrow's wing and his bluish-grey eyes, which had narrowed to slits and were hazy with morphia. Much of the lower half of his face had been shot away and what remained was hidden beneath a large white gauze bandage.

He looked at Rowan and made a sound in his throat. She smiled at him. 'Your mum and dad are on their way,' she said gently. 'They'll be here soon, Alfie.' She had told him this several times before but couldn't tell whether he had taken it in.

Another choking, guttural sound.

'They're coming down on the train. They won't be long, I promise.'

Alfie's family lived in Staithes, on the North Yorkshire coast. It would take them a day to travel to the hospital in Kent so that they could be with what was left of their son.

They were in a corner of the ward, screens barricading them off from the other beds. The familiar sounds of the hospital, the hurrying footsteps of the other nurses and the moans of patients and squeak of bed wheels and rustle of starched sheets seemed to have faded into the distance. After long days of caring for the burned, injured, shocked and exhausted from Dunkirk, Calais, Le Havre and now St Nazaire, Rowan felt drained. The ward sister had instructed her to hold Alfie's hand and talk to him. She had always thought of herself as a good conversationalist, but what chit-chat did you make with a dying boy?

A watery light filtered through the blue fabric screens as he made small restless movements. She said, 'Do you have any brothers and sisters, Alfie?'

A slight nod. One of his arms was encased in bandages; Rowan was holding his other hand. Infinitesimally, he raised three fingers.

'Three sisters?' she guessed. 'No? Brothers, then. Lucky you. I bet the four of you have fun. I've never been to Staithes. It sounds a lovely place.' She was about to ask him whether he and his brothers swam in the sea, but censored herself just in time. Alfie had been rescued from the wreckage of a ship sunk by German dive bombers off the French coast. A pale riming of salt from the Channel still clung to his hair.

She said, 'I went to school in Yorkshire. My Dad used to come at half-term and take me and my sister out for a walk and a cream tea. Best scones I've ever tasted. I hated school, though. I never liked being told what to do. Like the army, I suppose. And nursing.'

He made little, agitated noises and the hand she was holding twitched. 'I'm going to try and make you more comfortable,' she said. 'I'll plump up your pillow a little. See, I won't disturb you at all. There, is that better?'

Her voice seemed to soothe him. As she talked of summer holidays and the games she and Thea had played, the ice creams they had eaten and walks they had taken, he became calm again. Whenever she ran out of things to say Alfie began to squirm and to make the hoarse, inhuman grunts, interspersed by choking sounds. Rowan scoured her brain and talked about something, anything. Eventually his eyes closed and she let her voice drop as she continued stroking his hand. She was murmuring to him, the same words over and over again, like an incantation or a lullaby, that it was going to be all right, that his mum and dad were on their way, that she was here and everything was going to be fine.

Rowan had been nursing for almost nine months. St Anne's hospital was on the south bank of the Thames. Her first day had been a jarring succession of shocks mixed with bewilderment. Rising at six in the morning had been a shock, as had the starchy, uncomfortable, old-fashioned uniform and the breakfast of porridge and slabs of bread, taken with fifty other twittering and complaining nurses. And then, the ward. As a new probationer, she had been the lowest of the low on Women's Medical, and rightly so, because she had known nothing. She had spent the day alternating between hovering like a fool because she hadn't known what to do next, and having orders barked at her that she had no idea how to carry out.

But she had loved it. She had left the ward that first evening in a fug of tiredness, her head reeling, the ward sister's scorn echoing in her ears. And yet the day had passed in a flash because throughout she had been interested and absorbed. How dull so much of her former life seemed in comparison, how futile and without purpose! The discovery had startled and delighted her. Somehow, she had fallen on her feet at last.

In April, as the Phoney War ended, she was moved to a sector hospital in Kent. The collection of huts and tents was set up away from the capital, to deal with the anticipated casualties of conflict. Six weeks later the nurses and porters were ordered one morning to clear the ward. The ambulant patients were discharged and the convalescent sent to nursing homes.

And then the ambulances arrived, endless convoys of them, ferrying soldiers evacuated from Dunkirk. Until that day, the war had been a headline in a newspaper or a dull piece on the wireless, to be switched off in favour of dance music. Perhaps Rowan had felt a flicker of anxiety now and then for Thea, but not too much because Switzerland's neutrality had reassured her that whatever happened, her sister was safe.

Dunkirk changed everything. Those shocked and mutilated soldiers were the face of retreat, of defeat. Rowan cut off filthy, ragged uniforms and bathed grimed and salty bodies. She found herself dealing with shrapnel wounds. She had not been trained to remove shrapnel, but all the trained nurses were busy and someone thrust a pair of tweezers into her hand and told her to get on with it. So she set to work, digging fragments of metal out of heads and backs and limbs. Sometimes the soldiers screamed when she removed a deep piece of shrapnel, but more often they remained silent, the patches of pallid skin that were visible beneath the oil and dirt becoming even paler. The ridiculous conventions of hospital nursing – lining up the bed castors so that they pointed to the centre of the room, polishing brass handles twice a day and the constant tidying of lockers – were forgotten about. A day or two passed and added to the smell of blood and oil was the sweet scent of gangrene. When the news of the fall of Paris came, one of the French soldiers on the ward turned his face to the wall and wept.

Alfie's breaths were coming further and further apart. There was another frightful choking noise and the ward sister slipped between the screens. She was a sister who liked to find fault and was a stickler for rules, but she said, gently, 'The poor boy's gone, Nurse Scott. It's over.' And Rowan saw that it was.

A flying officer from the nearby R.A.F. base gave Rowan and her fellow nurse, a red-faced, jolly girl called Jenkins, a lift into London in his MG. Rowan had a drink with the flying officer and Jenkins in a bar in Covent Garden before parting from them to go to the flat.

She checked in her pigeonhole for letters but there was nothing from Thea. She held her breath as she went upstairs, an old superstition left over from her childhood. *If I can hold my breath until I'm in the flat Thea will be there.*

But she wasn't. Rowan let herself into cool, echoing rooms. They had been empty too long and there was a musty smell. She washed out a bottle of soured milk from the fridge and opened windows to let in air while disappointment and anxiety churned inside her. Then she switched on the geyser and ran herself a lukewarm bath. She soaked for a while to rid herself of the smells of the hospital before climbing out and wrapping herself in a large towel. After closing the windows and drawing across the blackout curtains, she lay down on the bed, thinking she might take a nap.

She had been working for ten days on the trot; she had

started her shift at seven that morning. But her thoughts intruded, memories of the last few days at the hospital, of Alfie Claybourn's pleading eyes and his hand, twitching in hers, and after a while she gave up trying to sleep and began to dress.

She put Cole Porter on the gramophone and picked out a peach-coloured silk bra and camiknickers. She lit a cigarette. Where on earth was Thea? Why hadn't she come home? Was she still safely in Switzerland? Or was she somewhere in the chaos of France, lost and frightened and in danger of capture? Someone at the hospital had told her that there had been civilians on Alfie's ship, the bombed ship. Rowan prayed that was untrue. The thought of Thea covered in oil and blood or in pieces like that poor boy, made her feel sick inside and she stubbed out her cigarette.

She sat down at the dressing table and did her face, then pinned up her hair in a smooth roll. Then, silk stockings, a coral satin gown and the white velvet jacket she had bought from Edwina. Her bag, with purse, powder compact and keys. She examined her reflection in the mirror as she clipped on earrings. There, if you ignored her red, raw hands, she looked almost like her old self.

Rowan let herself out of the flat. She didn't lock the door in case Thea came home. She often left it unlocked so that her friends could use it when they were in London for a night or two, on leave or in transit. The place was taking on an unfamiliar air, with odd things – a vial of perfume, a man's navy-blue jersey, a paperback or two – abandoned there.

Artemis and Maurice Wilton were in the American Bar at the Savoy. Artemis embraced her. 'I had a bath,' Rowan said dubiously, 'but I'm afraid I still stink of hospital disinfectant.'

'You don't at all, darling, you're perfectly divine, as always.' Artemis ushered her to a seat. 'Come and sit down. You must be *shattered*.'

A waiter poured champagne and they chatted of this and that. Maurice had a position in the Ministry of Supply and Artemis was working for the Women's Voluntary Services. She had helped to organise the battalions of women on the south coast who had greeted the survivors of Dunkirk with food and drink; she had herself cut hundreds of slices of bread and stood on a station platform passing mugs of cocoa to the soldiers in the railway carriages.

Artemis asked Rowan, 'Have you heard anything from Thea?'

Rowan shook her head. 'Nothing.'

'You mustn't worry.'

'*Artemis*. You've *seen* them. I've seen them too.' Rowan could no longer suppress her anxiety. 'I've spent the last couple of weeks nursing those men. Thea will be trying to come home. I know her, I know she will. She might be anywhere.' She turned to Maurice. 'If she's captured, what will happen to her?'

'She'll be interned. That means she'll be imprisoned as an enemy alien.'

'And then?'

'I don't know,' Maurice said gently. 'I'm sorry, Rowan. One hopes the usual civilities would be observed.'

'At the hospital, someone said something about a ship sinking off St Nazaire . . . and I wondered whether . . .'

Maurice lowered his voice. 'Rowan, there was a huge loss of life, which is why they're keeping it under wraps. Morale, you see.'

'Do you know whether there were any civilians on board?'

'I'm afraid there were. We don't know how many. We may never know.'

Artemis patted her hand. 'Thea is very sensible,' she said firmly. 'She's probably stayed put. I would, if I were in Switzerland. Think of all that delicious chocolate and cheese.'

Rowan knew that Artemis was trying hard to cheer her up so she smiled and they spoke of other matters.

Later that evening, walking home, she acknowledged that she had not until today truly thought it possible that she might lose Thea. A part of her had been convinced that eventually, even if it took another week or two, Thea would come home. But she couldn't kid herself any longer. Young men and women were dying all the time. Alfie had been only a year older than Thea. Ships bearing British, French and Polish soldiers, and British civilians too, had been bombed and sunk off French port after French port. If the government had made the decision to keep the loss of the ship under wraps, then thousands may have died.

The clouds parted and a ragged shaft of moonlight illuminated a great, silver barrage balloon, beautiful and ominous, bobbing in the sky. Rowan passed by a square garden. The night air was warm and scented with roses. It appalled her to think that, having saved Thea from drowning off Corran all those years ago, the sea might yet have swallowed her up.

Briskly, she walked the remainder of the way back to Macklin Street. Out of habit, she checked for letters in her pigeonhole, then went upstairs. As she approached her flat she saw the narrow line of light that glowed beneath her front door. Her heart pounded. It could be anyone, she reminded herself as she turned the door handle. It could be Nicky or Patrick or Davey Manningham, on leave from the army and needing a bed for the night, anyone.

She went into the sitting room. There was a rucksack on the floor and a smallish, humped bundle on the sofa. Joy and relief flooded through her.

'Thea!' she cried.

While she soaked her feet in a bowl of warm water, Thea told Rowan about her journey. Rowan was in the kitchen, making toast and scrambled eggs.

'St Malo was rather odd.' Thea grimaced as she tugged a plaster off her big toe. 'There were shops selling smart clothes and handbags, just like shops do, but the streets were full of masses of tired and filthy people. Everyone was trying to get away. I was okay because I have a British passport, but they were turning people away. And then, when we were all on board, some planes tried to bomb us.'

Rowan stuck her head out of the kitchen door. 'Oh, Thea, how terrifying.'

'It was completely terrifying. The R.A.F. drove them away.'

'Thank God.'

'Did all the ships get through from St Malo? Do you know, Rowan?'

Her sister came into the sitting room. 'A friend told me about one that was sunk. Masses of casualties.'

Thea's heart gave an agonised jolt, but then Rowan frowned and said, 'No, it was St Nazaire, I think, not St Malo. Yes, I'm sure it was St Nazaire.'

Relief rushed through her. She prayed that Cormac had reached England safely on the next ship across the Channel. On her journey home it had occurred to her that she had fallen in love with him. She had never been in love with anyone before and was unsure whether it was possible to care so deeply for someone you had known for less than a day. But she knew in her heart that it was. Her feelings were raw to the touch, as sharp and lacerating as the blisters on her feet. She had fallen in love with him, perhaps, the very first time she had seen him, unconscious and lying in the dirt at the edge of a French field.

'Here.' Rowan put a mug of tea beside her. 'Drink this. Your supper's nearly ready.'

'Thank you.' Thea rubbed her foot with the flannel and the water turned grey. 'I was hideously seasick,' she said. 'I thought it might not be as bad on a big ship, but it was, it was awful. I was expecting to feel some sort of, I don't know, affinity, or patriotism, when we disembarked, when we were on British soil at last, but all I could think of was how utterly relieved I was not to be sick any more.'

Rowan came into the room with a plate of scrambled eggs. 'Let me see your feet. Poor old Thea, what a mess. Eat up, then you can soak in a hot bath, and afterwards I'll sort your feet out.'

'How about you? Are you all right?'

'I'm fine. So happy to see you again.' Rowan sat down beside her. 'We had a lot of soldiers from France at the hospital. I've been so worried.'

Thea scooped up a forkful of egg. 'I thought I'd messed it up. I thought I'd left it too late.'

Rowan squeezed her shoulder. 'It sounds a horribly eventful journey.'

It had indeed been horrible. Her journey had taught her things about herself, some of which she would rather have not known. But there had been moments too that, looking back, she treasured. The lift of her heart as she had seen the sea. And Cormac's voice: *Thea, I'm not going to leave you.* And his kiss.

But she did not explain any of this to Rowan. It all seemed too fragile and too difficult to put into words. And she was exhausted beyond measure and though she hadn't eaten properly for days, it was all she could do to lift the fork to her mouth.

So she said only, 'I'm so happy to be home. Just so happy.'

In bed that night, she still seemed to feel the up-and-down motion of the ship. Though she had called out her address to Cormac she did not know whether he had heard her. Perhaps she would never see him again.

But that thought was too dreadful to contemplate. Unbearable that she should lose him so soon after finding him. She could not let herself believe that. Groggy with exhaustion she closed her eyes, and his face flashed in front of her inner eye so that his were the features she saw as she drifted off to sleep.

Chapter Thirteen

July–September 1940

Stuart had enlisted in the Navy, which meant that Sophie now had room for three lodgers. Since the outbreak of war, her clientele had altered. Gone were the travelling salesmen and the spinsters and widows fallen on hard times; instead, Mr Reynolds, a quiet, unassuming man who worked at the Admiralty, had joined the household in April. His colleague, Miss Cornish, was her second lodger. Much the same age as Sophie herself, tall, stout and forthright, Miss Cornish was cheerful and friendly. She liked to 'muck in', as she put it, and insisted on helping clear the supper table each evening.

Lastly there was Captain Kazimierz Wajszczyk, who had been billeted on her in June. Captain Wajszczyk was Polish. He had fought to defend his country on the German invasion of Poland in September 1939, and then, when Russian troops had also marched in and defeat had become inevitable, he had made his way through Hungary to France. There he had battled on as part of General Sikorski's Polish army in France. After the French capitulation, he had escaped via one of the southern ports to England.

Sophie guessed Captain Wajszczyk to be thirty-five or thereabouts. He was tall, with straight light-brown hair, very handsome in a cool, chiselled way. There was a steeliness in the grey-green eyes. Despite her best efforts, Sophie repeatedly mangled his surname, with its unforgiving clusters of consonants. She sensed him trying to suppress his irritation. Sometimes she chickened out and addressed him as 'Captain'.

He was tidy and neat and she had to do little for him other than provide meals, wash and iron shirts and occasionally run a duster over the mantelpiece and windowsills in his room, Duncan's room. He polished his own boots, brushed his own coat and tunic. Invariably polite and uncomplaining, his customary greeting to her was an elegant bow. He went out early in the morning and arrived back at the house late at night.

So he was no trouble at all, really. And yet Sophie suspected Captain Wajszczyk thought his current way of life, and her home, beneath him. She wondered whether there was a castle, or something like that, in Poland. There wasn't much she could do about the food. Butter, sugar, bacon and meat were now rationed. Though she had always prided herself on her housekeeping, Mrs Leonard had left in April to work in an aircraft factory, which meant that Sophie had had to take over her tasks. She had also volunteered to help out at a First Aid Post, unearthing her rusty nursing experience and attending classes where she practised treating people pretending to be air-raid casualties.

Earlier in the year the boys had dug up a portion of lawn for another vegetable patch. The fresh vegetables were a boon but necessitated hours of weeding and watering. Every minute of every hour was taken up with one task or another. The scarred grass and the great, humping Anderson shelter meant that even the garden wasn't looking like itself any more. She was afraid the roses would have to go, too. Sometimes, when she looked at her home through Captain Wajszczyk's eyes, she could quite understand why he didn't think much of it.

Captain Wajszczyk was leaving the house as Sophie's neighbour and dear friend Viola Foster arrived. In passing, he gave her one of his extravagant salutes. Divesting herself of her gas mask in the hallway, Viola raised her eyebrows at Sophie.

'Was that the famous Polish officer? He's very handsome.'

'I suppose he is.' Viola gave her a look and Sophie laughed. 'He's far too young for me. Just a boy.'

'Hmm,' said Viola. She had brought with her a basket of strawberries, which she put on the kitchen table. 'The birds have nibbled them but they'll be good for jam,' she said.

Because it was a fine day they hulled the strawberries outside, sitting side by side on the low wall that surrounded the terrace. Viola's shorts revealed her thin, tanned, bony legs. Sophie was wearing a red cotton dress, much the same shade as the strawberries. Since Captain Wajszczyk had arrived, she had made an effort with her dress – not because of his handsomeness, not at all, but because she did not wish to feel herself included in the many objects of his disdain.

As Viola relayed the contents of a letter she had had from Michael, her elder son, who was at an army training camp in Yorkshire, Sophie's mind wandered. It had been wrong of her to describe Captain Wajszczyk as a boy. He was not a boy, he was a man, and a man who must have seen and very probably done terrible things.

'Sophie?' said Viola.

She jerked out of her thoughts. 'Sorry. Sorry, Vi, what did you say?'

'Only that we're about done here.'

They went into the kitchen. Sophie tumbled the strawberries into the big pan with the sugar and lemon juice while Viola filled the kettle and put it on the stove.

Viola said, 'Have you heard from Duncan?'

'I had a letter a few days ago and Sally dropped in yesterday. Duncan phoned her the night before. She said he sounded all right.' Duncan and his girlfriend, Sally Fleming, had become engaged in April.

'That was good of her, coming round.'

'It was, yes.'

The heavenly, summery scent of the fruit began to fill the kitchen. Sally's family, the Flemings, lived in Richmond-on-Thames. Sally travelled into town daily to work at the B.B.C. The previous evening she had called in after work. Sally had stayed for supper; afterwards she and Miss Cornish had insisted on doing the washing-up.

Before Stuart had left home, he had helped Sophie move from the drawing room the two large brown leather armchairs and a small chintz one into the study, turning it into a sitting room for the lodgers. Yesterday evening, Sophie had sat there, making conversation with Mr Reynolds and Captain Wajszczyk and drinking tea, while all the time great peals of laughter had issued from the kitchen. 'What a great gel,' Miss Cornish had commented after Sally had gone, and Sophie had agreed.

There had been a time when she had been envious of Duncan's close relationship with the Flemings, and of his fondness for Sally's mother, Eva, in particular. But that time

228

was long gone. Sally made him happy, and for that she, Sophie, would always love her and be grateful to her.

'If you give me the Kilner jars I'll scald them,' Viola said.

Sophie perched on a stool and handed down jars. She said, 'Sally's half my age yet I can't imagine her ever being at a loss. When I think of myself at twenty-one, so incompetent, so unsure – and then, falling for Hugh! What a fool I must have been!'

Viola poured boiling water in the jars. 'Hugh was very clever and he fooled a lot of people. None of us had a clue what was going on with him. You've no reason to think less of yourself.'

Sophie clambered down. She gave the pan a stir. 'I don't trust myself any more. I'm a poor judge of character.'

'Nonsense,' said Viola briskly. 'You mustn't let what he did put you off men. Easier said than done, but you mustn't. Hugh had charm. He used it as a smokescreen. Underneath, he was ruthless.'

Married to him, her vision had been filled by Hugh. It was only now, in retrospect, that he seemed to be shrinking.

Viola said, 'Shall I label these?'

'Please.' Searching in a drawer for labels and a pen, Sophie said, 'Stuart still hopes that Hugh had some acceptable reason for marrying me. Before he went to Portsmouth he asked me whether his father might have had amnesia, whether he might have had a knock on the head in the trenches and, I don't know, forgotten he was married or something.'

Viola grimaced. 'Oh, Sophie. Poor Stuart, that's so sad.'

'I can't say what I think to him. I can't say that the truth is that Hugh was self-centred and greedy and took what he wanted. Stuart still misses him dreadfully.'

Sophie rested her palms on the edge of the sink, looking

out at the garden. Often she felt that she would never get to the bottom of Hugh's deceit. When, a year ago, she had first met Hugh's daughters, she had discovered that he had been brought up in a town near Glasgow. He had inherited the stationery business from his father. There had been no Devonshire rectory, no repressively religious upbringing – all that had been a lie, like all the other lies. Of course, she had no way of knowing whether what Rowan and Thea believed to be the truth was in fact true. Hugh might have lied to his daughters as well. He might have been brought up in London or Leeds or some far-flung outpost of the Empire. None of them knew. They kept in touch, she and Rowan and Thea. It seemed to her important that they did so, and not only because it was a rejection of the barriers Hugh had so laboriously put up between them. Thea and Stuart poured out their hearts to each other, and if her own contact with the girls – between a bigamous wife and her lover's daughters – was confined to the occasional polite card and brief, factual letter, it seemed to Sophie a marvel that it existed at all.

She gave the strawberries another stir. Viola said, 'Has Duncan met Hugh's girls yet?'

Sophie shook her head. 'He doesn't want to.' She thought that Duncan might never want to meet his half-sisters. It was perfectly understandable.

Sophie asked after Viola's husband, Doug, and her lover, Arnold.

'They've both joined the Local Defence Volunteers so I have to be terribly careful to remember who's doing what.' Viola added dryly, 'Doug's having the time of his life. He adores dashing round Hampstead Heath, shouting at people and feeling frightfully important. Arnold hates it. He says he couldn't shoot a German parachutist if his life depended on it.'

Sophie tested the jam for its set, dolloping a teaspoon of it on to a china saucer. When she pressed the edge of the blob with her fingernail it wrinkled. Viola poured the jam into the Kilner jars and Sophie placed circles of waxed paper on top. While the jars were cooling they went outside and sat in the deckchairs and drank tea.

Each night, after completing her tasks, Sophie sat on her own in the drawing room and was overwhelmed by loss. She put off turning on the electric light for as long as possible, partly to save electricity and partly because she disliked being enclosed by the blackout blinds. Sitting in the half-light, she felt her solitariness and lack of rootedness in her pounding heart and hot, panicking anxiety.

She fell into the habit of listening to music in the evening. She was too tired to read but she curled up on the sofa, listening to Mozart or Offenbach, the gramophone turned down low so as not to disturb the lodgers. She was working her way through her record collection. She did not expect to find solace. Distraction and a filling of the silence would do.

One evening, she was listening to a record of Beethoven sonatas when there was a tap at the door. She opened it to see Mr Reynolds.

Assuming the music was too loud, she was about to apologise when he said, 'Forgive me, Mrs Craxton, but I wondered whether you would consider leaving the door open? I do so enjoy Beethoven.'

She invited him into the drawing room and they listened to the music together. He told her a little about himself. His

Christian name was John, he had a widowed mother in Aylesbury and a younger brother in the Merchant Navy. He had volunteered for a tank regiment but had been turned down because of a spinal condition.

Over the ensuing fortnight, she discovered that John Reynolds was passionate about the Romantic composers. They didn't talk much, he was a quiet man. Miss Cornish – Vera – joined them now and then, beaming and beating time to the music. It was better, Sophie discovered, to listen to music in company. There was solace in that.

Vera Cornish was out visiting her married sister in Earl's Court and Captain Wajszczyk had left the house first thing in the morning and had not yet returned, when, one evening, John tapped on the drawing-room door.

'I hope I'm not intruding, Sophie, but I found this in a shop in Tottenham Court Road.'

'This' was a recording of Schumann's piano concerto. Myra Hess had embarked on the Intermezzo when Sophie heard the front door open. Assuming Miss Cornish had returned to the house, she rose to ask after her evening.

Captain Wajszczyk was in the hallway. He made a showy bow. The sleeves and shoulders of his uniform glistened with rain. They exchanged greetings and then Sophie asked him whether he would like some supper.

'I have dined, thank you, madame.'

'A cup of tea, then?'

'Thank you, but no, I have this.' With a flourish he produced a brown paper bag.

'What is it?'

He opened the bag and the aroma of coffee beans pervaded the hall.

'Coffee!' she exclaimed. 'How splendid.'

'A gift from a friend. I, um, mend a bicycle . . . a . . .'
A waggling motion of his fingers as he searched for the
word. 'Une crevaison.'

'A puncture.'

'Puncture.' He repeated it carefully. 'Do you have a . . .'
This time, a rotating motion of the hand.

'A coffee grinder? Yes, of course.'

'I make coffee for us.'

He followed her into the kitchen. He was too tall, or
perhaps there was something too extravagant about him for
the modest room. He didn't fit; she felt he was out of scale.
She found the grinder and made to take the beans but he
shook his head.

'I do it.'

'Captain, I do know how to make coffee.'

'But you drink tea, madame.'

'My husband was a great coffee drinker.'

'At home, I make the coffee.'

She understood, then. 'You're homesick. That's why you
want to make the coffee, because it will remind you of
home.'

A flicker in his finely shaped, grey-green eyes. 'Yes.
Homesick.' He put a fist to his chest. 'A pain, here. I think
you are the same, madame. You pretend to be happy, you
smile, but you are not.'

Flustered, she said sharply, 'I'm anxious about my sons.'

'Ah, yes.'

She sat down at the table while he ground the beans.
There had been a time when she had worried that Duncan
would ride his bicycle too fast and be mown down by a
lorry. Or that he would meet some unsuitable girl or develop
a liking for strong liquor. Or, after Hugh, that he would run

away from home and go off to fight in Spain. All these worries had paled into insignificance this summer. Duncan was flying Spitfires with the R.A.F. The Luftwaffe was raiding southern England daily, bombing radar stations and fighter airfields in preparation for the invasion. The air battle being fought over the southern counties would decide whether the United Kingdom retained its freedom. The combatants of the battle, that thin, air-force-blue line of defence, were young men in their late teens and early twenties, young men like Duncan. They should have been playing cricket or going to university or fooling around with girls in dance halls, but instead they were daily risking their lives. They plummeted into the Channel and drowned or they burned to death in fireballs on Kentish fields. Oh yes, there was a pain in her heart.

Captain Wajszczyk flung open cupboard doors, searching for something. 'Coffee will make you feel better,' he said. 'It makes everyone feel better.'

He took out a small saucepan, then a sieve, and put the sieve on the saucepan and poured boiling water over the grounds. Sophie arranged the coffee set, pink with a gilt trim, a wedding present from her mother, on a tray and found milk and sugar. Captain Wajszczyk carried the tray into the drawing room.

The three of them drank their coffee listening to the final movement of the concerto. Sophie sat on the pink-and-green chintz sofa, quiet John Reynolds to one side of her and flamboyant Captain Wajszczyk to the other. Now and then John hummed a phrase under his breath. The Polish captain's fingers tapped the sofa arm as Myra Hess's fingers raced over the keys. Sophie saw the scattering of golden hairs on his wrist, his tanned and sinewy hand. Now and then her shoulder brushed against his, a small, charged contact that jerked her attention away from the music.

When the record ended, he insisted on carrying the tray of coffee things to the kitchen. He offered to wash up but she put her foot down and he said goodnight to her and went upstairs.

John asked her whether she played the piano. She did, she told him, but was a very mediocre pianist.

'And I'm a very mediocre tenor,' he said. 'So we should get on well.'

They started with a book of English and Scottish folk songs and progressed, via 'Linden Lea' and 'All in the April Evening', to Gilbert and Sullivan. John Reynolds had a light, pleasant tenor voice. Sophie enjoyed accompanying him. Now and then they sang duets.

One evening, Vera was their audience as Sophie and John tackled 'Fair Moon to Thee I Sing'. They were halfway through the aria when, from the corridor, another voice joined in. Captain Wajszczyk appeared in the doorway. He sang with a rich, unexpected baritone, his phrasing was good and his expression serious. The two voices wove together, making something that melted the heart. Sophie fluffed a note or two.

She played the final chord. 'Goodness, Captain Wajszczyk,' she said. 'I had no idea you were such a fine singer.'

'My father admired the operas of Gilbert and Sullivan. I have sung these songs since I was a boy. If you would permit . . .' He came to stand at her shoulder. Leaning over her, he turned the pages of the score until he came to an aria from Iolanthe.

'Perhaps this one, madame?'

She played 'Spurn Not the Nobly Born'. Both men sang. When they had finished, Vera applauded.

'Splendid!'

They had embarked on 'Take a Pair of Sparkling Eyes' when Sophie heard a key turn in the front door. She lifted her hands above the keyboard, where they trembled. Then she dashed into the hallway.

'Duncan!' she cried.

Her elder son dumped his kitbag in the hall. 'Forty-eight-hour pass,' he said. 'I thought I'd come home.'

She flung her arms round him. He swayed and she released him. She took a step back, noting his pallor.

Gently, she brushed his dishevelled hair from his forehead. 'Food first or bed?'

'Bed, Mum. Too tired to eat.'

She had not noticed Captain Wajszczyk slip upstairs, but now he came down, carrying a bundle of his things. 'I sleep downstairs,' he said.

'Captain . . .'

'I clear the room.' He nodded at Duncan.

A great many Polish airmen, the captain's fellow exiles, were, like Duncan, taking part in the Battle of Britain. 'Thank you,' she murmured. 'So kind.'

She and Duncan went upstairs. Sophie changed the sheets while Duncan was in the bathroom. He came back into the room, toppled on the bed like a lopped tree, and fell asleep instantly. She unlaced his boots and put them beside the bed, then drew a blanket over him. She remembered how, when he was one or two, he had fallen asleep in a moment, like this. How practised she had been at putting him in his cot without waking him, and how she had carefully lowered him in. She remembered the perfection of his features, the pale skin with its flush of pink and the transparent, veined eyelids.

She took a pillow and blanket out of the airing cupboard and returned downstairs. John and Vera had gone to bed and Captain Wajszczyk was in the lodgers' sitting room. He had taken off his tunic and undone the top buttons of his shirt. His bare feet looked pale and vulnerable.

She said, 'You should sleep on the drawing-room sofa.'

He took the blanket and pillow from her. 'I am too tall, I think. I sleep here, on the floor.'

'Thank you. It was good of you to give up your room.'

He shook his head. 'Not my room, your son's room.' He looked at her. 'You are happy tonight, I think, Mrs Craxton. Is good to see you happy. When you are happy you look very beautiful.'

In the dim light, she flushed. 'Nonsense.'

'Is true.' Turning away from her he dropped the pillow on to the rug.

That night, she couldn't sleep. The feeling of joy and release that Duncan was safely at home, if only for forty-eight hours, was overwhelming. Beneath her joy she was already afraid of him going back. She longed for the war to be over, for Hitler to say to himself, *Actually, it's not worth it*, and for everything to return to how it had been before.

She thought of Captain Wajszczyk, lying on the rug in the lodgers' sitting room. She wondered whether he tossed and turned on the hard floor or whether he had the soldier's knack of being able to sleep wherever he found himself. What he dreamed of. Who he dreamed of. She thought of the V of tanned skin at the open collar of his shirt and the angles at his jaw and throat. She wondered what it would be like to go to bed with him, and what sort of lover he would make. She thought he would be generous and that he would know how to give a woman pleasure.

Duncan slept for fourteen hours and then woke, blurry-eyed, and ate the contents of the larder. It was a fine day and in the afternoon they sat in the garden. They talked of this and that and every now and then he dozed off in the sunshine. He didn't speak of the war or of his day-to-day business of hurtling into the sky and engaging enemy aircraft in combat. Nor did he speak of the friends he had lost.

Sally came round after work and the three of them had supper together and then Duncan and Sally went out dancing. The following morning, Duncan dug out another chunk of lawn for vegetables. Then he went off to Richmond, for supper with the Flemings.

He left Gilbert Street very early the next day. A tooting of a horn told them that his lift was outside the house. When Sophie opened the front door, a chill tumbled into the room.

He embraced her. 'Don't watch me go, Mum,' he said. 'I don't want you to watch me go.'

So she didn't. She returned to the kitchen and washed up his breakfast things, then made a pot of tea. She went outside and sat on the terrace wall, cold in her sleeveless summer dress, hugging her knees. The new vegetable patch made a raw gash in the grass; in the distance, high in the sky, bobbed the swollen silver shapes of barrage balloons. She drank the tea feeling as if someone had taken a spoon to her ribs and gouged out her heart.

John was away on business in the north and Vera had gone to a church social. Sophie served Captain Wajszczyk his supper in the dining room.

238

Afterwards, he cleared away his plate and glass to the kitchen. 'I will be Vera,' he said, as he put the things in the sink.

Sophie smiled. The flash of humour was uncharacteristic of him. Much of the time he seemed to take himself, and the world, very seriously. Understandably.

He rolled up his sleeves and washed the dishes. Sophie dried. 'Vera always has a cup of tea with me after we wash up,' she said, when they were finished. Though she said it lightly, she was aware of a tension between them.

His lip curled, showing her what he thought of tea.

'Or,' she said, 'I have brandy, Captain Wajszczyk.'

'Kazimierz.'

'Casimir,' she attempted.

A grimace. 'Maybe you call me Kaz.'

'Am I not pronouncing it right?'

'Hmm,' he said. There was in his expression the implication that he was employing great tact. 'Is very charming, but no. Kaz is better. Easier for the English.'

'If I'm to call you Kaz, you might find your way to calling me Sophie. "Madame" is rather formal.'

He gave her a slanting look. 'Sophie,' he said, testing it out. 'In Polish, Zosia.'

Zoh-cha, or something like that. She thought it had a carefree, frivolous sound. Might Zosia have more fun than Sophie?

They went into the drawing room. She asked him whether he would like to listen to some music and he chose a recording of Chopin's mazurkas.

'My father used to play these,' he said. 'My mother and I, we would dance the mazurka.'

'In your castle in Poland?'

239

'Castle?' He gave her an amused look. 'No, not a castle.'

'A house like this, then?'

'Not like this. Some land . . . an orchard, a fish pond.'

'A manor house.'

'We were not rich, you understand, Zosia, not . . .' that waggling of the fingers '. . . not . . . what is the word?'

'Showy? Ostentatious?'

'We were not showy. But a good place. A fine place.' His expression darkened. 'I think Russians are living there now.'

'What happened to your family?'

'My mother died when I was fourteen. My father . . .' A lift of the shoulders. 'I don't know. I hope he is in Hungary.'

'Will he be safe there?'

'I hope so. We have friends in Budapest.'

The music filled the room, fast, stirring and plaintive. Listening to music with Kaz was very different to listening to music with John. She could not relax with Kaz. She felt taut and wound up. She sensed in him some emotion suppressed, barely under wraps.

He said, 'And you, Zosia, is hard for you without your husband.'

She couldn't help herself, she made a disparaging sound.

A raise of the thin eyebrows. 'No?'

'Believe me, Kaz, I'm better off without him.'

'He was . . .' He tapped his brandy glass.

'Hugh liked a drink, but no, it wasn't that.'

'Then he had a lover.' He slung an arm along the back of the sofa, behind her. 'So he was a fool.'

She was tired of minding explaining about Hugh, and tired of avoiding explaining about Hugh. It tied her in knots. Kazimierz might think her stupid, he might think her wanton: she didn't care.

'Hugh had two wives,' she said. 'At the same time, you understand, Kaz. I was the second one.'

He rose to fetch the brandy bottle. Standing over her, frowning, he poured a measure in her glass. 'Is okay in England, two wives?'

'No, of course not.'

'He lie to you.'

'Oh, yes. Over and over again.'

'And he is dead now?'

'Hugh died two and a half years ago.'

'You, um . . .' He made a flicking motion with his hand. 'You hit him on head with a, how you say, *une pelle*—'

'A spade. A shovel.'

A quick glance in the direction of the rear of the house. 'And you bury this, this Hoo, in the garden.'

She laughed, at his ludicrous pronunciation of Hugh's name as much as anything. 'I'm afraid not. Perhaps I should have. But no, he died of pneumonia.' She pointed a hand at her chest in case of confusion.

He smiled at her. 'You have exciting life, Zosia. You are not ordinary woman.'

'Well, that's one way of looking at it.'

'A good way?'

She considered. 'Perhaps. Do sit down, Kaz. You are *looming* rather. It's making me feel nervous.'

'I apologise.' He put the brandy bottle back on the sideboard and sat down beside her.

She was aware of a sense of release, of some of the tension draining away. She wasn't sure whether it was because she had at last been able to laugh about Hugh (Hoo) or whether it was the brandy. Both, maybe. She had had a glass or two of something-or-other every evening in the months following

Hugh's death because without a drink she couldn't sleep. Then, one day, she had stopped, seeing that Duncan and Stuart should not, on top of everything else, have a mother who was permanently three sheets to the wind.

She said, 'It's funny how life turns out, isn't it?'

'Funny?'

'I mean strange. Odd. No good brooding about it.'

'It faut chercher la consolation où l'on peut.'

'Yes, exactly.'

'Such beautiful hair you have, Zosia.' He drew the back of his hand very gently down her blonde curls. 'Like silk.'

She realised – had realised a while ago – that he intended to seduce her. She had the same intention – it was, after all, she who had suggested the brandy. One must find consolation where one can.

She heard the front door open and close. Vera was in the hallway, fussing about a late bus. Sophie offered to make her a cup of cocoa.

Vera took the cocoa upstairs. Sophie cleared up then glanced in the drawing room. It was empty, the two glasses abandoned on the coffee table.

She went up to her room. She changed into a pale-blue silk nightdress she hadn't worn for ages and sat on the bed, waiting for the sounds of the house to die down. Kaz thought her out of the ordinary; for a moment or two she was afraid he was wrong, that she was so very ordinary, a coward who was afraid of what life had to offer. She was holding her breath, poised between one existence and another, unsure which way to turn. But then she eased open the door and stepped out into the corridor.

She didn't need to tap on his door. He must have been waiting for her because he came out to the landing. He ran his palms down her arms and she saw the glitter of pleasure and desire in his eyes. In her room, after he had closed the door behind them, he murmured, 'My beautiful Zosia.' His mouth brushed against her breasts, a light motion like a flicker of a bird's wing. The straps of her nightgown slipped over her shoulders, the blue silk fluttered to the floor.

He came to her room every night after that. They had their routine. Clattering sounds from the bathroom, the waterfall rush of the lavatory flushing, Vera's or John's feet padding off to their bedrooms – and then, silence. How wonderful silence felt, full of excitement and anticipation, while they both waited in a mutual, unspoken agreement. And then, the door opening. He was skilled at opening and closing a door without making a sound.

He was skilled at other things too, she discovered. Their lovemaking sessions were never the same twice. They did all sorts of things she had never done with Hugh. Afterwards, she lay spent and dishevelled in his arms and they whispered about this and that. She discovered that he was thirty-two years old and that his family home was in eastern Poland. He had studied law at university; there had once been an engagement, which his fiancée had broken off. They talked about the war. *Now comes the invasion*, he said, one night. *First they destroy the air force, then they bomb London, then the troops come. Like Warsaw.*

They never went out together; he continued to leave the house early and come back late. She had no idea what he did between. But the affair made her feel alive again, young again. She took joy once more in the blue of the skies, the opulence of a climbing rose and a tender passage of music. She felt a thrill of excitement on hearing Kaz's arrival at the house, his footsteps in the hallway. Now, when he bowed to her, she saw in his eyes a touch of humour and knowing complicity. She liked to ask him polite questions about his day as she served him his supper. She loved his answers, his accent, and the way he frowned as he concentrated in his attempt to improve his English.

She knew – always knew – that it would never last, but the affair was more than a distraction from worrying about Duncan and Stuart. As much as she was able to love anyone then, she loved Kaz. He was more wounded than she was and she wanted to comfort him for that. He had lost a country as well as his family. He knew what it was to have a piece ripped out of your life, to have it burned to cinders, erased as if it had never existed.

For some time there had been intermittent daylight air raids on London but in the latter half of August the night raids stepped up. In bed one night when the siren started to wail, she and Kaz quickly finished what they had begun and then Sophie, all fingers and thumbs, pulled on her clothes.

John and Vera were on the landing, bleary-eyed, John sporting a fawn dressing gown with a tartan collar, Vera with a shiny pink quilted bed-jacket over her nightdress. Sophie made a show of knocking on Kaz's bedroom door and then they all trooped down to the Anderson shelter. Kaz came down after the three of them were settled. They sat on folding chairs, wrapped up in blankets. A couple of hours later the All Clear sounded and they went back to bed.

A different kind of routine took over her life: the Thermos of tea made while she was preparing the lodgers' supper, blankets, torch, mugs and spoons, and a book and knitting put in the shelter, just in case. The stirrup pump and bucket of sand to hand in case incendiaries fell on the house. Gas mask and an old briefcase containing important household documents, birth certificates and insurance and suchlike, as well as money, door keys and a sponge bag with smelling salts, aspirin, cleansing lotion, lipstick, powder and a comb, all left where she wouldn't forget them. There was a quiet night or two when Sophie and Kaz made love with efficient, watchful silence, and a glorious afternoon when he came home early and found her on her own. Once, a hotel: undressing, she enjoyed the illicit, slightly sordid excitement of the small, shabby room. People were typing in offices and buying this and that in shops, and here she was, with her lover. It was extraordinary.

The nights interrupted by air raids were followed by days hazy with tiredness. You'd remember something you needed to do and then instantly forget it. Sophie wrote lists: buy potatoes, water tomatoes, don't forget Incendiary Bomb practice. Everyone was the same, you could see the weariness written on the pale, drawn faces of the passengers on the bus and the women queuing at the greengrocer's.

They were in the Anderson shelter one night when a bomb struck a house two streets away. They felt the impact as a pulse through the earth. John made a little sound and Vera said, very quietly, 'Dear God.' In the darkness, Kaz took Sophie's hand and with his thumbnail drew a soft shape on her palm. A heart, she thought.

One night they had made love and were lying quietly, wrapped in each other's arms, when Kaz said, 'I have something for you, Zosia.'

He took a small cloth bag out of his tunic pocket and gave it to her. Opening it, Sophie drew out a necklace, a fine, filigreed silver chain set with diamonds and garnets.

'Kaz, it's beautiful!'

'It was my mother's.'

She made to give it back to him. 'I can't possibly accept this, you know I can't. It's a family heirloom.'

He put his hand over hers, enclosing the necklace. 'After my mother died, I gave the necklace to Klara, my fiancée. When she broke off our engagement, she gave it back to me. I want you to have it.'

Sophie ran a thumb over a bevelled garnet. 'Then I'll keep it safely for you. And after the war, when you come home, I'll give it back to you.'

'Home?' His lip curled as his grey-green eyes contemptuously scanned the room. 'This is not my home.'

'I meant,' she said 'at the end of the war, when you go home to Poland.'

He lit a cigarette and with a sharp flick of the wrist extinguished the match. 'I don't know if I will have a home to go to. I don't know if I will have a country to return to. Perhaps the Russians will keep their conquered lands.' His tone was bitter. He drew on the cigarette, then gave a dry laugh. 'There is talk that they will send us Poles to Scotland, to guard the east coast from invasion. So, my dear, sweet Zosia, I would like you to put on my necklace. And when I am patrolling some cold, grey beach . . . or when, God willing, I can fight for my country again . . . I will close my eyes and see my necklace on your beautiful . . .' He put his palm to her chest. 'What is the word?'

'Bosom,' she said firmly. 'The polite word is bosom.'

Kaz clasped the necklace and the strands of silver slipped between her breasts. 'Beautiful,' he murmured. 'You look so very beautiful.'

*

And then, 7th September. Sophie was alone in the house. She was in the kitchen, scraping carrots, when she heard the warbling wail of the air-raid siren. She left a cake baking in the oven and went out to the shelter where she sat in the gloom, waiting for the All Clear to sound. After nearly an hour she risked a dash into the kitchen to rescue the cake and saw the huge, billowing column of smoke rising high into the sky.

Sophie went upstairs. A pale-tangerine glow had settled above London. From the easterly direction of the smoke she guessed that the docks were on fire. She stood motionless at the bedroom window watching, awed, frozen. The shrieking, rumbling chorus of the bombers went on.

The All Clear sounded at six o'clock. When Sophie emerged from the shelter she tasted in the air brick dust and caramel. Vera returned to the house half an hour later and John Reynolds shortly afterwards. Vera told them that the Beckton gasworks had been hit. Kaz did not appear and in the end Sophie served supper to the three of them. While she was washing up the supper things the siren sounded once more and the aeroplanes returned. Sophie, Vera and John trooped off to the shelter, where they remained until half past four in the morning. While the chorus of shrieks, sirens and explosions went on, and while she battled her own fear, she thought of Kaz, somewhere in the city, and prayed that he had found a place of refuge.

In the morning, she discovered that the bombers had struck the docks and warehouses of the East End. The Tate & Lyle barges on the Thames, with their cargoes of sugar, a rubber factory and a grain store, all had gone up in flames and were turned to blackened skeletons. A timber wharf at the Surrey Commercial Docks had made an inferno that blazed hundreds of feet into the sky. Smoke plumed from the still-smouldering fires.

When Kaz did not return to Gilbert Street that evening Sophie tried to tell herself that he was probably helping with the clear-up in the aftermath of the raid. Warnings and All Clears sounded throughout the evening and night. John Reynolds said, 'I hope the Captain is all right,' and Sophie said, 'Yes, I hope so too,' but neither of them said much else. Fear had settled beneath her ribs, heavy and sour, and nothing she did could dislodge it.

She spent the following afternoon at a W.V.S. rest centre, where she helped serve tea and buns to homeless families. Returning to Gilbert Street, she caught sight of a soldier standing by the gate to her front garden. She knew his uniform because Kaz wore the same one. She knew the little bow he gave her because Kaz had greeted her in a similar fashion. And she knew from the expression in his eyes that something terrible had happened.

The Polish soldier introduced himself to her as Major Kaminski. Sophie showed him into the house. In her sitting room, in the room where she and Kaz had sung together and where she had told him about Hugh and where he had stroked her hair, she learned that Kaz was dead, that the office in which he had been working had been struck by a stray bomb early on Saturday evening and that he had died instantly. Major Kaminski told her other things as well, that Captain Wajszczyk had been a hero and a true patriot and that he had carried out his duties with courage, selflessness and tenacity. But then she would never have doubted that.

The major left. Sophie went upstairs to her bedroom. As she took Kaz's necklace out of the cloth bag and clasped it round her neck, her hands shook. The diamonds and garnets gleamed against the pale fabric of her blouse. She went back to the sitting room and sat down at the piano. She put the Gilbert and Sullivan score on the stand and turned the pages to 'Take a Pair of Sparkling Eyes.' She picked out the melody, but then, as tears spilled from her own eyes, found that she was unable to read the music any more.

Kaz had lost so much: a family, a country, a future. She thought that they had understood each other, she and Kaz. They had both lost their history and had had to start from scratch. And somehow, from within the ragged remnants of their lives, they had found passion and love.

Chapter Fourteen

October 1940–July 1941

After a period of indecision, during which she couldn't think what to do (not much call for an archaeologist in a country hourly expecting to be invaded), Thea found, crumpled at the bottom of her rucksack, the letter that Grace Fainlight had given her. The addressee, a Mr Nicholas Grey, a civil servant, worked for the Ministry of Supply. She wrote to him and was eventually offered a position as a clerk/typist.

A few weeks into the London Blitz, her department was moved out of London to Wiltshire, away from the bombs. Their new home, Whiteridge House, was a large, undistinguished, eighteenth-century mansion on the edge of Salisbury Plain. Thea and the other girls shared attic bedrooms where the blackout never worked very well so that at night, going to bed, they switched off their torches and snuffed out their candles as quickly as possible. When they had to go to the bathroom they stumbled around, sending alarm clocks, tumblers of water, stubby lipsticks, stained powder-puffs and framed photographs of lovers in uniform crashing to the floor.

Thea didn't have a boyfriend so she didn't keep a photograph on the little brown leather suitcase she used as a bedside table. Cormac Jamieson had kissed her but she didn't have a photograph of him and he wasn't her boyfriend. Though she had tried to draw him numerous times, her sketches never seemed quite right. She was afraid that she was forgetting what he looked like.

On Thea's bedside table there was a stack of books and the stone axe-head from Corran. One of her room-mates, a girl called Davina, picked up the axe-head one morning. 'What've you got this lump of stone for, Craxton?'

'It's an axe-head. It's about ten thousand years old.'

'Crumbs.' Davina had attended one of those smart but useless girls' boarding schools where you did a bit of drawing and gardening and were taught how to get in and out of a motor car without showing your knickers. She yawned, then put the axe-head back on the suitcase. 'Hurry up. The toast will be cold if we don't get a move on.'

Thea kept the axe-head beside her so that she'd remember who she was and to remind her that she hadn't planned to sit in a cold drawing room with twenty other girls, bashing a typewriter for eight hours a day. Sometime in the future, however long it took, she was damn well picking up the life she'd only just begun to have. In the meantime, she found a role in the house. She was the one who took the spiders out of the bedrooms. There were a lot of spiders in Whiteridge House. There were girls who shrieked and stood on the beds while Thea gently cupped the poor beasts in her hands and took them downstairs. She always released them into the warmth of the scullery and kitchens, though she didn't tell anyone that.

She didn't mind Whiteridge House too much. She had

first gone to boarding school when she was six years old and was accustomed to the cold and lack of privacy. She liked to walk in the park, liked the brush of wet grass against her boots and the earthy scents of dead leaves and fungi. She got to know the rusty benches that were dotted round the grounds, where once, presumably, men in brimmed hats and long waistcoats, sporting a shotgun perhaps, had courted women in voluminous embroidered silk gowns. It was hard to find a quiet place indoors, so when she had a free hour she made for a damp bench and the deer and the rooks.

This was where she read her letters. Letters from Rowan, first from the hospital in Kent, and then, after she was transferred back to St Anne's, from London, where she was nursing victims of the Blitz. Letters from Peggy, who was living in Cornwall among a colony of artists. Letters from her archaeologist friends. The old team was scattered. Monty and Grace had remained in Switzerland but Lucy was still living in London, working as a secretary at the Ministry of Information. Will Towler from the Barbury Hill dig had joined the air force and was flying sea planes. Geoffrey King was an airraid warden in his home city of Bristol.

Letters from Helen, who had made a safe journey back from France and had since joined the Auxiliary Territorial Service. Max was in the army too, stationed in the north of England. They planned to marry before the end of the year. Helen's letters and those from Thea's other military friends arrived intermittently at first. It took the Services a while to sort out the efficient postage of tens of thousands of letters from lonely men in army camps, airfields or on board ship to their tens of thousands of equally lonely girlfriends, wives and friends. Then, someone must have organised something, because December brought a flurry of letters, though the mail services were still interrupted by bombs falling on mail trains and postal depots.

She had letters from Stuart, on a minesweeper patrolling the east coast. Thea and Stuart had agreed to be brother and sister, though they weren't, not at all. Stuart's mother was Sophie – kind, sweet Sophie – and Hugh Craxton had been his father. Whereas Thea's mother was Sigrid, Swedish and headstrong and beautiful and drowned at the age of thirty-five, and her father was – well, all she knew was that back in the 1920s he had lived on Corran. So there was no blood relationship at all. But still, she liked Stuart and he liked her and being brother and sister was simpler than trying to find another name for it.

Stuart was one of the few people who talked freely to her about her father, about the man Thea still thought of as her real father, who had brought her up and whom she still loved, in spite of everything. Stuart, like her, needed to make sense of it. Stuart was trying to understand why Hugh had done what he had, and so was she. She just had the added complication of Sigrid. Before Rowan had told her about Corran and her mother's lover, and before she herself had found out about Sophie, Duncan and Stuart, she had assumed that her parents had loved each other. Because you did, didn't you? Sigrid's untimely drowning, Hugh's grief: that great, tragic romance had underpinned her childhood and teenage years. Only it hadn't been like that at all. All her assumptions had been wrong. She didn't blame Hugh or Sigrid, people did what they did. But she wanted to know. She was trying to fill in the gaps, and so was Stuart, because he had loved his father too. Stuart's version of Hugh Craxton was in some ways the same as hers and in others quite different.

The only person who would be able to tell her more about Sigrid, the only person who knew about the affair that had led to her birth, was Sigrid's lover. If it hadn't been wartime, she might have gone back to Corran and dug round a bit, seen what she could exhume, searched for fragments buried in a long-cold earth. But right now that was impossible.

She received no letters from Cormac. *I'll write to you,* he had called out from the quayside as she had boarded the ship. But he hadn't. To begin with, living in Rowan's flat, Thea had eagerly anticipated his letters. Her heart had raced every time she had looked in the pigeonhole in the foyer. It had taken her long, painful weeks to accept that no letters were going to arrive.

St Malo had been noisy and chaotic and Cormac had misheard her address, perhaps. As far as she knew, all the ships that had left St Malo had got back to England in one piece. So if he had boarded ship at the port he should be safe, which was really the only thing that mattered. There were, of course, other possibilities. Cormac's unit might have been ordered on to another port. There might not have been enough room for them on the other vessels leaving St Malo. Ships leaving French ports at that time had been sunk with great loss of life. Thea tried not to think about that, nor to dwell too much on the head wound Cormac had sustained. She had talked to Rowan about Cormac, though she had not mentioned the hug and the kiss. She was unsure why not, but perhaps it was because a part of her had begun to be afraid that it might not have meant as much to Cormac as it had to her. Anyway, Rowan had told her that head injuries could be unpredictable and life-threatening. That was another thing she tried not to think about.

Cormac might have changed his mind about writing to her. The kiss might have been an expression of relief and happiness at seeing the ship in St Malo rather than anything else.

But it had meant everything to her. She might analyse it and try to dismiss the significance of it because she was afraid of rejection and hurt, but that just didn't work. Something had happened to her on that journey, something others might pass off as a consequence of the heightened atmosphere of those anguished times, but Thea could not. She had met a boy and she had fallen for him. She thought about him day and night. She longed to see him again, longed to kiss him, to hold his hand, or merely to have a glimpse of him.

Grace had once shown her two Beaker potsherds. She had placed them side by side and demonstrated how neatly they had fitted together. That was how she had felt when she was with Cormac. As if she had found a piece of herself she had not even known was missing.

Thea spent Christmas in London, staying at Rowan's flat. Rowan was on duty for much of Thea's three-day break, so Thea looked up old friends. Peggy and Gerald, who had drifted apart before the war, were seeing each other again. Helen and Max had married. Both couples continued to live separately for much of the time, the war having swept them up and deposited them in different parts of the country. Peggy and Gerald were staying with Gerald's parents for Christmas, while Helen and Max were spending their leaves at the Fainlights' Bloomsbury house.

Her friends' lives seemed to have progressed while hers had frozen solid. Her career had ground to a halt and she had not yet even had a proper boyfriend: a dismal record, she felt. Living so near to Salisbury Plain, she sometimes went with groups of girls from Whiteridge House to dances and socials at the army camps. She made conversation and danced, and sometimes she sat in a corner of the aircraft hangar or village hall, longing only to leave, wishing she had brought a book with her but knowing her friends would have thought her odd and unsociable if she had. Once, she overheard a group of soldiers talking about her. 'What about the little dark one?' one private had suggested to his friend. 'You mean the flat-chested girl?' the other had answered, giving her a disparaging look. So, Simon Pemberton might have thought her the possessor of a pair of fine eyes but that counted for nothing when coupled with a small bosom. She tried not to mind, but the comment stung.

And yet, if she was honest, she had felt little interest in any of the boys she had met. The truth was that she automatically compared them to Cormac and found them wanting. Perhaps she wasn't being very fair in finding all those other men unattractive and uninteresting, but that was how it was. Telling herself that she was being silly, that she should forget Cormac, didn't work. She couldn't forget him. He was there, piercing her heart as a thorn drives itself into the skin, and the truth was that though it might hurt she clung to it. The pain of memory and yearning was preferable to having nothing at all.

A sharp frost gripped London on the day of Thea's journey back to Wiltshire. No heating in a train which crawled to a halt in a siding and sat there for three quarters of an hour. Glimpsed through the strips of anti-blast tape on the carriage windows the west London suburbs had an opalescent quality, a burnished coldness. Roof tiles and roads had a glacial, impenetrable sheen and the sky was as pale and hollow as the interior of a shell. Six months before she had walked along baked French tracks and footpaths, surrounded by ripe wheat and leafy woodland, and the sun had scorched her shoulders and made rivulets of sweat run down her arms. It was impossible now to imagine warmth. All that seemed to belong to a different era. This winter had a relentless permanence.

Everyone in the carriage must have heard the grinding thrum of the aeroplanes but no one said anything. Thea thought about the Stuka that had screamed out of the empty sky and fired at the columns of fleeing people. She thought of Cormac Jamieson's hand in hers as they made their way through the crowds in St Malo. The train set off again and the knot inside her slackened a little.

She remembered Cormac saying to her, *I'm not going to leave you, Thea.* She wondered where he was. Whether he was kicking his heels in some cold army camp in Northumbria or Yorkshire, or whether he had been posted abroad, to the battlefields of North Africa. She prayed that he was alive and well. She wondered whether he thought of her too, wherever he was, in the hills or the desert. And whether their journey through France had meant as much to him as it had meant to her. More and more often the thought came into her head that she might never see him again.

The winter passed, and the snow melted and spring came. She hadn't thought to spend her war filling in billing forms for the Ministry of Supply, but somehow that was what had happened. Thea and a girl called Claudia Daniels spent their Sundays off cycling in the countryside. It relieved the boredom of Whiteridge House. Claudia was tall and raw-boned and had frizzy toffee-coloured hair and large, light, myopic eyes. She was a great reader and had an obsession with fossils. Claudia's bedside table was heaped with ammonites and belemnites, gathered from flinty Wiltshire fields and quarries.

They cycled to Cley Hill, where the raised earthworks and ditches were believed to date from the Iron Age. Inside the concentric circles Thea found a handful of dips and hollows, suggesting burials. She remembered the burials at Barbury Hill, the bones polished by time to the colour of bronze, and the rush of excitement she had felt, unearthing the antler pick from the ground. A sharp breeze made the grass on the hilltop shiver and bend. The gently undulating Wiltshire countryside spread out below them, and from her vantage point Thea saw concrete tank-traps scattered over the fields like grey boulders hurled from a volcano. A land girl led a horse and cart down a narrow lane. Thea wondered what it would be like, being a land girl. Surely less tedious than being a clerk in the Ministry of Supply, though with a lot more mud and cold and potato picking.

They were on their way home, cycling through a small village, when Claudia waved an arm in the air.

'Puncture!' she called out.

They braked and swung off their bikes. Claudia stooped to squeeze the tyre. 'I won't be a tick.'

Thea parked her bike and walked along the road, looking for a box in which to mail the letters she had forgotten to post that morning. She passed a church, a blacksmith and garage, and a clutter of thatched cottages in varying states of disrepair. Finding a post box, she extracted her crumpled letters from the bottom of her rucksack and tried to smooth them out. An army lorry had drawn up ahead, blocking most of the narrow road. A.T.S. women in khaki skirts and tunics were milling around outside it, chatting to each other and smoking cigarettes and leaning against a flint wall.

Claudia came to stand beside her. 'It's all right,' she said. 'It's only a slow puncture. I've pumped it up so it should do till we get home.' Then, after a silence, she said, 'Do you ever think about . . ?'

Thea followed her friend's gaze to the A.T.S. women, who were climbing back into the lorry. 'It would be awful,' she said.

'It would, yes.'

P.E. on freezing Tarmac squares, being yelled at by some sadistic gym-mistress type, and the least flattering uniform in the women's Services – awful didn't even begin to cover it. It would be crazy of her even to *consider* joining the A.T.S.

They cycled back to Whiteridge House. But it was funny how hard it was to get rid of an idea once it got into your head. It sat and niggled, like a lash caught in the eye as you endured the dull hours of typing and form filling. And Thea remembered how, when she was seven or eight, she had once deliberately run into a clump of nettles because she had wanted to know what it felt like. It had stung and hurt like hell, of course. Volunteering for the A.T.S., she thought, would be much like that.

But at least she would have tried it. And at least she might feel alive again.

On 11th January, Bank underground station suffered a direct hit. The blast travelled down escalators and stairs, killing and maiming everyone in its path, passengers and those sheltering from the air raid in the underground system. The injured were distributed between the hospitals, including St

Anne's. Rowan cut off charred, ragged clothing, putting it aside to help identification.

That night changed her. When, at last, she went off duty, she made her way to the dining room at the Nurses' Home but was unable to eat the breakfast put in front of her. The smell of burned flesh lingered in her nostrils. As the days went on, she continued to taste it in the back of her throat, no matter how many cups of coffee she drank or cigarettes she smoked.

The triage system that had been set up at St Anne's in the early days of the Blitz now worked with practised slickness. The wounded were stretchered by medical students into the clinical reception room and from there directed to specially equipped wards or to operating theatres or resuscitation rooms in the basement of the hospital. One evening in March, Rowan had already been on duty throughout the day, but when the raid began she paused only to change into a clean uniform before heading back to the ward. The stream of casualties seemed unending, the injuries mostly burns and blast wounds, a cross-section of London's shifting population. Medical teams organised blood transfusions and saline drips and junior doctors dressed wounds. Rowan was washing out trays in the sluice when someone told her that the Café de Paris, in the West End, had been struck by a land mine, killing many of the nightclub-goers as well as the leader of its resident swing band, Ken 'Snakehips' Johnson.

She didn't have time to worry whether any of her friends were among the dead and wounded because the casualties continued to pour in. In the early hours of the morning, the hospital basement shuddered as a bomb fell nearby. The electricity went off and the ward was plunged into darkness.

From a nearby operating theatre, one of the staff nurses called to her, 'Over here, Scott. Hold this.' A torch was thrust into Rowan's hand and she shone the light on to the operating table, where a surgeon was repairing a stomach wound. Like the rest of them, she had become practised at hiding her raised heartbeat, the thud of fear to the system.

The emergency generators switched on and the operating theatre lit up. A tray of surgical instruments had tumbled on to the floor in the darkness so Rowan gathered them up and set about re-sterilising them, using a primus stove. Then she returned to the ward, where she attended to a middle-aged woman who had been treated for a burned arm and who was shaking uncontrollably. Rowan had learned to recognise the different types of shock. Dangerous in its most severe form, when caused by injury or surgery, urgent medical intervention was required. Mild shock could be treated with warmth and rest and cups of sweet tea. 'Siren strain', some of the doctors called it. Rowan sometimes thought that all of them, patients and medics alike, were suffering from siren strain. You said I'm fine, I'm okay when someone asked you how you were, because everyone was in the same boat. If you'd had a truly awful, frightening, bomb-ridden night, and if you were missing your friends and family so much your heart ached, perhaps you might say, I'm feeling a bit second-rate.

By five in the morning the flood of wounded had dried up. When, a couple of hours later, she went off duty, Rowan found herself surrounded by a scene of devastation. London had for a long time been her sanctuary. She had fled to the city at the age of nineteen and distracted herself with romance and glamour and dancing. Following the failure of her marriage to Patrick, the Covent Garden flat had become her refuge. It was hard to see the city she had come to love so torn to pieces. A little drunk with exhaustion, she had to think twice before she was able to make her way back to the Nurses' Home.

Inside the building, a maid was brushing up heaps of powdery debris from the hall floor. As Rowan started up the stairs, a voice called out to her.

'Nurse Scott!'

Rowan turned. Home Sister was glaring at her from the foot of the stairs.

'Yes, Sister?'

'I believe you know there is a rule against leaving shoes on the bedroom floor, nurse.'

Rowan gripped the banister. Twenty-two hours on duty and she was being reprimanded about shoes. Unforgivable words teetered on the tip of her tongue.

A beat, then she managed a sweet, penitent smile. 'Yes, Sister. Awfully sorry, Sister.'

'Don't let it happen again.'

She went into her room and began to strip off her uniform. Anger roared through her head as she kicked off her shoes, then dropped her dress, belt, cap and black stockings to the floor. She lay down on the bed in her underwear and closed her eyes. Images from the evening flickered into her vision: the surgeon, sewing up the man's stomach, the woman with the burned arm, shaking like a jelly. And the dead of the Café de Paris, their swirling dresses grey with ash and dust, frozen in their last dance as the music died.

Duncan and Sally married in June 1941. The wedding ceremony took place at the Flemings' local church in Richmond-on-Thames. Duncan looked so handsome in his air force uniform and Sally was beautiful in a white lace gown made by her mother, Eva. The church was decorated with white and yellow flowers from Eva's garden. Capable, pretty and socially adept, Eva Fleming had been hugely appreciative of Sophie's offer to contribute the wedding cake.

Sophie wore a pale-blue shantung silk dress and jacket she had bought before the war. She concocted a little hat for herself from leftover ribbons and net. Poor Kaz's necklace gleamed opulently at her throat. Now and then she put a hand to it and touched the stones, reminding herself that she had been desired, and thought of Kaz and smiled to herself. And yet there were moments during the day when she felt superfluous, one of many guests. Sally's father, Giles, nobly circled the room with her a couple of times, though Sophie suspected that he loathed dancing, and that was sweet of him. But could there be any situation when one felt the lack of a husband more acutely than at one's child's wedding? Duncan was a proud man and it must have been hard for him to tell the Flemings that his late father had been a bigamist. But if Sophie thought she saw disdain and pity in Eva Fleming's bright smile and resolute good humour, she knew that was probably only in her imagination.

During the summer and autumn that followed the wedding, she realised that she was growing stronger. Despite the obvious heartache that had followed Kaz's death, she was losing her self-consciousness and becoming more confident. She thought about Hugh less. She often felt she had Kaz to thank for this change in herself.

These days she was too busy to dwell on the past. She got up at dawn to do the housework and gardening and to write to Stuart, on his minesweeper off the east coast, and Duncan, now based in Lincolnshire. Throughout the year she attended regular shifts at the First Aid Post, helping out with the initial reception of casualties. In the afternoons she volunteered for the W.V.S., serving tea and buns at rest centres and sorting out second-hand clothes for distribution to the homeless. Through the W.V.S. she came into contact with women from other social classes. From women who had lost their homes and all their possessions and sometimes, appallingly, a child or two, she learned a great deal about resilience and endurance.

And then there were the lodgers. Vera Cornish was still living in Gilbert Street but John Reynolds had moved on to a different part of the country. Kaz's room had remained empty for several months following his death, but now it was taken by a former colleague of Sally, a pleasant girl called Heather, who worked at the B.B.C. The third room was occupied by a naval man, Lieutenant Walker, who had lost an arm and an eye in the Battle of the Atlantic and now had a post at the Admiralty.

Feeding the lodgers took up more and more of her time and her garden was now almost entirely given over to the cultivation of soft fruit and vegetables. Before the war, she had grown vegetables only in the summer, but it had become a year-round necessity. Making the pickles, chutney and jam that would help keep them going through the winter also took time.

So she was learning to fight her corner. *Hugh pushed you around*, Viola had once said to her. *He was terribly good at getting you to do what he wanted.* Sophie didn't intend to let any man push her around. Not any more, not ever again.

Chapter Fifteen

February–October 1942

The train from London King's Cross to York was crammed full of passengers and the air was thick with cigarette smoke and the stale wool smell of wet military uniforms. It had been raining heavily when Thea left Rowan's flat that afternoon after a forty-eight-hour leave from the A.T.S. As the engine got up speed and pulled out of the sheltering canopy of the station, rain dashed against the carriage windows. Thea wormed her way along corridors, murmuring apologies, stepping over kitbags and suitcases and peering into compartments, though with no great hope of finding a vacant seat.

As she emerged from one of the rattling, rubbery tunnels between carriages her heart suddenly clenched. For a moment she thought she was imagining things. Standing right in front of her with his black, slightly curling hair, tanned face and those blue, blue eyes was Cormac Jamieson.

'Good Lord. Thea!' he cried.

'Cormac. It is you, isn't it?'

He flung his arms around her and gave her an enormous hug. And oh, the bliss of that moment. Between this embrace and that other one, so long ago, she had felt only half-alive.

'Wow,' he said, stepping back, looking at her. He, like her, couldn't stop smiling. 'I can't believe it. This is amazing. Wow, Thea. Sorry, I'm blethering on, but it's so marvellous to see you. How are you?'

'I'm fine.'

'Feet all right?'

She laughed. 'Oh, yes. How's your head?'

'Fine.' He drew her closer to him as half a dozen sailors squeezed by, complaining loudly about the lack of seats. As she brushed against the rough fabric of his uniform and breathed in the tang of his skin she was instantly back in the crowds at St Malo, his hand in hers as they made for the ship.

She said, 'I didn't know if you'd got back all right.'

'I was on the next boat out.'

I didn't hear from you. Why didn't you write to me? But then he said, 'I collapsed, more or less. Poor old Phil had to practically carry me on to the boat.' His eyes narrowed. 'You told me your address, didn't you, Thea?'

'Yes.'

'I flaked out on board and woke up in hospital in Southampton a day later. I couldn't remember it. I couldn't remember what you'd said to me.'

'It doesn't matter.' And it didn't, not any more.

'I couldn't even remember the name of the ship you'd boarded. All that last bit of the journey, it was all muddled up in my head.'

Her mouth was dry. 'But you remembered me?'

He looked at her, frowning, and said simply, 'Thea, I could never forget you.'

And her heart soared, and she knew that she didn't need to hold back any more, maybe never again, and she said, 'Nor me you.'

The smile returned to his face. 'Bloody miracle, meeting you here,' he said. 'I was afraid I might never see you again. And now, here you are. I bet your sister was relieved to have you back home from Switzerland.'

'She was, yes, awfully. She's still at St Anne's, still nursing. What about your sister, Cormac?'

'Nicola's fine. She's at home, on the farm, with Dad. There's a lot of blazing rows, I suspect. Nicola has a temper, like Dad.'

'Did you make up your disagreement with your father?'

'You remembered.'

Once she might have blushed, but the army had toughened her up. The ordeal of training with the A.T.S. for the past six months had knocked out of her much of her old shyness and embarrassment.

'Of course I remembered,' she said. 'I remember everything about our journey together.'

They moved aside to let more passengers through. The train, which had come to a halt miles from any station, gave a violent jerk and then set off again.

Cormac said, 'It's funny, isn't it, you'd think you'd want to forget it. There we were, both of us in pieces, afraid we'd never make it back to England. You'd think it would have been hell and you'd want only to put it out of your mind. But I've thought about it so much.'

And in the crowded, rattling carriage in the depths of a miserable British winter wartime, Thea found herself recalling the heat of the French sun, the smell of the dust and dry grass. She had nearly lost him so many times, she thought. That afternoon in France, she might have walked on by, might not have found the courage to help him from the roadside while the planes circled overhead. Or they might have been captured and imprisoned or have reached St Malo only to find that the port was under siege or all the boats had sailed. And then, after parting, they might so easily have never found each other again.

But she would not risk losing him another time. She knew, standing so close to him, aware of his physical presence and her own desire to touch him, to be held by him, that she must let him know how she felt about him, must not retreat into the reticence that had been bred into her by her secretive, fractured family, and that sometimes came all too easily to her.

She said, 'I don't think it was just, you know, wartime. Fear and the circumstances. People say that. But for me it was more than that.'

'Nor for me.' Again, gazing at her, his brow creased. 'I was okay once I met you, Thea. I mean, I was a mess and my head hurt a lot and I was desperate to get home, but when you were there, it was okay. It was as if I'd found my way again.' And he put up a hand to her face, as if to touch her, as if to check that she was real.

The sailors had slung themselves along the corridor; one of them noticed Cormac's gesture and nudged his mate and there were whistles and catcalls.

'Stow it,' Cormac said mildly to the sailors, and gave her an apologetic smile.

They decided to move along the train and find somewhere quieter. They came across the buffet and Cormac offered to buy her a cup of tea. The buffet car was packed but an airman shoved up on his seat to allow Thea room to sit down. It was starting to go dark, blackout time, so the blinds had been pulled down.

Cormac came back from the counter with two teas and something to eat.

'So you made it into the Royal Artillery,' he said, glancing at her white lanyard.

She was in an Anti-Aircraft battery, she told Cormac. 'I'm stationed at a practice camp. I'm a kine-theodolite operator.' It was interesting work and she knew that she was lucky to have been assigned to it.

'What about you, Cormac? Are you on leave?'

'Yes. I'm on my way back to Northumberland for a couple of days and then I'm off on manoeuvres in Scotland. Dad and me are all right now. He and Nicola have to do all the work on the farm these days.' He stirred his tea. 'The men who used to labour for us have joined the Forces. Army pay's lousy but farm labouring's worse.'

'What did you and your father quarrel about?'

'The farm.' He leaned in as an older couple joined the ever-lengthening queue at the counter. 'I told Dad I wasn't going to go in for farming and he blew his top. I'm the only son so he expects me to take over Crawburn. It's what he did and his father before him. But I haven't changed my mind. He thinks I have, and I stay quiet to keep the peace, but after the war I'll find some other way of making a living.'

After they had finished their tea and cake, they made their way up to the far end of the train, still looking for seats. Cormac walked ahead, forging a path through the crowded corridor. The furthermost carriage was the emptiest. A sailor dozed, sitting on his kitbag, and two soldiers crouched on the floor, playing cards. Cormac and Thea slotted themselves into a space near the guard's van.

She said, 'When the war started, I don't know, I had this idea that it would be over quite quickly, in six months or so. I couldn't help hoping that everyone would realise what a bad idea it was. But I can't see a way out of it, Cormac. Someone said to me they thought it could go on for ten years. *Ten years.*'

'What do you miss most?'

She rested her back against the compartment window. She missed lots of things. Oranges and decent coffee and lit streets and being able to walk into a shop and buy a needle and thread to mend an item of clothing. Having time to read. Being able to spend time with your friends, the people you loved. Not worrying that Rowan might be obliterated by a bomb while she was nursing at the hospital.

But she said, 'I miss my work. I miss archaeology. I miss it all the time. I feel as if I'd only just got started and then I had to give it up. Is that awful of me? So many people have lost family and friends. When I started working for Grace Fainlight, it was as if I'd found the missing piece of a jigsaw.'

'You'll go back to it after the war?'

'If I can. But it might not be up to me. Grace and Monty may not come back to England. They may decide to stay in Switzerland. Grace may retire, though I can't imagine that. Or maybe when the war's over there won't be enough jobs to go round, and what jobs there are will go to the men. I may have to start again from scratch.'

'But you'll do it.'

'Yes.' The summer she had spent at Barbury Hill had been the happiest of her life. She would find a way.

She asked Cormac what he missed. 'Home,' he said simply. 'Being somewhere I belong.'

In contrast, she felt rootless. She belonged nowhere, she thought.

The train drew up at a station and passengers spilled out

on to the platform. A couple of seats in a nearby compartment were now empty so they sat down. As the train continued its halting journey north, they talked about all sorts of things.

Then he said, 'I thought you might have met someone else.'

She looked up at him. 'No.'

'Thank heavens for that. Gives me a chance. Here, rest your head on my shoulder.'

The train squeaked and rumbled on. Cormac's shoulder was a solid, warm pillow. She would not have chosen to be anywhere other just then than with Cormac Jamieson in a cold train in the dark depths of wartime. She had spent so many months wondering if she would ever see him again and, as soon as she had, she had known how deeply attracted to him she was. It often took her a long time to feel comfortable with a person and yet she had felt at ease with him instantly. She did not feel she had to put on an act or pretend to be other than she was.

He woke her as the train pulled into York station. Blearily, she gathered up her belongings. He kissed her gently on the cheek before she left the carriage and asked her if he might write to her. Yes, please, she said, as she gave him her address. Yes, she would like that very much.

Their leaves never seemed to coincide, so Cormac and Thea got to know each other first through their letters. She wrote to him at length early on, telling him about Corran and her mother, and her mother's lover. *I don't know who he was. I don't suppose I'll ever know. And her father, Hugh. Sometimes he'd get down in the dumps, but when he was in good spirits he was wonderful to be with. Sophie (wife number two) says the same thing. I've visited her a few times,*

271

when I was in London. I like her, and though a lot of people might find it surprising, it makes it easier, talking to someone who knew Dad well – as well as anyone did, at least.

He told her about his family home, Crawburn. From the back of the farmhouse you can see the Cheviots, he wrote. They're blue or they're brown or they're orange or green or white, depending on the time of year, and they seem to fold over each other all the way to the sky. When we were kids, we'd stay out in the hills all day. We'd dam streams and try to catch fish and we wouldn't come home till after nightfall. Dad always yelled at us for staying out late but it didn't make any difference.

At last, the final day of Thea's leave coincided with the first day of Cormac's forty-eight-hour pass. He was in Yorkshire and she was staying in London, in Rowan's flat. After studying maps and railway timetables they settled on a small station on the London–Leeds line, a halfway point where they could meet.

In the carriage, Thea counted the stations. The name plates had been removed in the invasion scare so it wasn't easy to tell where you were, but at least it was summer, so easier to make things out in the better light and absence of fog. As they drew into each successive station, the passengers in her compartment debated whether this was such and such a place. Often someone would peer out of the window and call to the station master to check. As she drew closer to her destination the knot of excitement beneath her ribs tightened.

Cormac was waiting for her on the platform. After a flurry of greetings and exclamations – her train wasn't as late as she had feared it might be and they'd found each other, thank goodness – he took her hand and she felt a bubble of happiness rise inside her. Then he kissed her.

It was her first proper kiss. It was heavenly, and he clearly thought so too. They kissed again and again, standing in the shelter of the awning, oblivious of the passengers hurrying by them.

Eventually they pulled apart, both unable to stop smiling, and arm in arm went in search of a pub in the village. They went on holding hands while they had a glass of beer and a sandwich and talked. Their couple of hours together seemed to pass in a flash and Thea dreaded the moment when she would have to part from him. They eked out their last minutes together, back at the railway station, standing on the platform, making plans for when they would meet again. She hoped the train that would return her to camp would be late, but it was wretchedly on time for once. 'Here it is,' he said, and she looked down the rails and saw it coming towards them.

It drew up at the platform. Doors were thrown open and a huff of smoke masked the people alighting from the carriages. Cormac kissed her again, his mouth brushing her forehead, then her mouth, as his hands rested on her hip bones. She closed her eyes, losing herself in the taste and feel of him. They said goodbye and she climbed into the carriage. In the course of a day, everything had changed.

Outside the branch line station, Sophie paused for a moment, getting her bearings and shifting her baggage from hand to hand. Then she set off in the direction of Church Street, where Duncan and Sally lived. The village was in a low-lying part of Lincolnshire. Beyond the school and the fine redbrick houses and the church, Sophie made out fields and copses, grey in the approaching twilight and hazed with autumn mist. Charcoal trees shimmered against the gloom, and from their branches an owl called. Duncan was training pilots at the Lincolnshire airbase. He had been angered by the posting, regarding it as a demotion, so Sophie had kept her immense relief to herself. So, she suspected, had Sally. Before being sent to Lincolnshire, Duncan had been unwell with a series of chest and throat infections. Sophie had known that, after years of flying in combat, he was both physically and mentally exhausted. She guessed that his commanding officer had recognised that as well.

She had been travelling since first thing that morning. Her wicker basket and suitcase, which seemed to have grown heavier since she had packed them in London the night before, were filled with tiny knitted garments and things to eat and gifts from Viola and lodgers past and present. Her granddaughter had been born three weeks ago. Duncan and Sally had named her Rosalind Eva Sophie. The inclusion of her own name had touched her immeasurably.

Eva Fleming had been with her daughter at the time of the birth and had written to Sophie to tell her that all was well with both Sally and their baby granddaughter. Viola had offered to cook for the lodgers so that Sophie could go away. Vera Cornish had brushed off her concerns with an airy wave of the hand. 'We'll muddle along perfectly well, Sophie. I shall set up a rota of washing-up and dusting. Off you go.'

On the train, she had felt a mixture of nervousness and anticipation. She had found herself remembering the birth of her sons, the violent demands of the body and the great tidal waves of emotion. Hugh had been away on business when Duncan was born so Sophie's mother had helped out, but he had been in London at the time of Stuart's birth. As soon as the nurse had cleaned his son up, Hugh had held him in his arms. And he had wept. Sophie remembered that he had wept. There had been times these past few years when she would have brushed that off as fakery, but as she neared Duncan and Sally's house, a small, modern, semi-detached cottage, Sophie felt able to acknowledge that Hugh's tears had been genuine.

She opened the gate. A curtain moved aside and there was Sally, waving to her, and in her arms was a small, white bundle. Seeing her granddaughter, Sophie felt an onrush of longing and delight. She hurried up the path. The front door opened and she and Sally embraced on the front step. She went inside the house and put down her cases and took off her coat and Sally put the baby in her arms. Sophie looked down at the tiny, pale, perfect face. 'Oh, Sally,' she began, and then was unable to speak any more. Tears trailed down her face, but they were tears of joy. And Sally patted her shoulder and left her to get to know her granddaughter while she went off to make them both a cup of tea.

Chapter Sixteen

March–September 1943

A dozen of them were crowded round the table when, one evening at the end of March, Rowan arrived at the night-club. From several conversations going on at once she picked out Nicky Olivier, talking loudly and dogmatically about poetry.

'Of course, the form dictates the content.'

'Do you think so?' This from a man in army uniform, sitting across the table from Nicky. He had thick straight brown hair, small, deepset eyes and a long nose that ended in a bulbous oval tip. It was a face, Rowan thought, in which all the bits did not quite match. It was a likeable face, though.

'You don't think it's the other way round?' the man said.

'Not at all.'

'If I was going to write a poem I'd think of what I wanted to say first and then choose the most suitable form.'

Nicky leaned towards him. '*Are* you a poet?'

'No. Are you?'

'Certainly not.' Nicky pursed his mouth. 'I despise poetry.'

Standing at his shoulder, Rowan tousled Nicky's hair. 'Nicky writes about poetry,' she said to the soldier. 'He's a famous critic.'

'An oxymoron, dear Rowan.' Nicky patted her hand. 'Can a critic be famous? I don't think so. Ask the man in the street if they can name a single critic and the answer will be no.'

'F. R. Leavis,' said Denis Charlbury.

'You are not the man in the street, Denis. You holiday in St Moritz and drive a Morgan. You have a flat in Belgravia and a house, I believe, in the country – Hampshire or some such benighted place. As I'm virtually penniless, I have a far greater claim than you to being the man in the street.'

Denis snorted. 'Gloucestershire. My place is in Gloucestershire. It's currently full of ageing relatives and dogs.'

'Rowan, you look divine.' Nicky put an arm round her waist.

'Thank you, sweetie.' She gave a wave of greeting to her friends then offered her hand to the man Nicky was arguing with. 'I'm Rowan Scott.'

'Alex Moore. Delighted to meet you. Let me get you a drink.'

'You mustn't listen to him, Alex,' she said, slotting into a seat. 'He's only doing it to get attention.'

'How can you criticise poetry if you dislike it?'

'I didn't say that I disliked it.' Nicky jutted out his chin. 'I said that I *despised* it. That's entirely different. It's easy to write about what one despises, it fires one up. Indifference, on the other hand, sends one into a stupor. Besides, how can anyone say that they "like poetry"?' He affected a pallid lisp. 'It's like saying you like food. Surely one admires some things and loathes others. For instance, I adore squid and detest apples.'

Rowan said, 'How are you, Nicky?'

He made a woebegone face. 'Utterly down in the dumps, darling. They've made me a lieutenant, can you believe it? Lieutenant Olivier. They can't have noticed how inept I am at marching up and down and running round mountains and all the other frightful things one has to do. I detest and loathe the army. If it wasn't for the fact that I'd detest and loathe a military prison even more, I'd desert.'

Rowan murmured comforting words. A waiter bought another bottle of champagne to the table. She ran a thumb over the palm of her hand, worrying at a piece of dry skin. Davey Manningham asked her to dance. They went downstairs to the floor of the nightclub, where the women's brightly coloured frocks were a foil to the men's khaki and blue. Davey was a good dancer, they always danced well together; while she danced, she forgot the hospital and the events of the day. Afterwards, she did her face in the Ladies' Room. Half the lightbulbs had gone, making the application of lipstick and powder hit and miss.

When she returned to the dance floor, she saw that Davey was chatting to Bobbie Wharton. Rowan went upstairs but did not go back to their table. Instead, she stood on her own to one side of the balcony, resting her arms on the rail and looking down at the dancers and the swing band. Her love affair with Bobbie Wharton seemed a lifetime ago, an ill-chosen but ultimately unimportant interlude.

A voice said, 'May I join you?'

Rowan looked round. Army uniform, broad shoulders, hooded eyes and hair the red-brown of autumn leaves. He was a few years older than her, perhaps. Something watchful about him.

'Yes, of course.'

He came to stand beside her at the balcony. 'You're Rowan Scott, aren't you? I'm Josh Makepeace.'

'Hello, Josh. How do you know my name?'

He smiled. 'I asked Alex.'

'Is Alex Moore a friend of yours?'

'We've known each other for years. We met on my first day at boarding school, when I was fourteen. Alex took me under his wing.'

'He seems very pleasant. Are you in London long?'

'Just the one night. You live here, don't you?'

'You seem to have done a fair bit of reconnoitring, Josh.'

He rested his arms on the rail, next to hers. 'It's the best way. Know your enemy and all that. Though I hope we're not going to be enemies.'

Rowan felt a flicker of an old excitement. It took her by surprise; it seemed a long time since she had felt that instant connection with a man, that pull, that sense of urgency.

She said, 'I hope not, too.'

'What do you do?'

'I'm a nurse.'

'Do you live in?'

'Not any more, thank goodness. I was supposed to, before I passed my nurse registration exams, but I used to escape to my flat as often as possible.'

He raised his eyebrows. '"Escape"? Were drainpipes and bathroom windows involved?'

'I'm afraid they were, but it wasn't as daring as it sounds. It was only a first-floor window.'

'What was wrong with the Nurses' Home?'

'If you'd ever had to listen to half a dozen women moaning

about their varicose veins, you'd know.' She considered him; it was hard in the dim light to tell the colour of his eyes but she thought they were green. She noticed that in spite of having, like herself, a redhead's colouring, he was tanned. Which didn't suggest a desk job.

She said, 'I suppose you've slept in worse places.'

'One or two. But soldiers are perfectly capable of moaning about their ailments too.'

'Where are you stationed, Josh?'

'Oh, here and there. I move around.'

Though his answer seemed off-hand she knew what it meant. *I can't tell you where I'm stationed or what I do.* Something hush-hush, then.

He asked her where her flat was and she told him that it was in Covent Garden. She said, 'My friends often stay there when they're in London. I love seeing them. There's nothing like the company of your oldest, dearest friends, is there?'

'Would you like me to escort you back to your table?'

'No, not at all, I didn't mean that.' Rowan looked down at the dance floor, where couples were dancing to 'I've Got You Under My Skin'. 'To be honest, I'm feeling rather anti-social tonight,' she admitted. 'I don't think I'm in a nightclub mood.'

'I can't tempt you to dance, then?'

'No, I'm afraid not, though this is one of my favourite songs.'

'I'll keep quiet, then, so that you can listen to it.'

And he did. This she thought rather remarkable. So many men felt obliged to fill a silence.

She said this to him as, once the number was over and they had decided to leave Signorelli's and look for a restaurant, she was collecting her mackintosh from the cloakroom.

He said, 'I've been on my own quite a bit recently. I was afraid I'd forget how to make conversation.'

It was hard to be on your own in a London at war. Everyone was always in a state of transit, which was why Rowan let any of her friends who happened to be around and needed a place to rest their heads use the Macklin Street flat. Sometimes when she turned up there, there might be half a dozen people sleeping on the beds and on the sofa or the floor.

She said, 'I'm afraid my conversational skills are a little rusty as well. I could talk to you at length about bedpans and dressings but it wouldn't be awfully interesting.'

'Don't you think that if you're talking to the right person, anything they say is interesting?' His hand brushed her shoulder as he helped her on with her mackintosh. It was as if a small electric charge flickered between them and the shock of it lingered as they went outside.

Though the time of nightly air raids was long past, London was still subject to frequent bombardments. Rowan looked up automatically at the sky. She noticed that Josh did so too. A light drizzle fell, dampening the rubble and debris in the bomb sites and the damaged roads and pavements. In the clouded opaque darkness, Josh Makepeace made his way easily round obstacles. The qualities she had detected on meeting him, of alertness and watchfulness, seemed intensified out here.

He took her to a small restaurant on Piccadilly. A waiter showed them to a corner table, tucked away out of sight. 'Your favourite table, Captain Makepeace,' he said, before leaving them alone with the menus.

'It's one of my bolt-holes,' Josh explained. 'When I'm in London I often eat here. It might look shabby, but the food is excellent.'

It was, but she couldn't eat it. She moved the fillets of fish round the plate with her fork, acutely embarrassed, hoping he wouldn't notice, hating herself for the wastage and her own stupidity.

But he touched her hand and said quietly, 'Would you rather we left?'

'Please.' Her face flamed.

He had a word with the waiter and they rose and left the table. Out in the street, she blurted out, 'I'm so sorry. I'm so hopeless tonight.'

'It doesn't matter a jot.'

'I wouldn't blame you if you were fed up with me.'

'I'm not.' Pausing, he turned to face her. Shadows cut into his forehead and incised the sides of his strong, well-shaped mouth. He said, 'Rowan, I don't often make a beeline for a girl. I'm not saying I'm some sort of shrinking violet, nothing like that, but life recently hasn't given me much opportunity for anything other than work. And perhaps that's how you feel too. Nursing must be one hell of a job. Maybe it's enough for you now, and if so, I'll leave you in peace.'

'No.' She put a hand on his sleeve. 'No, I don't want you to do that.'

'Good.' He took her arm as they set off down the pavement. He said, 'When I saw you tonight, in the nightclub, I thought . . .'

'What did you think?'

'That you were very beautiful. And that you were someone I'd like to know better. Shall we go to my flat? Would you like that? It's not far away.'

While they walked, he told her about his family. When he had been a boy the Makepeaces had lived abroad, in Austria, Italy and then France. It sounded an interesting, itinerant existence, dictated by his father's work as a diplomat. His mother had enjoyed travelling; the sociable life of an ambassador's wife had suited her. Josh and his two elder brothers, Peter and Ronald, had had a great deal of freedom. Their mother had believed a rough-and-tumble life to be suitable for boys, and until they were in their teens Josh and his brothers had been placed in whichever local school came to hand.

She asked him where his brothers were now.

'Peter's on submarines,' he said. 'And Ronald is somewhere in the Middle East. Egypt, I suspect.'

'And your parents? Do they still live abroad?'

'No, thank heavens. They have a house in Suffolk. It has some land, which allows my mother free rein for her passions. She adores gardening and horses. And you, Rowan, do you have family?'

'I have an ex-husband, Patrick.' She felt the need to make things straight between them as soon as possible. Attitudes to divorce were changing as the number of broken marriages increased in wartime but condemnation had not completely disappeared. She didn't think he would judge her but you never knew.

But he said, 'That must have been difficult.'

'It was, it was hugely difficult. I'll tell you about it someday, Josh, but not now. It's done and dusted and I've put it behind me.'

They were making their way through the tangle of narrow streets behind the Strand. She said, 'My parents are both dead but I have a sister, Thea, whom I love dearly. And I have two half-brothers, one in the navy and the other in the R.A.F. I don't really know them. In fact, I've never met the elder one. I only found out they existed a few years ago, just before the war.'

Josh unlocked the door to a house and let her inside, into a hall cluttered with bicycles and yellowing items of post. The tiles were cracked and dusty and the carpet on the stairs they climbed was worn through in the middle.

His flat was on the top floor. Inside it, as he was taking her coat, he said, 'My paternal grandfather, Frederick Makepeace, was a dissolute old devil. He had a mistress in Paris. Or a handful of mistresses, who knows? He used to go over to France whenever he was fed up with my grandmother, which was rather often. My grandmother didn't think much of that and cut up a fuss. I'm told she used to throw things at him – Sèvres porcelain, carriage clocks, that sort of thing. The story is that that's why we haven't much in the way of family heirlooms. No doubt it's an exaggeration and more likely they were sold off to pay debts. Anyway, Sarah Makepeace was a famous beauty. John Singer Sargent painted her. I've always suspected she took her revenge in the obvious way. My father doesn't look much like his brothers.'

Rowan smiled. 'It's a relief to meet a man whose family is as disreputable as mine.'

'I suspect most families are disreputable if you pick away at the surface. Do please sit down, Rowan. Would you like a drink?'

'Please.'

The room he showed her into was neat, the books tidily arranged in a glass-fronted cabinet, a copy of The Times folded on a side table and a pen beside it, the crossword completed.

But the fabric of the building had been badly damaged. Deep fissures snaked through the plaster on the walls and one of the windows was covered in hardboard.

Josh passed her a brandy. 'The place took a battering in the May nineteen forty-one raid,' he explained. 'The house behind us was wiped out. A few yards closer and there wouldn't have been much left.'

Rowan took a sip of a Calvados that tasted divinely smooth and old. 'Were you here?'

'No, thank God, I was away.'

'I feel such a fool about the restaurant. I think I'm all right, that I'm hungry, and then I find that I'm not. It was much worse a couple of years ago, when it started. We had casualties sent to us after the Bank underground station bomb, you see. It was dreadful, Josh, truly dreadful, and afterwards I couldn't eat. I think I'm over it, and then, at the most damnably ill-timed moments, it happens again. It's so silly.'

'It's not silly at all,' he said gently. 'That was a ghastly business. Shock does strange things to people, I've seen it myself. You're on the front line, Rowan, and that makes it tough.'

'I'd have quite understood if you'd run a mile, faced with a woman floored by a serving of plaice à la meunière.'

'Oh, you won't get rid of me that easily.' He gave her a slow, easy smile. 'And now I'm going to cook us something. You can eat it if you want to, but if you'd rather not it doesn't matter at all. My mother's sent me a pound of bacon. Keeping pigs is her latest thing.'

A delicious aroma drifted into the room as Rowan wandered round, glancing at Josh's belongings. Unexpectedly, she felt a pang of hunger. She noticed that some of his books were in foreign languages, French and German and Italian.

She called out to him, 'Do you speak all these languages?'

He put his head round the door. 'Yes. When you're a child, languages just sink in. And once you've picked up one or two, others are easy.'

The room had a sparse, masculine air and she suspected that that he didn't use it very often. Though at first sight it appeared to tell her little about him, there were nevertheless clues as to who Josh Makepeace was.

He put a plate of bacon sandwiches on the coffee table. 'Tell me about your work,' he said. 'Why nursing? What is it that you like about it?'

'The patients, mostly. They put up with so much and yet they still manage to laugh about it. And I like to do things well, and nursing's useful, particularly now, and I like that.'

'Whatever you do, do it to the best of your ability, that's my motto.'

'Exactly. So you may as well do something worthwhile. It hasn't been easy. I made such a mess of everything in my first year.'

He reached for the brandy bottle and topped up their glasses. 'Tell me what you're afraid of, Rowan.'

'How do you know I'm afraid of anything?'

'Everyone's afraid of something. They might pretend not to be, but they are.'

He had slung his arm along the back of the sofa. She was very aware of his proximity. Move an inch or two and they would touch. Lean towards him and she knew he would kiss her. Now she was able to make out the colour of his eyes. They were an unusual greenish-brown, almost bronze, lightened by flecks of gold.

286

'For instance,' he said 'I dislike confined spaces. I could never have joined a tank regiment.'

What was she afraid of? She said slowly, 'In the past, I've been afraid that everything might fall apart. And that I'd never find out what I was supposed to do with my life. But now . . . I'm an absolute liability if I'm bored, Josh, that's for sure. Maybe that's what I'm most afraid of – boredom. When I started nursing, I think I was trying to prove to myself that I was capable of sticking at something. But then I found out that I loved it. Anyway, it would have been too tediously predictable to throw in the towel. Nurses are forever threatening to give in their notice.' She had passed her exams the previous autumn. She was now a registered nurse.

'Keep buggering on, that's the thing.'

'Exactly.' Rowan realised that she had, almost without noticing it, eaten a sandwich.

'Must be satisfying, helping people.'

'Often it is. I wish we could do more for the patients and their poor relatives, though. We patch them up and if they make it through we send them away to cope with it on their own. Girls who are so badly scarred they'll never look pretty again and lads who'll walk on crutches or be stuck in a wheelchair for the rest of their lives. The bereaved, too. We've hardly time to give them comfort. We mop up the worst of it, that's all we can do, and they have to learn to deal with their loss by themselves. It feels so wrong.'

'All you can do – all any of us can do – is our best.' He gave a low chuckle. 'That sounded terribly trite, didn't it? Perhaps I should take up writing morale-stiffening columns for the Sunday papers.'

He took down a photograph from a shelf. The image was of a beach, a pale sandy bay embraced by high rocks.

He said, 'When I was seventeen, I decided to walk to Crete.'

'Is that possible?'

He grinned. 'Not completely, no.'

'How long did it take you?'

'Nearly six months. I decided I'd had enough of school. I walked out. I told the headmaster beforehand, so it was all above board.' His eyes sparked. 'Rather a lot of annoyance all round, as you can imagine. My mother was furious with me. There was Ronald in the army and Peter in the City, both doing sensible things, and there I was, tramping round Europe. She sent Peter after me, to try to persuade me to come back.'

'But he didn't succeed.'

'No, certainly not. I was an obstinate little blighter. I made it in the end, though parts of the journey were hellish. I went down with food poisoning a fortnight in, in some little French town, and got near to giving up then. It was only the thought of my nearest and dearest saying I told you so that kept me going. I worked my passage but even so I ran out of money quite a few times. And once I went for a couple of days without water, which was unbelievably awful as well as unbelievably stupid. The worst time was when I was hiking through some hills and I fell and broke my arm. I was in the middle of nowhere and I ended up having to travel for two days before I could find a doctor to set it. But I wouldn't have missed it for the world. It was eye-opening. I'd turn up in some poverty-stricken little place no one had ever heard of in the mountains and someone would always invite me for supper and give me a place to sleep for the night. You realise that most people are decent, given the chance.'

She pictured him, seventeen and stubborn, hiking through isolated areas where old customs reigned and almost-forgotten languages were spoken. She said, 'Why did you do it? To see if you could?'

'That's about it. To test myself. And to see the world, of course.'

'What were the best bits?'

'The landscape . . . the people.' He put the photograph back on the shelf. 'When I finally made it to Crete I found this secluded little beach and ripped off all my clothes and walked into the sea. God, it felt good.' His gaze met hers, full of humour. 'I still had my arm in a sling.'

'I'm picturing you, Josh, walking into the Mediterranean, wearing only a sling.'

'It would have been a sight,' he conceded. 'I was completely filthy and I had a bright red beard. Anyway, when I got back to England I went to a crammer and took my exams and went on to university. People thought I'd got it out of my system. But I'm not sure one ever gets these impulses out of one's system.'

As he talked, his fingers gently kneaded the little bones at the nape of her neck. Again, she felt that crackle of electricity. She said lightly, 'You're not such a bad conversationalist after all, you know, Josh.'

'I'm glad you think so.'

Then he kissed her. His kiss reached deep into the core of her, awakening old desires and longings.

Someone hammered on the door. 'Captain Makepeace! Captain Makepeace!'

'Damn it,' Josh muttered.

'Who is it?'

'My neighbour, Mr Lyons. He's been a wreck since the

289

bomb.' He ran his fingertips down the curve of her cheek. 'Forgive me, Rowan, I'll have to see to this.'

She stood up. 'I should go.'

'Must you?' He frowned.

More door knocking. 'Captain Makepeace, Poppy has gone!'

'Josh, you should answer it.'

While he dealt with his neighbour, Rowan looked round for where she had put her bag. She was being sensible, she told herself. She had only met Josh Makepeace a few hours ago. She, too, was a creature of impulse and in the past some of her impulses had rebounded on her.

The neighbour, Mr Lyons, sounded distraught. Poppy was, Rowan gathered from the conversation on the landing as she checked her face in her powder compact mirror, a cat. Footsteps on the stairs – and then a loud, protesting miaow. Shortly afterwards she heard Josh's voice, saying, 'It's all right, Mr Lyons, I've got her.'

Mr Lyons thanked him profusely. Josh came back into the room and closed the door behind him.

'Poor man, the wretched creature never goes far, but he panics. You won't change your mind, Rowan?'

'I really must go. It's late.'

'Of course.' He fetched her coat. 'I have to go away tomorrow but I hope we can see each other again.'

'I'd like that very much.'

He held out her coat to help her into it. Slipping an arm into a sleeve, she breathed in the salty, lemony scent of his skin. Suddenly her reservations seemed foolish and petty. She wanted to see him again, she had no doubt about that, so what was she waiting for? Josh Makepeace was a linguist, fluent in several European languages. He was fit and adventurous and his reluctance to talk about his work made her conclude that Intelligence was the most likely outfit for a man of his skills. If she was right, then it was probable that he was doing dangerous work, and it was also likely that he would be sent out of the country. She might never see him again. Why on earth would she wait, why be coy, why heap regret upon regret?

Somehow – she was never sure quite how it happened – she brushed against him as she was putting on her coat. And then they were kissing again, wild, passionate, needy kisses, and she was ripping off her coat and he was pulling her to him, and his fingertips were tracing out the hollow of her backbone as he drew down her zip of her tangerine silk gown.

And so it began, the love affair that changed her life. They woke at five in the morning and made love again, slowly and luxuriantly. Afterwards, wrapped in each other's arms, they talked. Above them, Rowan could see the rafters through the damaged ceiling and chinks of starlit sky between the tiles.

She told him her story. 'Patrick and I, we thought we loved each other, but we didn't. I don't think either of us knew anything much about love. I was only twenty-one. You think you know but you don't. Patrick's a good man, but we weren't right for each other and we only made each other unhappy.' Six months ago she had run into Patrick, who was serving in the navy. He had told her that his old school friend Colin Slater had been imprisoned by the Japanese following the fall of Singapore. Patrick had been sick with worry for him.

She told him about Simon and about her journey through Europe with Christopher Page. And Lucian and the motor accident, that painful, self-inflicted episode. She spoke about a trip she had taken when she had been a small child with her mother, to Sweden, and her fragmented memories of a large, light country house, and her grandparents, who had been kind, quiet people. She had the idea that in Josh Makepeace she had found a man she could say anything to, a man who thought and felt much the same as she did, and who shared her fear of the life half-lived.

She asked him whether he had ever been married or engaged. There had been a girl once, he told her. Marriage had been mentioned but in the end it had come to nothing and they had drifted apart. His girlfriend had wanted a house and babies. 'She told me I wasn't a serious person,' he added wryly, as he lit two cigarettes. 'And she was right. I think I've become a serious person since, but I wasn't then.'

They drifted off to sleep again and did not wake until mid-morning. After cooking her breakfast he saw her back to her flat in Covent Garden. They kissed, clinging to each other, unwilling to let each other go, and then she stood on the pavement and watched him until he was swallowed up by the other pedestrians.

Time passed, and she became accustomed to the pattern of their affair. The phone call or the note left at her flat, followed by a brief, snatched meeting. An hour in a quiet little restaurant or a few stolen moments walking through London's ruined streets. And then the emptiness and the missing him and the worrying about him. Once, she was dancing at Signorelli's with Davey Manningham when Davey smiled ruefully and released her, and Josh, whom she hadn't seen for months, swept her into his arms. The band began to play again: 'I've Got You Under My Skin'. She rested her cheek against his as they danced, breathing in his cold, outdoor scent. She saw how thin he looked, how drawn. They kissed as the dancers circled round them.

Clouds streaked the evening sky and a brisk wind worried at the cigarette ends in the gutters as Thea walked out of Salisbury station. The hotel where she and Cormac had arranged to meet for dinner was on the far side of the road. In the foyer, a porter directed her through winding, mud-coloured corridors to the restaurant. The room was large and high-ceilinged and most of the tables were already occupied. Thea scanned the room, looking for Cormac.

A waiter approached her and she explained that Lance-Corporal Jamieson had reserved a table. He thumbed through the reservations book.

'Do you know if he's here, yet?'

'I don't believe so, madam.'

She was shown to a table by a window. A chair was pulled out for her, a menu handed to her. Opening it, she made a pretence of reading it, but kept looking to the door. It had gone eight. Cormac had told her that he expected to arrive at the hotel by half past seven.

For the last two months he had been stationed at Bulford, taking part in manoeuvres on Salisbury Plain. Though they were geographically nearer to each other now, their meetings were rarely straightforward. Trains were late or didn't run or his leave or hers was cancelled at the last minute. Thea was aware of an irony: had she still been at Whiteridge House, they could have seen each other far more often.

The waiter returned to the table. Would madam care to order a drink? She declined, thanking him.

She was coming to loathe these stuffy restaurants, where

293

the formalities of the pre-war years were clung to in spite of shortages of both staff and food. She knew that Cormac disliked them too. They met in them because you could count on there being a Station Hotel or Railway Inn or at least a buffet with butterless buns and a single teaspoon chained to the counter for communal use, in all but the smallest, meanest town or village.

Thea drank some water. The restaurant door opened; she glimpsed a khaki uniform and her heart sprang. But it wasn't him. She looked down at the menu. Baked veal chop, grilled fish, cold sliced chicken and ham. A couple, the woman in a fur-trimmed coat and little green hat, the man in naval uniform, came into the restaurant. Thea wondered whether they too were familiar with railway stations the length of the country, with busy London interchanges and provincial stations with wooden awnings and well-tended flower beds, and the tiny halts in marsh and fen and wold where the trains stopped only twice a day and you didn't meet another soul.

Half past eight. There was a time when she would have found it mortifying, waiting for a man in a restaurant, when she would have felt the awkwardness of her situation and imagined the other diners staring at her. When she would have opened her book and tried to blot out her nervousness and doubts by reading, though she wouldn't have been able to concentrate. But those times were gone, and all she felt was an aching longing to see Cormac. She never doubted him. She *knew* him, had known him, she often thought, since she had knelt beside him on a French roadside and fallen for the swoop of an eyelid, the whorl of an ear. She remembered that once – it seemed an age ago – she had longed to yearn for a man. She hadn't realised then how painful it would be, how evenings like this could chill her with desolation.

A cold draught seeped through the window. The wind was getting up, the blackout rattling against the pane. The waiter, who looked old and tired, returned to her table.

'Perhaps some soup, madam?'

Whether Cormac made it or not, she would have to go back to London tonight. She had only a few shillings on her and hadn't eaten since midday, so was hungry. She glanced at the menu. She could afford a bowl of thick vegetable soup for sixpence. She placed her order and thanked the waiter. Half a dozen people grouped round a table on the far side of the room were shrieking with laughter and calling out for glasses of beer. On a corner table another girl, wearing the uniform of the W.A.A.F., was sitting on her own, like Thea. Their eyes met and the girl gave Thea a watery smile.

Gone nine. She had the idea of asking at reception whether a message had been left for her. Leaving her book and cap on the table, she went to the foyer. There was a queue at the reception desk; Thea took her place at the end of it. An R.A.F. officer – drooping moustache, top button of his tunic casually undone – sat in one of the leather armchairs, a drink in front of him. Thea felt his eyes running her up and down.

The receptionist told her that there was no message for her. 'He's stood you up,' the R.A.F. officer said to her as she walked past him. 'I'll treat you to a drink, love.'

'No thanks,' she said politely.

In the Ladies' Room she washed her hands and gave her hair a quick tidy. If she left it long enough Cormac might be waiting at the table by the time she got back. That was what happened, you waited and waited, and then, when you'd almost abandoned hope, he turned up.

Cormac wasn't there. Thea drank the soup. The W.A.A.F.'s date, a ginger-haired GI, had turned up. Ever-increasing numbers of American servicemen were congregating in British towns and villages, rehearsing military manoeuvres on British hills and beaches. US troops had hugely swelled the numbers of the Forces in Britain, all of whom were preparing for the coming battle for the liberation of Europe. Some day, one day.

In the autumn of 1942, the second Battle of El Alamein had marked a turn in the fortunes of the Allies. A once seemingly endless succession of defeats had been replaced by a series of victories, first in North Africa and then Italy, where after fierce fighting the Allied army had at last established a foothold in mainland Europe. By February 1943 Stalingrad had been retaken and Russia had begun to reclaim its conquered cities. Victory was becoming not a far-off dream, but a real and tantalising possibility.

Diners were beginning to leave the restaurant. The hands of the clock moved relentlessly towards half past nine. Thea's last train was at ten past ten. She felt a pang of intense longing and disappointment. These were the times she lived for and when they didn't work out she felt scoured inside. She pretended to study the menu again. She hadn't thought it would be like this. She hadn't thought that love would leave her feeling as desperate as this.

The waiter asked her if she would like to order a main course, adding that the kitchen was about to close. Thea asked for the bill. She paid her sixpence and left a couple of pennies for the waiter, then went back to the foyer to collect her coat. People were putting on coats and paying bills and asking about taxis and buses. As she slipped an arm into a sleeve the door opened and she saw Cormac.

Her heart leaped; they embraced. 'Thank God, you're still here,' he said. 'Did you get my message?'

Thea shook her head. 'No, nothing.'

'Damn them, I phoned. The train was cancelled. I had to scrounge a lift on the back of a motorbike.'

As they went outside, he put his arm round her waist. 'I was afraid you weren't coming,' she said.

Standing on the dark pavement, he cupped her face in her hands and kissed her. 'Never be afraid of that,' he murmured. 'I'll always find you, one way or another, I'll always be there for you, wherever you are. I'll never let you down. I love you.'

'And I love you too. I love you so much.'

A cool breeze rustled dead leaves in the gutter. Thea closed her eyes and they kissed.

To Sophie's immense joy, Stuart had appeared on her door-step without warning, just as she was dishing out the lodgers' supper, a vegetable pie followed by a mock-apricot flan. The apricots were really carrots and there was potato in the pastry, but the alternative would have been a potato milk pudding and she drew the line at that. Stuart offered to help with serving. Vera said she would do it so that Stuart and Sophie could have the chance to talk, but Stuart insisted.

He was at the sink, washing up, when she came back into the kitchen after giving the lodgers their cups of tea. She sensed his anxiety.

He said, 'I need to talk to you about something, Mum.'

Vera, who had been about to come into the kitchen,

turned on her heel and left, quietly closing the door behind her.

Sophie picked up a tea towel. 'Fire away.'

She saw him draw himself up, as if to guard against blows. 'I'm married, Mum,' he said.

She managed not to drop the glass she was drying. She stared at him. 'Married. You mean, you're engaged to be married?'

'No, Mum. Ruby and I got married on Saturday.'

Ruby? Who on earth was Ruby? She had never heard of a Ruby. Carefully, she put down the glass.

Stuart said quickly, 'I thought I'd better come here and tell you first.'

'Married,' she said again.

'I love her, Mum. She's so beautiful and sweet. I love her so much. We got married in Liverpool, where she lives. It was only us and a couple of people off the street for witnesses.'

'But why?' she cried. 'Why the rush? And why didn't you tell me?' How had some grasping harpy managed to get her claws into her Stuart? The shock of it made her reel. Married.

Stuart looked down at the suds. 'The thing is, Ruby's expecting a baby.'

Sophie sat down at the kitchen table. 'Oh, Stuart,' she said quietly.

'Aren't you pleased about the baby?' he said angrily. 'You were pleased about Rosalind.'

It's not the same at all. She managed to bite the words back. She knew that if she said the wrong thing now she might lose him for ever. Stuart thought he was in love with this girl, this Ruby.

She made a superhuman effort. 'Of course I'm pleased. I adore babies and I'd love another grandchild, Stuart, truly I would. It's just rather sudden. And a lot to take in.'

He drew his dripping hands out of the washing-up water. 'Shall I make us a cup of tea?'

'Yes, please.'

She watched him, her boy, only twenty-one years old, as he filled the kettle and put it on the hob. He had her temperament and her golden-haired and blue-eyed looks, and they had always been so close. She had sometimes pictured the girl he would marry. Someone like her, someone she could talk to. She could have wept.

But she said, 'When's the baby due?'

'In March.'

Which meant, Sophie thought, managing a rough calculation, that this girl – that Stuart's wife – must already be three months gone.

She said, 'Does Duncan know?'

'I phoned him. He said I should come and talk to you in person.'

So at least one of her sons had some sense. Stuart made the tea and put a mug in front of her. Since joining the navy, he had a neat competence with all sorts of tasks. He was not her boy any longer, of course, he was a man, and a man capable of carrying out a hard and dangerous job. But still. Though he had tried to grow a naval beard last Christmas it had been a wispy affair and Duncan had teased him out of it. And he still had the odd teenage spot.

He opened the door to the garden; fresh, summery air wafted into the kitchen. He leaned against the jamb and took out a packet of cigarettes. All Sophie could think of was that he had thrown his future away.

She said, 'How long have you and Ruby known each other?'

'Six months.' Stuart spun the spent match into a flower

pot. 'It's six months since we met, but if you count it up, we've only had nine days together.' He said this as though it was marvellous, even creditable.

'How old is she?'

'Nineteen.'

Nineteen. 'And what do her parents think? She has a family, I assume?'

'Her dad's in the Merchant Navy. Her mum threw her out. She's been sleeping on her sister's sofa.'

While Sophie knew that she should have said, as Stuart wanted her to, the poor thing, something like that, she could not bring herself to do so. Instead, she felt a stab of dislike.

Stuart's face softened. 'I knew she was the one the first time I saw her. You'll love her too, Mum, honestly you will.'

'Yes, I'm sure I will.' She managed that, at least.

He said, awkwardly, anxiously, 'One of the bedrooms is spare at the moment, isn't it, Mum?'

She stared at him. 'Only,' he added quickly, 'Ruby hasn't got anywhere to go. She can't go home. I thought she could come here.'

Good God, so she was expected to put up this girl . . . Sophie cleared her throat. 'Your wife will always be welcome in our home, Stuart.' The word 'wife' felt odd, lumpy and unfamiliar.

For the first time in their conversation, Stuart smiled. 'I'll go and fetch her, then, shall I?'

'Fetch her?' she repeated, at a loss.

'She's waiting at the Blackbird Tea Rooms.' He dashed out of the front door.

Sophie had pictured a conniving little minx, tartily dressed and pleased with herself for ensnaring Stuart, but Ruby wasn't like that at all. She looked even younger than her nineteen years and was small and extremely skinny, and her childish, beaming face lacked any trace of powder or lipstick. She was wearing a cherry-red dress with white cuffs and collar that hung off her narrow frame, and a hat, a squashed brown felt beret that Sophie guessed to be her best, put on to meet her mother-in-law. Beneath the hat, her flat, dark hair turned up at the ends. She made Sophie think of Olive Oyl.

Her first words to Sophie were, 'It's ever so nice to meet you, Mrs Craxton, but I think I'm going to be sick.'

Stuart yanked her off to the downstairs cloakroom. Awful sounds ensued. Stuart came back into the kitchen and said to Sophie, 'She keeps being sick. All the time, Mum.'

'Poor thing.' This time she said it with feeling. 'Some women are, I'm afraid. Put the kettle on again, would you, Stuart?'

Ruby emerged from the cloakroom, white-faced but smiling. 'Ever so sorry, Mrs Craxton.'

'It doesn't matter at all. I'll find you some crackers to nibble and that'll do the trick. Come and sit in the garden. You'll feel better in the fresh air.'

She and Ruby went outside. While Stuart made the tea and Sophie put out deckchairs, Ruby wandered around the garden, exclaiming. 'What a smashing little table! Cor, what a lovely garden! There's real raspberries over here, Mrs Craxton!'

'Sophie. Please call me Sophie. Do sit down, dear. You must be worn out after the journey.'

Ruby sank into a deckchair. 'I thought it was never going to end. I kept having to dash off to the lav. A man gave me his seat. That was ever so kind, wasn't it?'

Stuart came out with the crackers and tea. Ruby fell on a cracker. 'Everything I eat I throw up,' she said, nibbling. 'I don't know how the baby manages to get bigger.'

Not a glimmer of a bump was visible beneath the folds of the cherry-red dress. Stuart sat down beside Ruby. They held hands.

'It's so kind of you to let me stay here, Sophie,' said Ruby. 'I won't be any trouble, I promise. Stuart told me you take in lodgers. I can help with the housework and the cooking. I'm good at that, honestly I am.'

Large dark-brown eyes gazed at Sophie, swimming with tears. Stuart put his arm round Ruby and hugged her. 'It's all right,' he murmured. 'It's going to be all right, isn't it, Mum?'

And she found herself reaching across and patting Ruby's small, bony hand. 'Of course it is. It's going to be fine.'

Her fears receded. That Ruby cared so much about Stuart's happiness, and that he cared equally about Ruby's, melted Sophie's heart. Her imaginary daughter-in-law, the girl she had once pictured Stuart marrying, faded away and was forgotten about.

Ruby's face lit up whenever Stuart came into the room. He was solicitous of her comfort, bringing her cups of tea and finding cushions for her back. Whenever they were together they held hands or wrapped their arms round each other. Stuart liked to scoop her on to his lap, where she rested her head against his shoulder.

They were good together, Sophie could see that. With Ruby, Stuart seemed more sure of himself. He had always been a sensitive and caring boy and perhaps it suited him to have Ruby to worry about. If she was not conventionally beautiful, she had nevertheless an appeal, a charm. You would have to be very hard-hearted to withstand Ruby's warmth and enthusiasm for any length of time. And after all, Sophie reflected, she herself hadn't exactly thought long and hard before marrying Hugh.

After Stuart went back to sea, Sophie took Ruby to the clinic, to be weighed and measured and issued with cod liver oil and orange juice, and to see her doctor, who rather uselessly recommended plain food and weak tea, all of which Ruby vomited up again. Sophie made sure Ruby ate whatever she could face as soon as possible after being sick in the hope that some food might stay down. It may have helped because after a while, Ruby stopped being quite so violently unwell and acquired a small but definite bump.

The house was different with Ruby inside it. Her gratitude to Sophie for having taken her in, and her admiration of both the house and garden, were unending. Unfailingly cheerful, she was a whirlwind of energy. She liked to help round the house, and though Sophie begged her to rest instead, she came to realise that Ruby preferred to be occupied. The second eldest of a family of seven brothers and sisters, she was accustomed to helping in the home and was quick and competent. She whizzed over tiled floors on her hands and knees, sitting back on her haunches to admire her work. 'There, that's brought out the shine in it,' she would say. She peeled potatoes and scraped carrots in record time and her chilly little hands were expert at pastry. After a few weeks, Sophie found it hard to imagine the house without her.

Though she looked fragile, Sophie sensed a toughness in Ruby, the consequence of battles fought at a very young age. 'Me mam just gave up,' she confided in Sophie one day, when they were turning out the larder. 'Seven kids in ten years – can't blame her, really.' A pickle jar was buffed to within an inch of its life. 'Me sister Angie and me used to come home from school and we'd find Mam in bed and our Frank crying in his cot. We used to take turns stopping at home and looking after him. I'm not going to be like that. I'm going to have two kids and that'll be that. Stuart agrees. And we're going to have a nice house with a garden and a cat and a dog. We're going to be a proper family.'

Chapter Seventeen

October 1943–March 1944

In October, Thea travelled to Northumberland to meet Cormac's family. Cormac met her at Hexham station and from there they took another, smaller train out of the town. Through the window, she glimpsed hills, purple with heather or rust-red with bracken, their summits streaked with cloud. Alighting at a tiny branch line station, they waited for a bus. Eventually it arrived and took them to the village of Lawton. Leaving Lawton behind them, they walked hand in hand up a narrow road into an open countryside of steep hills and dark-green valleys.

Their route took them past a large stone house, set back from the road. A crimson slash of Virginia creeper sprawled up its façade, partly curtaining some of the windows. To either side of the building, cypress and box cast gloomy shadows on a lawn that appeared to grow more thistles and ragwort than grass. The courtyard and gravel drive were pocked with yellow puddles; to one side of it lay a heap of bottles and rusty tin cans. The name, 'Langhill House', was incised on a stone plaque to the side of the rusty wrought-iron gates.

'That's the Grevilles' place,' Cormac said. Thea remembered that Cormac had told her that the Greville family owned much of the land in the vicinity of Crawburn, including his uncle and aunt's smallholding.

After Langhill, the road petered out, becoming a furrowed track that continued to climb uphill. Rounding a bend, Thea caught sight of a bicycle rushing down the track towards them. As the wheels rattled and ricocheted on the ruts the dark curls of the young woman rider bounced.

'My sister,' Cormac said. He waved to her and called out, 'Nicola!'

With a screech of brakes the bicycle came to a halt and Nicola Jamieson jumped off. An inch or so taller than Thea, she was slim and wiry and shared her brother's striking dark looks. Her eyes were lighter and greener than Cormac's, a pale aquamarine that stood out against her tanned face.

'You must be Thea,' Nicola said. 'Cormac's told us all about you.' She rolled her eyes, grinning. 'Honestly, *everything*. At length.'

Cormac said mildly, 'Shut up, Nicola.'

His sister threw him a teasing look. 'I've been expecting a mixture of the Mona Lisa and Marie Curie. Brains *and* beauty.'

'Don't take any notice of her, Thea. How's things?'

'All right.' His sister added, 'Dad's in a right mood.'

'Any particular reason?'

Nicola shrugged and began to push her bicycle back up the track. 'We had another letter from the Ministry of Agriculture telling us we should be growing wheat on Whin Fell. I've told them nothing but furze and grass will grow there. If they send that nosey-parker woman round again, Dad'll blow his top.'

'How's his cough?'

'Better. He's all right, Cormac. Can't do as much as he used to and gets het up about it, that's all. You know what's he's like.'

'How's the farm? Are you managing?'

'Of course I am,' Nicola said touchily. 'I get on fine when no one's bothering me.' Then, her features softening a little, she said, 'I'm glad you're home. Maybe it'll take Dad's mind off griping at me, the miserable old beggar.'

'It's good to be back.' Cormac squeezed Thea's hand. 'Look, there's Crawburn.'

Above them, high on a hillside, a whitewashed farmhouse was tucked into the slope of the land, like a book neatly fitting on to a shelf. A gable stood to one end of the building and a jumble of outhouses and barns to the other. Several grey slate roofs, of differing heights, were punctuated by tall white chimney pots. Black-framed mullioned windows looked down on to a higgledy-piggledy garden made up of a series of terraces, linked by narrow cinder paths and stone steps. On one of the lower terraces a rambling rose scrambled over an apple tree. Higher up, beside a stone bench, terracotta pots contained the last of the summer's scarlet geraniums.

'It's beautiful,' said Thea. And it was. Coming here after months of living in army camps, she felt as if she could breathe again. Here, she could remember who she was. Gunner Thea Margaret Craxton was able to take a step or two back.

'The garden was Mum's,' Cormac told her. 'Nicola keeps it going.'

'Dad's a slash-and-burn merchant when it comes to gardening.' Nicola propped her bicycle against the wall of an outhouse. 'I don't let him near it. The Min of Ag woman told me I should use the terraces for peas and beans. I told her what she could do with herself.'

The front door opened and two black-and-white border collies bounded across the flagstones to Cormac. Then a man came out of the house.

'Hello, Dad.' Cormac raised a hand to greet his father.

Robert Jamieson was tall and thickset. His blue eyes were sharp and enquiring and peered out from beneath a mane of shaggy grey hair. He gave Cormac a nod, then turned to Thea.

'Welcome to Crawburn, lass.'

Pleasantries were exchanged, then Robert Jamieson addressed his son. 'Your Uncle John and Aunt Cathy are here. They invited themselves to supper so that they could see you.'

'They're not here to see Cormac, Dad.' Nicola gave Thea a sly look. 'Everyone wants to see the girl our Cormac's fallen for at last.'

Cormac glared at her. Nicola said something about making sure the supper wasn't burned and dashed off. Robert Jamieson asked after Thea's journey and she said that it had been fine. Cormac and his father talked about the farm as they went into the house.

The kitchen was a big room with a settled, mellow air. The floor was tiled in grey slate, hollowed by years of foot-fall. The low ceiling was supported by large black beams and the depth of the windows revealed that the farmhouse walls were more than a foot thick. Iron teapots and pans hung on hooks suspended from the ceiling and the kitchen was dominated by a vast fireplace containing an old-fashioned black kitchen range on which Nicola was cooking supper. Rows of blue-and-white Delft pottery were arranged on the enormous farmhouse dresser and a tall glass-fronted cupboard contained copper flagons and earthenware jugs. On the big, circular black table there stood six lovely old glass goblets the colour of cranberries.

The tick of the grandfather clock in one corner of the room was almost inaudible beneath the scraping of pots and pans and the Jamiesons' chatter. While the introductions were made, Nicola crouched at the range, stirring the contents of a stew pot and calling out orders to Cormac, who was laying the table.

Uncle John was thinner than his elder brother, Cormac's father, but he had the Jamieson colouring and features. His wife, Aunt Cathy, was a small, lean woman with a face as red and seamed as a withered apple. Questions were fired at Thea. Where did her family come from? What did she think of Northumberland? Had she visited the county before? Where was she stationed? Which regiment was she in and what was a kine-theodolite and how long had it taken her to learn to use one?

'Told you Cormac's girl was brainy,' Nicola said, stabbing a knife into a potato.

More questions, this time about London and the Blitz and Rowan. Then Aunt Cathy said, 'Where did you two meet?'

'In France,' said Cormac. 'In nineteen forty.' He placed spoons on the table. 'I wouldn't have made it back home without Thea.'

'Oh, rot.' Thea blushed. 'That's not true. You kept *me* going. It was that way round.'

'Not so. If it hadn't been for you, I probably wouldn't have come to until some German soldier had prodded me. I'd be in a prison camp now.'

Nicola, who was counting out plates, interrupted another barrage of questions. 'You should show Thea her room, Cormac. Supper's nearly ready and I daresay she'd like the chance to sort herself out.'

Cormac took her kitbag and Thea followed him through the house. Crawburn's rooms led off from each other without corridors between them. The floors were on varying levels, as were the ceilings. Now and then, Cormac ducked to avoid banging his head on a doorframe, a movement so fluid Thea guessed he didn't have to think about it any more.

'People added a room or two on to the house whenever they felt like it,' he told her. 'So some parts of the house are a couple of hundred years old and others are fairly recent. Back in the seventeenth century, when they first built the place, they'd have kept farm animals downstairs where the kitchen is now.'

They went up a narrow, winding staircase to the upper floor. As Cormac showed her into a bedroom, he gave her an apologetic smile. 'Sorry about the grilling.'

'You're very lucky, having a proper family.'

They kissed, and she ran the pad of her thumb over the back of his neck, rubbing the springy little curls. She would have liked to have stayed there for ever with him, enclosed in his arms in the quiet space, but from below, someone shouted his name.

'Got to go,' he said, grimacing. 'One day, I promise you, love, it'll be just you and me.' He kissed her again. 'Supper will be ten minutes or so. If you can't find your way back to the kitchen, listen out for where all the noise is coming from.'

As Thea took a frock out of her bag and shook out the creases, she thought about the Jamiesons. She had liked them very much, especially Nicola, and any nervousness she had felt, going to meet Cormac's family for the first time, had been dispelled. She had noticed that they were not a hugging family. Both she and Cormac had been greeted by his father, uncle and aunt with shakes of the hand. Nicola had welcomed the brother she hadn't seen for many months with a pat on his arm. But beneath the teasing and joking Thea had recognised true affection and warmth.

As she washed and changed, she took stock of the room. The bedroom was small and charming and looked out over the front garden. The window was at a drunken angle – in fact, the entire room and its contents appeared to lie at a slant. Two legs of the bed had been propped up on blocks of wood, presumably to prevent the sleeper rolling out, and the floor sloped down to a large alcove containing a chest of drawers, a washstand and jug of water, soap and a towel. Someone – Nicola, Thea guessed – had put jam-jars of flowers by the washstand and on the drawers.

Thea felt the history that was soaked into the fabric of the house. It was there in the faded, sprigged, quilted cotton bedspread and the frayed rag rug and in the worn, graceful objects she had glimpsed in the kitchen cupboards, which must have been treasured and used for generations.

She washed and changed and went downstairs. Supper was lamb stew and mashed potatoes followed by an apple pie. To begin with the talk was of the farm. Robert Jamieson went red in the face as he told Cormac about the rulings imposed by the Ministry of Agriculture in their drive to increase farm yields so that the nation could become self-sufficient in wartime. Other squabbles went on, Uncle John disputing his brother's use of a field, Nicola and her aunt falling into a disagreement over whether or not apples should be parboiled before they were put in a pie.

'Anyway, it's delicious,' Thea said, but she wasn't sure whether anyone had heard her.

Then Cormac's father said, 'Sounds as though old Greville isn't long for this world.'

Cormac looked up. 'Charles Greville is ill?'

'Dying, they say. The doctor's calling at Langhill every day.'

Nicola passed round a jug of custard. 'Marian Kerr told me that Mrs Greville's sent for Rufus.'

'Rufus is in the army, isn't he?'

'He's stationed on Salisbury Plain, like you, Cormac.' Nicola put the pie dish on the counter and sat down. 'Perhaps you'll run into each other one day.' She smirked.

Cormac explained to Thea, 'Rufus is Charles Greville's son. He's a few years older than me. You remember Langhill, it was the house we walked by earlier on.'

'Rufus is married now,' said Aunt Cathy. 'A London lass. When did they marry, John?'

'How should I know?' John Jamieson said, uninterested.

'Five or six months ago,' said Nicola. 'She's called Madeline. She has yellow hair and big blue eyes and looks like a puff of wind would blow her away.'

'No sign of a baby yet,' said Aunt Cathy.

'Give them a chance,' Uncle John muttered.

Aunt Cathy pursed her lips. 'She didn't give me the time of day when I saw her in the village.'

'Maybe she didn't know who you were.'

'Everyone knows who I am. Thinks herself Lady Muck, that one.' Aunt Cathy helped herself to custard. 'Rumour is the Grevilles had hardly a penny left to their name and that's why Rufus married the lass. She brought money to the marriage.'

'Charles Greville never could pass on a bet on the horses,' John agreed.

'They've let that house go to rack and ruin.'

'The road's in a poor state,' said Cormac.

Robert scowled. 'I wrote to Greville about it but I've not had a word back.'

'If he's ill, Dad—'

'*She* could have had the courtesy to reply, couldn't she?'

Cormac, in a blatant attempt to change the subject, asked after his cousins, Francis and Jack, John and Cathy's twin sons, and the conversation moved on. Light streamed through the window-panes, making shimmering squares on the slate floor.

When supper was over, Thea offered to wash up. Cormac and Aunt Cathy offered to help as well but Nicola told them she would rather have Thea.

'Aunt Cathy always tells me I'm doing it wrong,' she explained to Thea when the others had gone off to sit in the snug. 'And Cormac will stop Dad and Uncle John picking a fight with each other.'

While Thea washed up, Nicola made a big pot of tea and carried it through to the snug for the others. When she returned, she shut the door behind her.

'Ciggie, Thea?'

'No thanks.'

'Tea, then.' Nicola refilled the kettle and put it on the range. She lit a cigarette and gave a sigh of relief as she propped herself against the door, smoking. She said, 'Well done. You've survived so far. You mustn't mind me. Dad tells me I open my gob and a load of rubbish comes out.'

'It must be hard work, running this place.'

'It's never-ending. Dad can't do so much on the farm now and it puts him in a bad mood. Not that he was ever any help in the house. Before the war, a girl I used to go to school with used to come up and give me a hand but then she went down south to work in a factory. She'll earn twice as much as we could pay her here.' Nicola propped her cigarette on a saucer and began to dry the glasses, polishing them with brisk efficiency. 'It's the winters that are hard, when the snow cuts us off. Mind you, I could never live anywhere else.' She put the glasses in the cupboard, then said stiffly, 'Thank you for looking after Cormac in France.'

'Honestly, I meant it, I didn't really do anything.'

'Cormac doesn't make things up. If he says you helped him, then you helped him. It would have killed Dad if he'd ended up stuck in a prison camp for years on end.' Nicola sorted cutlery into a drawer. 'Is your room all right?'

'It's lovely.' Thea smiled. 'Heaven after sleeping in a Nissen hut. Did you put the flowers in the room?'

'Aye.'

'They're so pretty. Thank you. It's good to meet you all at last. Cormac's told me so much about you.'

'He's madly in love with you, Thea.'

'And I love him very much.'

'Good.' Nicola's expression was fierce. 'Because I'd have killed you if I'd thought you were messing him around. Cormac's always looked out for me. Don't bother with that pan, Thea, we'll leave it to soak. Let's take our tea outside. It's warm enough for you, isn't it? I can't face sitting with those old gas-bags. Let Aunt Cathy poke her nose into Cormac's business for a change.'

They put on their coats and took their mugs of tea out to the uppermost terrace. Nicola sat down with a sigh on the stone bench.

'It's nice to have another girl to talk to,' she said. 'There

314

are too many men in this family. I think Dad forgets I'm a girl half the time.'

'Do you have friends nearby?'

'One or two.' Nicola looked down over the terraces. 'Not so many now. A lot of them have gone away to join the Services or to work in a factory. And anyway, what with the farm and Dad I haven't time for friends.'

'What about a boyfriend?'

Nicola snorted. 'Look at me.' She waved a hand at her fawn breeches and old plaid shirt. 'I hardly look like a girl any more. Why would any boy bother with me?' She gave a half-smile. 'Last time I saw Madeline Greville in Lawton, she was wearing a white lace dress and a pink hat. White lace! What use would a white lace dress be to me? I'd mess it up, feeding the pigs or mucking out the stables.' Then, lighting another cigarette, she said, 'A couple of years ago, there was this idiot, Lennie, who used to keep on at me to go to the pictures with him.'

'Did you go?'

'Once or twice. His family's from down in the valley. Lennie's nice enough. But he's abroad now, in Italy, I think. He'll have forgotten me by the time he comes back, with all those pretty Italian girls.'

Cormac came out of the house and joined them on the terrace. Nicola remembered something to do in the house and scooped up the empty mugs and hurried down the garden.

Cormac put his arm round Thea. 'Okay?'

'Okay.' She kissed him.

'Shall we go for a walk? There's something we need to discuss.'

'Tell me.'

315

'Not yet.'

A gate in the dry-stone wall behind the terrace led to a meadow. Cormac pointed out landmarks: fields and hills and streams and valleys, one of which contained Bane Rigg, where John and Cathy Jamieson lived. The woodland that spread along the hillside was called Low Chase. They took the path that led through the trees. It was a magical place where dappled light spilled between pale-trunked birches, and where the air smelled cold and pungent, of fungi and fallen leaves and damp earth. This part of Northumberland was not much wooded, Cormac told her, but Low Chase had been there for centuries. In spring, wild garlic and wood anemones blossomed on the banks and in the glades. There was rumoured to be the remains of an ancient settlement, hidden among the trees.

'Stone Age or Iron Age,' Cormac said. 'I can't remember which. Your department, Thea. I come here when I need to think. When I was a kid, I knew every single tree in this wood. The Grevilles own Low Chase but we've always used this path to get to Bane Rigg, Uncle John and Aunt Cathy's house.'

They came out of the shadow of the trees. Cormac pointed out Langhill House, below them.

Cormac said, 'So what do you think of Crawburn?'

She smiled at him. 'I love it.'

'Could you see yourself living here?' A change in his tone, an uncertainty in his expression, and he took something from his pocket.

'Marry me, Thea,' he said. 'Will you marry me?'

Thea saw the ring box. He opened it. Inside was an engagement ring, with a small emerald set between chips of diamond.

She didn't hesitate. 'Yes,' she said. 'I will, yes.' They kissed, and her heart seemed about to burst with joy.

They were married six weeks later in a simple register office ceremony. Thea wore a cream silk frock and pink velvet coat that had belonged to Rowan and which Rowan had altered to fit her. Cormac's father and Nicola travelled down from Northumberland and Rowan had a day off from the hospital. Much to Thea's delight, Helen was able to attend the ceremony. She also invited Sophie and Stuart and Ruby. As they came out of the register office, Thea tossed her bouquet of sprigs of winter berries into the air and Rowan caught it neatly.

Rowan lent them her flat for their two-day honeymoon. The first time they made love it was divine. Despite a certain amount of nerves, Thea was soon able to relax in Cormac's gentle embrace and the second time he made love to her it was even better. In fact, it was utterly blissful. As it was the third and fourth time.

On the last morning they walked to Victoria Station. They said their goodbyes on the platform and Cormac saw her on to her train. And then, though she was now Gunner Thea Margaret Jamieson, life went on much as before, with the same complicated arrangements to meet that often fell through at the last moment. The army was supposed to give married couples leave at the same time but it didn't always work out like that.

They had three days at Christmas, when they stayed in a guest house in Surrey near the practice camp where Thea was stationed, and then Cormac went back to his regiment. In the new year, Thea began to feel unwell. At first, she thought it was something she'd eaten. Army food was plentiful but poorly cooked and tasteless, bread and spam and cabbage boiled to death. But when she wrote of her illness in a letter to Rowan, Rowan wrote back by return of post. *Thea, is it possible that you're pregnant?* And she thought of their honeymoon, and how they had only left the flat when they had needed to find something to eat, and felt silly for not having thought of it before.

She was having Cormac's baby and that was miraculous and wonderful, but along with excitement and delight, Thea was aware of more than a little trepidation. She and Cormac had nowhere to live. They had no home of their own. She supposed that eventually, when the war was over, they would find somewhere. Meanwhile, she would go back to Rowan's flat.

And though she liked babies, she had little experience of them. She had never been one of those girls who cooed over babies in prams. She remembered the first time she had met Grace Fainlight. Grace had asked her about her domestic situation. *There's no husband and babies?* – as if marriage and children might prevent you from pursuing a career in archaeology. Most married women did not go out to work. She wanted this baby, Cormac's baby, very much, but she had never stopped wanting to be an archaeologist as well. Sometimes it seemed as if her old ambitions had slipped into the background, almost as if all that, the Fainlights and Barbury Hill, had happened to someone else. Thea had always admired the Fainlights' marriage, Grace and Monty's shared interests and purpose, and their support for each other. Grace had both a career and a family. It was possible, she reminded herself, to manage everything.

Pregnancy was the one thing guaranteed to get you thrown out of the A.T.S. She staggered on for a couple of weeks, believing that she was cleverly disguising her sickness, and then one morning her commanding officer took her aside and demanded bluntly to know whether she was expecting a baby. Two days later Thea found herself in civvies again, thumbing a lift in an army lorry back to London, and Rowan's flat.

Though the air raids on London had continued throughout the war, they became far more frequent and severe in the 'little Blitz' of the cold early months of 1944. In February, Rowan and Josh borrowed a cottage from a friend of his called Diana Clare. Hidden in a clump of Hampshire woodland on the brow of a shallow hill, it was accessed by a quarter of a mile of muddy track leading off from a country lane. 'Good grief,' muttered Josh, as his sports car bounced and rattled on the frozen ruts. 'My tyres.'

Rowan unlocked the front door while Josh unloaded their cases from the boot. The small single-storey building was made of a patchwork of materials, as if the maker had used whatever came to hand: brick and wood and chalk and even a couple of metal advertising panels, one for Bisto and the other for Champion spark plugs, hammered on to provide protection against the weather. Inside, there were four rooms, none of which was a bathroom. A tin bath hung on a peg on the kitchen wall, and after some exploration Rowan discovered an ice-cold shack containing an earth closet behind the house. Children's toys were stacked in a corner of the sitting room and there were two cots in one of the bedrooms and small sheets and blankets draped over a clothes horse. Mrs Clare had left an explanatory note on the table. *The water comes from a well in the garden. Sometimes it freezes up but I put boiling water down it and that usually does the trick so you should always keep a couple of buckets spare, just in case. There are logs in the shed at the back. If you could replace whatever you use that would be marvellous as I need to keep the rooms warm for the babies.*

Josh drew water from the well while Rowan lit fires in the sitting-room grate and kitchen stove. He carried a bucket of water into the kitchen. She was standing at the sink, peeling potatoes.

'You'll get your beautiful coat grubby,' he said.

She was still wearing her cream cashmere, bought in Paris in better days. 'But I will freeze to death without it,' she pointed out. 'I should have brought my nurse's cape with me. Are you hungry?'

'Starving,' he murmured. 'Absolutely ravenous.' He threaded his hands beneath the cashmere coat and brushed his mouth against hers. Desire flared inside her. But when, having put the potatoes on to boil, she went into the sitting room, she found him asleep on the sofa.

He had turned up at her flat the previous day with no warning. There was never any warning. It had been a stroke of immense good fortune that for once her week's leave had coincided with his. She sat down beside him. She liked watching him sleep, liked seeing the rise and fall of his breath and the expressions that flickered across his face. She ran her fingertips over his brow, trying to smooth away the worry lines, and his eyes flickered open.

'Hello, Josh,' she said gently.

'It's you,' he murmured. 'I'm so glad it's you.' He took her in his arms and ruffled her hair. And then he fell asleep again.

He slept through most of the first day. Now and then he would wake and apologise for being a bore and suggest they go a walk, but by the time Rowan put on her coat he would have fallen asleep again. She didn't mind. It was enough that he was there and that he was safe. She cooked some dishes and he woke up and ate them and then went back to sleep.

Rowan put on her coat, hat and scarf and went outside and wandered round the copse, her boots crunching on the dead leaves, each one rimed with a white frill of frost. The air was still and icy and the ploughed fields that surrounded the house were pale and frozen. Mostly there was silence in this, the dark heart of the winter, but once she watched as a convoy of army lorries trundled through the narrow Hampshire lanes. And now and then a formation of planes flew through the skies, heading, she assumed, for the Channel. When she became too cold, she went back into the house and stacked up the fire and read one of Diana Clare's historical romance novels.

The next day Josh woke up properly, so they put on their coats and boots and walked down the rutted track. From the other side of the road a long carriage drive, bordered with horse chestnuts, led into parkland. Ahead of them, an elegant Palladian house was fenced off with barbed wire. A soldier approached them, but when Josh showed his identity card the man saluted and allowed them to continue walking.

She said, 'Was it awful?' and Josh said, 'Yes, pretty awful, this time.' He didn't look at her, but scuffed the dead beech leaves with his boots. When she began to speak again, he interrupted her.

'Let's not talk about it. I don't want you to know the things that I've seen. I'd rather forget about them. I'd like to keep you separate from all that.'

So she didn't ask him any more. There were hollows under his cheekbones and in the shrinking winter light his eyes looked grey. She rested her head against his upper arm and they walked on.

321

They returned to the cottage. Rowan cooked supper while Josh went to the shed at the back of the house to cut wood for the fires. She heard the repetitive hack of the axe, over and over again, as if he was getting something out of his system.

After supper, they went to bed. Apart from anything else, it was the only place in the house where one could be warm. He made love to her with great care and solicitude and afterwards she lay beside him, perfectly and blissfully content. They must have both drifted off to sleep at much the same time. Her sleep was deep and dreamless, the sort of sleep she used to have before the war, before she had become a nurse, but Josh moved and cried out and once he sobbed. She stroked his face, kissing and soothing him back to sleep.

The next morning, they drove to a nearby village. She wondered where he had got the petrol from. And where he had obtained the hamper of food and wine they had brought with them to the cottage. And in what nightmarish place he had spent the last three months of his life.

They bought milk and bread and then mooched about, searching through a junk shop, hooting with laughter at their finds. Josh bought a set of brass fire dogs and an old leather briefcase with a ripped handle that he planned to repair. And for her, a necklace of artificial pearls. She put it on and admired her reflection in a flyblown mirror.

Inside the village church, they found a tomb bearing the effigy of an Elizabethan lord and lady. Beside them, like miniature versions of their parents, their seven children were lined up.

'Peas in a pod,' said Rowan.

Josh said, 'Shall we have seven children?'

'Eight, maybe. Even numbers are better. And then, when we die, we'll have one of these splendid tombs.' Then she said, 'I never got pregnant when I was married to Patrick. That sort of thing was never much good between us, but I think perhaps I can't have children.'

'I wouldn't mind,' he said. 'No children or eight children, it doesn't matter. It's you I love, Rowan.'

They linked hands and went outside. They had lunch in a pub. Later, back in the car, he spoke to her before he started up the engine.

'Rowan, what I do . . .' He was frowning. 'It puts everything on hold. There are things I'd like to say to you, things I'd like to ask you, but I can't, not while I'm living like this. It wouldn't be fair to you. But I worry that this isn't fair either.'

She pressed his hand. 'Darling, I understand perfectly. And you must never worry about me. Keep safe for me, that's all I ask.'

Rowan cooked supper at the cottage. Afterwards, they sat by the fire, reading. To feel so perfectly in tune with a man, to be able to sit in companionable silence, interrupted only by the crackle of flames and the turn of a page was a delight to her. She knew her faults, her restlessness and her need to fill a quiet moment with talk or busyness, but with Josh none of that seemed to matter. She liked to look at him; often he would seem to feel her gaze on him and he would glance up at her and smile.

The next day, the temperature lifted a few degrees. The cold no longer stung her face when she went outside. In the morning, they walked in the parkland again, talking about their families and the places they had been. They didn't mention the future.

They went back to the cottage. After lunch, Josh went outside to cut more wood. Rowan was washing up when she heard the sound of a motor engine. She walked to the edge of the trees and looked down the slope. A large black car was heading up the track. Despair washed over her. It might not be that, she told herself. It might be the landlord collecting his rent or a delivery vehicle. From behind the house she heard the relentless beat of the axe.

The car stopped at the top of the track and two men got out. One was in army uniform, the other in mufti, wearing a grey overcoat and homburg.

Grey Overcoat mopped his forehead with a handkerchief. 'Bloody boneshaker,' he said, with a scowl. 'Bloody countryside.' Then, as Rowan came towards them, 'Mrs Scott? We're here for Captain Makepeace.' He tapped his foot impatiently and took out a cigarette case.

It's too soon, you can't have him, he's too tired, can't you see?

The man in military uniform gave her an apologetic smile. 'I'm so sorry, Mrs Scott. My name's Major Drummond. We wouldn't trouble you but I'm afraid it's urgent.'

She asked them to wait by the car. She wrapped her arms round herself as she made for the back of the house. She did not call Josh straight away but stood for a moment in the trees, looking at him. He was stacking up logs. She knew so well his tall, well-made form, his hair the tawny brown of the beech leaves, and his stance, which on first sight seemed relaxed but always had a contained energy. She wanted to scream.

'Josh?' she said softly, and he looked round and saw her.

'What is it?'

'Some men . . .' she said. 'A Major Drummond and someone else . . .' She broke off, biting her lip, and looked down.

324

He held her as she cried. After a while, she managed to force the tears back. He brushed the trail of her tears with a fingertip, then they kissed and they said their farewells in private. They walked back to the front of the house. Greetings and handshakes; Josh went into the cottage and in what seemed to Rowan no time at all emerged carrying a bag of his things.

'Charles will drive you back to London in the Morgan, darling,' he said to her before he got into the black car.

Major Drummond said, 'Shall I give you an hour to get ready, Mrs Scott?' and Rowan said, 'No, it's all right, ten minutes will do.'

She watched the black car shrink as it headed down the slope. Then she went into the cottage to pack.

Major Drummond drove Rowan back to London. She heard nothing from Josh, but then she never expected to. At the hospital, she was on days, on a Women's Medical ward, though sometimes, when there was a bad raid, she worked into the night as well.

In the middle of March, she was coming off duty, chatting to a staff nurse called Florence who worked on paediatrics, as they made their way through St Anne's corridors. Florence, a good mimic, was imitating the pomposities of one of the senior registrars. When they rounded the corner and saw the same registrar coming towards them they both collapsed into fits of giggles.

They were still laughing when they reached the out-patients' hall. Rowan caught sight of Josh's friend, Alex Moore, heading towards them.

She waved to him. 'Hello, Alex! Not ill, are you?'

'Not at all.'

She was about to introduce him to Florence when she

took in the expression on his face. Her smile faded and her heart made an odd sinking motion that left her breathless.

He said, 'Rowan, is there somewhere we can talk in private?'

And she knew. Shock ran through her. The moment she had dreaded since she had fallen in love with Josh Makepeace had come. And it was unbearable and wrong.

She said, 'It's Josh, isn't it? Tell me, Alex!'

'I'm so sorry, Rowan,' he said gently. 'But I'm afraid he's been reported missing.'

Chapter Eighteen

March–July 1944

Sophie, Ruby and Viola were in Sophie's sitting room, knitting blanket squares. 'I had an awful quarrel with Doug on his last day's leave,' Viola told them. 'He deliberately put the entire butter ration on his toast just to spite me.'

Sophie asked, 'How's Arnold?' Viola's lover, Arnold, had been bombed out of his Bermondsey rooms two weeks ago. 'Is he still living in the workshop?'

Viola bit off a length of wool. 'He washes in a bucket and shares a lavatory with the shop below. He never complains about it. I should hate it. I'd leave Doug if I had anywhere to go.'

'You're always welcome here.'

This was a conversation they had had many times before. Though Viola complained about Doug, Sophie suspected she felt obliged to stay with him until the war was over.

Ruby yelped and dropped her knitting. 'Going to the lav,' she said, and hurried, as far as she was able to, out of the room.

Viola looked at Sophie. 'Poor thing, she looks like a ripe seed pod, about to explode.'

'I'd better make sure she's all right.'

Sophie went out into the hall and sat down on the bottom stair. A great wave of heat flooded through her, scorching her face, and she pulled off her cardigan and flapped at her blouse. There was no doubt about it, she was going through the change of life. It seemed another thing to add to the currently endless list of life's inconveniences and exasperations, like not having enough soap or toothpaste and one's stockings being all darns and being short of hot water because there was hardly any coal to be had.

When Ruby did not emerge, she tapped on the lavatory door and called out, 'Ruby, love, are you all right?'

The door opened and Ruby came out, clutching a pair of knickers. 'I think me waters have broken.'

Viola phoned for an ambulance while Sophie helped Ruby change into clean clothes. Then she fetched Ruby's case, packed with her things. At the hospital, the nursing staff told Sophie not to wait, that it would be many hours before the baby was born, days perhaps, but Sophie told them she was going to wait anyway. Along with hot flushes the menopause had brought with it obstinacy and rage.

She was glad she had ignored the nurses because Ruby's son was born at two in the morning, after six hours of labour. More pig-headedness earned Sophie a few moments with Ruby and her new grandson outside visiting hours.

Ruby lay in bed, her face much the same hue as the pillowcase. A little grub of a newborn baby, swaddled in white, was in the cot beside her.

'Ruby, he's so beautiful.' Sophie patted her hand. 'So clever of you. How are you, darling?'

'I feel like me insides have been pulled out,' Ruby croaked. 'He's called Kenneth. He's a cracker, isn't he?'

And he was. Gently, Sophie stroked the small downy head with a fingertip. Kenneth's tiny red mouth pouted and pursed, searching for milk. An eye opened, dark and dazed by the journey he had undertaken. And the world seemed to stand still, war and loss and deceit forgotten, existence narrowing to an exhausted mother and a newborn baby in a small white room.

Sophie had a new lodger, a man called Ed Willoughby. His slight limp became more pronounced as he climbed the stairs after her when she showed him the vacant room. She heard the irregular da-dum, da-dum of his footsteps as he followed her along the landing.

Ed was a big bear of a man, in his fifties, Sophie guessed. He had kind brown eyes, tousled brown hair, silvering at the temples, and a gentle smile. You could not have said he was handsome but there was something pleasant about his features. He was always a little untidy, a little rumpled. His clothes were good but old – but then everyone's clothes were old now. He was a quiet man, but neither shy nor unfriendly. She had warned him that there was a young baby, her grandson, in the house, who woke at night, but Ed assured her that he liked babies and could sleep through anything. He was out most of the time anyway, working at a government research establishment, but once, when Kenneth was colicky in the evening and Ed was at home, he propped the baby against his shoulder and paced round the sitting room. Kenneth seemed to get the message because, with untypical obedience, he fell asleep.

At three months old Kenneth was a big, hungry baby. He grew bigger while Ruby became skinnier. Plump, blond and blue-eyed, he was indisputably the most important person in the household. Everyone in Gilbert Street adored him and admired his every new feat. When he was hard to settle, they passed him round, taking turns to try to soothe him.

In the afternoons, if the weather was fine, while Ruby was having a nap, Sophie put Kenneth on a blanket in the garden beneath the old pear tree. She sat beside him, doing the vegetables for the lodgers' supper or writing letters while he tried to roll over, failed because he was too fat, and then tried again, gurgling at her, pleased with himself. Often, the carrots were not scraped and the letters went unwritten because she was too distracted by her grandson's beauty.

Sophie took Kenneth out in the big old navy Silver Cross pram that had once been Duncan and Stuart's. He liked to watch the shafts of sunlight through the bobbing fringes on the canopy. That spring, there was a strange atmosphere in London. The return of heavy air raids had set them all on edge, reminding them of the early, dark days of the war. In the late afternoons, women and children and older people were once again queuing for shelter in the underground stations. The city was full of rumours: that the Second Front was imminent, that an army of unimaginable size was marshalling in southern England to take the war back to France, that swathes of southern and eastern England had been fenced off for the sole use of the military. Foreign soldiers, a great many of them American GI's, filled up the tables in the cafés and sprawled on the benches in the parks. Army lorries squeezed through narrow streets and alleyways, and in the countryside troops were constantly on the move, taking part in practice manoeuvres.

All this lent a poignancy to the fine spring weather. The flowers in Kensington Gardens seemed to Sophie more vividly coloured this year, and the sky a deeper, more shimmering blue. Something extraordinary was about to take place and no matter how hard she tried to distract herself from it her mind would keep flipping back to the future that was rushing towards them. She, who had lost a brother in an earlier war, kept her fearful thoughts to herself. What if it went wrong? What if the Allied Forces were repelled on the beaches of France? How would they bear the loss of life and the knowledge that the war must go on and on and on?

During the Great War, when she had been working as a Voluntary Aid Detachment, Sophie had taken her convalescing officers to Kensington Gardens. She had pushed them along these paths in wheelchairs or escorted them as they had learned to walk on crutches. She had helped them to a bench when they were too tired to go any further. Young men, ruined men, men whose lives would never be the same again. She thought of Duncan and Stuart and dread ran through her and she pushed the pram faster.

She should have been knitting, Thea supposed, but she needed to do something that occupied her mind, and so, as her pregnancy progressed in that exceptionally fine May of 1944, she often wandered off to sit in Green Park, taking some of her old archaeology books for company.

Her thoughts drifted. To Rowan, who had heard nothing more of Josh. Thea shopped for food and cooked their dinners, mended Rowan's stockings for her, tried to keep the flat civilised when Rowan's friends were staying there, and listened night after night while Rowan talked about Josh. Anything to make it easier for her sister. And yet she was afraid that nothing made it easier. *I'm not going to fall apart*, Rowan had said to her, sitting on the sofa and trembling with shock that first night, after Alex Moore had told her that Josh was missing. *When he comes home, he'll need me to be strong.* Thea knew that Rowan hoped that Josh was in hiding somewhere in France. It was a desperate, yearning hope, and she suspected that Rowan believed that if she wanted it powerfully enough then it would come true. If the Second Front liberated France then Josh would be found safe and well and they would be happy again: Rowan hadn't said all this but Thea knew it was what she was praying for.

And then there was Cormac. The glorious weather continued, heat settling in a soft blanket over London. Towards the end of May, he phoned her to tell her that he had a few hours' leave. She met him at Waterloo Station. Hundreds of other soldiers were spilling off the trains. This was their embarkation leave, Cormac told her as they left the station, and in spite of the warm day Thea felt cold with fear.

The restaurants and pubs were crowded with men in uniform saying goodbye to their wives and sweethearts. Sitting in a small, dusty park, the only place they could find some privacy, Thea took Cormac's hand and placed it on her belly. 'Feel that,' she said. Her baby's movements had seemed a slight thing to her at first, like a minnow twisting its tail, but over the past weeks they had grown stronger.

He smiled, then said, 'Go to Crawburn to have the baby, Thea, please. You'll both be safe there.'

She shook her head. 'I can't. I have to stay with Rowan.'

He took her hands in his. 'I don't know how long I'll be away. It could be months, it could be a year. I'd feel happier if you were at Crawburn. Nicola and Dad want you to go there.'

She kissed him. 'I can't leave Rowan, not now, not after Josh. You understand, don't you?'

It was the nearest they had come to quarrelling, and she

hated that. Not long afterwards they had to say their farewells. Cormac leaned out of the carriage window to wave to her and she watched from the platform until the train vanished out of sight. She remained there long after it had gone, long after the other women on the platform had hurried past her.

She had one more letter from him and then, silence. The armies were enclosed in their marshalling areas, cut off from their wives and families. The trains stopped running; where, only a few days earlier, the big London stations had been crowded, they were now echoing and quiet. On 5th June came the news that Rome had fallen to the Allies. The next morning's bulletin told the British people that paratroopers had landed in France. Throughout the day, in shops and in cafés, wirelesses were switched on permanently. Wherever you went, rooms fell silent during the B.B.C. news bulletins. As the morning and afternoon wore on, news announcers told of the landing of thousands of Allied troops on the French coast between Le Havre and Cherbourg.

There was relief that it had begun at last and apprehension as to what it might mean. Thea thought of Cormac, shut up in a ship with hundreds of other soldiers, crossing the Channel, soon to be debouched on to a French beach. The B.B.C. announced that relatives would receive a card from the troops who had gone to France on D-Day. Thea waited. She couldn't concentrate on the archaeology books any more and her stitches slipped off the knitting needle.

That cold, cloudy, dismal June, London had been under assault from a new weapon, the V-1 rocket missile. Their nerves were now doubly frazzled, by daily news of the battles in Europe and Russia and by the ominous buzzing of the rockets that plunged into London, day and night.

Sophie came back to Gilbert Street one day to find Ed Willoughby in the kitchen, fixing a chair that he had upended on the floor.

'I hope you don't mind,' he said. 'I found some tools in the cupboard under the stairs.'

'It's wobbled for about three years so I don't mind at all.'

'There.' He set the chair on its feet and gave it a rock and it remained firm and steady. Sophie thanked him. Ed asked her whether she would like him to have a look at the china cupboard. It was in the style of a French armoire and hadn't been the same since Duncan and Stuart, play-fighting one day when they should have been old enough to know better, had knocked it over.

'I'd be delighted,' she said.

They emptied out the plates and bowls and Ed carried it outside and laid it on the terrace. She noticed how easily he lifted the big old cupboard, as if it weighed nothing at all. Sophie unpacked her shopping, then made him tea and a sandwich and took out a tray to him.

'Goodness,' she said. 'It isn't squint any more.'

He stood back. 'That's better, I think.'

'Do you do this sort of thing for a living?'

'I used to, before the war.' He thanked her for the tea. 'I had a workshop. I used to renovate furniture and make new pieces from old wood and special items for commission. If you had some paint, I could smarten this up.'

'I've only bits in the bottom of tins.'

'That's all right. I can do something with that.'

'I wouldn't want to impose on you, Ed.'

'It wouldn't be an imposition.' He ran a hand down the cupboard. 'I'd enjoy it.'

334

She sat down at the wrought-iron table. 'What do you do now?'

'Camouflage,' he said. 'I make things look like something else. It's not so different to what I used to do. They wouldn't have me in the Forces because of this.' He tapped his leg.

'What happened?'

'I was shot. In nineteen eighteen.' He gave a dry smile. 'It was the last week of the war, it was all almost over and I managed to get a couple of bullets in the thigh.'

'My husband, Hugh, was wounded in the arm at the Battle of Picardy.'

'Did he make a good recovery?'

'His arm healed, more or less.' She considered. 'If that's what you meant. I've wondered if it changed him. I've wondered if he was a different person before the war.'

'Oh,' he said gently, 'I think we were all different people before the war.'

Somehow, from a few unpromising odds and ends of paint, Ed worked a miracle. The cupboard, which had been a bruised brown, became pale blue and cream with garlands of roses and honeysuckle above the arches of the doors. A fat bee bumbled into a trumpet of honeysuckle. It awed Sophie that a big man like Ed could produce such delicate work.

'Oh, Ed,' she said, when he carried it into the kitchen and put it in place.

'Ever so pretty,' Ruby said admiringly. She had Kenneth tucked under an arm and was counting out cutlery.

'It was a pleasure.' He left the room.

Ruby raised her eyebrows at Sophie. 'He likes you,' she hissed.

'Oh, nonsense,' said Sophie, embarrassed. 'He's just trying to help.'

Ruby took out spoons. 'He likes you.'

A couple of days later, Ed asked her if she would like to go out for a drink.

Sophie's first instinct was to politely refuse. But he said, 'Just one. Half an hour. I know you're busy,' and she thought of the chair and the cupboard. It had been a long time since she had she been out.

Sophie changed into a frock and brushed her hair. She had no lipstick left but scrubbed out the corners of her powder compact to dull the shine on her face. A few last drops of *Je Reviens*, squeezed from the bottle, and she looked at her reflection in the mirror. Her hair needed a wash and she had freckles on her nose. *Oh well.*

They went to a nearby pub. Ed found a table and went off to buy beers. They talked about their families; Sophie told him about Stuart and about Duncan and Sally and Rosalind in Lincolnshire. Ed showed her a photograph of a smiling, curly-haired woman with two little boys, his daughter, Bridget, who lived in Lancashire, and his grandsons, twins called Max and Lewis. His wife, Jenny, had died of cancer eight years before. 'It was hard,' he said. 'You get used to it, don't you, you can be happy again, but something like that, it cuts your life in two.'

He asked her how Hugh had died. Pneumonia, she said, and then found herself telling him everything, about Hugh's other family, his daughter Rowan, who was a nurse, and Thea, who was married and expecting a baby. She even told him about Sigrid, and Sigrid's lover, who had been Thea's father, and he seemed to take it all in and didn't ask her to repeat anything, which she thought rather impressive. She hadn't planned to explain to him all this complicated family history but somehow ended up doing so. Perhaps it was because Ed was so easy to talk to, or perhaps she had at last got Hugh in perspective. All the things she had done since Hugh – the lodgers, the First Aid Post, the W.V.S., dear Kaz and of course her daughters-in-law and grandchildren – had crowded in front of Hugh's betrayal, pushing it into the background.

She said, 'Stuart thinks that Hugh must have had shellshock.'

'He may be right. I suspect we all did, to some extent.'

'He says that Hugh can't have been thinking straight when he married me.'

Ed frowned. 'Sophie, none of us came through the trenches believing in whatever we'd believed in before the war. There were plenty who stopped believing in anything at all. Everyone got through it however they could. I knew men who took shortcuts, who lied and stole. They did whatever they thought would let them stay alive. They felt they'd been cheated and they had no compunction in cheating back.'

On the way home, he asked her what she planned to do after the war.

'I expect I'll go on much as before,' she said. 'My family . . . the lodgers. What about you?'

'I'll start up the business again.'

'Furniture repairs?'

'And house restoration. There'll be a lot of work for me. It makes a difference, don't you think, what colour you paint a room and what furniture you put in it.'

She got used to having Ed round the house. After five years of war it looked distinctly down at heel. But Ed fixed the loose piece of skirting board and did something ingenious that meant the Anderson shelter no longer filled with water when it rained. When a storm brought down the runner beans he held them up while she tied them to the supports. If he came home early enough and the lodgers and Kenneth were settled, they would go for a walk and maybe a drink. Tiredness was ingrained in all of them, all of the time. You were more tired some times than at others, that was true, but you were never not tired. The news bulletins, which prompted terrible fluctuations of hope and despair as the Allies battled their way through Normandy, were tiring enough. And on top of that there was everything else.

Ed told Sophie that he was being sent away from London to work in Southampton. They were clearing up after supper. Vera was washing and Sophie was drying. From the sitting room came the sounds of Ruby, trying to comfort Kenneth, who was howling.

'Oh, Ed,' she said.

Vera said, 'When are you going?'

'The day after tomorrow.'

Sophie put a plate in Ed's cupboard. She always thought of it now as Ed's cupboard. 'We'll miss you,' she said.

'And I'll miss you. Very much.'

'Do you know how long for?'

He shook his head. 'Weeks or months, I don't know. You should let out the room.'

He seemed to be about to say something else, but then Ruby opened the door. 'He feels hot,' she said. 'Do you think he's hot, Sophie? Look at his poor little face, all red.'

The phone rang. Ed said, 'I'll get it, shall I?'

Ruby and Sophie took Kenneth upstairs, to see whether a bath might help. By the time Sophie returned downstairs, Ed had gone out.

*

A few days later, Vera was out at choir and Ruby was settling Kenneth, who, it had turned out, had an ear infection. Ed offered to help Sophie in the kitchen. Washing a plate, she said, 'You've been such a help, Ed.'

'I'm glad.' He was putting baking tins in a high cupboard. He could reach them easily; she had to use the stool. 'I've lost count of the number of places I've stayed in these past few years,' he said. 'Some have been okay and others pretty dire. But there's been nowhere like this.'

'So sweet of you to say so. I always think my lodgers must miss their families dreadfully so I try to make them feel at home.'

'It's you,' he said, shutting the cupboard door. 'I've been happy here because of you, Sophie.'

The doorbell rang and Sophie went to answer it. A W.V.S. friend had brought a little family in tow, a mother, Mrs Wright, and two school-age children, bombed out of their home that afternoon. Could Sophie put them up for the night? This was something she did now and then to help out. She made up makeshift beds in the lodgers' sitting room, cooked the Wrights some supper, and sorted out items for them from a bag of second-hand clothing kept for this purpose. It was past nine by the time she had finished. Sophie made herself a cup of tea and sank into an armchair in her own drawing room. The next thing she knew, she had jerked awake in the darkness, the blackout not yet drawn, the tea still beside her. She drank the cold tea, sitting in the dark, then sorted the blackout and went upstairs to bed. The clock in the hall told her that it was gone eleven. She stared at Ed's door. It seemed to her that they had not finished their conversation. She thought of knocking but decided it was too late. He might be asleep.

The following morning, she was cooking breakfast when Ed came into the room. He had dressed smartly, in a suit and tie, though, she thought fondly, he still managed to look dishevelled.

He said, 'I wanted to thank you for looking after me so well.'

'Ed, you looked after us.'

They said their goodbyes and he went away. Her spirits dived. Then the door opened again. She looked up.

He was standing in the doorway. 'I can't do this,' he said. 'I can't just walk away from you, Sophie. I want to see you again. What do you think?'

'I don't know.' Suddenly, she felt panicked.

She saw his expression alter. 'Of course, I understand,' he said.

She tried to explain, the words falling in broken phrases. 'It's not that I don't like you . . . I do, very much . . . It's just that . . . but I'm not sure . . . I'm not sure I could think about . . . not again.'

Ed took a pen out of his pocket and wrote on a scrap of paper. 'This is my address,' he said. 'If you were to write to me, Sophie, then I'd like that a great deal. And if I don't hear from you then that's okay too, I'll accept it, and I won't bother you again.'

As soon as he left the house, regret flooded through her. Why on earth hadn't she said, yes, please do keep in touch because I like you enormously and the house isn't going to feel the same without you, and I wish you weren't leaving.

She folded the piece of paper on which Ed had written his address, took it upstairs and tucked it into the top drawer of the chest in her bedroom. She put on a hat and scarf and shortly afterwards she, Ruby, Kenneth and the homeless family left the house. Sophie accompanied Mrs Wright and her children to the council offices while Ruby took Kenneth to the clinic. After she had left Mrs Wright filling in forms, Sophie went to the shops. She was in the butcher's when she heard the buzzing of the first V-1 rocket of the day, closely followed by the air-raid siren's demonic howling. She abandoned the queue and ran with everyone else to the shelter of a nearby underground station. Sitting in the dusty gloom, she mentally replayed her conversation with Ed. She had stood there, a stolid lump, saying hardly anything. And yet, along with annoyance at herself, she felt hopeful. She would write to him that afternoon. She would try to explain why she had hesitated and why fear had stopped her speaking, fear of letting herself love again.

At last, the All Clear sounded. She was wondering whether to go back to the butcher's and start queuing again when she overheard someone say that a V-1 had come down in South Kensington. As she rushed home, she failed to suppress her terror. She should have sent Ruby and Kenneth to the countryside, she thought. London wasn't safe for them any more. She had been foolish and selfish keeping them close to her.

As she approached the corner of Gilbert Street, she saw the plume of smoke and heard the shouts of the firemen. She was running now. *Please God, don't let them have gone home, please, please God.*

She turned the corner. There was a gap in the row of houses where her home had been and her hands flew to her mouth. She couldn't even pray any more. When she stumbled forward, an Auxiliary Fire Service worker stopped her.

'My grandson . . . my daughter-in-law . . .' Tears were streaming down her face.

341

'That's them over there, isn't it, love?'

She looked up, and there was Ruby with the pram, on the far side of the road. Her legs went to jelly, heat washed over her from head to toe, and she leaned against the wall and closed her eyes.

A crater in the road marked where Sophie's next-door neighbour's house had taken a direct hit. Her own house had had the roof and much of its upper storey neatly sliced off, as if a sharp knife had been taken to the bedrooms and bathroom. Surrounding her home were dusty, smoking heaps of bricks, shattered wood and tile, all soaking wet from the firemen's hoses.

Her solace was the knowledge that Ruby and Kenneth were safe. That, and the kindness of friends. Phone calls were made, telegrams sent. Neighbours rallied round to provide spare nappies and clothing for Kenneth. Vera Cornish trailed with her from rest centre to council office to bank, and sat with her in queues while she filled in forms to replace lost ration books and identity cards and cheque books and claim government grants. Viola bought train tickets and Ruby and Kenneth were dispatched to Lincolnshire and the safety of Duncan and Sally's house. There were only two bedrooms in Duncan and Sally's house, which must now house three adults and two babies, so Sophie remained in London, staying with Viola. Fragments of her past life were rescued from the debris and returned to her: an encyclopaedia, its pages glued together with water and dust, her writing case and Kaz's necklace. She rinsed it in Viola's kitchen sink, washing away the grime. The clasp had been bent out of shape but apart from that it had survived the disaster.

She went back to Gilbert Street a couple of days later. A neighbour gave her a cup of tea and another bagful of her belongings, salvaged from the ruined upstairs rooms. Afterwards, Sophie crossed the road to look at what remained of the home in which she had brought up her family. Barricades walled off the damaged building from the road. The lower storey of the house seemed more or less intact but the upper storey had been reduced to rubble.

Sophie's gaze drifted over the devastation. There was a leg from her dressing table and there was a ceramic basin, broken in half. Shards of coloured glass jars from the bathroom sprinkled the debris like dusty jewels – and there, chillingly, was the headboard from Kenneth's cot, complete with a painting of a bunny. Some strips of fabric, which might have been clothing or curtains, they were too wet and stained to tell, were draped in pinkish-brown folds, shrouding the pile of rubbish that much of her home had been reduced to. Not a drawer or handle from the chest in her bedroom remained. The piece of paper on which Ed had written his address was lost for ever. *If I don't hear from you I'll accept it and I won't bother you again,* he had said. So that, Sophie thought, was that.

At Viola's house, they sat at the kitchen table, going through the bag her neighbour had given her. Sophie took out an empty powder compact. Then a dressing gown the raw yellow of brick dust. Then some books and a wooden lamp base.

Beneath these things, something else. Sophie made an exasperated sound. It seemed the last straw.

'What is it?' said Viola.

'My photograph album.' Sophie took it out of the bag. 'Oh, Vi,' she said, dashing away a tear. 'Of all things, that they should rescue *that*!'

*

Rowan remembered the conversation she and Josh had had when they had agreed that whatever you did, you should do it well. So she tried to do her job well and to make sure that Thea, who was seven months pregnant, kept in good health, and she kept in touch with those friends of hers who had remained in London. *Keep buggering on*, Josh had also said, so that was what she did, though a void had opened up in her heart.

Something had gone wrong with the drop, Alex had told her, that night he had broken the news to her. *I'm not supposed to tell you, but Josh was parachuted into France. Our people over there were meant to pick him up from the drop zone but he didn't make it. The pilot said the weather had deteriorated and a wind had got up, so he may have been blown off course.*

The wind might have blown his parachute into a river or lake. Josh might have landed badly and been injured. If he had been captured, he would have been shot as a spy. These were things she tried not to think about. On a good day she managed, more or less, but on a bad night she imagined his parachute floating down through the night sky like a dandelion seed, and the wind knotting him in the branches of a tree.

She didn't *feel* that he was dead. He had gone missing only four days after they had parted at the cottage. She had returned to work by then and yet she had felt nothing. On those good days, she was certain that if something had happened to Josh she would have *felt* it. She didn't tell anyone else that, not Alex or Artemis, and not even Thea, because, though they wouldn't contradict her, she was afraid to see pity in their eyes. The only person she shared her conviction with was Josh's mother, who felt the same.

Julia Makepeace wrote to her. *Josh sent me your address before he went away. I should like to meet you, Mrs Scott.*

They arranged to meet for tea when Julia was in town. Julia Makepeace was formidable – beautiful, charming, well mannered and well turned out in a light wool skirt and beige cashmere cardigan, but formidable. She poured out tea and passed a cup to Rowan.

'Josh is clever and sensible and resourceful,' she said. 'He'll hunker down till it's safe to come out of hiding.' She spoke with ferocity, and her gold-brown eyes – Josh's eyes – glared at Rowan as if she was daring her to disagree with her.

'He can see in the dark,' agreed Rowan.

Julia Makepeace chuckled. 'He can indeed. Always could, the rascal. Do you want any of this?' A plate of cakes was offered to Rowan.

'No, thanks.'

'Can't eat? Neither can I. I'll wrap them up in a napkin and you can take them for your friends. Nurses are always hungry, so I'm told.'

As the Allied armies enlarged their foothold on the French mainland, Rowan followed their progress on a map. Julia was right, she thought, Josh was clever and sensible. If anyone could survive being parachuted into enemy territory, it was Josh.

On the bad nights, the voice in her head taunted her with the knowledge that no matter how resourceful you were, there was no armour against fate.

She had her habits, her superstitions. If she didn't look out for him when she came out of the hospital . . . if she didn't hope for a letter or phone call . . . if she didn't count on anything at all, in fact . . . then he would be all right. Josh had had his own ways of touching wood. That was why he had said, *There are things I'd like to say to you but it wouldn't be fair.* He, too, had been wary of hoping for too much.

345

Alex was back in England by now, recovering from wounds sustained in Normandy. Rowan visited him in hospital, sat by his bedside and saw the mess shrapnel had made of his once-pleasant and unremarkable face. After he was discharged, he called round at her flat once or twice a week, moving carefully because of his broken ribs. Often they talked about Josh.

Rowan tried not to think of the life they had not had. She tried not to think of the home they would have made and the years they would have spent together. And not to mind that she was not pregnant, like Thea. But on a bad night, she couldn't stop herself. If she had been expecting his baby, she would have a piece of him to hold to her heart, to get her through the dark months and years ahead.

Sophie found it hard to know what to do with herself. *Unsettled* hardly came near it. Doug was home on leave and she didn't like to be in his way so she tried to keep out of Viola's house during the daytime.

Sometimes she visited friends, but often as not she wandered aimlessly round the streets. *What will you do after the war?* Ed had asked her, and she had said, *I expect I'll go on much as before. The lodgers . . . the house.* Not now you won't, she told herself grimly. The house was uninhabitable, the lodgers dispersed, her daughter-in-law and grandson packed off to Lincolnshire. Her worldly goods, rescued from the lower storey of the house and smeared and gritty with dust, were dispersed round the sheds and garages of kind neighbours. All Sophie now owned were the clothes she stood up in, some bits and pieces Viola had given her, a cracked powder compact, a garnet-and-diamond necklace, a lamp that would probably never work again, an encyclopaedia that was largely illegible, and a photograph album she hadn't opened for years and had thought many times of putting in the stove. But how could you throw away pictures of your infant sons?

She would have to start again. And yet she seemed to have run out of steam. She was *displaced*. She had heard the word often enough throughout the war, applied to refugees and the bombed out – and Kaz, of course – but hadn't properly understood what it meant. Now, she never felt she was in the right place. It was as if she was always looking for somewhere and was unable to find it.

Sometimes she felt oddly lightheaded. No house to clean, no nappies to change, no garden to weed. Work had occupied her day and night for the last six and a half years, first the struggle to make a living after Hugh had died, and then the war. But now, nothing. Mixed in with shock and grief and confusion, was a fleeting relief.

The album niggled at her, a leftover, unfinished business, mocking her from its place in the bedroom (Viola's son Tom's bedroom, with its old model cars and school annuals and cricket bat). She remembered, shortly after Hugh's death, trying to cut out his image from a photograph. Clumsy with anger, the scissors had slipped and she had ended up slicing through a baby Stuart and she had felt terrible.

One of her walks took her past St Anne's hospital. She bought a postcard in a nearby newsagent, wrote a message on it, and asked a porter if he would deliver it to Rowan Scott. The following day, a letter arrived at Viola's house, inviting her to Rowan's flat.

Rowan let her in. Thea, who was very pregnant, rose from an armchair to kiss her cheek. Sophie asked after Thea's health, and then they spoke a little about Thea's husband in the army, somewhere in the fighting in France. While Rowan was in the kitchen making tea, Thea murmured to Sophie that Rowan's lover had gone missing and that she didn't want to talk about it, and so when Rowan came back into the room with the tray of tea things, Sophie changed the subject and told them about Gilbert Street.

'Your lovely house,' said Thea sympathetically, when she had finished. 'I'm so sorry, Sophie. How awful for you.'

'If you're short of somewhere to stay, you must come here,' said Rowan. 'I can always find room for another.'

So many people had been so kind to her, but this, the offer of a bed for the night from Hugh's daughter, as if it was a natural thing to help out one's father's distressed mistress, floored Sophie and almost reduced her to tears. She thanked Rowan in a muffled way and took the album out of her bag and put it on the table.

'They salvaged this,' she said. 'It's the one thing I'd have been quite happy to have gone up in smoke. I can never think what to do with it so I end up not doing anything at all.'

Thea opened the album and smiled. 'Oh, *Sophie*,' she said, looking down. 'It's Dad, isn't it?'

A photograph of Hugh Craxton in army uniform. Sophie, standing beside him, was wearing a white frock with a lace collar.

'I was so young then,' she said. 'Just twenty-one. Hugh wanted a picture of me to take back to France. I was nursing. I was a V.A.D., the lowest of the low.'

'Bedpans and bandaging,' said Rowan, putting a cup and saucer in front of Sophie.

'And polishing.' Sophie picked up the tea cup. 'We were always polishing. I can't remember why. We weren't allowed to do any real nursing. The V.A.D.s who were sent to France did everything, of course, but I was working in a private nursing-home. We were glorified skivvies . . . and the ward sisters were dragons. One used to regularly reduce me to tears. She even made the men, the patients and the visitors, quail.'

'Did Dad quail?' asked Thea.

Sophie shook her head. 'No, not Hugh. No one could make Hugh quail. He wasn't afraid of anything. He always did exactly what he wanted.' She sighed. 'I've put aside some of the photos for Stuart. I won't mention it to Duncan, he won't want to talk about it or even look at it. But I thought you might like to see them. I don't know what to do with it. I hate to think that I'll end up carting the wretched thing around with me, but I can't seem to get rid of it either.'

Thea said, 'I'll keep it for you, if you like.'

'Would you?'

'Yes. It's our history too, in a way.'

Thea turned the pages. Sophie caught glimpses of Hugh: in his walking tweeds, holding Duncan in his arms or standing beside a sandcastle on a beach.

Rowan said, 'I wonder whether he really loved any of us.'

Thea turned to her. 'He did, Rowan. He loved all of us. Just think of the effort he went to, having two families and trying to keep us apart. Why would he go to all that trouble if he didn't care? And it wasn't only because he didn't want to be found out. As Sophie said, Dad wasn't afraid of anything.'

'Hmm,' said Rowan. 'Perhaps.'

Thea turned another page. Sophie felt a sense of relief, having passed on the album. Did she think that Thea was right, and that Hugh had loved them all? She couldn't be sure.

*

Josh filled her thoughts; daily, Rowan followed the progress of the armies in Normandy in the newspapers and on the wireless, tracking the battles on a map of France in the flat. Though she tried not to hope too much, as the area of France held by the Allies grew larger and as the tide of war in Europe turned at last, she couldn't help it. They must find him soon. Leaving the hospital each day through the Outpatients' Hall, she felt on edge. She could no longer stop herself searching through the crowds for Alex. He had promised to let her know as soon as he heard any news. She would know from the expression on his face whether it was good or bad.

At the hospital, they were treating casualties from the V-1 raids. There was also a measles epidemic. Rowan was working nights on a fever ward, away from the main body of the hospital. She and a probationer nurse had sole care of thirty-two spotty, sneezing, coughing, snuffling, highly infectious children, babies in oxygen and steam tents and five- and six-year-olds with bronchitis and pneumonia and corneal ulcers. At night, when there was an air raid, all the children had to be taken down to the basement shelter. The older children must be woken and wrapped in blankets, the very sick babies taken out of their oxygen tents and carried down in a nurse's arms.

One night, the All Clear had gone, and they had just finished tucking the children back in bed on the ward, when the siren went off again. Rowan's junior, a thin, bespectacled Cornish girl called Trevelyan, the daughter of a vicar, raised her eyebrows.

'What a lousy night,' Trevelyan said.

They wrapped the children up again and took them back to the basement. Rowan returned to the ward to collect a very sick baby, who had been in an oxygen tent with breathing difficulties for the last three days. There was the usual cacophony: the bombs, the ack-ack. It *was* a lousy night, she thought, and she felt lousy. She had a headache and was afraid she was getting a migraine. They were very short-staffed, many hospital nurses having volunteered to go to France to care for the wounded troops. No one had time to go off sick.

She was lifting the baby out of the tent when a bomb fell nearby and the building shook violently. Rowan fell to the floor but managed to keep the baby cradled in her arms. Shaken, she scrambled to her feet and hurried to the basement. Sitting in the windowless space, holding the infant, her head ached and her throat prickled. It came to her in a sudden, dark plunging of the soul, that all her hopes had been futile. If Josh had been in hiding, they should surely have found him. The area of France into which he had been parachuted had been liberated by now. It would be better to accept that he was dead instead of torturing herself. She had hoped for months now, and she was too tired to hope any more. Her heart hurt and tears burned in her eyes.

Two hours later, the All Clear went off and once more they carried the children back to the ward. A tea trolley came round but Rowan couldn't swallow anything. The hours until the end of her shift seemed interminable. She longed to cushion her head on her desk and sleep. When, at last, her shift was over, she put on her cape and left the ward, walked to the nearest underground station and collapsed on to a train. She knew that she needed to buck up before she got home to Thea but tonight it was hard. Hot, itchy and exhausted, she alighted at Covent Garden and walked to Macklin Street. She was too warm; she peeled off her cape.

Thea must have heard her open the door because she came to meet her. 'Rowan,' she said, and took her hand and led her into the sitting room.

Alex Moore was there. 'Listen, Rowan,' said Thea gently, and squeezed her hand.

Rowan's heart was pounding in her ears. Alex said, 'He's alive. Rowan. They've found Josh and he's alive and he's going to be all right.'

The room went dark green and hazy; she swayed and would have fallen had not Alex caught her.

When she opened her eyes, she was lying on her bed. Alex was beside her. 'Thea's making you tea,' he said.

'*Tell me*,' she whispered. Tears were streaming down her face.

'He's going to be all right,' Alex said again. He was smiling. 'He broke his leg on the drop and he's had a bad time but he's coming home, Rowan.' Then he said remorsefully, 'I gave you a shock. I'm so sorry.'

She felt lightheaded with happiness and lousy both at the same time. She shuffled up the pillows, undid a cuff and peered at her arm.

'It wasn't you, Alex,' she said. 'You've given me the best news in the world.' She looked up as Thea came into the room. 'Thea, have we had measles? No, stay there, don't come near me, darling, I might be horribly infectious. Do you remember, Thea, if we ever had measles?'

The soldier sitting in the carriage opposite Thea lifted her case down from the luggage rack and opened the door for her. She thanked him. On the platform, deep in the heart of the Northumbrian countryside, she breathed in sweet, warm air.

352

She left the station to wait outside at a bus stop. Strands of cloud blown through a clear blue sky made mirror images, olive patches on the light-green hills. Rowan was in an isolation ward at the hospital, suffering from measles, and as neither of them could remember whether she, Thea, had ever had the disease, she had been quickly bundled off to Northumberland, to stay with Cormac's family at Crawburn.

The bus arrived and she climbed in and paid her fare. Sitting in the seat, she put a hand on her belly, feeling her baby move. He or she would be born here. Her son or daughter would grow up where Cormac had grown up, and that pleased her. Her child would put down roots here and would be part of a big, loving family. And there would be no more secrets.

PART THREE

LEAVING THE ISLAND
1945–1946

Chapter Nineteen

October 1945–January 1946

The upper storey and roof of the Gilbert Street house had been repaired and Sophie, Stuart, Ruby and Kenneth had moved back in a fortnight ago. Stuart was at work that afternoon, and while Ruby and Kenneth were out visiting friends, Sophie measured the windows for curtains. The wet-dog smell of plaster lingered in the upper rooms. Because paint and paper were hard to come by, many of the walls were still a raw pinkish-brown.

Though the war had ended, rationing had not. There were shortages of everything. Because she knew how lucky they were to have a roof over their heads again when so many other families were homeless or squashed in with relatives, Sophie kept to herself her feeling that the house was no longer the same. And yet she could not dispel the conviction that something had been lost. Only the downstairs rooms seemed to contain her memories. She moved through the house, tape measure, pen and notebook in hand. There, in the hall, she had met Ruby, whom she had quickly come to love, for the first time. There, in Hugh's study, now the lodgers' sitting room, she had begun to uncover the extent of his deception. There, in the drawing room, poor Kaz had stroked her hair. *Such beautiful hair you have, Zosia. Like silk.*

Sophie went into the kitchen and clambered up and knelt on the draining board to measure the back window. The garden, too, had seen better days. All that remained of the old pear tree, which had come down in a summer storm, was a scar in the grass and the logs that Stuart had cut. The previous week, Stuart and Duncan had dismantled the old Anderson shelter, stacking the sheets of corrugated iron and steel in the shed, out of Kenneth's reach. Sophie had swept up the autumn leaves and Stuart had dug over the vegetable patch. Friends and neighbours had given her seedlings for winter vegetables and she had planted them. These days, when she dug the garden, her spade struck bricks and shards of tile. A heap of them was stacked by a wall. Stuart planned to use them to make a sandpit for Kenneth and his little brother or sister, who was due in six months' time.

The kitchen, a room filled with light and memories, had always been at the heart of the house. Here, in this room, she had told Viola about Hugh, and here Viola had startled her by telling her that she had a lover. Here, after the war in Europe had ended, Viola had informed her that she had decided to leave Doug and go and live with Arnold. And here, only yesterday, Viola had tucked a strand of her limp, greying-brown hair behind her ear as she had said, 'It's been a murderous few months, Sophie, simply murderous. I didn't think the boys would take it so hard. But I had to leave Doug and I can't regret it.'

Duncan and Sally's second daughter, Isobel, was now six months old. Duncan had left the R.A.F. and was working at Croydon airport. The family was staying with the Flemings in Richmond until they found a house of their own. Stuart was currently working in a hotel, doing odd jobs, but in September he was to go to university to study engineering.

Sophie scrambled down from the draining board. One more window, a small one in the pantry. Sophie let her fingers trail over Ed's cupboard as she passed it. Somehow, miraculously, it had survived the explosion. She recalled Ed standing in the kitchen doorway that day he had left Gilbert Street, the day the V-1 rocket had obliterated the house next door. Memory, beautiful and cutting, consumed her. *I can't just walk away from you, Sophie. I want to see you again.* Whenever she passed a junk shop, she went inside it, hoping that she might find Ed there, polishing wood or painting some heavenly wreath of flowers. But she never had. He might have moved to Lancashire to be near his daughter and grandsons. He might have met someone else. He might be married. He had probably forgotten her.

At the flat, Rowan changed out of her uniform into a tweed skirt and a pearl-grey jersey. She put on her coat, tied a scarf round her neck and went to meet Josh in a pub in the Strand.

The public bar was a place of dark wood and etched windows. Some of the panes of glass were cracked and taped. There was no fire in the grate and the door flapped open, letting people in and out. Automatically, she steeled herself as she looked round for Josh, and then hated herself for doing so. Part of her always hoped that this time it might be all right, that he might be having a good day, that he might be getting back to his old self. But hope had worn thin recently. Josh had come home from France a year ago and during that time she had learned to sense his mood in her first glimpse of him. If it was one of his worst days, he would not have come to the pub at all.

She caught sight of him, sitting at a small, circular table. He looked pale and tired and was drawing a pattern in a spill of beer with a matchstick. She put a smile on her face and crossed the room to him.

'Hello, darling.' She kissed his cheek and sat down.

His smile was a twitch of the mouth. He said, 'How was your day?'

'Not too bad. Busy. I was glad to see the end of my shift.'

'Gin and tonic?'

'Please.'

He went to the bar. Sometimes she was able to tug him out of whatever dark place he was in. She tried not to look at him as he stood in the queue because she knew he hated her to worry about him, that it made him feel useless and ashamed, but she felt anxious because she knew he disliked crowds. She wished she had suggested somewhere quieter.

He came back to the table. As he put the glass in front of her, she noticed that his hand wasn't shaking. That was a good sign.

He sat down. He said, 'I quit the job.'

Her heart sank. For the last two months, Josh had been working for a friend in the City. 'It doesn't matter,' she said brightly. 'Plenty more jobs.'

'Of course it matters,' he said, with a touch of anger. 'I feel so bloody useless.'

Before the war, Josh had worked for a wine merchant, travelling for much of the time on the Continent. Since he had returned to England he had taken a series of office jobs. None had lasted.

'Sorry,' he said, lowering his voice and reaching out for her hand. 'It's my fault. But I couldn't stand it.'

'It wasn't right for you, that's all, darling. You'll find something better soon, I know you will.'

'It gave me a headache.' He tapped his temple. 'Here.'

'You're still getting the headaches?'

'Now and then.' He added quickly, 'Don't tell me to go back to Dr Clayton. He thinks it's all in my mind, I can tell he does.'

'Actually, I was about to say something boringly predictable about drinking enough water and getting out in the fresh air.'

This time, his smile reached his eyes. She said, 'Have you thought any more about Alex's wedding?' At the end of November, Alex was to marry a nurse he had met while serving abroad.

'I should do,' Josh said. 'Alex has always been very decent to me.'

'I'd love to go. It'd be fun to have a weekend in the country, wouldn't it? I'll see if I can change my leave.'

A burly man, winding through the tables and carrying two pints of beer, jostled against Rowan. Beer slopped from the glasses.

Josh jumped out of his chair. 'Look out, you oaf!'

'Who're you calling an oaf?' The man glared at Josh. Josh's fists were clenched.

'It's all right,' said Rowan, placating the man. 'Sorry, no harm done. It's all right, Josh.'

'You want to watch your mouth,' said the burly man before heading off.

Josh muttered, 'Too many people. Do you mind if we go?'

Rowan stood up, brushing beer from her skirt. The brief normality of their conversation had been shattered. After such an episode, it would take Josh a while to regain his equilibrium. She wanted to jab her high heel into the burly man's foot as they left the pub, but restrained herself.

They walked to the Embankment. Their best conversations often took place during walks. It had occurred to her, dispiritingly, that that was because they weren't looking at each other. She heard herself start to talk again in the bright tone of voice she often found herself using with him.

'It's good to get out. I've been stuck inside all day. One of the other staff nurses was off sick so I had to work through my break.'

Josh said nothing. Rowan made another conversational foray to which he did not respond and then they walked in silence. A gibbous moon hung over the Thames, its reflection slithering along the oily water, illuminating the ships and the coal barges moored near the hollow ruins of the warehouses.

She said, 'Is your head aching now?'

'No, not now.' His gaze whipped round to her. 'Don't nurse me, Rowan. I can't stand it.'

She was tired and on a short fuse, and the words escaped before she could stop them, sharp and stinging. 'Would you prefer I didn't speak at all?'

He shrugged. 'I don't mind.'

'Did you call Mr Hennessy?'

'Did I call Mr Hennessy . . . For Christ's sake, Rowan, you're doing it again!'

'You didn't, did you?'

'No.' He turned to face her. 'Why would I see another bloody shrink when the first two were worse than useless?'

'Because this one might be different. He might be able to help. Please, Josh, won't you consider it?' When he did not reply, she began, 'He's supposed to be good. He's worked with men like . . .' She caught herself, rephrasing rapidly. 'He's worked with other military men.'

But he had lost none of his sharpness. 'With men like me,' he said bitterly. 'Nutters. Loonies. That's what you were going to say, wasn't it, Rowan?' A smile hovered round the corners of his mouth, as if he was taking some pleasure, at least, in catching her out.

'No, Josh.' She closed her eyes. 'That's not what I was going to say.' Suddenly, she couldn't bear it. 'Look, I should go,' she said. 'We're not doing each other any good tonight. I'll call you tomorrow.'

She kissed his cheek and then walked away from him. When she looked back, tears blurred her image of him. He was standing in the same place, leaning against the wall. The miserable thought crossed her mind that tonight he might do something stupid, throw himself into the cushiony brown mud below or pick a fight with someone. But she kept on walking.

In July 1944, while the battle for Normandy was still raging, Allied troops had found Josh hidden in a small underground chamber below a barn. He had been there for two months, supplied with food by the brave farmer who had owned the barn. He had been able to leave his hiding place only at night, while everyone had waited for the Allied Forces to liberate that part of Normandy.

Five months before that, in February, a Frenchwoman had found him after the parachute drop that had gone wrong, lying in a ditch, delirious and with his right leg badly broken. The woman had taken him to her home in a village at dead of night on the back of a farm cart. A doctor had seen him, had treated the injured leg as best he could and had then got in touch with his friends in the Resistance. For the next two and a half months Josh had been moved from one hiding place to another, a series of outhouses, cellars and attics, until he had ended up in the pit beneath the barn.

It had been Alex Moore who had told her this. Josh had never spoken to her about it. Rowan's skin had crawled when Alex had told her about the pit. She had remembered Josh telling her that he disliked confined spaces.

Ahead of her, she saw someone emerge from Middle Temple Lane. Recognising him, she called out, 'Patrick! Patrick, it's you, isn't it?'

He turned. 'Good Lord, Rowan.'

'Hello, Patrick.' They kissed.

'You look as beautiful as ever.'

'Hmm. You're very flattering. I feel horribly worn out. But you, you seem well.' In the light of the street lamp, she saw that Patrick's fair hair had receded and greyed and there was a network of lines around his eyes.

She said, 'Where are you going?'

'Waterloo Station. I'm living in Guildford now, with Dad. Walk with me, won't you? It's so good to see you, Rowan.'

'Guildford . . . But what about Elaine?' Elaine was Patrick's sister. She had always cared for their ailing father.

'Elaine is married,' he said, surprising her because she had assumed Elaine to be a confirmed spinster. 'She has a child, a boy. He's two years old.'

'Is she happy?'

'Very much so.'

They were heading back along the Embankment, towards

Waterloo Bridge. 'I'm glad,' she said. 'And your father? How is he?'

'He's very frail now. But bearing up, you know. And you, are you still nursing?'

'I'm a staff nurse. I get to tell the juniors what to do.'

'I imagine you make a very good nurse.'

'Do you, Patrick?' She gave him a stare. 'I can't think why. I wasn't a good wife.'

'I don't think either of us was much good at marriage, were we?'

'No, we weren't.'

'You haven't had another bash at it, then?'

'No.' She hesitated, then said, 'There is someone. I love him very much, but it's been difficult. And you?'

He shook his head. 'No, no one. Colin . . .' he said. 'Do you remember Colin?'

'Colin Slater, your school friend, yes.'

'He died. He was in a Japanese prisoner-of-war camp. I'm writing a monograph about him, about his life. He was an exceptional person and I hate to think he'll be forgotten. I shall have it produced privately if no one will publish it. His family and the school will want a copy, if no one else.'

She put her hand on his sleeve. 'Patrick, I'm so sorry. How sad for you. You're right, he *was* an exceptional man,' she added.

'Thank you. You get used to things, don't you?'

Did you? she wondered. She raged about what had happened to Josh. This evening she had failed to bottle it up. All that hoping and yearning when he had gone missing . . . and yet it had come to this, this half-life, this damaged remnant of the man she loved. There were times when she was afraid he would never get better. Tonight was one of them.

She looked at Patrick. 'You used to find your father trying,' she said.

'Perhaps I've mellowed. Or perhaps I understand him better. We tick along, Dad and I. There's plenty of work for me in Guildford and I enjoy being an uncle enormously.'

At Waterloo Bridge they parted, with resolutions to keep in touch that Rowan knew neither of them would take up. She continued to walk back along the Embankment.

Josh had been discharged from the army on medical grounds earlier that year, in January 1945. He had recovered physically, more or less. Though his right leg was now an inch shorter than the left, he was still fit and active. Mentally, though, he remained very unwell. Whatever you called it – shellshock, siren strain or a nervous disorder – he was suffering badly. Rowan had treated enough shock victims of the Blitz at the hospital to be familiar with the symptoms. Josh hated being in crowds. He tired easily and suffered from headaches and his sleep was restless and disturbed. He struggled to concentrate and was permanently on alert. Incidents such as the one in the pub, when a sudden movement or noise or piece of carelessness on a stranger's part startled him, caused him to leap to his feet as if about to fight for his life.

She had always known that it would take time. She had given him gentle encouragement when he had attempted to go back to work, though in her heart she had known he wasn't ready for it. She had tried to persuade him to consult a psychiatrist, with little success. She suspected that he was afraid a psychiatrist would make him confront horrors that were unbearable to him. Josh was trying to shut away the past, to close himself off from difficult emotions, but they kept bursting through his defences. He was trying to navigate his illness by himself while he was too unwell to do so. He was a stiff-upper-lip sort of man, from a family who felt it self-seeking to ask for help and undignified to admit weakness. Makepeaces coped. The trouble was, Josh wasn't coping.

She walked to his house and rang the bell. Mr Lyons answered the door and let Rowan in. She climbed the stairs and tapped on Josh's door.

Josh opened it. Seeing her, he let out a breath and embraced her. They stood there for a long time, wrapped in each other's arms.

They went into the flat. It looked much the same as it had the first time she had been there, after she had met Josh that evening at Signorelli's. The rooms were still sparse and tidy but nothing had been repaired. Rowan thought that the flat, like Josh, was stuck in time, frozen, unable to move on.

'Forgive me, please, darling,' she said. 'I was feeling ratty. It's been a bit of a day.'

'No, it was my fault. It's never you, never.' He stroked her hair.

'Pour me a coffee, would you?'

He put a cup on the table in front of her and sat down on the sofa beside her. He pressed his fingertips against his forehead. 'Sometimes I feel like a grenade's about to go off,' he said. 'A grenade in my head. It's not the pain that bothers me so much, it's the waiting for it, the feeling that something awful is about to happen.'

It was the most he had ever opened up to her and it gave her a tiny fragment of hope. 'It's an illness, Josh,' she said. 'And it will get better, I promise. I know everyone keeps saying that and it must be utterly tedious and hard for you to believe, but it will just take time.' As she spoke, she wondered whether she was telling him the truth. Some of the big mental hospitals still housed shellshock patients from that earlier conflict, the Great War. She suppressed a shudder.

'I can't see another shrink,' he said. 'It must seem irrational to you, but I can't. I would just clam up. It would be a waste of time.'

She threaded her fingers through his. 'Okay. It's not irrational. And I do understand, honestly, darling. It took me more than ten years before I was ready talk to anyone about my mother. So I still hold the record.' She paused, then said, 'Would you think about going to Suffolk to live with your parents for a while? You know Julia and Bill would like that.'

'This sounds like a last-ditch attempt to get me to sort myself out.'

His tone was bitter and she found it hard not to flinch. 'No, Josh, that's not what I meant at all,' she said. 'But I don't think you're ready to work yet, and I do honestly believe you'd be better off in the countryside. Just for a few months, till you turn a corner.'

'What would I do there? What would I do without you?'

'I could find something nearby. There must be a cottage hospital or a nursing home where I could get work.'

He looked exhausted, the skin around his eyes grey and crêpey. 'I can't ask that of you.' A long silence, then he said, 'I'd like to ask you to marry me, Rowan, but how can I when I can't even earn a living?'

Useless to say that she would be happy to earn for both of them. Makepeace men were the breadwinners. She knew he wouldn't consider it. Instead, she said, 'There's no rush.'

'I'm a bloody wreck. I'm afraid I'll always be a wreck.'

'You won't.' She pressed her face against his chest. But

she, too, felt despondent and there were tears in her eyes again. She murmured something about putting more milk in her coffee and went into the kitchen.

He followed her. 'I love you,' he said. 'I love you so much.'

'And I love you too.'

And then they were stumbling through to the bedroom, the coffee forgotten, tearing off each other's clothing, their longing for each other intense and irresistible. Afterwards, he fell asleep, his head on her breast. This was how they communicated best, this wordless joining of body and soul, their love for each other conveyed through touch and pressure and caress. Sometimes she was afraid it was all they had left.

Posting letters in the village of Lawton, Thea caught sight of Madeline Greville on the far side of the road. A tall, fine-boned woman, her straight platinum-blonde hair was almost the same shade as her white fox-fur hat. Rumour was that Madeline was expecting a baby; just now her slender body was hidden beneath the folds of her tartan coat. Thea considered the feud between the Jamiesons and their nearest neighbours, the Grevilles, to be tiresome and unhelpful, though she kept that thought to herself, particularly at the moment in light of fresh resentments recently stirred up. She called out a good morning and Mrs Greville gave her a startled stare before murmuring a response.

Thea pushed the pram out of the village, along the Langhill road. Polly was restless, straining to get out. At fifteen months old, she had just started walking. Thea gave her daughter her keys to play with and Polly dropped them out into a puddle. To distract her, Thea pointed out a crow, some sheep and the collie that was rounding them up, and made the appropriate animal sounds. She said, 'Your daddy's coming home soon, Poll.' Polly held her hand out for the keys again and chewed the metal ring. Her blue knitted hat was coming off, revealing her wild dark curls. Thea was delighted that her daughter had inherited Cormac's curls rather than her own straight hair. The weather had turned overnight and it was a bitterly cold day, frost greying the grass on the hillside, and Thea considered tugging the hat down but that would draw attention to it, which would be fatal because Polly would then pull it off entirely. 'Your daddy's coming home,' she repeated. 'Only a few more days.' She smiled and Polly smiled too. Thea's separation from Cormac – a year and a half now – was a raw ache, sometimes in the background but always there. She gave the big old pram an extra shove over a badly potholed section of the road.

Her route took her past Langhill House, the Grevilles' home. The slash of scarlet paint daubed over the wrought-iron gates seemed a blood-red challenge, an insult. Thea chewed her lip, looking at it, and walked on. The Jamiesons thought Madeline Greville stand-offish but Thea wondered whether she was merely shy. Charles Greville, Madeline's father-in-law, had died during the war. After the conflict in Europe had ended, his widow had moved out of Langhill to live near her daughter in the south. Charles's heir, Rufus, and Rufus's wife, Madeline, had taken up permanent residence at Langhill. All this Thea had heard from Cormac's Aunt Cathy, who knew everything. Aunt Cathy had also told her that Madeline Greville had been brought up in London and that her father owned a bank. If Madeline Greville was a true city girl, the sort who loved shops and restaurants and theatre-going, mightn't she feel lonely at Langhill? Though Thea had been brought up in a city she had always felt at home in the countryside and had been able to cope with moving to an isolated part of Northumberland. There were things she missed: museums and libraries and her friends – and Rowan, of course. And her work.

Becoming part of a big, disputatious family . . . now, that had taken her a while to get used to. The Jamieson household was noisy and busy and people were always trying to talk to you and tell you what to do. Boarding school and the A.T.S. had accustomed her to communal living, but not to the lengthy arguments or level of nosiness practised by the Jamiesons. The personal questions, the comments on the way one baked a pie or changed a nappy; all this Thea had struggled with. Their curiosity, and the advice that accompanied it – the Jamiesons were great ones for helpful advice – were kindly meant, Thea knew, but even Nicola, who seemed happiest in the seat of a tractor or hauling a bale of hay, had seen fit in the early days to comment on Thea's care of her baby daughter. Thea didn't mind too much because she knew that Nicola adored Polly, would do anything for her, was almost a second mother to her, and was happy to take over after a bad night or when Thea needed a few moments to herself. And anyway, Nicola was herself now married to Lennie, who had been released from the army in 1944, after having been wounded in Italy. They too had a baby daughter, Janet, who was just six weeks old.

Along with Robert Jamieson, Crawburn now housed Nicola, Lennie and Janet as well as Thea and Polly. Robert had given the big bedroom he had once shared with Cormac's mother to Nicola, Lennie and Janet. Thea and Polly slept in the room with the sloping floor, overlooking the garden.

Thea loved her daughter with a deep and abiding passion. From the moment Polly had been born in a bedroom at

Crawburn in September 1944, she would have done anything for her, would have given her life for her without a moment's hesitation. She could lose herself, watching her baby sleep, taking delight in the curve of a rosy cheek and the shadows her lashes cast on her satiny skin. That sort of love nourished, but it also flayed. So much of what was involved in pregnancy, birth and motherhood had been a shock to her. In spite of conscientiously reading up about childbirth and infant care during her pregnancy she had quickly discovered herself to be utterly ill-prepared. The books seemed to her evasive to the point of dishonesty. They had used the word 'discomfort' to describe labour pains. They had not told her that when her baby cried it would hurt, and when she couldn't work out why she was crying, that it would hurt more. They had skimmed over the terrible exhaustion of night feeds. Four weeks after the birth, when she had at last felt capable of walking to Lawton, she had given all the books to a jumble sale.

She hadn't thought motherhood would be like this. And she had missed Cormac desperately. It would all have been so much more bearable had she been able to share her joy and fatigue with Cormac, if she could have shared some of the work and the worry with him.

She hadn't realised how much time a tiny scrap of humanity could take up. She had fed, changed and settled the newborn Polly, then cleared up the mess, and by the time she had finished clearing up the mess Polly had needed feeding again. Polly hadn't dropped a night feed until she was five months old, hadn't achieved anything remotely resembling a routine during her first six months. By that time, Thea was in a permanent muddle of tiredness. She wore mismatched socks, took a mouthful out of a cup of tea and then forgot where it was. If by some miracle she had ten minutes' peace to open a book, she would find herself reading the same sentence over and over again. And even then it failed to make sense. Not one of the jobs she had taken in an earlier life that now seemed impossibly distant, neither secretarial work nor waitressing nor archaeology, nor even the army, demanding though she had thought them at the time, had been anything compared to looking after a newborn baby.

The first time Polly had fallen asleep on her breast, a peaceful warm bundle, and the first fleeting smile: those had been turning points. She must be doing something right, she had reasoned. Polly's gaze had followed her when she moved round the room, as if she was something wonderful. That she was a beautiful and bright little girl was, Thea felt, a stroke of enormous good fortune. The wild Jamiesons and restless Sigrid might have combined to make an entirely different kettle of fish. Of course, there was a great big blank in Thea's family tree. Perhaps Polly's grandfather, Sigrid's lover, had been cheerful, black-haired and blue-eyed, like Polly.

At fifteen months old, Polly had yet to meet her father. As part of the Allied Forces, Cormac had fought his way from the Normandy coast to Berlin. After the war in Europe had ended in May 1945 he had remained in Berlin, helping to keep the fragile peace in a city of hunger and ruins. He had missed his daughter's first smile, her first step and first word. Two days ago Thea had received word that he was to be discharged from the army. At last, he was coming home.

Thea pushed the pram into the courtyard. Nicola came out to meet her. She gathered Polly into her arms. 'Hello, lovey,' she murmured. 'How's my beautiful girl?'

They went into the house. Thea asked after Nicola's Janet, and Nicola told her that she was asleep. Nicola offered to take Polly upstairs for her nap while Thea chopped vegetables for dinner. Raised voices were coming from the snug. Returning to the kitchen, Nicola said, 'She went out like a light.'

'Thanks, Nicola.' Thea nodded in the direction of the snug. 'What's going on?'

'Uncle John came round.'

'What about Jack and Francis?' Jack and Francis were Uncle John and Aunt Cathy' sons, twins in their early twenties. They were two hot-tempered, rash, black-haired and blue-eyed rogues, who enjoyed playing practical jokes and having a few drinks. Thea couldn't help liking them, though they were born troublemakers. Just now, when she thought of them, it was with a weary exasperation.

'They're not here, thank goodness,' said Nicola.

'Shall I make the soup?'

'It's okay, I'll do it. You should take your coat off, Thea, it's too hot in here for a coat.'

'I might go out for a walk if you don't mind keeping an eye on Polly.'

''Course not. You know I never mind. You don't need to ask.' Nicola gave Thea a glance. Her frown faded and she seemed to thaw a little. 'You all right?'

'I'm fine.' She slipped her feet back into her boots. 'I just can't seem to be able to sit still.'

Nicola flung some butter into a hot pan. 'It's giving me butterflies too, waiting for him,' she said, as Thea went out of the door.

Thea headed up through the terraces. She needed a proper walk among grass and trees, instead of a slow plod pushing

374

a pram. She needed to keep a lid on the tension that was boiling up inside her. Since she had received Cormac's letter, she had fizzed with excitement. Mixed in with excitement and joy was some apprehension. You couldn't go through what Cormac had experienced without it changing you. She knew that she, too, had changed. They were neither of them the same people who had parted on a railway platform a year and a half ago. If you added up the time they had spent together, what would it come to? Four weeks . . . five?

There were marriages that had soured or broken up in the aftermath of a returning soldier's homecoming, everyone knew that. Thea had only to think of Rowan to be aware of the pitfalls that lay ahead. Josh had returned to England at the beginning of the year, and yet he and Rowan were neither married nor engaged and they still lived apart. There was love there, Thea could see that there was, but could it survive the gulf that the war had opened up between them?

Throughout the war, she had written to Cormac daily. Even on the day of Polly's birth she had managed to scribble a couple of lines. There had been times when a week or more had passed without a letter from Cormac arriving at the farm, anxious times, but then a flurry of post would fall through the letterbox into the hallway. His letters filled two shoeboxes, and in them they shared their hopes and fears. Cormac had written to tell her that a fellow Northumbrian in his regiment, Phil Coleman, whom Thea had met briefly more than five years ago, in St Malo, had offered him work in his small engineering business on the outskirts of Hexham. Phil repaired motorcycles and manu-factured spare parts for them. Cormac hadn't yet told his father what he planned to do when he came home.

Since she had come to live at Crawburn, Thea had made

sure to pull her weight. She had conscientiously studied books on household management and was a far better cook than she had been before her marriage. But she suspected she would never make a great one. Crashing around the kitchen bad-temperedly, Nicola produced sponge cakes of wonderful lightness and doughy, delicious bread. Thea's cakes and bread tended to fall flat. Aunt Cathy often commented on that. Privately, Thea thought there was something soul-destroying about the repetitive minutiae of housework. It was necessary work, important work, but it did not satisfy, and perhaps her heart wasn't in it.

She took the path across the crisp frosty grass of the meadow, into the woodland. She loved the wild, remote countryside that surrounded Crawburn, and was especially fond of the woodland at Low Chase. The dark, cool quiet reminded her of the forest in Normandy through which she had travelled in 1940 when fleeing France. She had found the site of the remains of the ancient settlement that Cormac had told her about on the evening he had proposed to her. Large stones, velvety with moss, in a small clearing deep in the heart of the forest, formed a roughly circular enclosure. She would have liked to have sunk a small explora-tory trench to confirm her theory that the structure was from the Iron Age, but the land did not belong to the Jamiesons. Rufus Greville owned Low Chase. Instead, she was sketching the enclosure and she had begun to make an accurate plan of it. Sometimes she brought her trowel and scraped away at patches of earth not visible from the path. She planned to send a description of the site to Grace once she had completed the work.

She sat down on one of the mossy stones. Grace and Monty Fainlight had returned to London shortly after the war had ended. Helen and Max were living with them in the Bloomsbury house, along with their three-year-old son, Rafe. So far Helen and Max had been unable to find a home of their own in which to live. After the enormous destruction of the war, housing was in desperately short supply, especially in the cities.

Everyone was short of money, too. Grace had written to Thea, telling her that she was trying to get together the funds to finance a dig in Wiltshire the following summer. Because of financial constraints it would be a modest venture, a re-examining of a small site Grace and Monty had worked on before. Grace hadn't yet offered her work but Thea suspected she would eventually. When Grace did, she would have to refuse. How could she leave Polly to travel so far away? It was out of the question. She hadn't told anyone about the dig, neither Nicola nor Cormac, and was trying to put it out of her mind.

Sometimes these days, glancing at the stone axe-head from Corran that she still treasured, and thinking about her career, she felt a flutter of panic. She never talked about it to the Jamiesons, who had been so kind to her, and she often felt ashamed of herself for minding so much that archaeology was no longer part of her life. There she was, married to a man she loved beyond measure, the mother of an adored, beautiful and healthy daughter, and living in a comfortable house in glorious countryside. The war had ended and she should be content. But what she had once had had slipped away with such frightening ease that she was afraid it was gone for ever. Could you consider yourself to be an archaeologist if six years had passed since you had practised any archaeology?

She came out of the woodland to the fields. Here, she

stopped to look down to Langhill House. Since Rufus Greville had inherited it, he had made alterations. You had to admire his energy. The house was shedding the grey, grimy carapace of Charles Greville's ownership and regaining its lost elegance. The drive and terrace had been weeded, the lawn mowed, and there were flowers in the border and the shrubs had been pruned. From somewhere a tin of white paint must have been unearthed because the window-frames and French doors now gleamed. Towards the end of the summer, passing Langhill's gates, Thea had seen Rufus sanding down the rusty ironwork himself.

Two months ago, Rufus Greville had informed Cormac's Uncle John that when his tenure of the Greville land at Bane Rigg ran out, it would not be renewed. Rufus's letter had dropped into the Jamiesons' lives like a lit match on dry tinder. Though John Jamieson had asked him to reconsider, Greville had refused and last week John and Cathy had lost the acres that they had farmed for decades. Recently discharged from the army, at a loose end and looking for mischief, Cormac's cousins, the twins Jack and Francis, had responded by throwing scarlet paint over Langhill House's shining white gates. This had happened two nights ago. Thea hated that the cousins should have done such a thing just before Cormac was due to come home. She resented that his homecoming was likely to be marred by arguments and worry.

She looked past Langhill House towards the road. Someone was making their way along it. She watched as the distant stick figure headed along the winding route, now and then lost behind a bank or the swell of the land, before re-appearing. She knew she should go back to the farmhouse; it was dinner time and Polly would soon wake up. And yet she was unable to tear her gaze from the man on the road.

A shiver ran through her. Clenching her fists, she took a shaky lungful of air. She ran down the slope and along the path on the far side of Langhill, her boots beating on the clumps of grass.

Reaching the road, her heart racing, breathless with joy, she called out, 'Cormac! Cormac!'

Seeing her, he too began to run. When he reached her, he swept her up in his arms. Kisses rained on her face and on her mouth. And she felt right again, something slotting back into place that she had missed so long she had almost forgotten to notice its absence.

Polly woke up from her nap and Thea carried her downstairs to the snug. Still sleepy, she sat on Thea's lap, sucking her thumb, giving this stranger, her father, sidelong glances. There was a tray of tea things on top of a chest of drawers, out of Polly's reach, and Nicola was passing round cups. Janet, Nicola's baby, made little noises in a Moses basket to one side of the sofa. Thea's gaze, like her daughter's, kept turning to Cormac. He was familiar and yet he was unfamiliar, hardened by experience and responsibility. He had secured a place on an earlier transport home, he had told her, had got through the bureaucracy that had officially released him from army service as quickly as possible and had travelled as far as York the previous day. *I couldn't wait*, he had said. *I had to see you. It's been so long.*

Robert, John and Nicola were talking to Cormac. 'Bane Rigg's nothing without that land,' John Jamieson said, giving his cup an angry stir. 'I'm not saying I approve of what they've done . . .'

'Silly beggars,' said Nicola.

'You're certain it was them?'

'Haven't seen them since. They haven't come home, Cormac.'

'They're lying low.'

'Has Rufus Greville said anything?'

'Not yet.'

'Bloody idiots.'

Thea finished giving Polly the bottle of warm milk she liked to have after her nap and she began to perk up. She slid off Thea's lap and toddled over to her toy box. She had just begun to walk and was unsteady on her feet. Cormac took Thea's hand.

Nicola said, 'You'll be all right in the old room for a while, won't you, Cormac?'

'We'll be fine.' Cormac watched Polly take a rag doll out of the box.

'It'll be a squash with the three of you,' said Nicola. 'The roof's letting in rain to the green room or you could have had that.'

'It won't be for long. Thea and I will be looking for a house of our own.'

'No need for that,' said Robert. 'Plenty of room here.'

'I know, Dad, and thanks, I appreciate it, but Thea and I need a home of our own. I've lived in tents and Nissen huts and slept in ditches or out in the open for too long.' As he talked, his thumb stroked her palm and she felt longing stir inside her.

Robert said, 'You're needed here, son, at the farm.'

'I won't be working on the farm, Dad.'

'Nonsense.'

'Nicola should have Crawburn. It's Nicola who put in all the work over the war.'

'Lennie's shaping up well, too,' said Nicola.

380

'I'll help out when you're short-handed, of course I will.'

'Magnanimous of you,' growled Robert.

'I've got a job, Dad, in Hexham, working for a friend who owns an engineering works.'

'What on earth would you want to do that for?' Robert's voice rose.

Janet began to cry. 'Honestly, Dad,' said Nicola crossly. Robert muttered an apology and Nicola rocked the Moses basket.

Cormac gave Thea's hand a hard squeeze and changed the subject. 'I made something for Polly.'

He took out of his kitbag a brightly painted wooden duck on a string, which wobbled comically when it was pulled along. Polly watched as Cormac pulled the duck back and forth along the rug. Then he held out the string to his daughter. A long pause, while Polly sized it all up, and then she pottered across the room and took the string and smiled at her father for the very first time.

Rowan was at a friend's house one evening, sitting on the sofa and leafing through a booklet aimed at expectant mothers. Her friend, Caroline Jenkins, was the red-faced, jolly girl who had been a probationer at the same time as Rowan at the sector hospital in Kent in 1940. They had kept in touch. She wasn't Jenkins now, she was Caroline Ross, married to a surgeon from St Anne's, the mother of a three-year-old son and with a second baby on the way. She was still red-faced and jolly, though.

'Frightful load of rubbish,' Caroline said, referring to the maternity booklet. 'I don't know why they dish these out second time round.'

Rowan was reading about the symptoms of pregnancy.

Tiredness . . . nausea . . . sore breasts . . . a missed period or very light period. She read the list again. Then a third time.

She realised that Caroline was speaking to her. She looked up.

'Are you all right, Rowan?'

'Yes. Fine. Sorry, long day.'

'I don't know how you stick it at St Anne's. I was sick to death of the place. I couldn't wait to see the back of it.'

Rowan attempted a smile. 'You must be so pleased about the new baby. How lovely for you and Alan.'

There followed some baby talk, to which Rowan struggled to respond sensibly, and then Caroline asked her whether she would like another coffee.

'Thanks, but no. I should go.'

From upstairs, a howl from Caroline's son. Caroline raised her eyebrows. 'Oh Lord. He has a sniffle, poor love. I'm afraid we're in for a bad night.'

Caroline saw her out and Rowan walked to a bus stop. Waiting for the bus, she was in turmoil. Again, she mentally ran through the list in Caroline's booklet. She had every one of the symptoms of pregnancy, had had them for weeks. She was terrified. She was ecstatically happy. She couldn't possibly tell Josh. She must tell Josh. She couldn't be pregnant. She knew that she was.

The bus arrived. Alighting from it, Rowan made for the Strand. No point putting off talking to him: it must be done so it may as well be done now. She found herself unable to predict how he would react. She was afraid he might feel he had been pushed into a corner.

One of the other residents was coming out of the building as she arrived so Rowan slipped in. At the top of the stairs, she tapped on Josh's door.

He let her into the flat and kissed her. 'I wasn't expecting you. I thought you were seeing Caroline.'

'I didn't stay long. Do you mind?'

'Of course not, it's lovely to see you. Drink, darling?'

'No thanks. Maybe a coffee. No, actually.' The thought of coffee nauseated her. 'Just a glass of water, please, Josh.'

As he ran the tap, he said, 'I'm glad you've called. I've been thinking.' He filled the glass. 'Perhaps you're right, perhaps I should go and stay with my parents for a while.'

'It might help.' She knew how difficult the decision must have been for him.

'I can't go on like this, I do realise that. I need to do something. I feel that I'm letting you down.'

'Josh, you're not.' She rubbed his arm.

'I shall miss you terribly.'

'Perhaps I should come with you.'

'Rowan, we've been through this before.'

'I think I'm pregnant.'

He stared at her. 'Pregnant . . .'

'Yes, I think so. Damn it, I'm sure of it. I've been feeling peculiar for weeks.'

He said nothing and disappointment washed through her. She spoke quickly. 'So stupid of me not to realise earlier . . . and me a nurse! But I didn't think I could have a baby.'

'Darling, I'm over the moon.' And she saw, looking at him, that he was. 'It's wonderful news.'

'It is, isn't it?' she said shakily. There were tears in her eyes.

'Sit down,' he said. 'Are you sure you don't want anything?'

'Perfectly sure. Don't fuss, Josh.'

He gave her a look, a flash of the old, funny Josh, and she smiled wryly. 'Yes, I know. Pots and kettles, all that. We'll have to settle for fussing over each other, at least till the baby comes. Then we can both fuss over him.'

'Him?'

'You Makepeaces only ever seem to father sons.' Josh's elder brother, Ronald, had three boys; the middle brother, Peter, had two.

'I thought you would mind leaving the hospital,' he said.

She sighed. 'The truth is, Josh, I'm feeling rather tired of the hospital. It's funny, but I haven't felt the same about nursing since the war ended. I don't mean that I'm not glad it's over, and I'm not saying for a moment that I'd want to go back to all that horror, but I've felt . . . flat, I suppose.'

'You didn't say.'

'I thought it would pass. I can't seem to find the same enthusiasm for it. Everything's different. Honestly, Josh, the probationers on my ward seem so young. And silly, most of them. They look at me as if I'm a leftover from a bygone age.'

She was sometimes afraid that they thought of her as an ancient old trout, stuck in her ways. It was depressing to find herself stepping into the shoes of the very people she used to laugh about when she had first started nursing. A few days before, talking to a couple of probationers about some of the techniques she had used when nursing in the Blitz, she had caught one yawning.

'People want to forget,' he said. 'The younger ones don't want to think about the war.'

'Yes, I know.' And she could see it through their eyes. It was understandable.

'I feel the same as you,' he said. 'The skills I learned, what use are they now? There are men I know who've gone off to meddle in tin-pot wars on the other side of the globe.

They're trying to get the excitement back in their lives. They don't know how to live without it. My nerves are too shot for that, but still, a part of me can see why they're doing it.' He took her hand. 'You want this baby, don't you, Rowan?'

'Yes, very much.'

It was hard to get her head round it, though. It wouldn't seem to sink in. She had accepted some time ago that she would never be a mother.

'I'm awfully old to be having a first baby, Josh,' she said. 'I'm thirty-two. And the whole business of bringing up a child seems awfully daunting.'

'You'll be a wonderful mother.'

Would she? You could start out with the best intentions and make a complete mess of it. Look at Sigrid – she had probably started out with the best intentions, too.

He kissed the top of her head. 'Look, we'll go to Suffolk. We'll work it out from there. Don't worry about anything. But we'd better get married, don't you think?'

'Yes, we probably should.' Again, she was close to tears. 'Yes – yes, please, Josh.' And he took her in his arms and kissed her again.

The first house on their list sold before they were able to look at it, snapped up by a family of six. During the weeks that followed, Thea and Cormac visited every property they could afford for sale or rent in the Hexham area. There were the rooms above a chip shop, which smelled of beef fat, and the cottage in the countryside with bedrooms so low-ceilinged Cormac couldn't stand up straight. There was the icy bungalow with black mould flowering on the walls. There was the flat where they were able to hear every word of the next-door neighbour's argument with his wife, and the small stone cottage, set among stream and valley, that had neither a bathroom nor running water nor electricity. And a smattering of others, all cold, depressing and impossible.

They viewed a terraced house in a village six miles out of Hexham. The garden was piled high with rubbish – a split, soaking mattress, an armchair with stuffing bursting out of the upholstery, wet cardboard boxes and heaps of tins and bottles. It looked, Thea thought, like a bomb site, though there were no indications that any bombs had ever fallen there. A man wearing stained corduroy trousers and with a cigarette hanging out of the corner of his mouth showed them round the rooms. On a sofa in the living room, a teenage boy slept beneath threadbare blankets. He pulled the blankets over his head when his father drew back the curtains. Every room smelled of sour milk and cats.

Leaving, they didn't speak to each other. The motorcycle sped out of the village. On a narrow, winding road, Cormac drew the bike to a halt and Thea slid off the pillion.

'Seven years in the army,' he said bitterly. 'Dear God. And this is what we have to choose between – living in a hovel or staying with my family. While men like Rufus Greville still run the show.' When he turned to her, she saw the anger in his eyes. 'This isn't what I wanted for us, Thea. And it isn't what I wanted for our daughter.'

Because Rowan was a divorcee, she and Josh were unable to marry in church. Rowan sensed disapproval: Makepeaces didn't do register-office weddings. Nevertheless, she felt it in many ways a relief. A short, quiet ceremony would be far less exhausting for Josh and would mean that for her there were fewer difficult reminders of wedding number one, to Patrick. Because the Makepeaces thought such marriages rather shady, they would get away with having it in London rather than in the wilds of Suffolk, and so it would be easier for their friends to attend. And anyway, Rowan mused, thinking of her father, the whole business of weddings, and how many a person could reasonably have in a lifetime, was a sore point with the Craxtons.

Rowan said to Thea, 'I'm afraid Josh will hate every minute of it.'

'Not everyone enjoys weddings,' agreed Thea. 'I was terribly relieved when mine was over.'

It was Rowan's wedding day. Thea was her matron of honour. Rowan looked at their reflections in the dressing-table mirror. She had put up her hair and threaded through it a cobalt-blue ribbon, the same shade as her grosgrain silk dress and coat. Thea had cut her dark hair short and feathery round her face and was wearing a small hat of the same mushroom-coloured satin as her long-sleeved frock, which Rowan had chosen for her at Edwina's shop.

Rowan stood up and looked in the mirror sideways on. There wasn't much to show for her pregnancy yet. Julia Makepeace had made her an enormous bouquet of winter leaves and berries which would hide the slight thickening of her waist.

Bill Makepeace was going to give her away. While Thea went to fetch the bouquet, Rowan found herself thinking about her father. How, before the war, he had fallen in love with the beautiful Swedish girl he had met in Paris, and how, nine years later, in a nursing home in London, he had fallen in love again. They had that in common, she and her father, the habit of falling in love. But she knew that this time, with Josh, it was for ever.

They took a taxi through the London streets. In an ante room, Thea helped Rowan smooth the creases out of her bridal outfit. Rowan took a deep breath and Thea squeezed her hand.

Bill Makepeace said, 'You look beautiful, my dear. Josh will be so proud of you.'

He gave Rowan his arm as they went into the room where the guests had assembled. Rowan saw Josh, ahead of them, next to Alex, his best man, and her heart beat faster. And as Josh turned towards her, love for him flowed through her, and she knew that this time, her marriage was going to last.

Chapter Twenty

February–May 1946

Thea pushed the pram home from Lawton. She was looking after Nicola's baby, Janet, as well as Polly, because it was the lambing season and Nicola was busy from morning to night on the farm. Janet had fallen asleep by the time they returned to Crawburn so Thea lifted Polly down from the pram seat, put up the cat net and parked the pram outside the kitchen door, in the shade of the overhanging roof. A fine rain was sheening the paving stones in the courtyard. She carried Polly upstairs and tucked her into her cot for her nap, then took the shopping into the house and put it away. She chopped vegetables for a stew and beat eggs, butter and flour for a sponge pudding and put them on the stove to cook. John, Jack and Francis were also at Crawburn, helping with the lambing, so she must prepare a large amount of food. She peeled potatoes and then whizzed round the kitchen, clearing up, before checking on Janet. Then she made herself a cup of tea and went to sit in the snug. She opened the book she had ordered from Hexham library on Mortimer Wheeler's excavations of Maiden Castle in Dorset and began to read.

She had reached the foot of the first page when she heard a wail. She closed the book and picked up Janet from the pram. She was warming the baby's bottle when there was a cry from upstairs. She fed Janet in the bedroom, sitting on the bed, reading a picture book to Polly at the same time. While she was reading, she thought about her friends. She had had a letter from Peggy that morning. Peggy had told her that Ralph and Nancy Wadham, who had lived in the Bloomsbury house where Thea and Peggy had shared a room, now had three children. Nancy spent more time in Wales with her mother than with Ralph in London, Peggy wrote. Peggy herself was still living in Cornwall. She had separated from Gerald. Thea would have liked to visit her, to make sure she was all right, but St Ives, where Peggy lived, was five hundred miles away, so that was impossible. Claudia Daniels, with whom Thea had joined the ATS, was living in York, not so far away. Maybe she could take a train over there one day. But she dismissed the idea immediately: the thought of catching a train – a series of trains – with a toddler and push-chair and all the paraphernalia needed – food and drink, nappies, spare clothing – to visit Claudia, who shared a small room with a friend, was beyond her. Claudia was working in a library. Thea pictured Claudia, sorting and stamping books, and felt a stab of envy.

After Janet had had her feed, Thea changed both babies' nappies. She was down to the last three nappies; she should have washed them earlier. She put the soiled ones to soak in the scullery sink. She settled Janet in her little chair and Polly at the table with crayons and scrap paper while she checked on the dinner. Polly was fractious – late afternoons were always her worst time – and sobbed when one of her wax crayons broke. Thea sat her on the draining board while she rinsed out the nappies. She had Polly balanced on her hip and was trying to lay the table when Janet began to cry. The potatoes were boiling over and the nappies needed putting on the clothes horse near the stove, to get the heat, or she would run out, so she put Polly in the playpen and adjusted the saucepan and then quickly rinsed out the nappies. Both children were howling lustily.

Nicola came in while Thea was comforting Janet. 'It's all right, I'll feed her,' she said. Nicola sat down in a chair, unbuttoned her blouse and took the baby. She looked tired.

'How was it?'

'We lost a pair of lambs. Dad tried and I tried but we couldn't save them.' The crying stopped as Janet latched on to the breast. 'Have you seen Dad?'

'Not yet.'

'You haven't heard, then?'

'Heard what?'

'Rufus has fenced off the wood.'

Draping nappies over the clothes horse, Thea turned to stare at Nicola. 'Low Chase?'

'Yes. He's had a couple of men out there all day, putting up a fence between our meadow and the wood.'

'He can't do that.'

''Course he can, Thea, it's his land. He can stop us going there whenever he likes. It's because of what Jack and Francis did. Rufus Greville doesn't like to be made a fool of. Anyone who passed Langhill would have seen that red paint over his gates. Apparently some folk made comments about it when Rufus was in Lawton, laughing at him behind his back, like. He'd have hated that.'

The door opened and Robert, Lennie, John and Cathy

came into the kitchen. 'I'll torch the bloody thing,' Robert was saying.

'Dad!' hissed Nicola. 'The children.'

'Sorry, love. I will though. I'll set fire to that fence.'

'And what's that going to solve?'

'What do you want me to do?' Robert's voice rose. 'Say yes, Mr Greville, do what you like, Mr Greville, we don't mind walking the extra mile round?'

'Stupid bugger,' Francis Jamieson said. The twins were peeling off their wet, muddy oilskins and boots in the lobby. 'Who does he think he is? We've always used that path.'

Janet began to cry again. 'Hey, love,' said Nicola softly, trying to coax the baby back on to the breast.

'You go and feed her in the snug, Nicola,' said Aunt Cathy. 'Get some quiet. I'll give Thea a hand with the dinner.'

The family sat round the table and Thea and Cathy served the dinner. Thea took Nicola a plate of food in the snug. Nicola raised her eyebrows to her. 'He'll do it,' she murmured. 'I wouldn't put it past Dad to burn that fence down. You should have heard him outside, he was that mad.'

Cormac came home from work while they were eating pudding. Thea had Polly on her lap so he took his plate of stew out of the stove and squeezed round the table, next to her.

His cousin Jack was saying, 'I'll give you the matches, Uncle Robert, if you like.'

Cormac's voice cut through the clamour. 'You won't touch that fence.' His eyes, cold and hard, moved from one twin to the other. 'You won't . . . and neither will you. You'll leave it be, do you understand?'

Francis Jamieson scowled. Jack said, 'I don't see why we should take this lying down.'

'I'll go and see Rufus Greville. Dad, Uncle John, just leave it, would you?'

More protests broke out. Tired of arguments, and with the headache that had been threatening all day pulsing at her temples, Thea used the excuse of Polly needing her bath and went upstairs. She ran the water and stripped off Polly's clothes and nappy.

Cormac came into the room and shut the door behind him. 'Has it been like this all day?'

'I don't know. I've been looking after the children.'

'Let me. You look like you've had enough.' He took a wriggling, naked Polly from her and lowered her carefully into the bath.

Thea shrugged and wiped her straggling fringe from her eyes. 'All these arguments . . . I hate it, Cormac.'

'I know. I'm sorry.' He was soaping Polly. He looked up at Thea. 'I'll find us a place of our own, I will, love, soon, I promise.'

'It's not your fault.'

She went downstairs to fetch the nappies. Folding them in the scullery she seemed to see herself, sitting at the table as the Jamiesons raged, not saying a word. She had turned into someone she hardly recognised. Someone who couldn't get through a page of a book without dozing off or being interrupted. Someone who thought about nappies and recipes rather than potsherds and antler picks. Someone who talked about weaning and rashes on babies' bottoms instead of discussing the fine detail of the problems involved in dating Iron Age settlements. Someone who was always tired and who was losing confidence in feeling that she was any good at anything.

She looked out of the scullery window. The rain was still

falling. She pictured the wet stones on the terrace and the narrow path of dark, trodden grass across the meadow. And a fence, cutting off Crawburn's land from Rufus Greville's. She thought of the Iron Age enclosure she had found in the woods, the mossy old stones and ditches, and the sketches and research she had begun in order to try to understand what had once stood there. The work had given her life here meaning, but now it seemed futile, a waste of time.

Sally had dropped round for a visit with the little girls; they were playing in Sophie's sitting room with Ruby and Kenneth. In the kitchen, one of the lodgers, a tiresome man called Mr Nuttall, was complaining to Sophie about the food.

'I thought I made it clear when I took the room, Mrs Craxton, that I have a delicate constitution. A little baked fish . . . a coddled egg even . . . is surely not too much to ask.'

There were neither fish nor eggs in the larder, but Sophie promised to attempt to source suitable food for that night's tea. 'If you would, Mrs Craxton,' said Mr Nuttall, who was a travelling salesman. Then, raising his eyebrows in the direction of the sitting room, he added, 'Oh dear, the noise.'

To prevent herself pointing out that that's what very small children did, they made a noise, Sophie fetched her shopping bag, ration book and purse, buttoned her coat and jammed on her hat. She went outside. It had been a harsh winter and the spring had arrived in fits and starts. Today, the fog had lingered. Sophie straightened the empty milk bottles and gave the brass door handle a quick buff with the sleeve of her coat. Then she closed the gate behind her.

She looked along the pavement and saw someone walking

towards the house, out of the mist. A man, tall and broad-shouldered, wearing a dark overcoat and blue scarf. The blurred figure resolved into Ed Willoughby.

She stopped, still, on the pavement. 'Ed!' she cried. 'Oh my goodness, Ed.' She was staring at him. She almost expected him to dissolve back into the fog.

He was smiling broadly. 'Is this a bad time?'

'No, not at all.' She held up her shopping bag. 'I have to go out, though, to buy fish for my lodger's tea.'

'May I come with you?'

'I'd love you to.'

They set off for the shops. Queuing in the fishmonger's, she noticed the changes in him. There were more strands of silver in his hair, at the sides and temples, and a few more lines round his brown eyes. His smile was the same, though, bright and gentle and generous.

She managed to purchase a piece of coley and a pair of kippers; he insisted on carrying her shopping bag for her. 'There's a tea shop over the road,' he said. 'If you had time . . .'

They went inside the tea shop. Ed placed their order. He said, 'How are you, Sophie?'

'I'm very well. And you?'

'Yes, I'm well, thank you. And the family?'

'I have another granddaughter. Isobel is Duncan and Sally's daughter, and she's a dear little thing. And Ruby is expecting her second baby in three months' time.'

Ed expressed delight and offered congratulations. He asked after the lodgers.

'Vera Cornish left last August,' Sophie said. 'She went to live with her sister in Birmingham. She's teaching at a girls' school. We write to each other regularly. So I've had to take in some new lodgers.' She would have preferred to give Stuart and Ruby the fourth bedroom for the children but money was tight. She took a small contribution from Stuart because he insisted, but his hotel job was not well paid and he needed to save money so that he and Ruby could one day have a home of their own. Anyway, Ruby was such a great help in the house that Sophie often thought she should be paying her.

The waitress arrived with a pot of coffee. 'The new lodgers aren't a patch on you and Vera, Ed,' said Sophie, as she poured. 'Mr Nuttall complains about everything and he is so very sure of himself. And then there's Miss Kerridge. She claims to be a ballet dancer. She comes back to the house at all hours and she's so untidy.' Miss Kerridge's room, which Sophie was obliged to clean daily, was a nightmare of discarded art silk underwear and grubby nylons and spilled powder.

She put down her cup. 'I can't like them, Ed,' she said, with a sigh. 'I was fond of my lodgers during the war. You and Vera and John and most of the others, I thought of you as my friends. Mr Nuttall told me that he was excused from military service on health grounds. There's something flabby about him. And one can't help wondering where Miss Kerridge gets her make-up and stockings from. Oh, dear.' She made an apologetic grimace. 'I shouldn't judge, should I?'

He offered her a cigarette; she took one. He said, 'I tried to find you, after the war. I wasn't sure whether I should call on you, after what we'd agreed, but I then thought I would anyway. I wanted to see how you were, at least. When I saw what had happened to the house I was afraid that something terrible had happened to you all. But then one of your neighbours told me that you were all right. They didn't know where you were living, though.'

'We moved around,' she said. 'At the time, it was difficult. But really, Ed, it could have been so much worse. We were so very fortunate.'

'I came back a couple of times after that. I don't travel to London all that often, but when I did, I'd call at Gilbert Street.' He paused and she sensed him weighing his words. 'If you hadn't been here today, I don't think I'd have tried again. Back in the war, after I left, I hoped you'd write to me, Sophie. It took me a long while to accept that you'd chosen not to. And in the end, going on hoping starts to feel, well, as if you're inviting pain. Courting it, almost.'

'It happened the day you left.' Sophie spoke quickly, as if suddenly afraid that she might be running out of time. 'The V-1. I was going to write to you that afternoon.'

He frowned. 'The same day?'

'Yes. You wrote your address on a piece of paper, Ed, and I put it in my chest of drawers upstairs, and then I went out. And when I came back, the top floor of the house was gone. And everything was burned in the fire or soaked and ruined by the firemen's hoses.'

He rubbed with a fingertip at the two deep lines scored between his eyes, as if trying to erase them. 'If you had written to me, what would you have said?'

'That I regretted hesitating. And that I like you very much. So very much.'

She saw him look to the side, as if catching his breath. The thought came to her that it was too late. She said carefully, 'Perhaps you've met someone else.'

'No.' A shake of the head. 'No, Sophie. You're not the only one with regrets. I could have written to you. I could have come to find you sooner. Rejection is so hurtful to one's pride, isn't it? I wanted to see you in person because I thought I'd be able to read your feelings on your face. I thought I'd be able to tell what you thought of me. You might open the door and I'd see, oh, I don't know – exasperation, perhaps. And in that case, I'd make some polite small talk and beat a hasty exit.'

'How we torment ourselves,' she said softly.

'Oh, yes. How indeed.'

They both must have moved at the same time, because their hands touched. It was easier to touch than to talk. It began to erase the misunderstandings. With her hand enfolded in his large warm one, she glimpsed a possibility of happiness.

'It was always hard for me to move on, because of Hugh,' she said. 'It took me a long time.'

'Not all men are like Hugh. I am not like Hugh.'

'I know that, Ed. But after Hugh died, I had to learn to manage on my own. It was hard, but I did it. I've met such wonderful people, so many kind, good people.'

'Why do you think he did it?'

She thought about Hugh – handsome, charming, damaged Hugh. 'Because he could,' she said. She had had a lot of time to think about it. 'Because opportunity flung itself in his path. Women were drawn to him.'

The waitress was cleaning the tables, Mr Nuttall's coley was warming in her shopping bag and the lodgers' tea was already late. Ed paid the bill and they left the café. As they walked back to the house, she tucked her hand round his arm and asked him to tell her about his wife, Jenny, who had died nearly ten years ago. He had loved her dearly, he said. They had met at a church social, when they were both eighteen. He described a cheerful, energetic woman, who had liked playing tennis and dancing.

'We used to go dancing together,' he told her. 'I was never anything special, but she was so good and she got me on my feet. I haven't danced since Jenny died. And I never thought I'd love again. I didn't think I had it in me. You're not the only one who's had to learn to live again, Sophie. It's taken me quite a while, too.'

An uneasy atmosphere hung over the farmhouse. Though Cormac had called on Rufus Greville to talk to him about the fence, Rufus had been obdurate, and so the fence remained, dividing Crawburn's land from Langhill's. A few afternoons before, Robert Jamieson had been to see John at Bane Rigg. The brothers had had several drinks together. Walking home in bad weather, Robert had decided to take the path through Low Chase. He had tried to climb over the fence in the dark, but had slipped and torn a muscle in his leg. As he slowly stumbled home he had been drenched by rain and, over the days that followed, the bronchitis he was prone to had returned. His condition had deteriorated and that morning he had been admitted to the cottage hospital.

Nicola broke the news to Cormac when he came home from work in the evening. 'I'll go and see him,' he said. He pulled his wet coat back on.

'Let me,' said Nicola.

'No, you stay here.' He kissed Thea and Polly and left the house again.

Thea put Polly to bed, then she and Nicola cleared up the kitchen while Lennie lit the fires in the snug and sitting room. The rain was driving down, hammering against the windows. Visiting hours at the cottage hospital were between seven and eight. Nine o'clock arrived and Cormac had not yet come home. Thea, Nicola and Lennie sat in the snug. For the Jamieson family, the evening was unusually quiet, their conversational forays quickly petering out. They were all worried about Robert, and though nobody said so, Thea suspected that each of them was afraid that Cormac had stayed on at the hospital because his father's condition had worsened.

At half past nine, Thea went upstairs to bed. She dozed off, surfacing at the sounds made by the wind and the rain. She was slipping into a deeper sleep when she heard the door open. Cormac came into the room.

'How's your dad?' she whispered.

'Stable, the doctor said.' He was pulling off his clothes. 'Weak, though. He could hardly sit up in bed. I hate seeing him like that.'

She saw him grab a towel and rub his hair. 'You're soaking.'

'Wet night.'

'You were a long time.'

'I had something to do.'

Polly murmured in her sleep and Cormac went to check on her. Then he climbed into bed and took Thea in his arms. His cold skin made her flinch. She drifted off to sleep again.

Cormac got Polly up the next morning so that Thea could have a lie-in. When she went downstairs, Cormac had gone to work. Nicola told her that she had phoned the hospital. Robert had had a quiet night. She put Janet in the pram and set off for the village.

Thea made a pie for dinner with a jar of the plums they had bottled the previous summer. Polly sat in her high chair beside her, playing with the offcuts of pastry. The post arrived.

There was a letter from Grace. Thea read it, then put it upstairs, tucking it behind the dressing-table mirror.

She heard a knock at the door. She opened it. A policeman was standing on the step. 'Mrs Jamieson?' he said.

When he was gone, Thea put the pie in the oven, picked the lumps of pastry off the floor and cleaned Polly up. Then she fed Polly her dinner of mince and mashed potato and put her upstairs for her nap. Nicola came back from Lawton and Thea told her about the policeman's visit. Rufus Greville had reported that the fence at Low Chase had been vandalised. That someone had taken an axe to it.

'It'll be the twins again,' said Nicola angrily. 'There'll be hell to pay for this. Those idiots.'

Thea didn't say anything. The policeman had asked her whether she had any idea of who might have damaged the fence. No, she knew nothing about it, she had said, reasonably truthfully. Nicola must be right, Jack and Francis would have hacked apart Rufus Greville's fence. It was the sort of thing they would do. Still, she wished she could stop thinking of Cormac, coming home late, towelling his wet hair, his clothes so sodden they had still been damp when she had put them in the wash that morning.

Cormac had more sense, she told herself. And yet recently he had seemed distant from her. It chilled her to realise she could not recall when they had last had a proper conversation. They had once been able to talk endlessly about anything.

He couldn't have done it. He wouldn't be so stupid.

In the afternoon, Nicola went to visit her father. Thea looked after the babies and got the tea ready. She thought about Grace's letter and she thought about Cormac, rubbing

his black curls dry. *You were a long time . . . I had something to do.*
Anxiety lay like a stone in the pit of her stomach.

Nicola came home from the hospital. Robert had seemed better, she said. He was sitting up and talking. She hadn't told him about the fence. Someone would, no doubt, Cathy or John probably, but it didn't do to get him worked up. After her visit, Nicola had talked to one of the nurses who had said that her father was responding to treatment.

Before he had left for work that morning, Cormac had told them that he would stay on in Hexham and see his father in the evening visiting hour. They had dinner and Thea put Polly to bed. She knelt by the cot, singing lullabies, as she did every night, 'Golden Slumbers' and 'Twinkle, Twinkle Little Star', repeated over and over again, softer and softer, until Polly slept. She wished she could remember the Swedish lullaby that her mother had sung to her but she couldn't. She wondered whether Sigrid had ever knelt beside her daughter's cot, her insides knotted with fear, wondering what her husband had done. Whether he had turned out to be different from the man she thought she had married.

Polly's eyes closed. Thea stood up, still singing softly, and read through Grace's letter again. Grace had offered her work later that year, in the summer. She was hiring as many of the old team as she could get together to take part in the excavation of the site of a long barrow in Wiltshire. Thea tried to suppress her sense of longing. She should tear it up, she thought, forget the person she had once been.

She couldn't face going downstairs but remained in the room, sitting on the bed, reading. She heard voices from the lower floor of the house; she recognised Cormac's.

He came into the room. He whispered, 'Is she asleep?'

'Just. How was your dad?'

'He's improving, thank God.' He took off his jacket, slung it over the back of a chair.

She waited for him to say something more but he didn't. Nicola or Lennie would have told him about the fence being vandalised. It was odd that he didn't mention it, she thought. Thea watched him unknotting his tie, rolling it up, putting it on the chest of drawers. He hadn't yet looked properly at her. It was as if, she thought, they didn't know each other very well.

She said, 'Did you do it, Cormac?'

His hand, undoing the top button of his shirt, stilled. Then he said softly, 'The wood isn't his to fence off.'

She pressed her knuckles against her mouth. Now he looked at her.

'Yes, he's got a piece of paper that says it's his, but you and I know, old places like that, they belong to us all. Rufus Greville is Low Chase's custodian, nothing more.'

She pushed her fringe back from her face. She needed a haircut, she thought. She needed to sort herself out, sort her life out. 'You didn't tell me. You did that without telling me.'

'I didn't want to worry you.'

'Rubbish. You didn't trust me.'

'That's not true. Rufus Greville has no right. And when I saw Dad like that in the hospital—'

'That's not the point.' Her voice was small and hard. 'You and I, we're supposed to share things. We have to be honest with each other. After everything we've worked for, everything we've got, you went and did that! How could you risk our future?'

'Our future . . .?' Now his eyes were chips of blue ice. 'What future? And what have we got, you and I? What have

403

we got after all those years of being apart? *Nothing*. We don't even have our own home!'

'We have each other. We have Polly. That's not *nothing*.' She wanted to cry and was furious with herself for doing so and squeezed her eyes tightly, forcing the tears back.

He went to stand at the window, moving the curtain aside an inch, his back to her. 'I thought coming home would be different. I've let you down.'

She stared at him. 'No.'

'I'm supposed to provide for you and yet here we are, stuck here, caught up in the middle of other people's quarrels.' He swung round to her. 'You're not happy, are you, Thea?'

Of course I am. But the words caught in her throat and she looked away. Only a few moments ago she had said, *We have to be honest with each other*.

'I love you,' she said. 'I love Polly.'

'I know that. But you're not happy.'

Moments passed before she spoke. 'I should be happy.' Her voice was small. 'I have Polly. I have you. I have a roof over my head.'

'Running a house bores you stiff, I can see it.'

She bunched up the patchwork quilt between her fists. 'I shouldn't find being a mother boring, though, should I?'

Shame flooded through her. She thought, my mother put us in a boat and took us out in a storm and I would have drowned if it hadn't been for Rowan. Perhaps being a mother hadn't been enough for Sigrid, either. And look at what had happened.

Cormac sat down on the bed beside her. 'Thea, you love her, and that's what matters,' he said gently. 'The rest of it . . . you don't have to love all that.'

'Plenty of women do.'

'Doesn't mean you do. If I'd wanted to marry a woman who was content with doing the cooking and cleaning, I'd have done so.'

Neither of them spoke for a while. Thea thought of the envelope she had put behind the dressing-table mirror. *We're supposed to share things.*

'Grace wrote to me,' she said.

'What did she say?'

'She's offered me work, this summer, in Wiltshire.'

'Then you must take it.'

'How can I?'

'We'll find a way. Nicola will help with Polly, you know that. And Aunt Cathy. And I'll take some time off work.'

'I wouldn't expect you to do that.'

'Why not? I'm her father.' He touched her hand, their first physical contact since he had come into the room. 'Working for Phil, it's fine for the time being, but I'm not going to stay there. I've realised that it's not for me, being indoors all the time.'

'You didn't say.'

'No.'

'We're rather hopeless, aren't we?'

'I don't think so.' The ghost of a smile. 'I think we're just sorting ourselves out. Don't you?'

She nodded. He gripped her hand. 'Thea, I don't want to be the person who limits you. I don't want to be the man who forces you into being something you're not. I've been thinking for a while that we should talk about moving away from here.'

'Moving away from Crawburn?'

'Yes.'

'I wouldn't ask that of you. I know how much you love it here.'

'I can learn to love somewhere else.'

She mulled this over. Then she said, 'Where would we go?'

'Somewhere we can start afresh. This place, it ties you up in a net. Maybe that's not such a good thing. It's all very well loving a place, but not if it holds you back. I can't seem to move on here. Wherever we end up, I'll love it, so long as I'm with you. That's all that matters to me.' His gaze roamed round the room and came to rest on her. 'Last night, I lost my temper. I never told you about what happened when I went to talk to Rufus Greville about the fence. I ended up feeling a fool for ever thinking I could change his mind. He treated me like a servant, like his inferior. He kept me waiting for half an hour, and when he did deign to see me, he didn't offer me a seat. He had me standing there, cap in hand, while he sat at his desk.'

'Oh, Cormac.'

They lay down next to each other on the bed. She hated that he had kept his humiliation to himself, that he hadn't felt able to confide in her. She hated that they had, for a while, forgotten how to talk to each other. Rufus Greville might press charges, the policeman had said so. The thought of Cormac in court appalled her. Thea still felt the pounding of her heart and the ache of anxiety in her gut. Cormac's hand ran down her ribcage and waist and over the swell of her hip, a gentle, reassuring caress, and after a while the small sounds in the room – Polly's soft breathing, the creaking of timbers and the rattle of rain against the window-panes – soothed her and she found a strength inside that came from the knowledge that so long as they were together, truly together, she could get through anything. And she nestled closer to him and began to unbutton his shirt and their lovemaking was silent and passionate.

All the next day she waited for the rap on the door. A movement in the yard outside or footsteps on the flagstones made her start and dash to the window to look out, her heart in her throat. But the policeman did not return to Crawburn. In the evening, John and Cathy came to the farmhouse after visiting Robert. Cathy told them that Madeline Greville's baby had been born earlier that day, that it had been a difficult birth and that Madeline and the child, a girl, had been rushed to hospital. The baby was thought to be very ill. Cormac, on hearing the news, fell silent. Later, when he and Thea were alone, he took her in his arms. 'I've been such a fool,' he said. 'God help me for ever feeling envious of Rufus Greville, the poor devil. I have a beautiful, healthy daughter and I have you. I have so much to be grateful for.'

Sunday lunch at the Makepeaces' house. Josh's two-year-old nephew, Freddie, a child of boundless energy, was hitting a spoon over and over again against the metal arm of his high chair. 'Don't do that, darling,' said his mother, Mary. Freddie kept on banging the spoon.

Mary's husband, Ronald, the elder of Josh's two brothers, drawled, 'See what you're letting yourself in for, Josh. Drive you nuts, children.'

Josh stood up. 'Going out for a walk,' he said. Grabbing a jacket from the back of a chair, he headed out of the house.

Rowan made to rise too, but Julia, Josh's mother, put a hand on her arm, staying her. 'Mary, Ronald,' said Julia. 'Why don't you take the boys upstairs to play with the train set?'

Mary and Ronald and their three sons headed up to the attic where Bill Makepeace kept his model railway.

'Ronald always was my least tactful son,' said Julia, piling up bowls.

'I'd better go after him,' said Rowan. 'Make sure he's all right.'

'I should leave him be. Josh just needs a few moments to himself. He's always been like that — wonderful company, but then he'd slip away so that he could be on his own for a while.' Blobs of trifle were spread round the high chair and table. Julia scraped up jelly with a spoon. 'Sometimes one remembers fondly the days when children were kept to the nursery,' she said.

Rowan and Josh had been staying with the Makepeaces for the last three months. Their home, The Sandlings, was a substantial redbrick house set in grounds of an acre and a half in the small village of Wintlesham. Behind the paddock where Julia kept her horse and a pony for her grandsons lay a landscape of sand, birch and gorse, threaded with a maze of winding paths that led to the crumbling Suffolk coast, and the sea. Rowan knew that Josh would be walking those paths now. He had done so every day since they had come to stay at The Sandlings. He would choose a route he had never taken before because that's what he preferred to do. No matter how much his yen for adventure had scarred him, Josh remained an explorer at heart. His head would be down against the whipping rain but he wouldn't notice the bad weather, he never did.

Most days Rowan walked with him. Sometimes they talked but at other times they said little, exchanging only the occasional comment about what they saw. Their walks were part of the pattern of life at The Sandlings. The Makepeaces' lives ran like clockwork, the routine masterminded by Julia. It had been good for Josh, Rowan had noticed, because it kept him busy without asking too much of him. Meals were at pre-ordained times; gardening and tending the horses, pigs and chickens and Julia's W.I. meetings and Bill's golf occupied the hours between meals. Bill liked to play a round of golf with Josh a couple of times a week. Sundays meant morning service at the pretty village church, sherry with the neighbours, and then lunch at one o'clock. Josh's brothers and their families often joined them. The pace of life was a shock to the system after London, and after the hospital. Rowan felt as if she had been running fast as for a very long time and had suddenly stopped. She should be bored, but she wasn't, not yet.

'He hasn't done that for a while,' she said. 'Just walked out.' She subsided, feeling despairing.

'He'll be fine.' Julia patted her shoulder. 'Ronald's three would sap the life out of anyone. I'm their grandmother and I adore them, but I still reach for the gin bottle the minute they go home.' She took the china into the kitchen and Rowan followed her.

'Josh is getting better,' Julia said. 'I'm sure you've seen that too, Rowan.'

'Sometimes I think he's recovering but then he seems to slip back.'

'Isn't that a common pattern with illness?'

'Yes, I suppose so.'

'He hasn't had a headache since the first week you came here. And you told me he was sleeping better.'

'It's me who wakes up now. This little thing, moving around.' Rowan put a hand on the small curve of her belly. She was six months pregnant.

'He's getting better,' said Julia firmly. 'He told me that he's looking forward to the baby. I've always thought that Josh would make a wonderful father. Go and sit in the sun room, Rowan, and I'll bring you some tea. You know the doctor said you needed to rest more.'

'I'll help with the clearing-up.'

'Dear me, I used to cater single-handed for dinner parties of thirty when Bill and I were stationed in Ooty. This won't take me two ticks. Run along now.'

Rowan did as she was told and went to the sun room. At the rear of the house, the ramshackle structure of wood and glass was invariably chilly but always light and airy. Bill and Josh had both had a go at the holes in the roof, but it still leaked when it rained.

On The Sandlings' walls were portraits of illustrious Makepeaces. They had fought in colonial wars, they had forged careers in politics, they had been travellers or rene-gades. Some of Josh's forebears had been painted in military redcoats or evening dress; others, more dubious characters perhaps, were got up in fanciful versions of local costumes, in turban or djellaba. Rowan didn't doubt that any of those Makepeace forebears could have made a meal from scratch for thirty in Ooty, wherever that was. The Makepeace family history exuded self-assurance and a sense of infallibility. Sometimes she thought that was part of Josh's problem.

But Julia was right, she reflected. He was getting better. Because his recovery had been gradual, it was easy to skate over the improvements. He was less jumpy and did not tire as quickly. It was obvious to Rowan that an outdoor life suited Josh. During their long hikes over heathland and pebble beaches, she had sensed him trying to walk his low mood away.

She drank the tea that Julia brought her and then she must have dozed off. She was woken by the back door opening. She sat up.

Josh came into the room. His jacket was soaked and the rain had darkened his hair. 'Hello, darling,' he said. 'Are you up to a walk?'

'Now?'

'Yes. I've found somewhere rather wonderful. I'd like you to see it.'

Rowan put on her mackintosh and boots and they went outside. The clouds had thinned and between the squalls of rain the pale spring sun gleamed now and then on the wet lawn and on the grey branches of the beech hedges. They headed through the back garden and alongside the paddock, towards the heathland. Gorse to either side of them and birch trees like sentinels. On her own in this sprawling wilderness she might have got hopelessly lost but Josh had a sense of direction like a homing pigeon's.

He slowed his pace to match hers, taking her hand and warning her of the exposed roots and rabbit holes that made the ground treacherous. Though she was thrilled about the coming baby, she was not, Rowan had discovered, one of those women who enjoyed being pregnant. She disliked the physical limitations that pregnancy imposed on her. Her doctor's admonitions to rest irritated her, but what irritated her far more was the fact that he was right. These days, she tired easily.

The path wound through a box wood, all twisting pale-yellow trunks and leathery dark leaves, and then they were back on the heath. Another quarter of a mile or so and the countryside changed again, gorse and birch giving way to deciduous trees. The wind had dropped and the rain fell lightly, soft drops tumbling vertically on to the undergrowth.

'Look,' he said.

A suggestion of brick and flint and the glitter of a windowpane. In this place where land disintegrated into sea, the house that lay ahead of them seemed to shimmer.

'Oh, Josh,' she said. She smiled, looking at it. 'It's rather magical.'

'Isn't it?'

They walked down the slope to the flint-and-brick wall that surrounded the building. There was a gate in the wall. Josh began to tear off the strands of ivy that bound it shut.

'Josh, we mustn't!' She was whispering, as if some unseen listener was round the corner. 'Someone might come.'

'It's empty.' He unlatched the gate. 'I had a good look round earlier.'

Curiosity propelled her after him and Rowan found herself in a walled garden. What had once been a lawn was now grass a foot high and gone to seed, dotted with wild daffodils. A thicket of shrubs and climbers fanned out through the old flower beds. The house appeared to be L-shaped, a stepped gable making up the shorter stroke of the L and a long two-storey wing jutting from the side of it. Tucked into the angle made by the two wings of the house was a terrace.

They walked across wet paving stones blotched with lichen. Dead leaves rippled in water dimpled by the rain in a rectangular pond; a huge rambling rose scrambled up the back wall of the house, to the height of the roof. French doors led into the room overlooking the terrace. Josh tried the door handle while Rowan squawked a protest. They were locked. She peered through a window.

They walked round to the other end of the building. A kitchen garden, a greenhouse with a glass roof where half the panes were missing, letting in the rain. A shed, an overflowing water butt standing beside it, and a brick-built structure, in front of which was a series of railed enclosures.

'Kennels,' said Josh. 'For guard dogs. The house must have been requisitioned during the war. By the R.A.F., perhaps, out here in Suffolk.'

Here was a side door, its green paint peeling. Again, Josh tried the handle. Then he took his penknife out of his pocket.

'Josh!' she hissed.

He twisted the narrow blade of the knife in the lock and the door opened.

'Josh, we can't!'

He smiled at her, over his shoulder. 'Come on, let's have a look inside.'

They found themselves in a narrow lobby. Russet fragments of dry leaf swirled across a black-and-white-tiled floor. A khaki water bottle hung from a coat peg and a dog's lead lay curled like a snake on top of a boot rack.

Behind the lobby was a corridor leading into a series of empty rooms. At the windows, blackout material hung in tattered folds next to faded brocade and chintz curtains. Rowan imagined how in fine weather the silvery Suffolk coastal light would pour into these rooms, which were square and substantial without being overly large.

Josh ran a fingertip through the dust on a mantelpiece. 'It must have been empty for quite a while.'

'I wonder what it was before the war. A farmhouse, perhaps. Oh, Josh, come and see this.'

She was standing in the doorway of the room she had

413

seen from the terrace. Wallpaper patterned in faded green lozenges of stylised strands of ivy reflected the dark-green leaves of the climbing rose around the windows.

'Imagine sitting in here on a summer's day! Imagine two plump sofas – yellow and green, yes, I'd do this room in yellow and green. Two sofas and some armchairs.'

'Definitely your department, soft furnishings,' he said, wandering round. 'I daresay I could sort out the gin and tonics.'

They explored the remainder of the ground floor. A door that jammed bore the marks of boot-prints where the R.A.F. officers must have kicked it open. In a corridor, names and dates had been scrawled above a dado rail. The old wooden floors were dulled by a layer of dirt and dust; pinholes punctured a wall in a circular fashion, showing where a dartboard had once hung. A few items of furniture remained, uncomfortable metal chairs that Rowan assumed the R.A.F. had brought with them. The only other pieces were built in to the rooms. Along one side of the kitchen wall was a dresser, painted cobalt blue. The row of tiny drawers along the front of the dresser contained, Rowan discovered, odds and ends. Safety pins, a stub of pencil, an empty match box, a reel of cotton.

And buttons. She scooped out a handful. Made of crystal and coloured glass, they sparkled in her palm. 'Josh, come and look at this,' she called out. 'Some of these look really old.'

No reply. She glanced round. He was not in the kitchen. 'Josh?' she called again. She put the buttons back in the drawer and went to look for him.

She found him in a corridor that led away from the kitchen. A trapdoor, set into the floor, lay open. Steps ran down into the blackness of a cellar. She heard his laboured breathing; when she said his name again he looked up, but she did not think he saw her. She knew that he was remembering the pit beneath the barn in which he had hidden in France.

'Josh?' she said.

'I messed up.'

'Josh, it's okay, I'm here.'

'The drop, Rowan. I messed it up.' He stared at her, his eyes anguished.

He had never talked to her about that last, disastrous mission into occupied France. On the few occasions she had tried to speak to him about it he had batted the subject angrily away. She took his hand and steered him away from the cellar, back into the kitchen. There was a tin mug on the dresser; she rinsed it, filled it with water and gave it to him.

His gaze fixed on the drops that slid down the window-panes. 'It was raining,' he said. 'Heavier than this.'

'In France.'

'Yes. It was all right when we left England. A fine night, no wind. But the forecast can't have been correct because by the time we were over the Channel, the weather had turned.'

'That must have made it difficult.'

'Yes.' He dropped his head. 'It all went wrong, Rowan.' He closed his eyes tightly.

'Have some of the water, Josh.'

He took a few sips and his breathing seemed to steady. He wiped his mouth with the back of his hand. 'The wind blew me sideways.' His voice was quiet and she had to strain to hear. 'I couldn't see well because of the damned rain. I

415

didn't react quickly enough. I hit the corner of a roof of a building as I came down. Some damned ramshackle little hut in the middle of nowhere, I should have seen it, but I didn't. If I'd seen it, I might have been able to pull away from it. If I'd been just a couple of feet over, it would have been all right.'

'It wasn't your fault, Josh.'

His gaze moved to her, unblinking. 'It was. I thought the damned chute wasn't responding, that there was something wrong with it, and I looked up, and then I hit the hut.'

He put his hands over his face. 'Every mistake you make puts a dozen others in danger. I lost count of the people who put their lives on the line to help me, and all because I wasn't concentrating and made a stupid mistake. There was a girl, just a schoolgirl, sixteen or seventeen, little thing, pigtails and glasses. She used to bring me food when I was hiding in a shed somewhere, when my leg was bad. And suddenly she didn't come any more. I didn't ask what had happened to her. I didn't need to.'

When she took his hand she felt his muscles vibrate like a string wound too tightly. 'Listen to me, Josh,' she said gently. 'It was dark and wet and you were worried about the parachute. It could have happened to anyone.'

'Yes, but it happened to me. Just to me.'

'There may have been something wrong with the parachute. You don't know that there wasn't. The weather forecast was incorrect, you said that yourself. The aeroplane may have been blown off course. So it wasn't just you.'

He made a hopeless gesture. 'It comes down to me. It always comes down to the person responsible for doing the job.'

'Yes, I see that, but, Josh, if it had been Alex, if exactly

416

the same thing had happened to Alex, what would you have said to him?'

He frowned. 'What do you mean?'

'If Alex had made a small error of judgement on a bad night, would you have condemned him for it?'

He looked down at his hands. He muttered, 'I don't know.'

'I think you do. I think you'd have told him that mistakes happen and he shouldn't blame himself. I think you'd have forgiven him. Perhaps you should think about forgiving yourself.'

He was silent for some time. Then he gave his head a quick shake as if to clear it. 'I panicked, Rowan. I've always been able to tell which direction north is. I knew I'd hurt myself badly that night. My leg wouldn't work at all. I knew I had to get rid of the parachute but every time I moved it was so excruciating I thought I was going to black out. It felt like hours before I managed to cut the harness. I stuffed the chute by the wall of the blasted shed. You're supposed to bury it but I couldn't. I knew I had to get away somehow but I couldn't tell what direction to go in. I had to drag myself across the ground. I'd memorised the layout of the drop zone but because I'd been blown off course I just couldn't . . .' He ran his tongue over dry lips. 'I couldn't work out where I was. I thought I was going to die there, in some bloody little hell-hole corner of France, on my own in the rain.'

'Poor Josh.'

He ran a fingernail along a groove in the draining board. 'All that time I was in France,' he said softly 'I never really knew where I was. They moved me around. I could only go out at night. I don't know whether it was something to do with being shut off from the sun, but I couldn't get my bearings. I tried to work it out from the stars, but I was lost.' Another longer silence, then he said, 'I've been struggling to find my way ever since.'

'Darling, we'll work it out together.' She put her arms round him, resting her head against his shoulder.

Minutes passed and then he said, 'I wouldn't have blamed you if you'd called it a day.'

She stroked his face. 'I love you. I love all of you.'

'I'm not sure I can go back to what I was before.'

'You don't have to, Josh.'

'I don't think I can face working in London any more.'

'That's all right. We'll stay here.'

'But then I think, I need to find something to do. I can't do nothing.'

'You won't. I know you. You'll find something. Let's not worry about it now. Let's have a look upstairs.'

As they climbed the stairs, he said, 'You and my parents . . . I don't know what I'd have done without you. I've been so lucky.'

Lucky, she thought, and she wanted to scream with rage at the thought of all he had endured: the physical agony and the mental anguish. But she pressed her head against his arm and said, 'I love you too.'

'I feel I'm asking too much of you, immuring you in deepest, darkest Suffolk.'

The sun was breaking through at last and shafts of light quivered on the oak floor on the landing. 'Maybe I'm ready for a change as well,' she said.

'Could you think of staying here?'

'To live?' She considered. 'Yes, why not?'

'Because you're a city girl. Because you're miles away from your friends and from Thea.'

'If we found somewhere of our own they could come and stay with us. Your friends, too, Josh, of course.'

'There's one or two I'd ask down here if we had a place of our own. Men who are in rather a mess, like me.'

'That's a good idea.'

'Put our home to good use.'

'We used to see them at the hospital,' she said slowly. 'Men who'd been in the Forces and were brought into Casualty. Maybe they'd got drunk and ended up sleeping on the pavement in the cold and were frozen to the marrow. Or they'd got into a fight. I used to try to talk to them, to find out if there was any way I might be able to help, but there was so little any of us could do.'

An idea was hovering on the edges of her consciousness; she was struggling to grasp it. Out of the window of the biggest bedroom, she saw the glimmering horizon of the sea, not half a mile away.

'Look at that view, Josh. Just look at it.'

'I know. You could fall in love with it.' His gaze fixed on the sea. 'I wonder if this house is for sale?'

She shot him a glance. 'Worth finding out. But could we afford it?'

'I have some money. My grandfather left it to me. It would be a good place to bring up a family, don't you think?'

It would, she thought. Could she live here, so far from the sort of life she was accustomed to? She had told him that she wanted a change. Could she cope with a change as huge as this?

'It's a lovely big garden,' she said. 'And the beach, so near.'

'Yes.'

'The house is in rather a state. It would need a lot of work.'

'I could do that. I'd like to do that.'

Like seizing a mote of dust floating in the sun, she reached out to the thought that was tantalising her. 'We could use it as a respite home,' she said. 'Ex-soldiers who were unwell could come and stay with us here. We could start with your friends. We'd give them somewhere peaceful and beautiful to stay and they'd have the chance to recover. You'd run the home, Josh, and I'd do the nursing side of it. We could get help if we needed it. You're not the only one who needs something to do. I know I'll have the baby, but I'll need something to keep my brain going as well. All those years working as a nurse – I can't just waste that.'

'A respite home . . .' He frowned.

'What do you think?'

He drew her to him. 'I think it's a marvellous idea.'

Rowan looked round the room. She imagined it furnished in soft blues, greys and gold that would echo the landscape that surrounded them. More images: vases of delphiniums in the big front room, the sound of a child's footsteps on the stairs and the French doors open to the terrace as the scent of roses wafted indoors.

He said, 'Could we live here? Would it be completely berserk to think of buying this place?'

Sophie went to see Ed, near Lewes. Wild rose and honeysuckle sprawled through the Sussex hedgerows. A sign outside the barn said, *E. Willoughby, Cabinet Maker and Furniture Restorer*. The weatherboarding of the barn was stained black; to one side of the building were tall double doors, through which, presumably, carts and farm machinery had once driven.

Ed's living quarters, a kitchen, sitting room and two

bedrooms, were at the rear of the building. He made a pot of coffee in the kitchen, which he had fitted out with units made of reclaimed wood. They went into the workshop, a large, airy expanse at the front of the barn, which smelled of resin and sawdust, and Ed showed Sophie his latest commissions, a rocking-chair with a carved backrest, a circular table made of timber of a soft golden colour.

A customer called about an order. Sophie left Ed to it and went to sit on a bench in an area of grass to the side of the building. This was one of her favourite places. Sunlight fell in shimmering green columns through the branches of the elm trees and cow parsley spread itself about in a cream-coloured froth. The warm air bore the sharp tang of nettles.

Inside Ed's workshop was a long bench on which stood paints, papers and jam-jars of brushes. He had told her that this was where he did his decorative work. Sophie remembered that when she had been at school she had liked art. She had been good at it. She had wanted to go on to art college but then the war had come and poor Harold had been killed and she had become a nurse instead. She had coloured and drawn with her boys, when they were little, but since then her only painting had been of walls and window-frames. Ed was keen that she take it up again.

Ruby's second baby, a girl, Leah, had been born six weeks ago. Sophie planned to give the Gilbert Street house to Stuart and Ruby. Mr Nuttall and Miss Kerridge had been given notice that the Bed and Breakfast establishment was to close. Ruby intended to re-open it in the future, when the children were older.

After months of searching, Duncan and Sally had found a house near Croydon airport, where Duncan worked. It was a nice detached villa with bay windows at the front, rough round the edges, but then, wasn't everything? Sophie had talked to Duncan about giving Stuart the family home and Duncan had said, yes, of course, Mum, that's fine, but what about you? She had begun to tell him about Ed, about what a wonderful man he was, how solid and supportive and honest, and how much in love they were, but Duncan, who was fitting a row of bookshelves in the sitting room of his new house, had interrupted her. Stu told me about him, he said. It's fine, Mum. The only thing that matters is that you're happy. Are you going to get married? A little flummoxed by the discovery that a conversation she had imagined would be difficult had turned out to be surprisingly easy, she had said that yes, they were, in the autumn, she expected. She had glossed over the fact that she would probably be living with Ed at the barn before that, living in sin, she supposed, but she suspected Duncan could work it out for himself.

Ed's customer completed his business and left. Sophie and Ed had lunch sitting outside and afterwards went for a walk. The barn was on the edge of the South Downs; from the top of the hill, they looked down to Lewes, a couple of miles away. Sophie pictured herself walking to Lewes on a fine day, doing a little shopping. She imagined the two of them living in the bright, open space of the barn.

There, among the dog-roses and the honeysuckle, he kissed her. An inconvenient hot flush ran through her and she had to untuck her blouse and flap it to get some air. 'It's my age,' she said, but he knew that, was used to it, and had already gone into the house to fetch her a glass of water. She drank it and the heat passed and they kissed again. And then he put up the *Closed* sign by the workshop and they went indoors, and to bed.

*

Thea was pushing Polly up the Langhill road. Polly was in the pushchair, bribed with a biscuit. She preferred to walk, but walking took ages because Polly liked to examine every pebble and blade of grass and could happily spend half an hour admiring some sheep in a field. Today, Thea must get back to Crawburn, to pack.

She caught sight of a woman ahead of her, pushing a pram. She recognised Madeline Greville from her flaxen hair. The Jamiesons had heard nothing more from the police; Rufus Greville had not pressed charges. Neither had the damaged section of fence been repaired. Thea supposed that in the drama of Rufus's daughter's birth, six weeks ago in April, all that had been forgotten.

'Hello!' Thea called out.

Madeline Greville looked back. 'Good morning, Mrs Jamieson.'

'May I have a peek at her?'

'Yes . . . yes, of course.'

Thea admired the baby in the pram. 'She's beautiful,' she said. 'What a pretty little girl.'

'Thank you.'

'I hope she's well, now.'

'The doctor says she has a heart murmur. He doesn't think it's anything to worry about, but Venetia didn't breathe at first when she was born and . . .' The words faltered. Madeline touched her daughter's face, as if to check the warmth of her skin.

'So frightening,' said Thea.

'I worry, all the time.' The words were a gasp.

'You do, when you have a baby. And you, are you well?'

'Yes, thank you.' Violet shadows had printed themselves beneath Madeline's light-blue eyes. 'Though I'm very tired.

423

She was only five and a half pounds when she was born and she needs to catch up.'

'The night feeds are exhausting, aren't they?'

'They are, yes. How old is your daughter now, Mrs Jamieson?'

'Polly will be two in September.'

Madeline smiled. 'Such pretty curls.'

'I know. She's so lucky. Shall we walk together?'

They headed up the road, side by side. Polly made baaing sounds as they passed a flock of sheep. Madeline Greville said suddenly, 'You don't come from here, do you?'

'No, I was born in Glasgow.'

'How do you find it, living here? I find it very quiet.'

'Actually, Cormac and I are moving away. We've found a cottage to rent in Wiltshire.'

'I hope—' Madeline broke off, her pale skin stained by a flush of pink. She seemed to alter what she had been about to say. 'I hope you're both happy there,' she said. 'I'd prefer to move back to London. Rufus hasn't made up his mind yet. I feel there would be better care for Venetia in London. We'll always keep Langhill House, naturally. We'd come here for summers.'

'It's a beautiful place.'

'Yes.'

They had reached the gates of Langhill House. Thea said, 'It would be nice to think that both our daughters will play here, in the fields and the woods. It would be nice to think that, in the future, they might be friends.'

Madeline unlatched the gate. 'I hope so, yes.'

They said goodbye and Thea headed on, up the track. Tomorrow, she, Cormac and Polly were to take a train to the south of England. They would stay overnight in London, in Rowan's flat, and then the following day they would travel on to Wiltshire and move into a rented cottage. Cormac would look after Polly while Thea worked for Grace. The dig was only a few miles away and she could easily bike to the site. Cormac had promised to teach her to ride his motorcycle. They had been told there was the possibility that they would in the future be able to buy the cottage. If everything worked out Cormac had all sorts of plans for it, so Thea was keeping her fingers crossed.

Chapter Twenty-One

September–October 1946

The wedding reception was held at the barn. Planning their wedding, Sophie and Ed had agreed to invite only those close to them, but when they added up their family and friends it came to more than eighty guests. The marriage ceremony was held at the register office in Lewes; afterwards, the guests arrived at the barn in dribs and drabs, by car and bus and taxi. Those who did not object to the occasional squall of rain walked from Lewes through the fields. Ed had opened up the big double doors at the side of the building and he and Sophie received their guests there. All these people she loved, she thought, as they gathered together. Ed's daughter, Bridget, and her family, Duncan and Stuart and their families. Friends of Ed's and her own friends, Viola and Arnold and women from the W.V.S. and the First Aid Post. And the lodgers, of course. Vera and her friend Mavis travelled down from Birmingham, John Reynolds from Manchester.

And Rowan and Thea and their families. Sophie had a qualm, at the register office, when Rowan introduced herself to Duncan, but he merely smiled and shook her hand. And now they were standing to one side of the throng, each with a child in their arms, Rowan's Jamie and Duncan's Isobel, and talking away as if it was normal, as if they had known each other for years. Which they had, in a way, though they had not spoken to each other before this morning.

Their conversation was a little sticky at first, but then, when Rowan mentioned the house and what they were planning to use it for, Duncan, who in looks reminded her so disconcertingly of her father, unbent and seemed interested.

'It's a good idea,' he said.

'I hope it'll give them a breathing space. So often we hurtle about, don't we, not allowing ourselves time to think things through. *Sweetie*,' she said to Jamie, who had the hiccups. He was eight weeks old and the most beautiful baby boy in the world, with his dark-blue eyes and fine haze of bright red hair. She propped him on her shoulder.

'Where is it?'

'Near the Suffolk coast, about four miles from Dunwich. Neither of us can think what to call it. The local people know it as White's Farm, which is rather dull. Josh suggested calling it The Place of Last Resort, but I told him that might not help the men's morale. I like Holly House. There's an enormous holly tree at the front.' Automatically, she scanned the barn, looking for Josh; she saw him, on the other side of the space, talking to Cormac. 'One of Josh's friends is staying with us just now,' she said. 'He's our first guest. He's perfectly delightful.'

'There was a chap in my squadron in the R.A.F.,' said Duncan. 'Bit of a sad case. I visit him now and then.'

Jamie was rooting about, making little hungry sounds, so Rowan excused herself and spoke to Sophie. Sophie directed her to a quiet bedroom with a comfortable chair

427

where Rowan could feed him. By some miracle, Rowan felt, considering his parentage, Jamie had turned out to be an undemanding baby. He fed and slept, fed and slept.

For the wedding breakfast, they sat round the series of trestle tables that Ed had put up in the workshop. Sophie and Ruby had prepared the food. Ruby, along with Stuart and the children, had been staying with them for the last two days to give a hand. Rowan and Josh's extraordinarily generous wedding present had been a couple of cases of wine, unearthed from some Makepeace stash. Jugs of autumn leaves and berries were dotted along the tables, which were covered in simple white cloths.

Conversation roared round them. Ed took her hand. 'Enjoying yourself?'

'Enormously,' she said. 'And you?'

'Every minute of it. Though I have to admit that I can't wait for them all to leave, so that I can be alone with you.'

She gave a little sigh. 'Oh, yes. I know what you mean. It's all perfectly delightful, but I feel exactly the same.'

Thea found Rowan in a corner of the workshop, looking at chairs. 'I wondered whether Ed would make us some dining chairs,' Rowan said. 'We have ex-army chairs at home. Julia keeps threatening to give us some frightful upholstered things from The Sandlings.'

'Where's Jamie?'

'Asleep in his pram. Josh is keeping an eye on him.'

'You are lucky, having a baby who sleeps.'

'I know,' Rowan said smugly.

'How is Josh?'

'Very well. Surprisingly well. Doing all the practical things in the house suits him. I've told him he can always have a career as a plumber or electrician once he's finished our house.' She looked at Thea. 'What is it, darling?'

'I found something,' said Thea.

'At your dig?'

The dig should have been completed by now, but on the penultimate day of August they had sunk a small exploratory trench to one side of the long barrow and had discovered the remains of a timber circle. Grace had succeeded in getting permission to investigate the site further. Thea was helping to carry out the painstaking process of removing the layers of earth and she was recording the artefacts they had found: a worn tooth, fragments of bone, a flint scraper. Throughout the summer, she had worked for Grace Fainlight three days a week. While she worked, Cormac looked after Polly. This unconventional arrangement suited them both and they were buying the cottage that they had been renting. A small, redbrick, detached house, built in the 1930s, it stood in a large plot of land that ran down to a chalk stream.

'Not at the dig, no,' Thea said. She looked round the crowded room. 'I need to talk to you. But not here.'

The rain had ceased but sharp gusts of wind still tugged at the leaves on the elm trees. There was music from a gramophone and some couples were dancing. As Thea and Rowan walked up the lane, away from the barn, the melody became softer.

Thea was wearing the outfit she had worn to Rowan's wedding. She tried to keep her mushroom-coloured satin shoes out of the mud. She said to Rowan, 'Do you remember that when you were clearing out your flat to sell it, you found my old rucksack?'

Rowan wrinkled her brow. 'It was in the back of a cupboard.'

'I hadn't used it for years. One of the shoulder straps had worn through so I bought a new one with my first wage packet from Grace. I must have thought I'd emptied it out when I put it in the cupboard. Then I started working for Grace and forgot all about it. Anyway, when you sent it to me, I checked the pockets and I found this.' Thea took a book out of her handbag. Rowan glanced at it.

'*Leaving the Island*,' she said, reading out the title.

'Yes. It's a book of poems. It was given to me years ago, before the war, when I went to Corran. But I never read it and I must have stuffed it into the rucksack and then forgot I ever had it.'

Thea remembered the low, whitewashed house and the man in the garden, who had given her directions to Portmore. And the stone gannet and the leaping fish carved into the tree trunk. Lorcan Richardson had told her he was a poet and a gardener. But what else had he been?

'This man, Lorcan,' she said, indicating the author's name, 'he gave it to me. He gave me a stone axe, too.'

'That's nice,' said Rowan, in a humouring-Thea tone.

'All the poems are about Corran.'

For the first time, Rowan looked properly at the book. 'Have you read them?'

'I have, yes. There's one called "The Grey Dancers". That's a Neolithic site on Corran. I visited it when I was there.'

Curious to see what Lorcan Richardson had written about the stone circle, she had turned the pages to the poem. And shivers had run down her spine, ice-cold fingers that had beckoned her back into the past.

She turned to the page and showed it to Rowan. 'Oh,' Rowan said, very softly. The word was like a sigh.

'The Grey Dancers' had a dedication: *To Sigrid.*

'Oh, Thea.'

'It's a love poem. It's about love and loss.'

Rowan skimmed the page, then looked up at Thea. 'And you think . . .'

'I do, yes. He was the right sort of age. He had straight dark hair, like mine.'

'If he was Mamma's lover . . .'

'Then he could be my father.'

They leaned side by side against a five-bar gate that overlooked a field. Questions floated through the air like falling leaves but neither of them said anything. Lorcan Richardson's poem described the point when the dancers on Corran had been turned to stone. A heaviness of the limbs, a resistance as a hand moved through air. Skin taking on the glitter of sandstone and granite and feet that became weighted to the earth. A heartbeat slowing, solidifying, ceasing. Dancing and drowning, Thea thought. There was movement and then there was stillness.

The following month, the three of them travelled to Corran. They stayed in a guest house in Portmore overnight; in the morning they walked up the narrow streets behind the harbour. Soon they were in open countryside. Glassy, reed-fringed tarns reflected the streaks of cloud that hung round the soft purplish-grey mounds of the hills. Cormac carried Polly on his shoulders, striding over the tussocky grass.

Thea saw the house ahead of them. Behind it was the green cliff and the sapphire sea. She saw that a man was in the garden. He was taking down old bean poles, stripping off shrivelled black tendrils. As she approached the house, he turned and saw her.

She waited by the gate. Lorcan Richardson walked down

431

one of the narrow, winding paths towards her, and then he stood still. He gave her a long look. 'Thea?' he said.

'I wrote that poem a long time ago,' Lorcan said. 'I wrote it five years after your mother died. When I gave you a copy of Leaving the Island, it was, I think, like placing a message in a bottle.'

'It took a long time to reach me,' she said.

'Yes. But I'm so glad it did.'

They were in the sitting room of Lorcan's house. On the long, deep windowsill were pieces of driftwood, pebbles with holes in them, crystals, and a bird's skull, the bones as thin as paper. The room was painted white, like the exterior of the house. Sunlight fell through the windows on to faded rugs the blue-green of the sea, and on to a desk, heaped with papers.

Lorcan sat down across the low table from her. His sister, Eilidh, had brought them a tray of coffee but neither of them had touched it. Cormac had taken Polly to the beach with the cave and the diving gannets.

He said, 'Do you want to know what happened?' and she nodded.

'Please. I'd like you to tell me.'

'The first time I saw your mother was in nineteen twenty. She was hauling her sailing boat up on to the sands. She was strong and tall and beautiful and her hair was the colour of raw silk and it flared in the wind like a banner. I think I fell in love with her then. I wrote a poem about that too, about seeing Sigrid and the Iduna on the shore, but I've never published it and I never will. I went to give her a hand with the boat and we got talking. And that was the start of it.' He looked out of the window. 'I used to come to her house in the evenings, after your sister was in bed. You could say that it was wrong of us. But the only answer I can give is that when we were together it didn't feel wrong.' He gave a small smile. 'Some people scoff at the idea that a person can fall in love at first sight. They think it the invention of sentimental poets like me. But I know that you can, and that it's not a soft thing, it's hard and ruthless, like the cut of an axe.'

Thea thought of a soldier tumbling off a motorcycle by a dusty French field. Kneeling beside him, she had been entranced by the curve of a jaw, the sweep of an eyelid. 'Yes, you're right,' she said.

'Ah, you too?' This time his smile was for her, and she felt a bond with him, a sense that in finding him she might understand herself better.

Lorcan went on, 'A lot of people would judge us for it. Sigrid was married, and she had a child. She had bought the house on Corran and the Iduna with money she'd inherited from her grandparents. She told me that she'd needed somewhere of her own. She loved to sail and to swim and to walk. She told me she liked to be outdoors, that she felt more alive when she was outdoors, and that being in the city, in Glasgow, made her feel trapped.' His voice dropped and he looked away, out of the window. 'She was very unhappy, Thea. The marriage wasn't happy.'

'My father was unfaithful to her. He'd met someone else, in nineteen eighteen.'

Lorcan returned his gaze to her. 'Ah. Sigrid was never sure. I wonder whether it would have been easier for her, whether things would have been different, if she'd been sure.' His expression darkened. 'It was not just selfishness on my part, the pleasure of being with a woman like

433

Sigrid. I could see what her marriage was doing to her. I saw how it constrained and limited her. It was hard to witness that, Thea. I thought I could give her a life that suited her better – arrogant of me, perhaps, but that was what I thought, that I could make her happy. I wanted her to come and live with me here, on Corran.'

'She loved the island, didn't she?'

'Yes, so much.' His eyes sought out hers. 'But what she loved most was her daughters, Rowan and you. You should never forget that you were at the centre of her life.'

Thea looked down then at her knotted hands and pressed her lips together tightly. Lorcan gave her some moments to recover herself before he spoke again.

'I knew as soon as I saw you that you were mine, Thea. I could see it. And Sigrid knew it too. I tried to persuade her to leave Hugh but she wouldn't. I think it was tearing her apart. The day she died, we quarrelled about it. I begged her to leave Hugh, I implored her, but she refused. And Rowan saw us. God help me, I will never forgive myself for that.' He poured the coffee, passed her a cup. 'But that morning . . . I was angry. I walked away from her and I came back here. I was living on my own back then, Eilidh only came to live here later. I found out later that day what had happened. One of the fishermen saw the accident from the shore. The boat struck the reef and Sigrid was thrown into the water. They thought she'd hit her head on the rocks. She never had a chance.'

'Poor Mamma,' Thea said softly.

'Yes.' He was silent for a long time, then he said, 'It would have been quick. They say drowning's a gentle death. But at the time it seemed so cruel. She was always so alive. It seemed an outrage that she should be extinguished like that.'

He let out a breath. 'For a great many years I blamed myself for what happened. More than once, Sigrid had told me she was ending our affair. But then she'd come back to the island and it would start up all over again. I should have found the courage to break it off, I should have left the island myself instead of forcing her to make a choice that was impossible for her. That was what I thought.'

There were tears in Thea's eyes again. She said gently, 'But it was hard for you too. You loved her.'

'I did, so very much.'

'After Mamma died, why didn't you try to find me?'

He shook his head slowly. 'I wanted to. I longed to. But there were many, many reasons. You might have resented me, even hated me. Your sister certainly would have, I think.'

'To begin with, yes,' said Thea. 'But not now. Rowan would understand now.'

She and Rowan had learned about love, she thought. How it came upon you unawares. How it buffeted and sometimes betrayed you. How, if you clung on to it, it might transform you.

Lorcan spoke again. 'Besides, it wouldn't have been fair to Hugh, would it, to have lost his wife in such a way, and then for me to turn up on his doorstep, claiming to be the father of one of his children. No, that would have been wrong of me. But I always hoped. I always hoped you'd return here one day.'

'When I came here before, did you know it was me?'

'No.' He tilted his head to one side and smiled at her. He had a nice smile, she thought. Was it strange to see her own features reflected in someone else's? Was she drawn to him? He was her kin. She was a part of him.

'Though perhaps it crossed my mind,' he said. 'Perhaps I

had an inkling. As I said, I always hoped. And I don't give away my axe-heads lightly.' He offered her a plate of biscuits; she took one. 'It's a comfort, Thea, seeing you so well, so happy and beautiful, like your mother. Sigrid was a vivid and wonderful person. I've never loved another woman like I loved her. I have mourned her so long. She's still here for me and I've stayed on Corran because of her. I see her walking across the hills. I see her on the shore, laughing at the waves.'

They drank the coffee and talked some more and then they walked to the cliff, to meet Cormac and Polly. They spoke of his work and hers, about the dig, and about the cottage in Wiltshire and the business Cormac planned to establish there, a plant nursery. The wind beat against them and whipped up white tops on the waves. She was walking in step with this man, her father. She thought that she would enjoy getting to know him. She had the sense that a story begun long ago was being taken up again, and that it would go with her into the future,

From the top of the cliff path, Thea looked down to the beach, to where Cormac and Polly played on the sand. Sigrid would have stood like that, in the ice-cold water, skimming stones. Sigrid would have told her and Rowan the names of the flowers dancing in the breeze and the seabirds rising up from the rocks. Sigrid had taught her things that had stayed with her ever since and that she, in turn, was teaching her own daughter. Sigrid had tried to leave Corran but had ended up staying here for ever. You might leave the island, thought Thea as they headed down the path to the shore, but it remained inside you, drawing you back to it, over and over again.